# DONUT
# FALL IN
# LOVE

# DONUT FALL IN LOVE

Jackie Lau

**JOVE**

NEW YORK

A JOVE BOOK
Published by Berkley
An imprint of Penguin Random House LLC
penguinrandomhouse.com

Library of Congress Cataloging-in-Publication Data

Names: Lau, Jackie, author.
Title: Donut fall in love / Jackie Lau.
Description: First edition. | New York: Jove, 2021.
Identifiers: LCCN 2021012850 (print) | LCCN 2021012851 (ebook) |
ISBN 9780593334300 (trade paperback) | ISBN 9780593334317 (ebook)
Subjects: GSAFD: Love stories. | Humorous fiction.
Classification: LCC PR9199.4.L3825 D66 2021 (print) |
LCC PR9199.4.L3825 (ebook) | DDC 813/.6—dc23
LC record available at https://lccn.loc.gov/2021012850
LC ebook record available at https://lccn.loc.gov/2021012851

First Edition: October 2021

Printed in the United States of America
1st Printing

Interior art by Vi-An Nguyen
Book design by Ashley Tucker

For George, who read lots of books with me

# CHAPTER 1

**W**hen Ryan Kwok woke up on Tuesday morning, he discovered his abs had become a social media sensation.

It had started with a scathing review of his latest movie.

> The best part of *That Kind of Wedding*? Ryan Kwok's abs. But the last thing Canada needs is another actor named Ryan.

It was his first leading role, and the critical response had been a bit of a mixed bag—okay, leaning toward negative—so this review wasn't exactly a surprise.

The review didn't appear in a major publication, but the author had started a thread on Twitter dedicated to his abs, cataloging their obvious beauty and many talents, complete with close-up shots from the trailer and his Instagram account. She appeared to be quite a fan of his abs, even if she liked nothing else about the rom-com.

And that thread? It had gone viral.

He'd had a spike in Instagram followers.

#StarringRyanKwoksAbs was trending.

People were discussing the roles his abs could play in movies, how they should appear in postapocalyptic and period pieces alike.

When he'd gone to bed at eleven last night, there hadn't been a whiff of this.

And now . . .

Well, he couldn't help but laugh.

"Good job, boys," he said, looking down at the body part that was now gaining international fame. If he was honest, they weren't quite as glorious as they'd been when *That Kind of Wedding* was filmed. In the past four months, he'd been following his diet and workout routine . . . mostly. But the past four months had been the worst of his life.

At least now the promotional tour was over. He'd struggled to fake a smile for late-night talk show hosts, given what was happening in his family and—

*Oh, dear God.*

Ryan's dad was going to see this, dammit.

Once upon a time, he'd assumed his father didn't pay attention. But a year ago, he'd caught his father looking at his Twitter account.

That was quite a shock, considering his father was anti-Twitter and all social media. In fact, Dad was anti a lot of things. He was also anti-stoner-movies, as Ryan had learned when he'd filmed *The Journey of the Baked Alaska*, though this hadn't surprised him one bit. And anti-sitcoms, which Ryan had known his whole life.

This hadn't changed when Ryan got his first break in *Just Another New York Sitcom* several years back.

Speaking of *Just Another New York Sitcom* . . .

He had a text from Melvin, one of his co-stars on the show.

**Please convey my congratulations to your abs.**

• • •

**LINDSAY MCLEOD WASN'T** used to seeing abs in her Instagram feed. Mostly she saw pictures of Toronto. And food. Lots of food.

She gave the photo a few seconds of attention and idly wondered if the man in question would ever eat anything as delicious as her chocolate espresso donuts, or whether such indulgences were strictly off-limits for this Ryan Kwok guy.

Then she uploaded a photo of her latest creation.

New donut alert! Here for spring: matcha tiramisu donuts

A couple of hours later, Lindsay was piping buttercream onto some chocolate raspberry cupcakes when Raquel came into the kitchen.

"Your mother's here," Raquel said, gesturing to the front of the bakery.

Excellent timing for once.

Ever since Lindsay's mom had moved downtown five months ago, she'd been popping into Kensington Bake Shop—the bakery Lindsay ran with her best friend, Noreen—on a semi-regular basis, and she had an uncanny ability to arrive at the worst possible moments. Last time, it had been literally a minute after Noreen had spilled cherry jelly on the floor, on a day when they were running way behind because of a malfunctioning oven.

But today, even though Noreen was away on her honeymoon, everything was in order, more or less. Lindsay could spare five minutes to talk to her mother.

"Oh, I should probably mention," Raquel said. "Your mother's not alone."

Yes, sometimes Lindsay's mom brought one of her friends into the bakery. She was always bragging about Lindsay's donuts, cupcakes, and other creations, and she wanted to show them off to everyone she knew. Sometimes it was a little embarrassing, but it was all good.

"In fact," Raquel continued, "I'm pretty sure she's on a date."

*Say what now?*

Lindsay washed her hands, then headed to the front. As always, the simple elegance of the shop made her smile. She and Noreen had argued for ages over paint chips; Noreen had eventually won, and Lindsay had to agree her friend had been right. The light blue was perfect. On the walls were two watercolors: one of donuts and one of cupcakes. There were only four tables—all cream in color—with small glass vases, each containing a single flower. Space was expensive in downtown Toronto.

Lindsay's mom wasn't seated at one of the tables. No, her Asian mother and an unfamiliar middle-aged white man were peering at the display cases.

The appearance of the man gave Lindsay pause.

He looked, well, a bit like her dad.

Not enough that she thought she'd seen a ghost, but it was a little eerie. Though his build was similar, it was his haircut more than anything else. That terrible haircut her father had gotten every six weeks at the local barber?

She'd never thought she'd see it again, but here it was.

*Oh, Mom.*

"The orange cardamom is my favorite," Mom said to her companion. She pointed at the display case to the left of the cash register, which contained today's eight varieties of donuts. "The filling is custard with a hint of cardamom, and the orange cardamom glaze is delicious. And that candied slice of orange? Mmm."

"Hi, Mom," Lindsay said. "Maybe you should work here. Your sales pitches are great."

"Lindsay, this is Wade. Wade, this is my daughter, Lindsay."

Lindsay would have stuck out her hand, but she was behind the glass display case, and it would have been awkward.

"Hi," she said. "Nice to meet you."

"You're giving me a weird look," Mom said.

"No, I'm not."

"Wade and I just had our first date at that Italian restaurant on Baldwin, and since we were in the area . . ."

Bringing a man to meet your daughter on your very first date seemed a little much. Especially when the daughter in question had no idea you were dating.

In theory, Lindsay was fine with her mother going on dates—yes, this was something she'd thought about before. Her father had been gone for seven years. Her mother had an active social life, and it was surprising this hadn't happened sooner.

But theory was different from practice.

Now that Lindsay was confronted—unexpectedly, at that—with a man her mother was seeing, a man who was not her father, she was digging her fingernails into her hands so hard they'd surely leave marks. And her mother was acting as though this was all no big deal.

"The chocolate espresso is really good, too," Mom said to Wade. "It's filled with a chocolate espresso custard—I think they should include the filling on the labels, don't you think? Because you can't see it. So they should tell people. I do recommend getting a donut, and not something else, because that's their *thing*." She glanced at the cupcakes, cookies, and squares to the right of the cash register before turning back to the donuts. "Lindsay, the matcha tiramisu—is that new?"

"Yes, today is the first day we're selling it."

"And the filling?"

"Matcha mascarpone cream."

Mom turned back to her date, who looked overwhelmed by the choices. "And I suggest getting a donut with a filling. The others aren't as exciting, aside from the one with cream cheese frosting, but they don't have it today."

Her mom was talking too much, which meant she was nervous.

Lindsay managed a small smile.

Eventually, poor Wade decided on the orange cardamom and Mom decided to try the matcha tiramisu. Lindsay left them alone with their donuts and coffee as she headed to the back to finish those chocolate raspberry cupcakes, but the perfect swirls of pink buttercream, garnished with chocolate shavings and raspberries, didn't lift her spirits. Nor did the aroma of fresh donuts—Beth was taking some out of the deep fryer now.

Lindsay's mother was dating. Her best friend was now married after a whirlwind romance. Of course she didn't object to either of those, but she didn't want things to change quite so much, so quickly.

Another thing that had changed recently: Lindsay's living situation. She and Noreen used to live in a cramped apartment within walking distance of Kensington Market. It had been chosen for its proximity to the bakery more than anything else, and they'd lived there together for nearly four years.

But now Noreen lived with her husband—or she would, once she got back from India—and Lindsay had moved into a building near Wellesley, with a roommate she didn't know at all.

At first she'd looked for a place to live by herself, but vacancies were low and prices were high in Toronto, so she'd started considering alternatives. This woman, Vivian Liao, was about her age. She owned a two-bedroom condo and was looking for a roommate.

Lindsay found the situation a little puzzling. Someone her age owning a *two*-bedroom condo in downtown Toronto? This woman must be making very good money at her job in finance.

Except she was renting out the second bedroom . . . so why hadn't she bought a one-bedroom place instead?

It clearly wasn't because Vivian wanted the companionship of a roommate. Vivian had been polite but not super friendly when Lindsay had toured the suite. Lindsay figured that would change once she moved in, but no. Vivian wasn't a terrible roommate . . . she was just a little distant and kept to herself, and she often seemed to be busy.

Which was fine. And it was Vivian's place.

But Lindsay had hoped to be friends with her new roommate, though she supposed things didn't always work that way. She was just used to living with her best friend, and the idea that a living situation could be like this—well, it had never occurred to her.

And now that her best friend was out of the country for a month, she could use a friend. Someone to tell, however briefly, about the day's events. *My mom showed up at the bakery today with a date. Who looked disconcertingly like my father.*

Lindsay didn't need a deep talk about her feelings. She could have just half laughed about it with someone, you know?

Except Vivian didn't know much about her. They'd had a short conversation about their careers, but that was about all. Vivian didn't know anything about Lindsay's family.

When Lindsay got home that day—though the place didn't quite feel like home yet—Vivian popped out of her room, still immaculately dressed in one of the pantsuits she always wore to work, and said, "I'm heading out soon to run errands. Just wanted you to know you have mail." She nodded at the small table by the entrance.

Huh. Lindsay had yet to receive mail at this address.

It was a wedding invitation—one of her friends from university was getting married to her longtime boyfriend—and had been forwarded from her old apartment, the place that still felt like home to her. That old apartment had been furnished with IKEA furniture, including a wobbly coffee table they hadn't assembled properly, and a large assortment of clashing throw pillows. The new apartment felt more grown-up, but nowhere near as cozy.

Lindsay brought the invitation into her room, then went to the kitchen and made herself a Havarti grilled cheese sandwich for dinner, as she'd done so many times before, in all the many places she'd lived. It had been her father's favorite.

As she thought of everything that had happened recently, everything that had changed, she couldn't help feeling like she was being left behind.

# CHAPTER 2

"How about I drive up to Markham this weekend?" Ryan suggested. "We can have dim sum."

On the other end of the phone, his father grunted.

Yup, that sounded about right.

"I have work to do," Dad said.

"Not all weekend, surely."

"I need to vacuum. Wash the towels."

Ryan sighed as he leaned back against the arm of his couch. "Okay. Fine. You don't want to see me."

He'd done as little traveling as possible lately, staying in Toronto so he could be there for his father and sister.

It wasn't going well.

Everything was off-kilter now, and he felt like he was stuck. He couldn't fix anything.

But for the next few months, until he started filming *For the Blood*, this was his priority: his family.

"Ah, don't be so dramatic." But Dad didn't disagree. "You can have dim sum downtown."

"You'll drive here to have it with me?"

"Not this weekend, no."

"Next weekend?"

"Aiyah, why are you bugging me like this?"

Well, Ryan didn't feel like providing a serious answer to that question.

"I was reading reviews of your movie," Dad said. "They're not great, did you know?"

"Yes, Dad, I know."

"Apparently you look attractive, though." Dad gave a derisive snort. "Good you are focusing on the important things in life. I have seen so many shirtless pictures of you today. That's all anyone seems to care about. Why do you post so many shirtless pictures?"

"A lot of them are from movies."

"And the ones on Instagram? You posted those yourself."

So Dad was anti-shirtless-pictures, too. Not surprising.

When he was a child, Ryan's father had basically been anti whatever Ryan wanted to do, and acting had been at the top of the list.

Dad's interests could be summed up as follows: engineering, nature documentaries, Canadian Tire, and CBC Radio. Whenever he read a book or watched a show, he wanted to learn something. He was a bit of a snob and didn't approve of most things considered "entertainment." A movie that just made you laugh or forget about your problems for a little while? To him, it was worthless if it didn't make you *think*.

Their relationship had always been difficult.

However, they'd reached an uneasy truce after Ryan's Golden Globe nomination, which was enough to make his acting career seem legitimate and had only earned a single "Why didn't you get an Oscar nomination instead?" comment.

And now Ryan's father had seen his son's abs' journey across the internet.

Ryan could appreciate this was awkward for him, but Dad

hadn't needed to bring this up—or google Ryan on a regular basis—though perhaps it was easier than talking about other things.

"You should make more movies like *Unraveling*," Dad said, naming the movie that had earned Ryan his Golden Globe nomination for Best Supporting Actor. A small-budget film that had been more successful than anticipated.

"I'll take your views into account, thank you."

"You sound sarcastic. But the last two movies you did—a stoner film and a rom-com?"

"I like doing a variety of things, *Dad*. You aren't my agent."

His mom, on the other hand, loved—had loved—rom-coms; she'd been happy when he'd gotten the role, and he'd been happy to star in that kind of film. Because when he was a kid, the people who looked like him in such movies were usually nerds who were the butt of jokes and laughed at for their accents.

And now his abs were trending! Funny how life worked.

Yes, the fact that he was a sex symbol, of sorts, *meant* something.

But although Ryan didn't say it to his father, he was worried about the response to *That Kind of Wedding*. The box office numbers weren't completely terrible, but they weren't great.

He was always disappointing his dad, but maybe this time, he'd disappointed every Asian person in North America. This movie could be a major setback. Movies about guys like him weren't allowed to flop. People would point at this single movie as proof that no more like it should be made.

That was what worried him, in addition to his chances of getting another role like that.

Most of the time, those fears stayed near the back of his mind. They weren't what was most important right now; they seemed inconsequential in comparison to looking after his family—and he was definitely disappointing himself there.

"How's work?" he asked his father.

"Why are you asking?" Dad made a sound of disgust. "You don't care."

Ryan bristled. "Well, I don't find your work terribly interesting, but . . ."

Everyone in his family was an engineer, and Ryan had flamed out of engineering school in spectacular fashion. He'd tried his best—for the first term, anyway—but it hadn't suited him at all, and he couldn't force himself to be something he wasn't.

"How *are* you?" he asked instead.

"What kind of question is that? It's a stupid greeting people use."

"But I'm not asking as a greeting. I mean it, really. How are you?"

"Hmph."

"Ooh, that's a promising start," Ryan said. "Let's explore that, why don't we?"

"For fuck's sake."

Though this wasn't the conversation Ryan had hoped to have, he got a perverse joy out of making his dad swear. It didn't happen often, and it was one of the few things he could do that his sister could not.

He was about to reply, but then he realized his father had hung up.

And because Ryan was in A Mood, he pulled off his shirt—always a great way to cope with life's frustrations—and snapped a photo of himself, focusing on his abs.

He wrote, I hear people like these . . . and uploaded the photo.

A minute later, he'd already gotten lots of likes and retweets, though they didn't bring him any joy.

He put his shirt back on and texted his sister to see how she was doing. She was nearly nine months pregnant with her first child.

When she didn't reply within ten minutes, he told himself not to freak out, then put on his shoes and sunglasses and left his condo. He walked quickly down the streets, needing to get out, needing to go somewhere, even if he had no idea where.

Down Bay to College, past a hand-pulled noodle shop and two sushi restaurants side by side. A McDonald's, a Starbucks, a tea shop.

And then he realized where he was going.

The independent coffee shop where he'd worked after getting his degree. He'd been a part-time barista as he struggled to get auditions.

But if he went there, he'd have to speak to people he knew, including his former boss, who still owned the place. She always enjoyed it when he stopped by—and he usually did, too.

Not today, though. He couldn't have that conversation now.

After being away for a while, he didn't have much in the way of close friends in Toronto. Only people who'd expect an easy smile from him, and he wasn't in the mood for that.

He'd lived in LA for a few years, until last fall, when he'd decided to move back to the Toronto area and bought his condo. He'd missed the city. And now it felt like . . . he'd subconsciously known what was going to happen.

Ryan turned onto Augusta, passing a craft brewery and a taco shop before he stopped in front of a bakery. The door was open, and it smelled so damn good. There were a couple of women sitting at the lone table outside the shop, eating cupcakes, and God, he *remembered*.

Not that he ever forgot.

But now he recalled the time he'd come back to Toronto for a few days after filming *The Journey of the Baked Alaska*. In his absence, his mother had become obsessed with baking shows, much to his father's exasperation. Dad had said it was stupid to watch baking shows if you were never going to bake—you weren't learning anything.

*Fine*, Mom had said. *Ryan and I will bake something.*

He hadn't protested. It had been a while since he'd seen his mom, and sure, whatever she wanted to do.

His mother had been a pretty good cook, but she'd never baked before. She'd selected a recipe for chocolate cupcakes from a random website. According to the excessively long description before the actual recipe, these were the "best ever" chocolate cupcakes.

That was certainly not how they'd turned out, though it probably wasn't the recipe's fault. Maybe the problem was that they hadn't followed the recipe closely enough, then had a lengthy debate about whether the toothpick came out clean when they stuck it in a cupcake. To be safe, they'd left them in longer. Quite a bit longer . . . until there was a faint burning smell.

His mother had fashioned a piping bag out of a resealable plastic bag, but somehow it had burst, and they'd gotten chocolate frosting everywhere. They'd also—and he would take the blame for this—started frosting the cupcakes before they'd cooled.

Many, many hours later, they'd finally finished a dozen cupcakes. The cupcakes hadn't looked like something from the baking shows with "good" bakers—no, they'd looked like something from *Baking Fail*.

His mother, laughing, had gone to the porch to get his father, who'd been reading some kind of "good for you" book that had won a literary prize.

*See? We did it*, she'd said. *Best-ever chocolate cupcakes.* Dad had chuckled—actually chuckled—and Ryan and his mom had eaten their not-so-great cupcakes while watching another baking show. Dad hadn't eaten a cupcake—he'd never liked sweets.

And that was a nice memory . . . but nice memories were painful now.

Because they couldn't make any more.

She was gone.

Ryan wasn't entirely sure why, but he felt like he had to go into this bakery, like eating a chocolate cupcake was somehow the closest he could be to his mother right now, even if these cupcakes were works of art compared to the ones they'd made together.

He strode inside . . .

And then someone shrieked, *"What the hell?"*

# CHAPTER 3

Lindsay hadn't needed this today. She really hadn't.

Of all the days . . .

That morning, her brother had called, and she'd freaked out. Trevor always texted, never called, and she'd immediately flashed back to *that* phone call, all those years ago.

As it turned out, nothing bad had happened . . . not really.

Trevor used to work as a geologist out in Alberta, but he'd gotten laid off and hadn't been able to find any work, so he'd moved back to Toronto and was temporarily living in the den of their mother's condo.

Probably *very* temporarily after what had happened today.

Her brother, after meeting an old friend about a possible job, had returned to the condo and discovered a sock on the door.

You know, the old college sign for having sex.

That was when he'd called Lindsay and totally lost his shit.

"Maybe it's, uh, not what you think," Lindsay had said unconvincingly, and then, because she'd figured he should know, she told him that their mother had brought a date into the bakery the day before.

The possibility of their mother dating and having sex had made Trevor's head explode. He hadn't simply been a little squicked out—no, he seemed to think it was wrong for her to date, though he refused to say why, and Lindsay had spent many minutes trying to explain, in her patient big-sister voice, that there was nothing wrong with this, but perhaps he and Mom should establish some, uh, rules. And though, in theory, she was glad her mom was dating, she was still uneasy about the whole thing, but she hadn't told Trevor about this.

Finally, she'd gotten back to work.

And then they'd run out of matcha tiramisu donuts.

With its pale green glaze and white chocolate decorations, her new donut flavor was the subject of many Instagram posts. The donuts were flying off the rack—which was great. It really was.

But she'd underestimated the number of donuts they'd require, and at one o'clock she'd realized she'd need another batch or they'd run out far too early. They had a bunch of special orders to fill, so they were pretty busy, but she'd made the donuts. Then she'd brought them out to the front, intending to take a picture—for social media—of the tray of pretty donuts before putting them in the display case.

Except as she'd been walking up to the window, a man had practically *flown* through the front door and knocked into her, and now twenty-three matcha tiramisu donuts were lining the floor of the bakery.

The last donut had somehow landed on his shoulder—how the hell had that happened? He picked up the donut, placed it on the nearest table, and turned back to her.

She crossed her arms over her chest. "Why don't you watch where you're going?"

"It's not like you were looking, either."

"I don't expect people to fly through the door out of nowhere."

"Flying is a bit of an exaggeration. There was a door. I used it."

"You barreled right in, as though you own the place. But you don't. It's *mine*." Sure, the building wasn't hers, but the business was.

The man took off his sunglasses and perched them on top of his head. Some kind of fancy designer glasses, and he was waltzing about—well, barreling about—as though the world was his playground.

There was a gasp behind her.

Lindsay looked back. The only other person in the shop right now was Raquel.

She looked forward again.

Ah. That explained Raquel's gasp. Because the man was really quite attractive. It pained her to admit it, but it was true. He was about her age, East Asian, a bit shy of six feet—and he was gorgeous. She couldn't explain what was so perfect about each of his facial features, but combined, the effect was stunning. He was well-built, too.

He should be in movies.

Whatever. Just another good-looking guy. Good-looking guys weren't precisely a dime a dozen, but there were many, and she'd enjoyed one—in much closer proximity than this—in the past month: she'd hooked up with a man she'd met at Noreen's wedding. So it wasn't like she'd had a long dry spell, though perhaps her sex life wasn't as active as her mother's . . .

Ugh. She wanted to slap that thought out of her head.

The man in front of her was wearing a pastel pink dress shirt, now covered in matcha glaze. He had a sort of dark, brooding thing going on, and it was at odds with his soiled attire.

That nearly made her laugh.

But then she glanced at the matcha tiramisu donuts scattered across the floor, the donuts she'd worked so hard to make. They still smelled wonderful, but they were ruined.

When she looked back at him, a peculiar transformation took place.

Not long ago, she'd watched a clip from a Superman movie, showing Christopher Reeve transforming into Superman as he took off his glasses and adjusted his posture.

Something similar happened in front her.

This guy had already removed his sunglasses, but now it was like a switch had flipped, and he went from brooding hero to relaxed, cheerful guy.

"Guess I'll have to take off my shirt," he said.

Behind Lindsay, there was another gasp.

What the fuck?

"I'll wait until I get outside, don't worry." He winked.

He seemed to be flirting with her. As though this would make her forget about the matcha tiramisu donut accident.

Yeah, right.

She also felt like he was making a joke she didn't understand, and she didn't like it.

"I needed those donuts," she said.

"They're just donuts." He shrugged.

"*Just* donuts? My donuts are amazing. They've been featured in . . ." Her brain promptly emptied. Her donuts had appeared in various magazines and blogs—and on TV. However, she could no longer remember the details.

She blamed his good looks.

And all the ruined donuts. It made her want to cry.

Plus her mom was dating and putting fucking socks on door-knobs and her roommate barely talked to her and she missed Noreen and . . .

All those things sounded silly, yet Lindsay had been barely keeping it together.

And she wasn't keeping things together anymore.

She might not remember all the media that had featured Kensington Bake Shop, but she remembered what was in these donuts.

"They're matcha tiramisu yeast donuts, fried to perfection and filled with matcha mascarpone cream and topped with a matcha glaze that took me a *long* time to get right."

"Hmm," he said. "I'm not sure about matcha tiramisu. For me, the espresso is such an integral part of tiramisu. I don't see that working."

He spoke in such a casual way, as though it was all no big deal.

But this bakery was her livelihood.

She pointed at the sad-looking matcha tiramisu donut on the table. "Try it."

"If you insist." He picked up the donut, took a generous bite, and chewed thoughtfully.

"Hmm," he said again.

"Is that so," she muttered.

"The donut itself is quite good."

"That's your expert opinion?"

"It is. The filling isn't bad, either, but it's still not my thing. Like I said, for me, tiramisu requires espresso. It's not the same without it." He put his hands in his pockets and rocked back on his heels. "I'll pay for the ruined donuts."

"Forty-two bucks a dozen, so . . . eighty-four bucks."

"Eighty-four bucks for donuts?"

"Is that too expensive for a guy like you?"

"A guy like me. What do you mean?"

She gestured to his clothes—though the effect was rather ruined by the matcha glaze.

"There are lots of ingredients in those donuts," she said, "and my time is valuable. You think anyone could make these? Could *you*?"

"Okay, okay. I apologize. I know it's not simple—there's no way I'd be able to make donuts that look so great." It sounded like he was mocking her, though, because he gestured to the donuts on the floor. "I tried to bake cupcakes once, and it did not go well."

A smile curved her lips—somehow, the thought of him baking cupcakes was amusing.

She promptly squashed down the smile. She would not be amused by this charming, handsome stranger.

He walked over to the cash register and pulled out a credit card. "I'll get a chocolate cupcake, too, so I can try your food properly. Actually, change that to a chocolate espresso donut."

"You really like your espresso, don't you?" She headed behind the counter.

"What's not to like? Anyway, you're still getting paid for your donuts. It's all good, right?"

"But I don't have the time to make more matcha tiramisu donuts today. People will come here expecting them, and they'll be annoyed when there are none for sale, and . . ."

God, she didn't usually lose her temper, but it had been such a long day.

If Noreen were here, Noreen would have diffused the situation.

Yes, he'd knocked into her, but it wasn't his fault she was having a bad day. Hopefully he wouldn't leave a Yelp review about this incident. Thankfully no one had been here to witness it.

She sighed, deflated. Nothing could be done to fix the situation now. They would have disappointed customers.

Maybe he was having a bad day, too. He'd been cheerful for the past few minutes, but you never knew what was going on underneath the surface, and he'd seemed rather dark when he'd come in.

He paid, and she handed him a chocolate espresso donut. It

was dipped in chocolate ganache and topped with a swirl of whipped cream and a chocolate-covered espresso bean.

He immediately took a bite. "Now, this is good."

A bit of the filling clung to the corner of his lips, but she resisted the urge to wipe it away.

"Glad it meets your approval." She couldn't keep the snark from her voice, but it appeared to roll right off him.

"It's not *just* a donut." He held it in the air and smiled at her. That was nearly enough to make her forget that this day wasn't going to plan at all—and he was part of the reason.

But in the end, she couldn't forget.

She watched him head out into the sunshine, and as soon as the door closed behind him, Raquel said, "OMG, do you know who that was?"

"Um, a clumsy guy with a nice smile?"

"That was Ryan Kwok. The actor." Raquel whipped out her phone and showed Lindsay a picture of some familiar abs.

*Oh.*

Lindsay had only seen his abs before, not his face. No wonder she hadn't recognized him.

Raquel went to his Twitter account, and sure enough, the profile picture looked like the guy who'd just walked out of Kensington Bake Shop.

His latest tweet was another shirtless photo, but this one showed his face. It had been posted less than an hour ago.

Well, it seemed posing shirtless was this guy's thing.

"Who would have thought he'd be clumsy?" Raquel said.

"I got mad at him, didn't I?"

"You did."

This day was just getting worse.

"He seemed kinda into you," Raquel said. "Despite everything."

"No, I think he was being a little flirty so I wouldn't get even more pissed."

It didn't matter. Lindsay doubted she'd ever see him again.

Time to clean up the floor before somebody slipped on one of those donuts and she had an even bigger mess on her hands. Then she'd get back to the kitchen, and when she took a break later, she would most certainly not look up what Ryan Kwok did other than take off his shirt, destroy her donuts, and insult the concept of matcha tiramisu.

"I'm sorry," she murmured to the destroyed donuts, and to a man who was no longer there.

RYAN LICKED HIS fingers. The donut was messy to eat, but worth it. Chocolate and espresso were always a great combination. The filling was sweet, but not too sweet, and with the whipped cream—sinfully delicious.

It had been a long time since he'd had a treat like that.

He was halfway back to his condo when he realized he should have offered to clean up the donuts he'd knocked on the floor. He came to a sudden stop on the sidewalk, and someone behind him yelled, "Watch it!" Warm liquid trickled down Ryan's back.

Well, now he had coffee on his shirt in addition to the matcha glaze. How lovely.

No matter what he did today, he seemed to make a mess of things.

Which was why he'd head home now. Given his luck, he'd probably ruin yet another tray of donuts if he went back to the bakery. He also doubted *she* would be happy to see him, and he suspected she wouldn't allow him to help clean up—if she hadn't already finished doing so.

He was pretty sure he was the one at fault for the ruined matcha tiramisu donuts, though the entire thing had been a blur. One minute, he'd been standing on the sidewalk, remembering the time he'd made chocolate cupcakes with his mother, and the next moment, someone was yelling at him for flying out of nowhere. He didn't fully remember what had happened, but he remembered *her*, because she'd been cute and pissed and extremely proud of her donuts.

To be honest, he hadn't been attracted to someone like that in a while.

He sighed and continued walking, a few people giving him funny looks, presumably because of his dirty shirt. Hopefully his sunglasses were enough to prevent anyone from recognizing him.

When he got home, he pulled off his shirt—and this time, it wasn't because he planned to take more pictures. He immediately put on a clean T-shirt, one that didn't smell like a bakery and a coffee shop.

Ryan felt a strong urge to do something useful, something other than arguing with his father or screwing up someone's hard work or worrying about what *That Kind of Wedding* had done to the state of Asian cinema in North America. He had a script to look over, which he'd been putting off. He'd do that after he checked his phone.

Still no texts from his sister, which was curious. Jenna was usually prompt at texting him back, and this was her first week of leave from work.

He pulled up Twitter and looked at the replies to the picture he'd posted earlier.

*What in the world . . . ?*

He peered at his phone, convinced he must be seeing things.

But he wasn't.

The most popular reply was from @RyanKwoksFather.

It said: When will you stop taking off your shirt and finish your engineering degree?

The account had a grand total of one tweet, and the profile picture was of a middle-aged man ice fishing.

Ryan recognized the photo. A few years ago, one of his father's colleagues had invited him to go ice fishing up north, and his father had gone because he enjoyed learning new things and wasn't bothered by the idea of sitting in the freezing cold for hours.

But even before studying the picture, Ryan had suspected it really was his dad.

*When will you finish your engineering degree?* was something he'd heard many, many times before, much to his frustration, though it had been a while. It was exactly the sort of thing his father would tweet at him . . . if his father ever got a Twitter account, rather than just looking at Ryan's tweets. Ryan hadn't expected this, given that Dad thought social media was everything that was wrong with society, but here they were.

@RyanKwoksFather followed only one "person" other than Ryan.

Cookie Monster.

Cookie Monster had been Ryan's favorite *Sesame Street* character as a young child, and he'd dressed up as Cookie Monster for Halloween when he was four.

There were already a hundred replies to his father's tweet, speculating on whether or not the account was legit.

Well, if Dad wanted to play this game, Ryan would play along.

And though his father's obsession with him studying engineering had bugged the crap out of him for years, Ryan felt good—mostly—about where he was in his career now, despite the response to *That Kind of Wedding*.

So he could laugh about it, yeah.

He quote-tweeted his father's response and typed, Yes, this is actually my father.

He wondered if Dad would have deleted his account by tomorrow or whether this would become a regular thing.

Ryan was about to put down his phone, but then he got a text. Not from Jenna, but from her husband, Winston.

**Jenna's in labor.**

# CHAPTER 4

"How do you feel about doing an episode of *Baking Fail*?" Bob's voice boomed over the phone. "The Canadian version. They asked if you were interested in a celebrity episode, and the usual five-thousand-dollar prize will be donated to a charity of the winner's choice."

"Oh." Ryan got up and paced his living room.

"You know what *Baking Fail* is, right? My wife loves it. They have not-so-skilled bakers try to make elaborate cakes and other things."

"I'm familiar with it, yes."

"They film in Toronto. They'd do it well before you're needed on the set of *For the Blood*."

It would be just a day or two of filming, and the host of the show was pretty cool—Ryan had met him a few times. And Ryan was good at laughing at himself and not taking it all too seriously.

At least, he used to be. But lately, he hadn't been his normal self.

"Ryan?" prompted his agent.

"I'll think about it. Give me a couple days."

They talked about a few more things before Ryan got off the phone.

It was hard for him to focus. Jenna was *still* in labor, last he'd heard. She didn't want any of them waiting around at the hospital, so he was at home.

But if Mom were alive, she would have wanted Mom.

It had been almost twenty-four hours. Ryan knew these things could take a long time, but considering the year his family had been having, he was half-convinced this meant something horrible was happening.

He tried to watch something on Netflix but just ended up scrolling through the options for half an hour, his mind constantly drifting back to the hospital. Finally, he put on Melvin Lee's comedy special, which he'd seen many times before.

When his mother had had something on her mind, she used to clean, but Ryan paid someone to clean for him, and his place was spotless. Nor did he have to cook; his portioned meals were in the fridge. He thought about doing an extra workout but couldn't seem to motivate himself.

He couldn't do anything, and he couldn't relax.

Not until several hours later, when he finally got some good news.

**JENNA WAS SITTING** up in bed, holding a little bundle wrapped in a green blanket.

"He's so tiny," Ryan said, coming around the side of the bed. Supposedly the baby was seven pounds, one ounce, but Ryan hadn't had a good sense of how small seven pounds was.

"He looks just like you did," Jenna said.

"You remember?"

"Yeah. Dad took me to the hospital to see you. It's one of my first memories. I was convinced there was something wrong with you."

"Gee, thanks."

"I was three. I had no idea what newborns were supposed to look like. I assumed you'd be similar to the doll Mom had given me—so I'd have my own baby to play with—but you weren't." She smiled at the tiny human in her arms. "Actually, he's more handsome than you." She elbowed Ryan, and he laughed.

He glanced at Winston, standing by the window, then turned toward the door.

And there was his father.

Dad was holding a small blue teddy bear, and he looked awkward as fuck. The bear, despite his stitched-on smile, looked like he wanted to leap from his arms. Dad came to stand on the other side of the bed, across from Ryan.

"Guess who's here?" Jenna said to the baby, who was awake—at least, Ryan thought he was awake. "It's your grandpa. Hi, Gung Gung!"

Dad seemed unsure of what to make of all this. "He can call me Stanley."

This was . . . possibly a joke? Ryan wasn't certain.

"This is Uncle Ryan," Jenna said, turning to face Ryan. "He's a big famous movie star."

He chuckled.

"Would you like to hold your nephew?"

"Um . . . okay?"

"You have to support his neck," Jenna said, placing the baby in his arms.

Ryan was determined not to fuck up this baby-holding business. The baby stuck out his impossibly tiny fist and didn't start crying, so he supposed it was going okay. Winston took a picture of him holding the baby.

"What's his name?" Ryan asked.

"We haven't decided. We had a name picked out, but now I don't think it suits him."

"That's what happened with Ryan," Dad said. "We were going to name him Christopher, but then your mother decided he didn't look like a Chris."

Huh. Ryan had never heard that story before.

It was hard to imagine having any name but his own, but if he'd always been Chris, he'd be used to it. Though the world didn't need any more young actors named Chris.

Or Canadian actors named Ryan, apparently.

"Come here, Dad," Ryan said. "You can hold him next."

Dad looked like he was going to protest, but then he came over and took the newborn from Ryan's arms.

Winston snapped another picture.

"Ah, why do you need to take pictures of everything?" Dad complained.

"You're holding your first grandchild for the first time, Dad," Jenna said. "It's an important life event."

"Hmph."

"Unlike the picture of fried chicken that Ryan posted on Instagram last week."

"Hey," Ryan said. "I don't eat fried chicken often. That was an important event, too."

Jenna laughed, but the mood in the room was off. Everything seemed . . . brittle.

*Mom should be here, and she's not.*

Nobody would say that; nobody would mention the last time they'd all been in a hospital together. They had to pretend things were okay . . . mostly. Because sometimes that's what you needed to go on.

"Now, this baby isn't your abs, Ryan," Jenna said. "You can't post pictures of him on social media willy-nilly."

Dad snorted.

"Actually, I don't want his face on social media at all."

"That's fair," Ryan said.

The baby started crying, and Dad appeared baffled, as though a crying baby was a truly bizarre thing.

"Here, pass him over," Jenna said, and the baby immediately calmed down.

"Hmph," Dad said, then suddenly left the room, pulling on his jacket as he went.

Ryan followed him. "Are you leaving now?"

"Why can't I leave? I came to the hospital and saw the baby. He looks like a baby. I think all is well. But I don't care much for small children, not until they can talk. More fun then. Can teach them to recite the periodic table."

"But it's your first grandchild."

"I know. I'm not an idiot, unlike the character you played in that stoner movie."

Ryan put a hand on his father's arm. "Are you okay, Dad?"

Dad shrugged him off. "Why do people keep asking me that? I'm fine."

"Isn't this exciting?"

"Babies are born every day."

Ryan wasn't sure why he bothered, and he wasn't in the mood to ask why the hell his dad had created a Twitter account, either. "Okay, see you later."

He went back into the hospital room, and his sister clearly hadn't been expecting him. She looked . . . completely different from how she had a few minutes ago, and he realized how much effort this must have been for her, after spending twenty-four hours in labor. He didn't want to stress her out.

"I'm heading out now, too." Ryan went over to the bed and brushed his finger over the baby's knuckles. "Nice to meet you, little buddy." He didn't know what else he was supposed to call the baby, seeing as he didn't have a name yet. "Text me if you need anything," he said to Jenna and Winston, not that he knew what they would need and what he could do.

He walked quickly through the halls of the hospital, the smell of disinfectant making him slightly queasy. He thought he heard someone say, "Isn't that Ryan Kwok?" and normally he might have turned and smiled, but not today.

Honestly, he was so out of it that it was a miracle he didn't knock down another batch of matcha tiramisu donuts—or some kind of expensive medical shit.

Once he was home, he returned to pacing the living room. And remembering what he'd seen the last time he'd gone to his parents'—his father's—house.

On the coffee table in front of the couch, there had been a knitting project, a half-finished yellow baby hat, which doubtless had sat there, unmoved, for four months.

The baby could have been wearing that hat today. Instead . . .

Why was Ryan so bad at this? Maybe he shouldn't have bothered to spend a few months focusing on his family. Maybe if he'd been working, it would have been better for everyone.

Then he remembered an interview he'd done for *That Kind of Wedding*. It had been so hard to act like himself—the version of himself that the world expected. Someone had asked him a question about diversity, and he'd almost lost it. He was usually pretty good at giving smooth and sufficiently thoughtful answers, but he'd wanted to scream about how white people didn't get asked these questions every damn time they did an interview.

It was like the loss of his mother had permeated all parts of his life, affecting everything he did. Things didn't roll off him the way they usually did. He was more irritable, even though he tried to make himself numb.

Ryan needed a distraction. He had some preparation to do for his next movie, but it wouldn't occupy all his time and he didn't like being alone with his thoughts. Not that he'd be able to completely free his mind of everything that was bothering him, but he needed *something*. Though he'd planned to take a break until *For the Blood*, he couldn't stand this anymore.

All right, he'd call Bob and tell him he'd do *Baking Fail*. He wished they were filming next week, but it would at least be something in his schedule.

That would give him a little time to practice, too.

The show was called *Baking Fail*. He was not expected to produce anything truly spectacular. But he'd have to be able to create something, not just stare blankly at the recipe. The bakers on the show might not be superstar amateur bakers, but they did seem to have a little knowledge, and the humor came from forcing them to do things that were truly ridiculous in small amounts of time. They'd probably be able to follow a straightforward cupcake recipe with a simple frosting—no elaborate decorations—unlike what he and his mom had done.

Okay, so he needed to get a little better at baking before the show. Cool.

Except he wasn't looking forward to it. Filling his condo with flour, sugar, and eggs, then sticking stuff in the oven—it was a solitary activity, and Ryan was already feeling lonely.

He immediately thought of his ill-fated trip to the bakery the other day and the woman who'd been carrying the tray of matcha tiramisu donuts. She'd flipped out on him for "flying" through the door and calling them "just donuts."

He'd been thinking about his mom, and there was obviously no comparison between losing your mother and losing two dozen donuts. The latter were replaceable and, for someone who actually knew what they were doing, probably didn't take too long, though

she'd said she didn't have any time to make more. Possibly she
hadn't been having a great day, and his clumsiness had been the
final straw.

But while they were bantering, he'd felt . . . not too bad, actually. Like himself again.

Yes, this would be the perfect distraction: he'd ask her to teach
him how to bake. There had been a sign on the door that said
"Baking Classes." He'd ask for private ones.

She hadn't recognized him, but he'd tell her who he was—he
wouldn't keep that a secret. He didn't intend for it to go anywhere,
of course; he just liked the idea of spending time with her. Of baking in the company of a pretty woman rather than staring brood-
ingly out the window. Like he was doing now.

He pulled up the website for Kensington Bake Shop. In the
"about us" section, there was a picture of her and a South Asian
woman, posing with two cakes. The first was an elaborate mer-
maid cake, which was a zillion times better than anything produced on *Baking Fail*—those blue and purple scales must have
taken forever. It probably tasted amazing, too. The other cake had
goddamn ruffles. How did one decorate a cake with *ruffles*? They
matched her apron.

The best part of the photo, however, was the wide smile on her
face. She hadn't graced him with a smile like that.

Well, there was still time.

She had long dark brown hair and dark eyes. Her name was
Lindsay McLeod, and idly he wondered about her last name. She
looked East Asian to him, and it wasn't the kind of name he'd expected her to have. There were many possibilities, but the one his
brain latched on to was the possibility that she was married.

Not that it mattered. He was hiring her to help him learn to
bake.

Though he suspected she was mixed race. That could also be the reason for the name—her father was white.

Ryan would visit her tomorrow morning. He was looking forward to it, and it had been a little while since he'd looked forward to anything.

And then he'd appear on one of his mother's favorite TV shows.

Yeah, he'd totally forgotten how much she'd enjoyed *Baking Fail*. He should have agreed to do it right away, and if he won, he'd donate the money to the immigrant and refugee health organization that Mom had supported. He'd already made a somewhat-significant donation, but more would be good, and it could give them some publicity.

After calling his agent, he checked Twitter again.

No tweets from his father.

# CHAPTER 5

Lindsay stared at the wedding invitation.

She hadn't even known that Eunice Kim was seeing anyone. They'd last met up a year ago, when they'd gone out for ramen with a few other university friends.

"Is something wrong?" Vivian asked.

Lindsay jerked her gaze up to her roommate, who was eating dumplings and looking at something on her phone. Vivian's skin was flawless—how complicated was her skin-care routine?—and her bob was perfect. And she hadn't gotten a speck of dipping sauce on her light blue shirt.

"You just sighed," Vivian explained, "and you seem more serious than usual. Never mind. It's none of my business."

Lindsay sat down at the kitchen table. "My friend Eunice is getting married."

"Ah." Vivian focused on her dumplings, and Lindsay figured that was the end of the conversation. It was already more talking than they'd done in the past three days. But then Vivian said, "Anyone named Eunice who's under the age of sixty has to be Asian."

"She's Korean."

"As is the only Eunice I know. But who am I to talk—have you ever met a young white woman named Vivian?"

Surely they existed, but Lindsay knew three Vivians and they were all Asian.

"*Pretty Woman*?" she said.

Vivian chuckled. "That movie's like thirty years old, and Julia Roberts is old enough to be your mom."

"Good point."

Lindsay had been in a slightly rotten mood. Things at the bakery were busy without Noreen, and a woman hadn't been happy with her special order today, even though they'd made *exactly* what she'd asked for—a pineapple-shaped chocolate cake with white chocolate buttercream. And then Lindsay had gotten her second wedding invitation in two days.

She was, of course, happy for Eunice. At least, she was trying to be.

But at the same time, Lindsay couldn't help feeling like she was stuck in life, while everyone else was moving on.

And today just so happened to be the day that Vivian strung more than two words together, which was nice. Lindsay was about to ask if Vivian wanted to have a beer and watch a movie, but then her phone rang.

It was her mother.

"I want to set the record straight," Mom said.

"Okay?" Lindsay figured she'd better head to her room, since she had no idea where this conversation was going and how long it would be. She mouthed "sorry" at her roommate, then poured herself a glass of water and brought it into her bedroom, along with Eunice's wedding invitation and her phone.

"Trevor told you about the whole sock-on-the-doorknob thing, didn't he?"

"Uh, yeah."

"I've since learned it doesn't mean quite what I thought it did."

"What did you think it meant?" Lindsay asked.

"Just a heads-up that you had a guest in the room."

"Uh-huh. And you have since learned . . . ?"

"That it means *sex*."

"Yeah, that's the standard meaning, as far as I know."

"Wade and I were not having sex," Mom said.

"Look, the details aren't important to me. You can do whatever you want."

"I thought about it . . . but it's hard, you know. I haven't had sex in so many years, and I haven't done it since I went through menopause, and—"

"Mom!"

"Do you think it's gross for old people to have sex?" Mom sounded defensive.

"It's not because of your age," Lindsay said. "It's because you're my mother, and it's awkward to talk about this with you."

"Are you like your brother? You think I shouldn't be dating?"

"No, I'm glad you're dating, but why don't you ask Auntie Deb instead? Or one of your friends? This—it's too weird. As is bringing a guy to your daughter's bakery on your first date."

Mom sighed. "Okay, I see your point. What's new with you?"

Lindsay was about to mention her friends' upcoming weddings, then snapped her mouth shut. Her mother would probably ask about Lindsay's dating life, and she wasn't in the mood for that.

"An actor came into the bakery," she said. "I didn't know who he was, but he's kind of famous, apparently. Ryan Kwok."

"He was in that movie *Unraveling* a few years ago."

"Yes. He was." She'd looked up his filmography last night. "He also made me drop two dozen matcha tiramisu donuts. People were asking for them all day, and we didn't have any because of *him*."

"Was he checking you out? Was that why he wasn't looking at where he was going and knocked over the donuts?"

"Mom!"

So much for avoiding this kind of conversation.

"Sounds like he really got under your skin," Mom said.

"It was the last thing I needed yesterday."

Lindsay talked to her mother for a few more minutes, then left her bedroom to heat up some leftovers for dinner.

Vivian, unfortunately, was back in her room with the door closed.


**"LINDSAY!" RAQUEL APPEARED** at the door to the kitchen. "Someone's here to see you."

"Is it my mother?" Lindsay asked, washing her hands.

Raquel bounced on her toes. "Nope, it's Ryan Kwok!"

Lindsay's stomach did a little somersault, which bugged the crap out of her. Sure, he was an attractive guy, but that was all.

"He asked for you by name," Raquel said.

Huh. Lindsay hadn't told him her name, though she supposed it wouldn't have been too hard to find.

She headed to the front of the bakery. Ryan was standing by the window, his hands casually slung in his pockets. He turned around as she approached, and dear God, he was even more handsome than she remembered.

"Hi, Lindsay."

"Hi, Ryan."

"So, you've figured out who I am, too."

"Yeah. Now I know why you made that comment about taking off your shirt."

He laughed.

Lindsay made a show of examining the floor. "Glad to see you haven't knocked over any matcha tiramisu donuts."

"Nah, I did that at another bakery today. Got it out of my system."

"Who else is making matcha tiramisu donuts in Toronto?" she demanded, even though she knew he was joking.

Perhaps she should stop giving him a hard time, but he didn't seem to mind.

It was a warm spring day, and he was wearing a blue polo shirt and jeans, those expensive sunglasses perched on his head once more.

"If I ever come across such important information, I'll be sure to tell you." He winked.

She wasn't *not* enjoying herself, but she was getting a bit annoyed with this conversation, truth be told. She had stuff to do.

"I have a proposition for you," he said.

Did he want to commission a fancy cake for his actor friends? That could be good for business. Maybe he wanted a butter pecan cake in the shape of his abs. One of those very realistic illusion cakes—though Kensington Bake Shop didn't do them. She suppressed a smile.

"I'd like you to teach me how to bake."

"Say what?"

"I don't know how to bake, and I need to learn."

"Why?" she asked.

"Apparently you've looked me up, and you know I'm a tiny bit famous . . ."

"Mm-hmm."

"I'm going to do a celebrity baking show."

"Which one?"

This seemed to be a big secret, because he leaned toward her, in the empty bakery, and whispered, *"Baking Fail."*

His breath tickled her ear. It was kind of nice, actually.

"You, uh . . . you don't really need to know how to bake for that one," she said, feeling slightly off-balance.

He shrugged. "Nowhere near as well as you, no, but I don't want to completely embarrass myself, and like I said, the last time I tried to make cupcakes, it didn't go well."

"Why were you making cupcakes?"

"Hey, don't look so surprised. My father thought it was stupid that my mom watched baking shows without actually baking, so she recruited me to help."

This mention of his parents . . . it made him seem like an ordinary guy.

"I don't need a comprehensive education, like at a culinary school," he said. "I just want you to help me with whatever I need, tailored for the show."

"Why me?"

"It's not like I know another baker."

She snorted. "It's not like you know me, either. I didn't even realize you knew my name until two minutes ago."

"Well, you yelled at me, so I know you better than any other bakers."

"I did not . . ." Her shoulders slumped. "I didn't exactly *yell* at you, but I was having a crappy day."

"As was I."

"I'm sorry."

"I should have offered to help clean up. Totally slipped my mind."

Yeah, it probably wasn't the sort of thing that a guy like Ryan Kwok needed to do often. Surely he had people to clean for him.

"But really, why me?" she pressed. "You didn't even like my matcha tiramisu donut."

"The chocolate espresso donut was really good." He flashed her a smile.

She felt like she was in a movie right now. This gorgeous famous guy was in her bake shop, his attention all on her.

"So, what do you say?" he asked.

"Well, Noreen usually runs the classes."

Was it Lindsay's imagination, or did he look slightly deflated? Probably her imagination.

"But she's on her honeymoon," Lindsay continued, "so if you want to start right away—"

"That would be ideal, yes."

"—then you'd need to do it with me. I'll have to email her and get back to you, though. See if she's okay with this sort of thing, since offering private baking lessons wasn't something we ever talked about."

"How many lessons do you think I'd need?"

"There are three rounds on the show, right?" she said. "Donuts, cupcakes, and cakes. I'm thinking two lessons each for donuts and cupcakes, three or four for cakes and decorating . . . Let's say eight. Obviously, I can't teach you everything in that time, but it should be a good start. I'll have to figure out a price with Noreen."

Ryan leaned forward, and her heart beat quicker at his nearness. He whispered a figure in her ear. It was high. Not obscenely high, but higher than what she'd had in mind.

She grabbed her phone. "What's your email? I'll be in touch in a couple days."

"Sounds good." He told her his email address, then slid his sunglasses back onto his face and strolled out the door.

*Did that just happen?*


**RYAN WAS FEELING** good about the baking lessons. Lindsay hadn't agreed yet, but he was pretty sure it would work out, and then he'd have a little distraction from the rest of his life.

That evening, he texted Jenna to see how she was doing, then uploaded the photo his sister had approved to his Instagram. It was a picture of him holding his new nephew, but his nephew wasn't really visible—it looked like Ryan was peering fondly at a bundle of blankets.

> Guess who's an uncle now? Got to meet this little guy for the first time yesterday.

Ryan's brand on social media was pretty straightforward. It didn't include any of the complicated shit. He was very aware of the image he projected publicly; it was a version of himself, but it wasn't everything.

Next, he checked his father's Twitter account—God, he still couldn't believe this existed.

His father had only tweeted the one time.

But people were quote-tweeting his father's response and saying how #relatable this was, because they had to deal with similar attitudes from parents.

Ryan was tempted to post another shirtless picture to see if he could prod his father into tweeting again. Maybe tomorrow. For now, he'd binge-watch old episodes of *Baking Fail* and try not to think about how excited his mother would have been that he was doing the show.

Instead, he'd imagine Lindsay sexily feeding him donuts . . .

# CHAPTER 6

Lindsay worked every Saturday, starting at six thirty in the morning. It was often the busiest day of the week at Kensington Bake Shop, and they usually had several special orders. Tomorrow would be another long day. It was the first Pedestrian Sunday of the year in Kensington Market, and those were always particularly busy—they'd make extra donuts.

After leaving the bakery that afternoon, she didn't feel like cooking, so she stopped at a sushi restaurant on College Street to pick up an assortment of maki, plus shrimp and vegetable tempura. More than she'd usually buy for one person, but not such a ridiculous quantity that she couldn't eat it all by herself if she needed to.

When she left the sushi restaurant, she took a few steps before coming to a stop.

She'd turned the wrong way—toward her old apartment rather than her new one.

She shook her head at her mistake, then started heading in the right direction, passing a new bubble tea shop and a not-so-new Korean restaurant with really good sundubu jjigae. She would have been tempted by that if it weren't for the sushi in her hand.

When she got home, Vivian wasn't in the kitchen or the living room. But if Lindsay put her ear to Vivian's door like a weirdo, she could faintly hear voices. It sounded like her roommate was watching a show.

What sort of shows did her roommate enjoy? What else did she do in her free time? Would she have preferred sundubu jjigae over tuna and salmon rolls?

After a minute of debate, Lindsay knocked on the door.

"Is something wrong?" Vivian asked.

Lindsay's heart sank. She didn't want them to talk so little that Vivian would assume there was something wrong when Lindsay knocked on her door.

"No, just had some extra sushi." Lindsay tried to sound upbeat. "You want some?"

"Oh, that's nice of you, but I'm heading out to a spin class in a few minutes."

Lindsay would eat her sushi alone—more for her this way—and that was totally fine. Though she'd wanted to eat with her roommate and tell her about her week. Did Vivian know who Ryan Kwok was? Would Lindsay need to show her #StarringRyan-KwoksAbs? Could they joke about a #StarringRyanKwoksAbs butter pecan cake?

After eating dinner, Lindsay had a shower and changed into pajama pants and a T-shirt. Then she flopped in front of the TV and pulled up Netflix. She knew exactly what she was going to watch: *Just Another New York Sitcom.* She couldn't help it; she was curious to see Ryan Kwok in action.

Unlike some shows set in New York, which featured people living in surprisingly nice apartments, *Just Another New York Sitcom* was about three men with student debt who rented a small two-bedroom apartment in Brooklyn out of necessity. Melvin Lee played a comedian of questionable talents with a passion for long showers and bubble baths—in other words, using all the hot water.

Juan Velazquez played an Afro-Latino elementary school teacher with an impressive array of hidden talents and knowledge. He was an expert on computers, baseball, macarons, eighteenth-century French poetry, and the etymology of swear words.

And Ryan Kwok? He worked in publishing and was very popular with women—because of course he was. Many TV shows had such a character, and *Just Another New York Sitcom* was no exception.

Ryan's character, however, could only pick up women when he was wearing glasses. The instant he took them off, he apparently became unattractive.

Ha. As if.

In Lindsay's opinion, he was equally hot either way.

She was on the third episode—the one in which Melvin Lee's character got a pet capybara named Dumpling without consulting his roommates, and it turned out that Juan Velazquez's character was an expert on large rodents and Ryan Kwok was scared of them—when she heard Vivian return.

She expected Vivian to head to her room, but instead, Vivian sat on the opposite side of the couch.

"Oh my God, you're watching *Janice*?"

Huh?

"It's *Just Another New York Sitcom*," Lindsay said. "I mean, that's the name of the show. Because it's set in New York, like many other sitcoms."

"Yes. J-A-N-Y-S," Vivian said impatiently. "*JANYS.*"

Oh. Is that what fans called the show?

"Right. Well, this is my first time watching it. I'm on—"

"Episode three."

On-screen, Ryan removed his glasses and took an impressive leap backward from the capybara. The capybara snarled. He put his glasses back on, and the capybara gave a soft mewl.

Melvin Lee started doing a bizarre chicken dance, which he

claimed capybaras liked—he'd seen a YouTube video once. Juan Velazquez then immediately corrected him on the preferences of capybaras.

"I know Ryan Kwok is the popular one," Vivian said. "I mean, look at him. I understand. But I always thought Melvin Lee was cuter. There's just something about him . . ."

Well, personally, Lindsay was Team Ryan. "It's amazing they cast two Asian actors as leads. Usually, there's only one, and they're The Asian Guy."

"Exactly."

Lindsay fiddled with the bottom of her shirt. "I met him."

"You *what?*"

She'd never seen her roommate so animated before. "Ryan Kwok, I mean, not Melvin Lee. He came into the bakery the other day and knocked over some donuts. I didn't know who he was, and I got kinda mad at him. But then he came back yesterday and asked if I could teach him how to bake for a celebrity baking show. So . . . yeah. That's happening now."

She'd emailed Noreen, who'd agreed Lindsay should do this. They'd use the money to purchase some much-needed equipment. The lessons would be on Mondays, since that was the day Kensington Bake Shop was closed.

Vivian was gaping at her, and Lindsay couldn't help but chuckle.

"You're . . . teaching Ryan Kwok . . . how to bake?" Vivian sputtered. Vivian, who was normally so well-spoken the rare times she opened her mouth.

"Yeah." Lindsay shrugged as though it was no big deal.

"What show is it for?"

"I don't think I'm supposed to say."

Vivian gave her a look, but Lindsay didn't crack.

"Fine, fine, be no fun," Vivian said.

Lindsay tossed a pillow at her, then realized what she'd done.

This was Vivian, not Noreen, and she and Vivian didn't have this kind of relationship. And rather than the random dragon, sushi-and-puppy, and "Stay Weird" throw pillows that had adorned the futon at Lindsay's old apartment, this pillow was solid maroon.

Vivian didn't toss the pillow back—as Noreen would have—but she smiled and lay down, tucking the pillow under her head, as though settling in for a long binge session.

And that was exactly what they did. They got through ten more episodes of *JANYS*, and Lindsay got to see Ryan Kwok interact with lots of women—both when he was wearing glasses and when he wasn't—and even find a second capybara, as well as a rat that would only eat jumbo empanadas. Vivian's favorite episode was the one with the Rube Goldberg machine that Melvin Lee made to dump foaming bath gel into the tub. Lindsay preferred the first capybara episode. During the infamous honey walnut shrimp episode, Lindsay also learned that Vivian didn't like shrimp and had visited New York City five times.

When Vivian went to bed, it was well after eleven, but despite her long day, Lindsay wasn't sleepy, and for some reason, she still hadn't had enough of Ryan Kwok. She wanted to see him when he wasn't in character, so she fired up her laptop and looked for videos.

She came across an interview he'd done after the release of one of his movies. It was on an American morning show, and about halfway through, after talking about his character's romance in the movie, the interviewer asked about his own love life.

He laughed it off and said that wasn't a priority right now.

Lindsay felt a momentary disappointment, even though it was foolish. It wasn't like she'd ever had a shot with him.

Next, she found an ad he'd done for winter coats. It was from several years ago, but it had been making the rounds on social media lately, presumably because Ryan Kwok was shirtless under that big winter coat, the zipper mostly undone. She rolled her eyes—

what an impractical way to dress for winter—before taking a closer look.

By the time Lindsay turned out the light, she'd watched several more videos. It was after midnight, and she had to be up at five thirty to make donuts. Tomorrow's varieties included orange cardamom, raspberry crumble, chocolate almond, and carrot pineapple cake donuts with cream cheese frosting.

But though she'd be a little short on sleep, she didn't regret her life choices.

· · ·

*Even though the Asian guy gets the girl for once, I wish this film had never been made.*

Ryan scrubbed a hand over his face as he read a piece on *That Kind of Wedding.* The journalist, Lester Cho, feared this movie's lack of success would discourage people from making movies with Asian leads, especially more rom-coms, proving these weren't simply Ryan's own irrational fears. Well, he'd known they were reasonable, but seeing someone else articulate them was different.

He wasn't allowed to fail.

And yet . . .

First of all, he didn't think the movie was as bad as Lester Cho made it out to be, and it wasn't completely tanking at the box office. And second of all, projects that failed were part of life in creative industries, right? Not everything would be a runaway success.

Lester Cho went on to praise *Just Another New York Sitcom.* On his list of TV shows that were canceled too soon, it was at the very top.

Ah, well.

It had been a terrible disappointment to Ryan when the show had been canceled after only one season. After a few years of roles like Postal Worker #2, Man in Bar #3, and Chinese Delivery Guy, it was his big break.

But five years later, he was over it. Mostly.

*Just Another New York Sitcom* had since developed a cult following. There was a fairly popular Facebook group, JANYSers United, devoted to it, and Lester Cho was apparently a member.

Ryan had an idea.

It had been a couple of days since he'd posted on Twitter. He took one picture of himself wearing glasses and one without, then tweeted, Which do you prefer?

People started responding immediately.

Ryan figured he should stop looking at social media and thinking about that article, so he made himself a cup of coffee. He lifted the cup to his nose and breathed in the aroma. Working at a coffee shop for a few years hadn't affected his love of the smell of coffee. Nope, not at all. As long as it wasn't spilled all over his clothes.

He breathed it in again. Fortification for what he was about to do next.

Calling his father.

He listened to the phone ring once. Twice.

After five rings, the answering machine clicked on. Although he had no intention of leaving a message, he waited for the recording to finish before hanging up.

"Hi, you've reached Stanley and Flora Kwok. Please leave a message and we'll get back to you soon. Have a nice day!"

His mom's voice. As though she were still here.

Dad hadn't changed the message, and Ryan liked hearing her voice, even if it hurt. He had two voicemail messages from her that he planned never to delete. One was just her telling him that she was running late and would be there soon, but he'd listened to it a dozen times.

He sighed and went back to Twitter.

The top reply to his recent tweet was from Melvin, but the second was from @RyanKwoksFather.

*This is what my son wanted to be when he grew up.*

Underneath, there were two pictures. One of Cookie Monster wearing glasses, and one of Cookie Monster without glasses.

I still want to be Cookie Monster, Ryan replied immediately. Who wouldn't? He's blue and furry and eats cookies all the time.

Not a minute later, his father responded with two words: dear god

Ryan was, frankly, shocked at his father's lack of capital letters and punctuation. Yes, it was Twitter, but that's just who Dad was.

He was less shocked—but annoyed nonetheless—that Dad hadn't answered the landline.

If Dad was tweeting, that likely meant he was home. He did have a smartphone—the telecom company had finally convinced him to get rid of his old flip phone—but he used it only for emergencies, and he didn't keep it turned on. There was no point trying to call that number.

Ryan sipped his coffee and considered texting Jenna, but she had a three-day-old baby. He didn't want to disturb her.

He was reading a lengthy debate on Twitter about whether the glasses he was wearing were the same ones he'd worn on *Just Another New York Sitcom* (they weren't, but yes, they were very similar) when his phone vibrated.

When he saw who the email was from, his heart skittered.

We can do the classes, but it'll have to be on Mondays, she said.

He was almost as excited as he'd been when he'd gotten the role in *That Kind of Wedding*. In fact, he nearly pumped his fist.

Which didn't make any sense. It was just baking classes.

With a pretty woman, but it wasn't like anything would happen.

Everything was out of whack these days—that was the only explanation. Ever since his mom had died, things that should mean nothing had taken on such significance. Voicemail messages, for example.

Good to know he could still get excited, though.

Of course, he'd been excited about his nephew's birth, too, but he'd been worried about Jenna, and he'd wished his mother were there at the hospital.

He read the email over, then sent Lindsay a text—she'd provided her number.

Hi, it's Ryan. Mondays are fine. We can start tomorrow?

After he sent it, however, he couldn't help wondering whether he should have phrased it differently. His message was straightforward and conveyed the necessary information, but did it have the right tone? And what tone did he want, anyway?

He read the ten words over and over until they were nonsensical, and then she replied.

Tomorrow is fine. We'll start with donuts?

Sure. Makes sense, since they're the first round. And your specialty.

He added a winking emoji and sent the message, then regretted his choice of emoji. Was it too flirtatious? What was he trying to do here?

I'll make the dough, she texted, and you can get here at two. I'll show you how to cut and fry them.

She must have watched *Baking Fail*, and not just the first few episodes. Initially, the contestants on *Baking Fail* had needed to make the donuts from scratch, but the baking fails were a little too inedible. So they'd moved donuts to the first round and had contestants replicate elaborate donuts, but with the dough and recipes provided.

In the cupcake round, they had to do everything from scratch, and in the final cake round, the contestants got to showcase their creativity . . . or lack thereof. They were given a few basic cake and frosting recipes and had to create something to match the theme.

But although making donut dough wasn't something he'd have to do, Ryan wanted to do it anyway. He didn't want to take the easy way out, and besides, he had time.

Lindsay agreed to his suggestion.

T minus twenty-four hours until donut making . . . and seeing Lindsay.

# CHAPTER 7

At the appointed hour on Monday afternoon, Ryan knocked on the door to Kensington Bake Shop. When Lindsay opened it a moment later, her gaze traveled over him slowly, and his skin felt like someone was pricking it with a pin.

Hmm. What a bizarre sensation. He really was feeling strange these days.

"Uh, hi," Lindsay said, then started walking.

He followed her upstairs.

She gestured at some aprons hanging from hooks. "Wouldn't want you to get matcha glaze on your clothes again."

He surveyed the aprons. Most were plain red or white, but there was one that stood out—the apron Lindsay had been wearing in the picture on the website.

He wanted to make her smile, so he picked this one. It was pink with ruffles.

She did, indeed, smile.

"Shall we get started?" he asked, tying the apron around his waist.

She nodded briskly.

He looked around. This appeared to be a special area for classes, not the main kitchen. There were six workstations. At one of them there was a recipe, as well as several ingredients. Sugar, eggs, that sort of thing.

"Where's the flour?" He didn't know much about donuts, but there must be flour in them.

Lindsay pointed to an enormous plastic container on the floor. Ryan had never seen so much flour in his life.

"I haven't given private lessons before," she said. "And. Um."

"I'm sure you'll do fine," he assured her, shooting her a smile. Not one meant to dazzle her, but to put her at ease.

"We'll each make a separate batch so I can show you what to do. Start by measuring the ingredients into each of the four bowls, as indicated."

He skimmed the recipe. It was more complicated than he'd anticipated. No wonder those ruined donuts had cost him eighty-four bucks.

"Why are there weights next to the volume measurements?" he asked.

"We measure by weight—it's more accurate—but home bakers often don't do that." She moved behind the counter at the front of the room and cracked an egg into a bowl.

Well, he better get started.

The problem was that, even though measuring ingredients shouldn't be difficult, he kept getting distracted by Lindsay efficiently moving around, measuring things out without looking at the recipe. Everything was automatic to her.

He lightly knocked the side of an egg against the bowl. It didn't crack. He tried again, much harder, and the egg white and yolk dropped onto the floor.

She already had a cloth in hand to wipe up the spill, but he refused to let her clean up for him. This was partly selfishness on his part—he didn't want her to think he was a stuck-up guy who considered himself too good for things like cleaning.

He might not do a lot of cooking these days, but he knew how to crack an egg.

Or at least, he thought he did.

As he reached down to take the cloth, his hand brushed hers, and he was struck with the strange urge to cover her hand with his and hold on. But he wouldn't, of course.

His second attempt at cracking an egg was better, and he finally managed to get two eggs in the bowl, as required.

In another bowl, he stirred the yeast into warm water and added a sprinkle of sugar. He'd never made anything that required yeast before.

"Leave it for a few minutes and it will get foamy," Lindsay said. "If it doesn't, that means the yeast isn't good anymore, but this yeast is definitely good."

Eventually, he got all four bowls ready, and she showed him how to combine everything, then fit the large bowl under the stand mixer.

This was the first time he'd seen a stand mixer in real life. It was one of those things he'd seen only on TV, on shows like *Baking Fail*.

Lindsay pulled out an attachment that looked different from what he'd expected. In fact, it reminded him of a certain fictional character.

Captain Hook.

"Ahoy, matey!" he said, picking it up. "Where's that rascal Peter Pan?"

She rolled her eyes and it looked like she was suppressing a chuckle.

Mission accomplished.

"It's called a dough hook," she said.

For some reason, he had trouble snapping the dough hook in place. Lindsay finally had to show him how to do it—he'd been turning it the wrong way.

Dammit, he felt like a clumsy mess today. Bakeries seemed to bring it out in him.

"Put it on low speed to start," Lindsay said, "then turn it up a bit."

He did as instructed and watched as the dough hook combined the ingredients in the bowl. There was lots of flour around the edge, though. He picked up a spoon and was about to reach into the bowl, intending to knock the flour closer to the center.

But before he could do so, he felt a warm hand on his wrist.

"It'll combine," she said. "Be patient."

"Really?"

"I'm the expert here, aren't I? I know what I'm doing."

"Aye, aye, Captain," he said with a smile.

She was smiling, too. They stared at each other, and for a moment, everything else seemed to disappear . . . and then he snapped out of the trance and looked back at his bowl.

Yeah, he certainly was in a weird mood these days.

"See how the dough is beginning to climb up the hook?" Lindsay said. "It's almost ready."

When she declared it was done, he turned off the mixer, and she showed him how to gather the dough in a ball and put it in the proofer.

"Now we wait for an hour," she said.

"An hour? I thought this proofing business only happened once the donut shapes were cut out of the dough." He'd seen contestants proof the cutout donuts on *Baking Fail*, hadn't he?

"It has to be done twice."

Geez, this donut-making business was more involved than he'd thought.

"What do we do while we wait?" he asked.

. . .

**LINDSAY HAD FELT** perfectly comfortable with Ryan Kwok before today. She'd had no problem telling him off for ruining her donuts. Even once she knew who he was, it hadn't been a problem.

But that was before she'd watched every episode of *Just Another New York Sitcom*, as well as *The Journey of the Baked Alaska*, in two days.

Now that she'd seen him on the screen, it was a bit hard to deal with the fact that he was here, in her bakery.

Pretending to be a pirate. Wearing a pink ruffled apron.

The apron looked good on him, of course—she couldn't imagine anything looked bad on Ryan Kwok. He had his arms folded across his chest, showing off his biceps, and it was a fine sight.

She swallowed. "What do we do now? Well . . ."

His character in *Just Another New York Sitcom* would definitely have been hinting at sex, and she'd seen him make out with several women on-screen.

His character in *The Journey of the Baked Alaska* would have done something really stupid while smoking weed. There would likely be a fire in the kitchen before the hour was up.

But in real life, Ryan Kwok wasn't like either of those characters. He might not know anything about baking, or even cracking eggs, but despite his lack of knowledge, there was a certain ease and grace to his movements, as though he knew he looked good no matter what he was doing.

At the same time, he could clearly tell she was a bit uncomfortable, and he was trying to make her feel more relaxed.

Ryan Kwok—she couldn't help thinking of him by his full name—was very much aware of other people.

There hadn't been an ounce of suggestiveness in his *What do we do while we wait?* but she couldn't help thinking of it now and flushing.

She blamed *Just Another New York Sitcom*.

And his ridiculous sex appeal.

But she had a job to do, and she'd do it.

"We'll make a quick vanilla glaze." She handed him the recipe. "Though we don't have to start quite yet."

"How did you get into baking?" he asked. "Did you know you wanted to do this when you were a kid?"

"I liked being in the kitchen and helping my parents, but I never seriously thought about it as a career. While I was studying history at university, I worked part-time as a waitress. It was quite a nice restaurant, and the pastry chef produced these incredible creations. The restaurant was also where I met Noreen, and she was planning on getting a diploma in baking and pastry arts management, and then . . ."

The truth was, Lindsay had thought it was a silly dream. But then her father had died, and that changed the way she looked at the world. The pleasure she got from baking things for other people, from trying different flavor combinations—it mattered.

Ryan's focus was on her, not on the recipes.

"Anyway." She swallowed. "After I finished my degree, we started the program together. What about you? How did you get into acting?"

"You didn't look at my Wikipedia page?" His eyes danced.

Oh, she was so busted.

"I, uh, might have done that." She'd learned a bunch of things. Like he was thirty-one years old and had grown up in Markham. "I also watched every episode of your show and one of your movies."

He looked down and laughed.

"So, I know you studied engineering for a year," she said, "then got a BFA."

"That's right. But I'd wanted to be in movies since I was a little kid."

"Why engineering, then?"

"It was a more sensible career path."

His easy manner had become a bit . . . forced. She hardly knew Ryan Kwok, but she was quite sensitive to the changes in him.

He smoothly turned the conversation back to her. "Did you start this place after you got your diploma?"

"No, I worked at a couple different bakeries before Noreen and I started it, but we'd always planned to do it eventually, though the plan evolved somewhat over the years."

"Yeah? That's cool. Were matcha tiramisu donuts always part of the plan?"

"No." She smiled at him. "That was a recent brilliant idea of mine."

Yes, she was starting to get used to this teaching-a-famous-actor business. She felt more at ease with him now.

**"NOW, PAY ATTENTION,"** Lindsay said, "because unlike making the dough, this part you'll have to actually do on the show."

Ryan watched as she tipped the dough—it had risen quite a bit in the last hour, like magic—onto her forearm, then carefully set it on the work surface, which she'd dusted with flour.

He liked watching her work. It was always enjoyable to watch someone who was really good at what they were doing, who made complicated things look effortless.

And he particularly enjoyed watching Lindsay. It had absolutely nothing to do with her being a beautiful woman who had a lovely smile.

Okay, maybe it had a little to do with that.

But he tried not to think about it. He was here to learn.

She showed him how to gently roll out the dough to the appropriate thickness, then cut donut shapes with the donut cutter.

He held up the small circle of dough from the center of one of the donuts. "Could we use these to make Timbits?"

"Well, Timbits are just what they call them at Tim Hortons."

"Fine," he huffed, pretending to be annoyed. "Regular non-Timbit donut holes."

That produced a bit of a smile—he'd become obsessed with making her smile.

"We can make some, sure," she said.

Once all the donuts were on a tray, she covered them in a light cloth and put them back in the proofer. Then she got out an enormous container of sprinkles.

The quantities of unhealthy ingredients were making his head spin. Like the amount of sugar in the vanilla glaze.

Ryan's diet was, for the most part, carefully planned. A delivery of special meals arrived at his condo twice a week; he just heated them up. He also had appropriate snacks and protein shakes. Sure, he did go out sometimes and post pictures of fried chicken on Instagram, but that wasn't the norm.

Twenty minutes later, Lindsay checked on the donuts. She placed one in his hand.

"Notice how it feels light for its size? They're ready to fry." She led him over to the deep fryers, which were already turned on and contained a frightening amount of oil. How much of that got absorbed?

Well, he'd stop wondering about such things. It wasn't like he ate donuts on a daily basis.

He and Lindsay placed a few donuts into the deep fryers.

Three minutes later—three minutes during which he was very aware of her standing next to him, her arm nearly, but not quite, brushing his—she checked the underside of a donut.

"Just the perfect color," she said.

They flipped all the donuts over and watched them cook for

another three minutes before removing them and putting them on a rack.

"Wow," he said. "They look like actual donuts." And they smelled great, too.

He shouldn't be so amazed—this was what he'd paid for, and he had every confidence in Lindsay—but he kind of was. He'd never made anything like this before.

And damn, there were a lot of steps in making donuts.

"When do you have to get in each morning?" he asked.

"Seven at the latest. We open at ten thirty."

"Do you make bigger batches of donuts than this?"

"Yeah, we have a bigger mixer downstairs, as well as bigger deep fryers," she said. "We'll let the donuts cool for a few minutes, but you can have a little taste now."

She picked up one of the donut holes and rolled it in a large container of what looked like cinnamon sugar. Then she stepped toward him and held it up.

He leaned in and opened his mouth.

And waited.

He quickly realized he was just standing here with his mouth open like an idiot. Why had he thought she'd feed him? Something about the position of her hand? He had no idea.

Whatever.

Ryan was okay with looking like an idiot. He'd make her laugh.

He quirked the corners of his lips up, as best he could when his mouth was hanging open, and waggled his eyebrows in an exaggerated fashion.

"You aren't going to feed it to me?" he teased, but since he kept his mouth open, it probably sounded like incoherent mumbling to her.

Sure enough, she did laugh.

He was about to take the fried dough from her hands, but then she lifted it forward until it slid between his lips.

It was warm, freshly fried dough, covered in sugar. It smelled heavenly, especially to someone who rarely allowed himself such things.

He wanted to eat it. Oh, he did. But for some reason, he couldn't get past the fact that her fingers were so close to his face, and he could stick out his tongue and lick the sugar off her fingertips.

Instead, he closed his mouth around the donut hole at the same time as he gently took the rest of it from her fingers, touching her briefly.

*Oh my God.*

The touch zinged through his body as he had his first bite of donut.

It was wonderful.

He wanted to kiss her.

*Where did that come from?*

The last time he'd kissed someone . . . well, it was on-screen, for all the world to see. The last time he'd kissed someone that *wasn't* part of his job—it took him a moment to remember.

Ah, yes.

A musician he'd met at a party, quite a while ago now. They'd gone out a few times, had some fun. That was how his relationships—and he was stretching the definition of "relationship" here—typically went. He'd focused on his career, more or less, for the past several years.

*One day*, he'd told himself, *I'll want more.*

In the last four months, however, even the thought of meaningless sex had lost its appeal, though it would be a good distraction.

He hadn't really been interested . . . until now.

But he'd hired Lindsay to do a job, and that was teaching him how to bake.

"Ryan?" Lindsay said at last. "Is the donut okay?"

Right. He remembered to chew.

"Delicious." A warm donut—how could it be anything but delicious?

"I was worried because you were standing there like—"

"Like I was analyzing all the complex flavors? The notes of yeast and flour and sugar?"

"Mm-hmm."

He washed his hands. "Now let's finish the donuts, shall we?"

They fried another batch. Then they dipped half of them in cinnamon sugar and half in the glaze. Some of the glazed ones were also dipped in rainbow sprinkles.

Several hours after they'd begun their lesson, he had a box of a dozen donuts. They weren't as pretty as the donuts he'd seen on Instagram—and they were less complicated than the ridiculous things on *Baking Fail*—but they were real, tasty donuts, and when he got home, he'd jot down some reminders to himself for the show.

Yes, the baking show was a comedy more than anything, but he had every intention of producing half-decent treats.

"Let's eat one now," Lindsay suggested.

Downstairs, she made some coffee and he selected a donut with sprinkles.

He'd made the dough and the glaze. He'd fried the donut himself.

And it tasted just perfect.

It felt good to do something productive. His schedule had been pretty empty since he'd finished the promo tour for *That Kind of Wedding*, and he'd felt like he was floundering, with nothing better to do than post pictures of his abs on Twitter. He was supposed to be taking some time off and helping his family, but it was a struggle.

"Was that okay?" Lindsay asked. "Was it the sort of lesson you were looking for?"

"It was great. Just what I wanted."

"Next week, we'll do filled donuts—I'll make the dough for you, to save time—and the following week, we'll start cupcakes."

He stilled, and some of the warmth he'd been feeling evaporated.

He'd have to bake cupcakes. It was silly to not want to make them simply because he'd made them once with his mom, but he couldn't help it.

Well, hopefully in two weeks, he'd feel more ready to tackle cupcakes.

Thinking of his family reminded him of something. "Could we make Nanaimo bars as well next time, if they don't take too long? They're my sister's favorite."

"Sure." Lindsay smiled at him.

He stood and picked up his box of donuts, which he'd give to the concierge in his building. "I'll be off now. Thanks again."

He strode toward the door, sliding his sunglasses over his eyes, and was about to step outside when he felt a hand on his shoulder.

"Ryan," Lindsay said, fingering a pink ruffle, "could I have my apron back?"

# CHAPTER 8

Noreen *Mathieson*—that was her new last name—leaned forward. "Enough about my honeymoon."

"Oh, I don't think so," Lindsay said. "You were away for a whole month, and we only exchanged, like, four emails. I need more stories about your family in India."

Noreen waved this away. "Later. Tell me about the baking lessons you've been giving this movie star."

"There's only been one lesson so far."

"And I've heard nothing about it. Spill! I watched one of his movies on the plane."

"Which movie?"

"The baked Alaska one. So, tell me all about him." Noreen rested her elbow on the table and put her chin in her hand, ready for gossip.

They were at Fantastical Brewing, a few doors down from Kensington Bake Shop. They'd been coming here regularly since opening the bakery, and this was probably the first time that more than a month had passed without them grabbing a couple of beers here.

Noreen was drinking a Centaur Baltic Porter and Lindsay had

a Unicorn Tears Sour. She'd been excited it was on tap—it hadn't been available since last fall. It was good to see her friend again, and they'd been lucky to snag a patio seat on a Sunday afternoon.

"We made donuts for our first lesson," Lindsay said, "with vanilla glaze and—"

"I don't want to hear about the *donuts*," Noreen said.

Lindsay laughed. After years of friendship, she knew how to get on Noreen's nerves.

"It was a little awkward at first." Lindsay sipped her beer. "I mean, I'm not used to giving private baking lessons, and I'd just binge-watched his show."

"Is he as handsome in real life as on-screen?"

"Oh, definitely."

Noreen smirked.

Lindsay ignored that. "He clearly didn't have much experience in the kitchen, but he didn't let it bother him. He was pretty easygoing. Not afraid to make a bit of an ass of himself. Made me laugh a bunch of times."

"Mm-hmm."

"I've watched a few of his interviews—"

"Just a few?"

"Yes, just a few," Lindsay said. "He comes across as a little cocky, but in real life, he isn't full of himself. Just comfortable in his own skin."

"As he should be when he looks like that."

"Really, he comes across as genuine. Even adorably awkward at times."

Yes, Ryan Kwok was paid to act for a living, but it hadn't felt like he was acting . . . although that could mean he was just a really good actor. He'd been nominated for awards, after all. How many Asian actors had been nominated for a Golden Globe? There couldn't be a lot.

Lindsay had started *Unraveling* last night, and it had been hard to watch, emotionally—a testament to how good he was at what he did. She still had to finish it.

"You like him, don't you?" Noreen raised her eyebrows over her beer.

"Maybe a little. I mean . . ." Lindsay made some ridiculous gesture meant to encompass Ryan's good looks and fairly down-to-earth personality.

Her best friend likely understood exactly what she meant. The advantage of knowing someone so well.

"You going to make a move?" Noreen asked.

"What? No! He's famous, and I'm an ordinary person. He's a little flirty—"

"Is he, now?"

"I'm sure it doesn't mean anything. It's just the way he is."

Lindsay's cheeks heated as she recalled when she'd held the cinnamon sugar donut hole up to his mouth. For a second, she'd thought he would kiss her.

But then the moment had passed.

It had all been in her imagination, surely.

"There's nothing wrong with a little harmless crush on the movie star who's taking baking lessons from you." Noreen shook her head. "Certainly not something I ever thought we'd be doing when we opened the bakery, but here we are."

"I do want to date again," Lindsay said quietly, spinning her glass around her coaster. "Like, have a boyfriend, not just hook up with guys on occasion, which is all I've been doing for a while now. Not that there's anything wrong with it, but . . ."

But she did yearn to have something more. She'd liked being in a relationship, back in high school and university. She'd had a couple of long-term boyfriends.

And then her father had gotten sick.

The cancer had been all through his body, and he hadn't had much time left. Lindsay's boyfriend had broken up with her a month after the funeral—she'd wondered whether he'd waited until it had been an appropriate length of time, whatever "appropriate" was.

*It's just getting too serious*, he'd told her.

She'd been disappointed, but not all that disappointed. She'd felt like something was off in their relationship, too.

In fact, she'd felt disconnected from her peers in general. She'd been twenty-two, and even though losing a parent by that age wasn't super uncommon, none of her friends had lost a parent. They didn't get it.

Still, her friendships from university had endured, but for some reason, she'd struggled to put herself out there again.

Lindsay had made no new friends since the age of twenty-two. She'd met Noreen a year before her father died; she hadn't made friends in their baking program after college. She felt like she couldn't connect with anyone she hadn't known for a long time, and she also couldn't stand to form close relationships with people who hadn't known her *before*, who only knew the *after*.

That extended to romantic relationships, too. She'd tried a few times, but it hadn't gone well. Four years ago, she'd given up and restricted herself to sex without romance.

But dammit, she did miss it.

Noreen squeezed her hand. "It'll be better now than it was a few years ago. You're in a better place."

Then why was she still struggling to make friends?

And why did dating scare the shit out of her?

Hmm. Perhaps she should stop reading advice columns and forums where women posted about their terrible dating experiences. Those used to comfort her and make her glad she was single, but they probably weren't helping now.

Yes, there were some crappy men out there, but there were good men, too. Her best friend was happily married to one, for example.

"I'm going to find someone for you," Noreen said. "Give me a little time. But tonight . . ." She grinned. "How about a trip to the movie theater?"

**THERE WAS SOMETHING** surreal about seeing Ryan Kwok on the big screen.

Lindsay had watched every episode of *Just Another New York Sitcom*, as well as *The Journey of the Baked Alaska* and half of *Unraveling*, in her living room. She was used to seeing Ryan Kwok in action.

But she wasn't used to watching him with a few dozen other people in the audience—the theater wasn't empty, but it was far from full.

And she wasn't used to seeing such a huge close-up of his abs. Why, they must be almost as tall as she was!

The woman in front of her sighed dreamily.

Lindsay, on the other hand, choked on her popcorn, and Noreen patted her knee.

Once she'd recovered from her coughing fit, she turned back to the screen, just in time to see Ryan Kwok, his shirt still unbuttoned to display his physical assets, gently sweep his thumb over the heroine's cheek and look at her as though she hung the stars in the sky, even if they were locked in a supply closet.

A rush of jealousy spread through Lindsay, much to her annoyance.

For God's sake, this was his job.

Besides, he wasn't hers, in any shape or form.

And now the couple had their mouths on each other, and Lindsay was unable to tamp down her jealousy, unable to stop wondering what it would be like if he touched her and kissed her like that.

She clenched her inner muscles and swallowed hard.

He was just so . . .

Well, fucking gorgeous.

His lips, the intensity of his gaze, the way his eyes crinkled at the corners . . .

Ooh, his shirt was coming off now, and she got a close-up view of his arm muscles. Nice.

Unfortunately, or perhaps fortunately—Lindsay was conflicted—the hook-up in the supply closet was soon interrupted by the groom's mother.

*That Kind of Wedding* was about a wedding where everything went wrong. Ryan Kwok played the best man and Irene Lai played the maid of honor, and they were desperately trying to prevent the wedding from being a complete disaster, despite the fact that they'd hated each other since having a one-night stand at a toga party back in college. Naturally, they also had to deal with their growing feelings for each other, in addition to several wardrobe malfunctions, a runaway goat, a runaway penguin, the mother of the bride getting burned during the tea ceremony, an unfortunate incident with bird's nest soup, wedding game shenanigans, and bad behavior from various family members—some fueled by alcohol, some not.

Overall, the movie wasn't bad. Yes, the script left a little to be desired, but it was enjoyable nonetheless. Not just because Lindsay knew one of the stars in real life, though he was definitely the best part of the movie.

And she was teaching him how to bake! How cool was that?

Okay, she definitely had a tiny crush on him, but it was only natural. Many people would feel the same way in her situation. It wasn't like anything was going to happen—and not only because his love life wasn't important to him. He probably still casually dated and had sex. With people more like Irene Lai.

Somehow, Lindsay would manage to get her dating life back on track, just not with a guy like him—hopefully Noreen would find a nice date for her.

By the time she got home, it was after ten o'clock. Vivian was in the living room, watching something on TV, when Lindsay walked in.

"I saw *That Kind of Wedding* with a friend tonight," Lindsay said.

"Yeah?" Vivian said. "How was it?"

"It wasn't a revolutionary piece of cinema, but it was fun."

Lindsay got ready for bed and picked out her outfit for tomorrow. No reason she wanted to look nice for the baking lesson. Nope, no reason whatsoever. Nothing too fancy, of course. Just her most flattering pair of jeans and a casual blouse with polka dots.

As she drifted off to sleep, she couldn't help thinking of a certain set of abs.

**"HI, LINDSAY!" MOM** said over the phone. "What's up?"

"Not much." Lindsay looked out the window of Kensington Bake Shop. Ryan Kwok was supposed to be here any minute.

"I wanted to tell you about this great new drink I had yesterday. Bubble tea."

"Um," Lindsay said. "What is this? Nineteen ninety-nine?"

"I figured you'd probably had it. Actually, I seem to recall you going out for bubble tea with your friends in high school. *I'd* never had it before, though. It seems like more of a young person thing, but Harold knew just the place to go."

"Who's Harold?"

"Oh, a guy I've been seeing," Mom said airily.

"What happened to Wade?"

"It's not like I made any promises to be exclusive. Though I've decided I like Harold better. I'll have to let Wade down gently. The poor man—I think he was more into me than I was into him."

"What else did you and Harold do on your date?"

"He took me to a noodle restaurant. It was quite good."

"And then did you go home and scandalize Trevor by putting a sock on the doorknob?"

"No, don't worry, we went for a *nightcap* at his place."

A nightcap. Indeed.

Lindsay did not ask for clarification.

"Don't worry," Mom said, "I won't bring him to the bakery this week. I understand it was a bit soon last time, but I think things might work out with this man."

"Well, that's great, Mom. I'm happy for you."

And she genuinely was, even if some complicated feelings were swirling inside her. Even if it was strange that her mother was dating a lot more than she was.

She glanced out the window. Nope, Ryan wasn't here yet.

"What kind of bubble tea did you have?" she asked.

"Passion fruit black milk tea—I think I got that right? With tapioca pearls and jellies, though the jellies were a bit hard to get up the straw."

"Sounds delicious." Maybe Lindsay should go out for boba soon. She and Noreen used to frequent a tea shop near their old apartment, but she hadn't been since she'd moved.

"Oh, I forgot to mention something about Harold."

*Please don't tell me how good a kisser he is. Please.*

"He's Chinese."

That was actually quite surprising.

Lindsay's mother was a bit of an Asian-hating Asian. It had

taken a while for Lindsay to comprehend the extent of her mom's internalized racism, but eventually it had become obvious.

It made Lindsay sad. The racism her mother had experienced as a child must have caused her to be this way, keen to reject her Chinese heritage and only date white men. Mom had had a bunch of boyfriends before she'd met Lindsay's dad, and every single one had been white.

So this was an interesting development.

Just then, there was a knock at the door, and a handsome face peeked through the window.

"Sorry, Mom, I have to go," Lindsay said. "Talk to you soon."

She ended the call and stepped toward the door.

"Hi, Ryan. Ready to make more donuts?"

But in truth, all she could think was, *I saw your abs at the movie theater yesterday!*

Hopefully she could get through this lesson without making it weird.

# CHAPTER 9

W e'll make a basic custard recipe that can be used as a filling for crème brûlée donuts," Lindsay said, "as well as a choc-olate espresso custard. Then we'll make vanilla glaze again, plus chocolate ganache."

Inside her head, however, she kept replaying scenes from *That Kind of Wedding* over in her mind. She couldn't help it.

"Sounds good," Ryan said. "By the way, I'd appreciate it if you didn't spread news of these lessons far and wide. At some point, I'll post about Kensington Bake Shop on social media, but not yet."

Lindsay nodded. "The only people who know are our employ-ees. And my mother."

His expression froze for a split second. "Your mother knows about me?"

"I was talking to her before you arrived. She told me she'd just discovered bubble tea."

He held her gaze for a moment and laughed softly.

And oh God, when he looked at her like that, it made her brain completely incapable of rational thought. He'd chosen the pink ruffled apron again, and he was wearing it on top of a blue Henley.

"I saw your abs last night!" she blurted out.

"Lindsay," he drawled, "the whole world has seen my abs. There's a hashtag for that."

"I know." She covered her face with her hands. "I've searched the hashtag on Twitter."

"Is that so?" he murmured.

"But that's not what I was doing last night. I went to see your movie with my friend. Your abs were in high definition and almost as tall as I am, and now I can't look at you without thinking about it."

She continued to cover her face with her hands, mortified. Why was she allowed out in public? There was just something about being alone in a kitchen with a movie star . . .

Fingers grasped her wrists and pulled her hands down from her face.

His eyes were dancing. He was so close she could feel the warmth radiating off him.

"Don't think about all that movie stuff," he said. "Besides, it's not like I'm as famous as Ryan Gosling or Ryan Reynolds."

God, he must think she was such a dork, but he was kind about it.

"I'm also the guy who ruined a batch of matcha tiramisu donuts."

"Don't remind me."

"Think of me like that," he said. "A clumsy guy who doesn't know how to bake. See? No reason to feel weird around me."

His fingers were still wrapped around her wrists. His touch was gentle and sweet—so different from how he'd touched Irene Lai in that supply closet.

He let go of her. "Did you like the movie? If you hated it, that's okay, you can tell me. My ego can take it."

"I did like it. It was better than many of the reviews suggested."

He nodded, then opened his mouth.

It was several more seconds before any words came out, though.

"I do worry," he said. "This movie isn't exactly a critical or box office success, and I'm worried what it'll mean for the future of such movies in North America with Asian actors."

"Yeah, I heard someone talking about that on a podcast a couple months ago. That the real test of the growth in films with Asian leads would be what happened when one flops."

"Which podcast is this?"

She told him, and he took out his phone to make a note.

"I'm thankful for the roles I've been able to get," he said. "When I was younger, there were two main options for Asian actors here: they had to be martial arts stars, or they were the butt of jokes. I told my dad I wanted to play James Bond when I grew up, and he said no way would that ever happen."

"What was it you liked about James Bond? The gadgets? The women?"

"I just thought he was really cool. Everything, I guess." He shrugged. "I begged my dad to let me take some kind of martial arts, but . . ."

She sensed his relationship with his father was a sore spot.

But then he brightened. "Anyway, I'm glad you like the movie. And my abs."

He returned his attention to the custard recipe, and she showed him how to separate eggs.

"Is separating the eggs really necessary?" he asked. "It seems like a pain in the ass."

She gave him a look. "Yes, it's necessary, as is knowing the difference between a teaspoon and a tablespoon, even if some contestants on *Baking Fail* believe otherwise."

He laughed.

"I've been watching some episodes for research purposes," she told him.

"You take your job seriously."

"Of course I do."

After they'd fried the donuts, she poked a hole in the top of a donut with a cake dowel, put the chocolate espresso custard in a piping bag, and squeezed some inside. Then she dipped it in chocolate ganache, added a swirl of whipped cream on top, and garnished it with a chocolate-covered espresso bean.

Just like the donut he'd bought the other week.

Once he'd made five of these, they started on the crème brûlée donuts. Her favorite. After filling each one with custard, she showed him how to dip the donut in the glaze, then caramelize some sugar with a little blowtorch, constantly moving it back and forth over the donut so it didn't burn.

Next, it was time for the Nanaimo bars. Lindsay had already put out the ingredients for the first layer, including coconut and graham cracker crumbs.

"This is a double boiler," she said, placing it on the range. "We'll start by combining the butter, cocoa powder, and sugar in it."

Ryan peered at it curiously, like he'd peered at the shamrock-green suit he was supposed to wear in *That Kind of Wedding*.

"It looks like a steamer," he said, "without holes for the steam."

They made the first layer and put it in the fridge to cool, then started on the second layer of the classic Canadian treat.

"It's custard-flavored buttercream," Lindsay explained. "Buttercream is definitely something you'll have to master for this competition. It'll likely come in handy in both the cupcake and the cake rounds."

"Huh. I had no idea what was in Nanaimo bars, other than sugar and chocolate. But I always liked them—though not as much as Jenna."

They were becoming more comfortable together. Lindsay was always conscious of where he was in relation to her, and his soapy scent was nearly as intoxicating as that of fresh donuts, but since the I-saw-your-abs-last-night incident, she'd managed to keep herself from doing anything too stupid. He talked about his work with her, and sure, that was the movie business, but she was getting used to it.

After the lesson, Ryan suggested they eat their baked goods and drink coffee, like last week. "Or is that too weird, now that you've seen my abs on the big screen?" He winked at her.

"I think I'll manage. But I have to clean up first."

"I'll help."

"No, no," she said, "you don't need to do that."

"I'll make the coffee, then. Or a latte?"

"Umm . . ."

"I do know how to use an espresso machine. For a few years, I worked as a barista at Rise and Shine." He jerked his thumb in the general direction of the coffee shop. "You know it?"

"I used to go there regularly when I was in university. Maybe eight years ago?"

"Then I may have made you a latte before."

"Oh, I never would have ordered something as fancy as a latte. Just drip coffee, or tea if it was late—cheaper than a latte, you know. I really liked studying there. They had a quiet upstairs where there were always lots of students working."

Curious she didn't remember him—surely she would have remembered a man like Ryan, right? Or maybe he'd worked early shifts. She hadn't exactly been an early bird in those days.

Ten minutes later, the kitchen was mostly tidied, and the aroma of espresso was calling to Lindsay. She went downstairs, and Ryan, still in the frilly pink apron, made a show of pulling out a chair for her. There was a plate with a crème brûlée donut and Nanaimo bar in front of her chair, as well as a large latte with . . .

"A swan?" she said. "Did you seriously make swan latte art?"

"I'm a man of hidden talents." He waggled his eyebrows as he folded himself into the chair across from her.

*Yeah, I bet you are.*

"Taking off your shirt and making latte art. A winning combination."

It felt like one friend teasing another.

He barked out a laugh. "Yeah. I suppose you could say that."

She bit into her Nanaimo bar and groaned. Damn, that was good. They sold these in the shop, but she hadn't eaten one in quite a while.

When she glanced up, Ryan was looking at her, well . . . a bit like the way he'd looked at Irene Lai in the movie.

Perhaps she was flattering herself.

But Lindsay couldn't shake the thought that she wasn't.

She pasted on a smile. "Shall we tackle cupcakes next week?"



**RYAN TOSSED THE** script on his desk in frustration. He had no interest in auditioning for the role of this Chinatown gangster. It appeared the main purpose of the Chinese character was so other characters could make racist jokes, half of them about his accent.

Yeah, no, thank you.

Once, he might have considered it for the paycheck, but fortunately, he was no longer that desperate. Why had his agent sent this to him? Did Bob think these were the only kinds of roles he could get after the reception of *That Kind of Wedding*? Ryan didn't believe that was true, but he couldn't help the thread of worry running through him.

He needed to have a talk with his agent. Bob knew Ryan was taking a break now, until the fall, but he was glad his agent had contacted him about *Baking Fail*, and if a really great script hit Bob's desk, Ryan wanted to hear about it. Not about stuff like this, though. The fetishization of the Chinese woman in the script was super cringeworthy, too. Ugh.

He was about to head to the kitchen when his phone buzzed. Mel had sent him a link. Ryan clicked on it.

*Oh no. Not again.*

It was an article about Melvin Lee voicing a character in an upcoming animated film. Ryan hadn't heard of the project, but he had no doubt Mel would be great in the role of—he read the line over again, just to be sure—killer penguin, the sidekick to Presley the Polar Bear.

But the reason Mel had sent the link? The photo.

They'd used a picture of Ryan instead of Mel.

This wasn't the first time the two of them had been confused, and Ryan had been mixed up with other Asian actors, even though the internet was *right there* to look up stuff like this.

There was already a firestorm on Twitter about it. Lots of tweets pointed out that Ryan Kwok and Melvin Lee looked nothing alike (true), and Asian people commented on their experiences of being mixed up with other Asian colleagues and classmates.

Other people told them to lighten up, it was an honest mistake. Just like they'd tell Ryan to lighten up about the racist jokes in the script on his desk, before complaining that no one was allowed to be funny anymore.

Ryan was about to tweet something, but then he sighed and put his phone down. He was tired of this shit. Besides, it was time to head to his sister's with the Nanaimo bars he'd made with Lindsay yesterday.

**WHEN RYAN ARRIVED** at Jenna's, the townhome was a disaster zone. Jenna was usually neat and organized, but her hair was pointing every which way, and there were dark circles under her eyes . . . and nothing was where it belonged.

A book on breastfeeding was perched precariously on the dining room table. He pushed it to the center of the table before it could fall, then passed his sister the container of treats.

"You made these?" she said.

"I'm taking classes. I told you, didn't I?"

She nodded, and he followed her into the kitchen, knocking into some kind of contraption—a bouncer?—on the way.

"Is he sleeping?" Ryan asked.

"Yeah. Finally."

Jenna set the container down on the kitchen counter and did a very un-Jenna-like thing: she pulled out a Nanaimo bar and stuffed it right in her mouth, without getting a napkin or plate first. There were crumbs on the table. Actual crumbs.

"Wow, this is surprisingly good," Jenna said. "You sure you made these?" She sent him a lopsided grin, and yeah, that was more like his sister. "These are the best Nanaimo bars I've ever had, and I consider myself a connoisseur."

"I'll tell Lindsay you approve."

"Lindsay, eh? Is this the woman who's teaching you how to bake for *Baking Fail*?"

"Yep, that's her."

Jenna had a strange gleam in her eye. Uh-oh. "What's *Lindsay* like? Is she a big fan of your work?"

"Well, she didn't know who I was when I walked into the bakery and knocked over her donuts—"

"This sounds like a rom-com you could star in."

*I don't know if I'm getting any more roles in rom-coms. Not as the lead, anyway. Maybe as the ethnic best friend.*

"Anyway," he said, "she's since watched *Just Another New York Sitcom* and went to the theater to see *That Kind of Wedding.*"

"I haven't seen it yet," Jenna said. "I'm sorry. As much as I want to see you deal with a bridezilla and chase a lamb through a church—"

"It's a goat, actually."

She gave him her classic big-sister look. It was hard for him to explain exactly what that look meant, even though she'd done it his entire life. Something like, *You're annoying and I'm thoroughly unimpressed with you, but I'll put up with you anyway because I love you.* Today, that look made him smile. It reassured him.

Just then, an ear-piercing wail filled the house.

Jenna's face fell. "He won't even let me eat a Nanaimo bar."

The wailing, by some miracle, got even louder—Ryan hadn't known seven pounds could be that loud. His new nephew sure knew how to project his voice.

"I'm coming, love!" Jenna called, rushing upstairs.

Ryan left half an hour later, feeling like he was getting in the way. He didn't know anything about newborns, and Jenna seemed frazzled—and she didn't usually like people seeing her like that. He wanted to help, but he didn't know how.

He wondered whether his father had visited Jenna since the hospital. Whether Dad, like Ryan, would feel rather helpless in this situation. Probably.

Mom, on the other hand, would have known what to do.

Next week, Ryan would make cupcakes, something he'd last done with his mother. He'd enjoyed his baking lessons with Lindsay thus far, but he wasn't looking forward to Monday.

Fucking cupcakes.

# CHAPTER 10

Ryan shouldn't have worried.

Cupcake week was going *great*.

Lindsay looked cute in the pink ruffled apron, the one he'd started thinking of as *his*. But she'd been wearing it when he showed up at Kensington Bake Shop today.

"I stole your apron," she'd said with a wink, and he'd laughed, even as that wink had done certain . . . *things* to him.

They were making two types of cupcakes: chocolate raspberry and chocolatey chocolate. The cupcakes were cooling on the rack right now. While they were in the oven, Ryan and Lindsay had made raspberry jam to fill the chocolate raspberry cupcakes and chocolate ganache—like they'd made for the donuts—for the other cupcakes. She'd refused to help him with the chocolate ganache, since he'd done it before, and it turned out pretty well, he thought. It helped that it only had two ingredients.

Now they were starting on the buttercream. Lindsay was going to make the raspberry buttercream in her stand mixer, and he'd do the chocolate buttercream in his.

"I was thinking," she said, "since you're such a fan of the chocolate espresso donuts, do you want to make it chocolate espresso buttercream instead?"

"You know how to make chocolate espresso buttercream?" he asked, but it was a stupid question.

Of course she did. She knew how to do everything in the kitchen.

Whereas he was just starting to feel comfortable with using the stand mixer.

"We'll add a little espresso powder," she said. "It's right . . . Dammit, Beth put it on the top shelf."

Ryan might not know much about baking, but reaching things on high shelves? This was something he could do. He was at least six inches taller than Lindsay.

"Allow me, m'lady," he said with a purposely terrible British accent—his accent coach would have covered her ears in pain— and a grandiose sweep of his arm.

It made Lindsay laugh, as he'd hoped.

Several minutes later, they both had all their ingredients in their bowls—butter, powdered sugar, cocoa powder, cream, vanilla, and espresso powder in his, whereas hers was pink from raspberry jam—and it looked like it was nearly ready.

He glanced over at her, in that cute pink apron, and their gazes held for a moment more than would usually be comfortable, but he didn't want to look away.

Yes, these baking classes had been a great idea.

When she declared the buttercream was done, he turned off the mixer.

"Try it." She handed him a spoon. "We can add more espresso powder if you like."

He dipped the small spoon into the buttercream and slid it into his mouth, closing his eyes to savor it.

It was, indeed, delicious, and he'd *made* that.

He was no expert at baking, but there was something soothing about it. Walking into the kitchen and walking out a few hours later with something tangible, something beautiful and tasty. Too bad everything in his life couldn't be this simple.

Though without Lindsay to guide him, it probably wouldn't be quite so soothing.

When he opened his eyes and put the spoon down, she was looking at him with a peculiar expression.

"You want to try the raspberry?" she asked.

He nodded, and she passed him a spoon with the pink buttercream.

It was good, but . . .

"Mine is better."

She rolled her eyes. "Who told you what to do and how much of each ingredient to use?"

"Oh, I know, I know." He grinned.

"You're just obsessed with espresso."

"You may have a point."

"*May* have a point?"

She showed him how to fill the cupcakes, half of them with the raspberry jam, and half with the chocolate ganache. The cupcakes on *Baking Fail* were always filled, presumably because it provided more opportunities for the contestants to screw up, so this was good practice.

Next, she showed him how to pipe the buttercream. She made it look effortless, but when he did it, the results weren't quite as beautiful, though by the time he piped chocolate espresso buttercream on the last cupcake, he was starting to get the hang of it.

Why had he worried about making cupcakes? It was all going swimmingly. Yes, the memory of baking cupcakes with his mother was at the back of his mind, but it was a manageable twinge, nothing more.

"Now we'll garnish them," Lindsay said, popping one raspberry on top of each chocolate raspberry cupcake. She passed him the chocolate-covered espresso beans for the other cupcakes, and they worked in tandem. At one point, his arm brushed hers, and when she got a little buttercream on her finger, he couldn't help wanting to lick it . . . or eat a raspberry from her hand.

But he didn't.

When they were finished, she swept her arms over the rack of chocolate raspberry and chocolatey chocolate cupcakes.

"I know which one you're going to eat," she said.

"Yeah, you know it." He reached for a cupcake with chocolate espresso buttercream.

"They're delicious, I promise. Best-ever chocolate cupcakes, if I do say so myself."

He stilled.

*Best-ever chocolate cupcakes.*

The recipe he'd made with his mother. That was what it had said. She'd described their burnt, hideous creations to his father with those exact words.

All of a sudden, it was no longer a twinge at the back of his mind.

For much of the past few months, he'd felt a bit numb, but now that numbness had been ripped off like a bandage, and he could see, so clearly, that afternoon with his mother, as though it was a movie playing right in front of him.

Something he'd never, ever get to do again. He wouldn't get to bake with his mom; he wouldn't go out for dim sum with her; he wouldn't receive any new messages from her.

He'd known all that, of course. She'd been gone for more than four months.

He'd known . . . and yet it was suddenly more real than it had been before.

It was like some part of his brain had been expecting him to wake up from this nightmare. She'd show up at his condo with food he didn't need, and it would all be good.

And now he knew that would never, ever happen, and the grief that he'd been trying to shove down . . . he could feel it in every cell in his body.

He staggered to the side and clutched the counter with one hand.

"Ryan?" Lindsay's voice seemed far away.

A tissue appeared in his hand, and he realized he was crying.

He was usually very aware of his body, but it was like a circuit was broken now and things weren't connected the way they usually were.

It took the utmost concentration to raise his hand to his face and dab at his eyes.

"Hey," Lindsay said softly. "You okay? Never mind, that's a stupid question." She rested her hand on his arm and squeezed.

He pulled her against him. She was real and present, and he needed to hold on to something.

"Is this all right?" he asked.

She put her arms around him and ran her hands up and down his back. Eventually, he stopped shedding tears and was left with an awful feeling of hollowness.

"I'll make you a latte." Lindsay led him downstairs and pushed him into a chair. She went back to the kitchen and returned a minute later with two plates, each with a single cupcake. The first was topped with raspberry buttercream—he recognized it as one of the ones she'd piped. The swirl of buttercream was shockingly perfect. The other, with chocolate espresso buttercream, was one of his. The swirl . . . well, it wasn't quite right. It was lopsided. He'd gotten lots of buttercream on the cupcake liner, too.

Focusing on these little details seemed to ground him.

The hiss of the espresso machine, the aroma of a coffee shop. These were good. Familiar.

Lindsay placed a cup in front of him and sat down. "Sorry, I can't do a swan."

He laughed because he needed to laugh, but it sounded tinny and weird.

"You don't have to talk," she said, "but if you want to . . . I'm here."

"My mom." The words came out before he could think, and his voice was raspy. "She died suddenly earlier this year and . . ." He shook his head. "We made cupcakes together once, not all that long ago, really. They came out terribly." He forced out a rueful chuckle. "'Best-ever chocolate cupcakes.' She said that, just like you did, and I . . ."

"Sometimes the little things can set you off."

"That's why I'm taking a break for a while and staying in Toronto. I'm trying to be there for my dad and sister, but I don't know what I'm doing."

Lindsay rubbed her thumb over his palm.

He squeezed her hand. "My dad and I were never close, and instead of talking to me, he grunts a lot and posts weird shit on Twitter. My sister was five months pregnant when Mom died. The baby is a couple weeks old now, and I just feel so helpless. And the baking lessons . . . I needed a distraction. My mom loved *Baking Fail*—that's why I'm doing it."

God, did his words even make any sense? Maybe he'd spoken a stream of gibberish.

But she nodded. "I know what it's like. It's a little different for everyone, of course, but . . ." She paused. "My dad died when I was twenty-two."

"I'm sorry," he said, his heart hurting for her. "We don't have to talk about this—"

"No, it's fine. Though it never entirely goes away."

Yes, he'd been told that, and it made sense—how could this ever completely go away?

"The first year was the worst for me," she said. "Still, it comes in waves. My mom started dating again recently, and it's been seven years and I support that, but it's weird. The first guy she dated looked a bit like my dad."

His father dating . . . Ryan shook his head. He couldn't wrap his mind around it. The thought of his father being with anyone other than his mom caused him to seize up.

But maybe, in a few years.

Okay, now he couldn't help laughing.

His father, going on dates? Signing up for a dating app? It was beyond the bounds of his imagination. Just the idea that his dad had ever been on a date in his life was kind of hilarious.

How had his parents met, back in Hong Kong? He had no idea.

"Sorry," he said, choking down the rest of his laughter. "I can see how it would be hard."

"Don't worry, it's fine. When my dad died, my grief made people uncomfortable, so I'd try to hide it, and then occasionally . . . I couldn't. But there's nothing wrong with letting yourself feel it, whether you end up laughing or crying. It's not healthy to push it all down."

"You're my baking instructor. This isn't your job."

"It's fine, Ryan, truly. I'd tell you if it wasn't. This . . ." She gestured between them. "It's as friends. How is your sister doing now?"

"I think she's a bit overwhelmed, and I'm not sure how to help. She liked the Nanaimo bars, though." He pulled out his phone and brought up a picture of him and his as-yet-unnamed nephew. One of the ones he wouldn't post on social media.

"Aww, he's adorable."

"Jenna said I looked just like that when I was born."

"So, an older sister?"

"Yeah, she's a few years older." He had a sip of his latte.

"Well, if your nephew takes after you, he's going to be a very cute kid."

"You think I'm cute?"

She blushed. "A *lot* of people think you're cute. I had to steal your favorite pink apron today so I wouldn't be overwhelmed by the cuteness."

"So that's why I'm stuck wearing this." He gestured at his red apron, which was covered in flour and chocolate ganache.

"Yeah, poor you." Her eyes flickered with amusement . . . but also understanding.

It had been a long time since he'd felt like someone *got* him like this.

"Do you have another film lined up?" she asked.

"Yeah. Not a big role, though." From a rom-com to a horror film—somehow, that seemed appropriate. He'd agreed to do it just before his mother had passed away.

But although Lindsay had changed the topic, he knew he could go back to talking about his mom at any time, and she would listen.

"There's something I've been curious about," she said. "Can I ask you a question?"

"Sure."

"The actors you make films with . . . are you friends with them? Like, you must spend a lot of time together on set."

"I'm friendly with many people, but the only person I've really stayed friends with is Melvin Lee. You know who's a total ass, though?"

"Juan Velazquez?"

"Oh, no. Juan's cool. He's been doing pretty well on Broadway. Haven't seen him in a while. Jory Tyler, on the other hand . . ."

Lindsay put a hand to her mouth and gasped. "Really?"

"Yeah. Total jerk to everyone on set."

"I liked his character in *The Journey of the Baked Alaska*. He wrote the script, right?"

"He's talented. But . . ." Ryan shook his head. "On the other hand, I really enjoyed working with Herbie Chin. He played my grandfather in a couple episodes of *Just Another New York Sitcom*."

"Yes! He reminded me of my grandpa, actually."

"He's had minor roles in films and television going back decades. He even met Anna May Wong once, you know? He was born in the US, but in every role until *JANYS*, he's had a foreign accent. A lot of villains—because that's what he could get. He once lost the role of an Asian man to a white actor."

"Things have definitely changed."

"Yeah, they have, even if the press keeps mixing up me and Melvin."

Lindsay rolled her eyes. "I can imagine."

Ryan should write to Herbie. The elderly man had been a mentor figure of sorts, and Ryan had helped him set up an email account, which he diligently checked once a day.

You never knew when it would be too late.

Another wave of grief passed through him, and he shuddered, even though he'd been smiling a moment ago.

Lindsay touched his hand. She didn't seem uncomfortable with any of this, and that was a nice change—different from his own family. But he didn't want to burden her too much.

"You'll probably never be the same again," she said, "but that's okay. Just the way it is."

Ryan went very, very still.

His character in *Unraveling* had been told something similar. Life was imitating art.

Though there were no signs of the zombie apocalypse.

Not yet, anyway.

Lindsay finished her cupcake and licked her fingers. "You going to eat that?" She gestured to the cupcake in front of him. "Because if you don't want it . . ."

She playfully slid the plate toward her, but he circled his fingers around her wrist. "Thank you," he said quietly, and then louder: "I worked long and hard to make that cupcake. Best-ever chocolate cupcake, right? No way am I letting you eat it."

She laughed and relinquished the cupcake.

He licked the imperfect swirl of buttercream on top. It didn't look the prettiest, but it did taste divine, and he wished he could bring a dozen to his mom.

The thought caused something to push on the hollowness in his chest, and yet it felt . . . slightly manageable now. Horrible, but somewhat manageable.

He bit into the cupcake. It was moist, not at all burnt, and concentrating on what he was eating—that calmed him.

Though the way Lindsay was looking at him had the opposite effect.

"Good?" She spoke with the confidence of someone who knew exactly what the answer would be.

And she should be pleased with herself. This was her recipe, and he couldn't have made it without her.

"Yeah, it's delicious," he said.

"You going to eat the other twenty-two cupcakes?"

"I might keep one for myself, but I'll give the others away."

"Could I keep a couple, if you don't mind? My roommate would be amused to eat a cupcake that Ryan Kwok made."

He laughed. "Sure, if you like." He finished his cupcake and sipped his latte. "What kind of cupcakes will we make next week? Have you decided?"

"I think so, but I'm not telling you." There was a look of mischief on her face. "It's a surprise."

"Lindsay . . ." He gave her his best smoldering look.

His smolder was quite fine, according to several movie critics, and was frequently discussed in #StarringRyanKwoksAbs tweets.

Lindsay, as expected, was not immune. Her pupils dilated and her lips parted . . . and God, she was pretty like that.

But she didn't cave.

"I'm still not telling you," she said. "Not even if you take off your shirt."

"Is that a challenge?" He removed his apron, then placed his hand on the hem of his shirt, but he didn't go any further. "I want to know what evil plan you have in store for me."

"Hey, I'm not *evil*."

"Villains always wear black . . . or pink ruffled aprons. It's a rule. Look it up."

She removed her apron and tossed it at him. "Let's just say the atmosphere in the kitchen next week will be a little closer to what you'll experience on the show."

"You going to round up some more actors who don't know how to bake? A couple judges and a host to comment on my progress?"

"You'll have to wait and see."

He wouldn't lie—he was a little alarmed. But he'd let her do this her way. And he was looking forward to next Monday regardless, because he got to see her.

She boxed up twenty cupcakes, then sent him out into the sunshine after giving his arm another squeeze.

He felt raw and a little disoriented, but all the murals in the market seemed brighter than usual, and he stopped to take a closer look at one with hot air balloons. The scent of grilled meat wafted out of a nearby café, and God, that seemed particularly potent today, too.

A little Asian kid on the other side of the street pointed at him, and Ryan was pretty sure he heard his name. The kid, who was maybe eight years old, started to run across the street, but his mom grabbed his hand just in time.

Ryan ambled over once the road was clear and crouched down.

The kid just stood there—for about two seconds—before saying, "Can I have your autograph, Mr. Kwok, please?"

The kid's mother produced a piece of paper from her purse, and he signed it and offered to pose in a picture with the kid, who nodded excitedly.

Ryan continued back to his condo in Yorkville, thinking about the fact that the mother had looked a lot like his own mom, twenty-five years ago, and it had been almost like stepping back in time.

He swiped a hand over his eyes and kept walking.

*You'll probably never be the same again, but that's okay.*

He hated that this was reality, wished he could visit his mother today, but he would learn to live with it, somehow. Make what he could of his life.

Like Lindsay had.

# CHAPTER 11

Lindsay was emptying the dishwasher when Vivian got home from work that day.

"How were today's baking lessons?" Vivian asked as she slipped off her shoes.

"They were good." Lindsay, of course, didn't tell her roommate that she and Ryan had had a long conversation about the loss of his mother. "He made you some cupcakes."

"He made *me* some cupcakes?"

"Well, there were two dozen, and I took a couple." Lindsay gestured to the Kensington Bake Shop box on the kitchen table. "I said my roommate would enjoy eating a cupcake that he'd baked."

Vivian pulled out a small plate and placed a chocolatey chocolate cupcake on it. Lindsay sat beside her but didn't help herself to a cupcake, since she'd had one with Ryan.

Eating cupcakes with movie stars. Just part of her regular life now.

"There's something really hot about a guy baking," Vivian said before taking a bite.

"Having studied baking and pastry arts with a number of guys, and after working in a bakery for so long, I'm mostly immune to it."

"Even to Ryan Kwok mixing up buttercream, or whatever this glorious stuff is?"

"Chocolate espresso buttercream. And no, I'm not entirely immune to him in a kitchen. Sometimes he wears a pink ruffled apron when he bakes, too."

"He's not insecure about his masculinity. That's good. My ex . . ." Vivian paused. "He baked."

This was the first time Vivian had mentioned an ex-boyfriend, or any other person in her life, for that matter.

"But wearing an apron—any apron—was a step too far for him." Vivian shook her head.

"He thought getting flour and chocolate on his clothing was manly?"

"Apparently. He only reluctantly started wearing an apron when I got him a *Star Wars* one. Literally the only thing I miss about him is the blueberry cheesecake he used to make."

Lindsay made a mental note to bake blueberry cheesecake for Vivian.

"That's why I have a two-bedroom condo," Vivian said. "My ex and I lived here together, though that didn't last long. Your room was the so-called office." She frowned before polishing off her cupcake and retreating to her bedroom.

Lindsay berated herself for not adding something about her own exes, although they were all ancient history now. That might have kept the conversation going a little longer.

But brief conversations here and there with Vivian—that was something.

And she'd spent a long time talking to Ryan today. She grinned as she thought about her idea for next week's lesson.

She was pretty sure she knew what she'd ask him to bake, but for research, she watched a few more episodes of *Baking Fail* and paid particular attention to the cupcake round. In the first episode, the contestants had to re-create salted caramel cupcakes with a vanilla buttercream. There was a caramel sauce filling, which they had to make themselves, of course.

So much could go wrong—and naturally, it did.

One person made the classic mistake of mixing up sugar and salt. Instead of lots of sugar and a little salt, she did the reverse. The first (and only) judge who tried it ran to the garbage can before assuring the contestant that he'd made this mistake before, too. Another person burned the caramel . . . as well as the cupcakes, since he had assumed oven temperature wasn't very important and hadn't set it correctly.

The third contestant added ice cubes to her buttercream, which made Lindsay cringe. She covered her face with her hands and peered at the screen through her fingers. What on earth was this lady trying to accomplish?

The fourth contestant didn't even attempt the caramel. Or the buttercream. But she seemed to be having a great time dancing around the kitchen, and she made a smiley face with melted chocolate on top of each cupcake.

Ms. Ice Cube won the cupcake round, since her creation was semi-edible and contained all the components, and there was much applause.

Next was the cake round, in which everyone was asked to make a unicorn-themed cake of their own design.

Lindsay had been asked to make several special-order unicorn cakes over the years. None of them had looked like the ones on *Baking Fail*.

Mr. Burnt Caramel decided to take an abstract approach to the theme, and his cake included lots and lots of rainbow sprinkles, but there was no actual representation of a unicorn.

Two of the others simply went for the unicorn horn and ears. Alas, Ms. Ice Cube's horn, which protruded from a nest of chocolate curls, was not sufficiently . . . stiff. It flopped over during judging, leading to many dirty jokes from the show's host, and Lindsay couldn't stop laughing. However, the judges did, for the most part, enjoy the taste of the cake, which they said was moist and chocolatey.

Ms. Salt Instead of Sugar was more ambitious and tried to cut her cake into the shape of a unicorn head. Unfortunately, she kept hacking off more and more cake to get the shape right, and by the end, there wasn't much left. She'd also gone overboard on the cotton candy flavoring.

In the end, Ms. Ice Cube/Flaccid Unicorn Horn was declared the winner.

Lindsay immediately started the next episode. In the first round, the contestants needed to make blueberry cheesecake donuts, which made her laugh in delight. She'd have to tell Vivian about this. The cupcakes in this episode were rosewater pistachio, and the pink buttercream was supposed to be in the shape of a rose on top of the cupcake—obviously that wasn't going to work out as planned. Someone would almost inevitably use too much rosewater and eating their cupcake would be more like eating potpourri.

However, Lindsay failed to anticipate that one of the contestants would slip on the mess they made on the floor and ruin all their cupcakes, though luckily, no body parts were broken. The cupcakes were the only casualties.

Well, she hoped Ryan wouldn't injure his beautiful self in her kitchen next week or make something revolting, since she'd be the one eating it.

But she could think of lots of ways to screw up the cupcakes she had in mind.

Or maybe he'd screw up in a completely unexpected manner . . .

. . .

*@RyanKwoksFather: This is not my son. Please do not be confused.*

The tweet included a picture of Melvin Lee doing stand-up.

Ryan chuckled. His father was addressing the Melvin Lee/Ryan Kwok mix-up, more than a week after it happened . . . so it was old news on Twitter. But Dad probably only checked Twitter about once a week, not every half hour like some people did.

The next tweet: *This is also not my son,* accompanied by a picture of Bruce Lee.

Ryan chuckled again.

After wasting more time, he put his phone down in frustration. He needed something to do. Maybe he'd call his dad and pick up the old family photo albums so he could scan in the pictures. He'd been thinking about it since yesterday's cupcake lesson with Lindsay. Looking at the old photos would be tough, but he really wanted a digital version of everything. Scanning pictures would be a good mini-project for him.

But when he'd called his father yesterday, there had been no answer; instead, he'd listened to his mother's voice telling him to leave a message.

Since it was so difficult to reach his father, why couldn't he stop over unannounced? Dad should be home—he never went anywhere in the evenings.

Ryan rubbed his hands together and nearly cackled.

A surprise visit from his son. Dad would *love* it.

It would be payback for all the times Ryan's parents had shown up at his place without warning. A regular occurrence, aside from the years he'd lived in LA. He suspected these had all been his mother's idea, however, and Dad had been dragged along to carry the boxes of food.

He couldn't show up empty-handed, so he put two of yesterday's cupcakes in a container, then made a quick trip to the fancy grocery store downstairs, where he bought bok choy and strawberries. Then he drove up to Markham, stopping on the way for char siu at the place his father liked. He also got some noodles. They could eat together, rather than Ryan having one of the premade, dietician-approved dinners in his fridge at home.

Ryan parked in the driveway of his childhood home, then picked up his small box of food from the trunk and knocked on the front door.

It took a couple of minutes, but Dad finally answered, a frown affixed to his face.

The frown only deepened at the sight of his son.

Great.

And yet, Ryan breathed out a sigh of relief. His dad not answering the phone was nothing new, but there had been a tiny fear at the back of his mind. What if something bad had happened and that was why Dad hadn't picked up?

"What are you doing here?" Dad demanded.

"Figured I'd visit my old man after his long day of work." Ryan slapped his father on the back.

Dad looked even more perplexed.

"It was not a long day of work," Dad said. "It was an average day."

"And you had time to tweet about your son."

Dad's expression changed from perplexed to horrified, as if Twitter was something that shouldn't be talked about in person. As if he hadn't expected Ryan to notice he had a Twitter account, despite replying to his tweets.

Ryan pushed past his father and into the front hall, setting down the food on the bench as he took off his shoes and put on the slippers he always wore when he was here.

He heard the TV, but before he could get to the living room, his father had turned it off, like he didn't want Ryan to see.

Interesting.

"What were you watching?" Ryan asked.

"Nothing," Dad said quickly.

"Sure didn't sound like nothing."

"A documentary on solar energy."

"Or were you watching a stoner movie? Or—God forbid—a sitcom?"

This was simply met with a glare.

After bringing the food to the kitchen, Ryan went to the living room. He was about to pick up the remote, but his father got there before him.

"Mind your own business," Dad said. "What I do in my own time is not important."

"Were you watching an erotic—"

"Aiyah, this is getting out of hand! Why are you here?"

"I told you, just visiting." Ryan paused. "And I want to get all the old photo albums. I figure I'll scan everything in."

"Ah, okay. But you should have called."

"You never pick up the phone. You're too busy watching mysterious TV shows and tweeting about Asian men who are not your son."

They were both silent for a moment, Ryan thinking about how differently this encounter would have gone if his mother were here.

"I'll get the albums from upstairs," Ryan said at last.

The albums were in his old bedroom, which his parents had redone a few years ago. He dumped the seven photo albums into an empty cardboard box he found in the closet.

When he got downstairs, his father was putting away the bok choy and strawberries.

"I don't know why you bought all this," Dad muttered. "I can take care of myself. And why did you bring me cupcakes?"

"I made them. I'm taking baking lessons because I'm going to be on a celebrity baking show."

"I really do not understand your life."

"Thanks."

"For example . . ."

Oh God. There were examples. Dad could go on for an hour.

". . . why do you retweet pictures of baby goats?"

Well, that wasn't where Ryan had expected this conversation to go.

"Why shouldn't I retweet pictures of baby goats? They're cute."

Dad just shook his head.

"You don't think baby animals are cute?" Ryan asked. "Ever? Did you see the video I retweeted with three baby goats prancing around?"

"I watched it. I expected it to include insightful facts about goats."

"Not everything is about gaining more knowledge. Are you really that unfamiliar with how things work on the internet?"

Dad made a sound of disgust, then started serving himself char siu and noodles.

They ate in silence for several minutes. Dad had always been a fast eater, and at family meals back in the day, Ryan had been the last one to finish eating, often because he'd been busy talking.

Ryan supposed it could be worse. His dad could be critiquing not just his retweets of baby goats, but everything about his career, and telling him to go back to engineering—and not only on Twitter this time—even though he'd failed out.

There had been significantly fewer comments about Ryan's career choice after his Golden Globe nomination, but Ryan feared he'd lose the little acceptance he had without his mother to interfere and argue with her husband. How would his family hang on without her?

"Have you visited Jenna?" he asked.

"No. She's busy. I don't want to bother her."

"Well, maybe ask her whether she'd like you to visit, rather than assuming?"

They finished their noodles, and Ryan pulled out the cupcakes.

"Try one," he said. "Even though you don't like sweets. Best-ever chocolate cupcakes."

He thought he saw a flash of . . . something cross his father's face, but possibly that was his imagination.

"Fine, if you insist," Dad said.

"This one has chocolate espresso buttercream and a chocolate ganache filling. The pink one has raspberry jam filling and raspberry buttercream."

Dad looked at him like he was speaking gibberish, and Ryan's lips twitched.

At last, Dad reached for the raspberry. "This one is prettier."

"Why, Dad, I didn't think you cared about such things. Of course, that's the one Lindsay frosted. Mine's not as pretty." He picked up the chocolatey chocolate cupcake.

Dad had a bite of his cupcake.

"What do you think?" Ryan asked.

"It's acceptable. Which baking show are you doing?"

"*Baking Fail.*"

"I saw an episode once," Dad said. "One contestant made a cake that looked like dog shit and apparently tasted like it, too."

"Mmm, I think I saw that episode."

"I hope you don't embarrass yourself. I guess it's good you are taking lessons."

"Yeah, but if I embarrass myself a little, who cares? It's all in good fun. But don't tell any of your Twitter followers that I'm doing the show. It's a secret for now."

Dad did not deign to reply. Instead, he started clearing the table. "You can go. Let me get back to my documentary on coral reefs."

"I thought it was a documentary on solar energy."

Dad froze.

*Ha! Caught you in a lie.*

"Why do you keep bugging me?" Dad asked.

"I hadn't visited you in two months."

"But you call me all the time."

An exaggeration. "You rarely answer. We only talk on the phone once or twice a week."

Dad had a point, though: it was more than they used to talk. Ryan had usually just spoken to his mother.

"I want to check on you," Ryan said. "Make sure you're doing okay. Can't I talk to my father?" His hand clenched on his cupcake wrapper.

He was good at charming people. How come his father was immune?

"I'm fine. See?" Dad gestured to himself. "If you want to make me feel better, make some intelligent movies for once. Narrate nature documentaries like David Attenborough."

For a split second, Ryan considered this, then wondered what on earth he was thinking. That wasn't his sort of thing.

"I'll take that into consideration," he said.

"You're being sarcastic."

"So?"

Dad didn't say anything more, and Ryan headed out a few minutes later, the photo albums in his trunk.

Talking to his father made Ryan feel like he should get over his mom's death. Dad hadn't explicitly said that, but he didn't seem to understand why Ryan would check up on him. Yes, Dad was surly, but no more so than usual. He'd always been like this.

Or had he? The thing was, Ryan didn't really know his father without his mother. He'd rarely spent time with just his father.

When Ryan got home, he immediately started on the photo albums. The first album contained an assortment of pictures from Hong Kong, including his parents' wedding. He set it aside for now and went to the second one. The first Canadian album. He started scanning in the photos from the beginning. There were three pictures per page, and on the fourth page, he found a picture of his mother when she was pregnant with Jenna. A quarter of the way through the album, Jenna appeared for the first time, squinty and wrinkled. There were various pictures of her being held by Mom, then one with Dad.

Ryan couldn't help flipping to the end of the photo album, to the first pictures of himself. He stared for a long time at the picture of him and his dad, then the first picture of the four of them. Jenna, age three, was half hiding behind a teddy bear, her finger stuck up her nose. Mom was smiling, though. As was Dad.

Ryan thought of all the photos that couldn't be taken.

Mom with Jenna's baby, for example.

Ezra, that was the baby's name. Jenna had texted the other day.

When Ryan looked at that photo, he also wondered what his parents had thought about the future. If they'd imagined growing old together and having a house full of grandchildren visiting on Chinese New Year.

They almost certainly hadn't imagined their son appearing in a stoner movie.

He chuckled as he remembered having to explain bongs and edibles to his mother after she'd watched the movie. His character had eaten too many special brownies, become utterly paranoid, and thought he was being attacked by a giraffe in the Alaskan wilderness . . . though the hallucinations might have been caused by the other drugs he'd taken. And somehow, the night had ended with him in bed with two models.

No, that movie hadn't made much sense, as his mom had pointed out.

Ryan's laughter grew and echoed in his empty, empty condo.

He flipped the page and found another picture of him with his mother. He wasn't an expert in baby expressions, but he was pretty sure Baby Ryan looked constipated.

*Mom, I wish you would tell me what the fuck to do about Dad.*

She'd probably berate him for swearing.

*I wish I could tell you about Lindsay.*

He stilled. When a tear fell on the album, he closed it and reached for a tissue, imagining his father's expression of disgust at his tears.

Dad would never do anything as emotive as crying.

Ryan felt like he should push the tears back, save them for the next time he had to cry on camera, but then he thought of his conversation with Lindsay, and he gave himself permission to feel this way for a little while.

He organized the photos he'd scanned and put away the photo album before checking Twitter. Dad hadn't tweeted anything, much to his relief. Or disappointment.

Ryan wasn't sure how he felt.

He considered tweeting a baby goat video and tagging his father, but then decided to email Herbie Chin instead.

# CHAPTER 12

**M**onday was Ryan's new favorite day of the week.

But Lindsay had an impish grin on her face as she led him to the upstairs kitchen, and it had him a little worried.

At the same time, he wanted to wipe that grin off her face with a kiss.

*Stop lusting after your teacher.*

Yes. She was the teacher and he was the student. It would be inappropriate.

He would not focus on how good her ass looked in those jeans, or how he wanted to run his hand through her dark hair, which was tied back and secured with a bow.

"So, today," Lindsay began, and he forced himself to pay attention to the words coming out of her lips, and not the lips themselves and how he could kiss them, "I've set up a special cupcake challenge for you. You'll have two and a half hours to make a dozen of these cupcakes, which is a generous amount of time."

"Thank you for your generosity," he murmured. He would need every one of those minutes to do more than a half-assed job, and it meant he'd get to spend more time with Lindsay.

"You're welcome." She gestured to a stainless-steel dome on the counter at the front of the room, then lifted it with a flourish to reveal three perfect cupcakes. "Lemon meringue cupcakes. A light lemon cupcake, filled with lemon curd, topped with meringue—which you'll need to torch—and a candied lemon slice. Looks easy, doesn't it?"

"No, it most certainly does not."

She laughed. "I know. Now, here's the recipe, and I've taken out all the ingredients you'll need." She pointed to a bowl of lemons, along with eggs, sugar, and various other things at his workstation.

"What will you do while I bake?" he asked.

She shrugged. "Watch. Possibly offer some insightful commentary, like on the show."

"The host of *Baking Fail* is a comedian. His commentary isn't what I'd call *insightful*."

"But he talks to the judges, and they know what they're doing. Anyway, I'm sure you can do it. Just remember everything I've taught you so far." She handed him an apron and patted his shoulder, and for a moment, he forgot all about cupcakes. "On your mark, get set . . . go!"

She retreated to a stool at the far end of the kitchen as he tied his apron and began looking over the recipe.

There were four separate recipes, in fact. One for the cupcakes, one for the lemon curd, one for the lemon slices, and one for the meringue, plus instructions for assembly. It wasn't clear which order he was supposed to do things in, and this was probably intentional.

He figured he'd start with the lemon curd, since that had to be refrigerated until firm. Although the candied lemon slices were supposed to dry for a while, too, he reasoned these were less important, as they were simply a garnish . . . Or maybe he was thinking about this all wrong.

He looked up at Lindsay, who sported a grin that was now closer to "evil" than "impish." It was still super cute.

*Stop getting distracted and bake!*

There were only five ingredients in the curd: egg yolks, sugar, lemon zest, lemon juice, and butter. It involved both separating the eggs and using a double boiler, skills he had perfected—ha!—in previous lessons.

He began zesting the lemons, something he'd never done before, then juiced them. The ingredients, aside from the butter, had to be combined in the double boiler for about ten minutes, until they reached the given temperature.

Ten minutes would have to do. The idea of using a thermometer for food was somehow a little intimidating.

As the ingredients cooked in the double boiler, he continued to whisk them, then wondered why on earth he was standing at the stove when there was so much to be done. The recipe implied he was supposed to keep whisking, however, so perhaps there was a reason?

"Contestant Number One, Ryan Kwok, known for his roles in *Unraveling* and *Just Another New York Sitcom*, has made the bold choice to begin with the lemon curd," Lindsay said.

Was she suggesting he shouldn't have started with the lemon curd? Or was she just messing with him?

She was probably messing with him.

The thought caused a strange curl of pleasure in his stomach.

"Ryan Kwok also starred in *The Journey of the Baked Alaska*. Tell me, Ryan, have you ever made a baked Alaska?"

"Can't say I have. In fact, I don't think I've even eaten it before."

"It's retro. I don't see it often. But maybe that will be your next challenge. Baked Alaska, and you'll have to make the ice cream yourself."

He turned to her in horror. She was still perched on the high stool, grinning.

Well, he was glad she was having fun with this.

"Who's Contestant Number Two?" he asked.

"Let's call him . . . Bartholomew. Bartholomew Smith. He's an Olympic swimmer who's won a bunch of gold medals and takes off his shirt more than you do."

Ryan raised an eyebrow. "Is that even possible?"

But he should probably stop flirting and—

Shit! The lemon curd!

It had now been ten minutes. He removed the thickened, slightly lumpy mixture from the heating element, added a little butter, and poured it into a bowl, as the recipe instructed. He then placed this in the fridge and got started on the candied lemon slices, trying his best not to be distracted by Lindsay.

The candied lemon slices looked fairly straightforward, thankfully. In fact, the hardest part would be thinly slicing them. The instructions said to use a mandoline, but wasn't that a musical instrument? Then he noticed an unfamiliar kitchen tool with a sticky note on it that said "mandoline" next to the bowl of lemons.

He had a sneaking suspicion he'd end up injuring himself on this, considering he had no idea how to use it, so he picked up a knife instead. A knife, at least, he'd used before.

His slices weren't perfect rounds, but that was okay. He brought sugar and water to a boil on the stove, and once the sugar had dissolved, he added his ugly lemon slices.

That had to cook for a little while, and in the meantime, he'd start on the actual cupcakes.

He preheated the oven and started measuring out the ingredients. Lindsay hopped off her stool and walked around, hands clasped behind her back. She stared for a long time at the lemon slices on the stove, then tilted her head this way and that as Ryan cracked an egg.

Her nearness was unnerving.

Usually, he didn't mind when people watched him do things. In fact, he often liked the attention, and he liked it now, too, but how was he supposed to make fancy lemon meringue cupcakes when she was watching him like this?

"Hmm," she said, in a rather frightening way, a way that suggested he was doing everything wrong. "Contestant Number Two has just put his cupcakes in the oven. Contestant Number One has some catching up to do."

He enjoyed that she could act this way around him and also that they could have deeper conversations, like last week. And he also enjoyed the shirt she was wearing today . . .

*Focus, dammit.*

Okay. He could do this. He mixed the ingredients together as instructed, and it wasn't long before he was pouring the batter into the lined cupcake tins and putting them in the oven. Fifteen to seventeen minutes, the recipe said.

Time to get started on—

Shit, the candied lemon slices!

He hurried over to the stove and looked in the pot. The lemon slices were slightly translucent, as they were supposed to be, and nothing was burning, so that was good. He took out the lemon slices with a slotted spoon and placed them on parchment paper.

"Are you sure you want to do that?" Lindsay asked.

"I'm doing exactly as the recipe says. I . . ."

He jerked his head toward her, and this time she was laughing.

Yep, she was messing with him.

And he totally didn't mind.


IT WAS RARE for Lindsay to be in the kitchen for more than two hours without actually doing any work. She was tempted to jump up and help Ryan, even though he wasn't doing too badly by himself. She kept her gaze on him, telling herself that she was being a good teacher and it had nothing to do with his handsomeness.

There were now twenty-five minutes left on the clock, and he was beating the egg whites and cream of tartar for the meringue. He still had lots to do.

She placed her hands on either side of her mouth and shouted— well, spoke slightly louder than usual—"Go, Ryan!"

He graced her with a ridiculously charming smile.

*He's a movie star! He's paid to do shit like this.*

Yeah, only natural she was attracted to him, but it didn't *mean* anything.

Though she did feel like they'd become friends, and she felt comfortable being a bit of a nut around him, which was unusual for someone she hadn't known for long.

He started gradually adding the sugar to the egg whites. He was supposed to do this once the egg whites had formed "soft peaks" but his interpretation of "soft peaks" was, well, much softer than it should be. She nearly told him so, then snapped her mouth shut. She was trying to re-create the competition atmosphere as best she could. And it was no big deal if the meringue was a little soft.

Ryan removed the bowl from under the stand mixer. "I think it's done."

He lifted the bowl up, and if she hadn't been distracted by his arm muscles, she would have stopped him from doing what he did next, even though she wasn't supposed to intervene.

But by the time she opened her mouth, it was too late.

Ryan's hair was covered in egg whites.

# CHAPTER 13

**R**yan had seen people do this on TV. Once the egg whites were whipped, they turned the bowl upside down over their head and the egg whites held their shape in the bowl.

Instead, it probably looked like he was washing his hair with too much shampoo. He felt like his himbo character in *The Journey of the Baked Alaska*.

When he got over his surprise and smiled at Lindsay, she cracked up.

He wasn't sure why he'd lifted the bowl above his head. Had he been trying to show off? Demonstrate he knew something other than what she'd taught him?

It wasn't like he was trying to impress Lindsay, was it?

Okay, it kind of was.

And it had gone terribly, but he was good at taking such things in stride.

"Why didn't that work?" he asked.

"Because you didn't whip the egg whites enough."

"But I'd been whipping them for a long time."

"They needed longer."

"At least my hair will be tasty now. How about you grab that blowtorch, I'll kneel down, and you can brown it a little?" He winked at her. "You can even garnish my head with a slice or two of candied lemon. Sprinkles for good measure."

She walked toward him, and his heart thudded in excitement. Maybe she'd lick the half-whipped egg whites off his face, the way she might lick frosting off a cupcake.

He deflated when he noticed the paper towels in her hand.

But then he got excited again when, instead of handing him the stack of paper towels, she lifted one to his face and started wiping him off.

Geez, these baking lessons were a damn roller coaster.

To his disappointment, she stepped back and said, "I think it'll be best if you stick your head under the sink. The staff washroom downstairs has a deep sink, so that should work."

He headed to the washroom and returned ten minutes later with wet hair and a mostly clean shirt and apron.

Lindsay's lips parted in an O.

"Did I miss something?" he asked.

"No, you look fine." Her voice sounded a little scratchy.

Ah. He understood. His hair was wet, and he probably looked like he'd just stepped out of the shower, although he usually didn't emerge from the shower in an apron.

She was far from the first woman to find him attractive, yet for some reason, her feelings mattered more than anyone else's.

He gave her a slow, lazy smile and watched her pupils dilate.

"Well, uh," she said. "You had twenty-one minutes left when you held a bowl of not-so-stiff egg whites over your head, so I'll give you twenty-one minutes to finish. Unfortunately, you'll have to redo the meringue."

Her voice was halting, slightly uncertain, and he couldn't help smiling again.

"Sure thing," he said.

He would separate the eggs and start whipping more egg whites, and as the stand mixer worked its magic, he'd use the cupcake corer, a piece of kitchen equipment he hadn't known existed until last week. Then he'd fill the cupcakes with lemon curd, top with the whipped egg whites, torch it, and add the sliced lemon.

Piece of (cup)cake.

Ha.

When there were five minutes remaining, the egg whites were about the consistency they'd been when he'd held the bowl above his head, which he was definitely *not* doing this time. He knew it wasn't quite ready, but he needed to frost the cupcakes. A piping bag had been set out for him, but there was no time for that. Instead, he dumped a spoonful on top of each cupcake, then went to town with the blowtorch, which he remembered how to use from when he'd made crème brûlée donuts.

"Thirty seconds!" Lindsay called.

Shit, shit, shit.

He grabbed a handful of candied lemon slices and hurriedly placed them on top of the cupcakes. They likely weren't as firm as they were supposed to be, but that didn't matter.

He was placing the final lemon slice when she said, "Time's up."

He held up his hands and stepped away from the rack. He took a deep breath as he looked between his dozen cupcakes and the three cupcakes she'd presented two and a half hours ago.

Hers looked significantly better, of course.

Lindsay hopped down from the stool and paced back and forth in front of his cupcakes, hands behind her back. Then she picked up a spoon and poked the meringue on top of a cupcake. "You needed to whip it for longer, and you were supposed to use the piping bag, not drop a spoonful on top. And the torching isn't very even." She pointed to a cupcake that looked a little burnt, then another that barely had any brown at all. "But the cupcakes do include all the components." She kept a straight face throughout her critiques. This seemed to be her baking-judge persona. Then she placed a single cupcake on a plate and pulled off the cupcake liner. She took a bite and chewed thoughtfully.

Why did he care so much about her verdict?

"The cupcake itself is baked perfectly."

He made a show of pumping his fist.

She had another bite. "The lemon curd tastes good, but the texture is a little off. I think your egg yolks started to curdle. The meringue tastes okay, but as I said, it's not stiff enough." She bit into the candied lemon.

He didn't know where to look. At her lips, or at the spot of lemon curd on her nose? God, he loved watching her eat. Loved watching her do anything, for that matter.

She smiled at him. "Not perfect, but not too bad. Certainly not an epic fail. Better than Contestant Number Two."

He'd never been so happy to win a competition against an imaginary person before.

"You gave me two and a half hours," he said. "I won't get that much time on the show."

"No, but you'll have a blast chiller, which will cool things quickly."

"I don't think that was my main problem."

"True, but you'll get lots more practice before then." She continued smiling up at him, and was it his imagination, or had she moved closer to him? She was no longer in judge mode.

They had four more lessons together. Four more lessons for him to practice. Four more lessons that he'd get to spend with her.

It didn't feel like enough.

And that bit of lemon curd on her nose was really bothering him. Not because it didn't look cute—it was rather adorable, in fact—but he was overcome with the urge to remove it.

He could hand her a paper towel, he could touch her himself . . . or he could lick it off.

When the tip of her tongue peeked out from between her lips, he couldn't help wanting her mouth on him. She was leaning toward him—or was that wishful thinking?

"Lindsay," he murmured, oh so quietly. He wasn't sure if she heard. Or was she attuned to every little thing he did, like he was to her?

And then he touched the tip of his finger to her nose and removed the lemon curd. The brief contact was enough to make them both inhale swiftly.

He wanted to slide his fingers into her hair, but instead, he stepped back from her. The last thing he needed was any kind of complication in his personal life.

But that didn't mean they couldn't spend more time together today.

"Do you want to hang out now?"

That sounded awkward to his ears, but how should he have phrased it? It wasn't like he was asking her on a date or—

"Yes," she said.

He smiled. He couldn't help being thrilled at the prospect of "hanging out" with her.

**"WHAT ARE YOU** thinking?" Lindsay asked as she and Ryan read over the tap list on the chalkboard next to the bar.

A part of her was like, *OMFG, a movie star wants to spend time with me!*

And another part of her was like, *Chill out, it's just Ryan.*

Because most of the time when she was with him now, he was just a guy to her. A very handsome guy, but a real guy, friendly and easygoing.

But now that they were outside the bakery together for the first time, she was very aware of who he was.

Did the paparazzi go after Ryan? Was he famous enough for that? He hadn't said anything, though he was still wearing his sunglasses. Surely Toronto wasn't like LA or London—except during TIFF—but there were still paparazzi here, weren't there?

"I'm getting the Unicorn Tears Sour," Lindsay said. "I recommend that one, if you're not sure."

"I'll get a Diet Coke," Ryan said.

Her stomach dropped.

When she'd suggested Fantastical Brewing, he'd agreed, but if he was ordering a Coke, maybe he didn't drink or wasn't in the mood for it today.

She'd respect his wishes. There was nothing wrong with not drinking, whatever his reasons. To maintain his abs, avoiding beer was quite sensible. Or he might have terrible Asian glow.

"We can go somewhere else," she said.

"It's all right. I don't mind being around alcohol. I just don't drink. No need for you to feel weird about having a beer or two around me."

But she couldn't help feeling weird about it. Besides, she came here with Noreen all the time. Well, less often than she used to, but she was still a regular customer.

"We'll go somewhere else," she said firmly. "Rise and Shine? Or we could have boba."

She hoped he'd pick bubble tea. In fact, bubble tea sounded better than beer to her now.

"Boba," he said.

She beamed at him. "Excellent."

The tea shop she liked was a ten-minute walk away. As they headed there, she thought a few people might be staring, but perhaps they didn't recognize Ryan and just thought he was really good-looking, which would be perfectly understandable.

They were closer together than they'd been earlier in the kitchen, aside from when she'd tried to clean whipped egg white off him, and when he'd wiped the lemon curd off her nose.

Had that really happened?

He'd touched her, and he'd asked her to do something with him afterward. Did that mean anything, other than them becoming friends?

She suspected it didn't.

But then he turned to her and said, "Is this the place?" and there was something about the way he spoke that made her think he wanted to wipe lemon curd off her again. That simple touch was etched in her brain.

She ordered brown sugar coconut milk tea with pearls—that was her favorite. He ordered peach green tea with jellies, half-sweet.

Fortunately, the table at the back was available. It was the most private table in the small tea shop, and if he faced away from the front, it was unlikely anyone would figure out who he was.

She'd have him all to herself.

Lindsay went to the washroom, where she splashed water on her face and made sure there were no remnants of lemon meringue cupcakes on her skin.

When she returned to the table, Ryan was staring at his phone with a peculiar expression.

"Is something wrong?" she asked.

Silently, he handed his phone to her.

Ryan had told her last week that his father posted "weird shit" on Twitter. It appeared his dad had the creative handle of @Ryan-KwoksFather, and someone had tweeted at @RyanKwoksFather, asking if Ryan had gotten his good looks from him.

His father had replied with, Judge for yourself, accompanied by close-ups of him and Ryan, both with the same brooding expression.

"People are calling my dad a silver fox," Ryan whispered.

Indeed, they were.

*OMG, he definitely got his looks from you. *fans self**

*You should be on the cover of a romance novel.*

*Silver fox alert!*

Lindsay couldn't help laughing. It was partly the comical look of horror on Ryan's face. He'd been all cool when he'd dumped the egg whites on his head, but this was a different story.

"How would you feel if these comments were about your dad?" Ryan asked.

"I—"

"Shit, I'm sorry. I forgot."

"It's okay." She thought back to the days when she'd had a father. "Yeah, I would have been disturbed, too. My friend in university, her dad was a prof, and on one of the professor-rating sites, they used to have chili peppers next to the names of professors that students had rated hot. The night she discovered her dad had a chili pepper, she got very drunk on tequila."

"This is my *dad*. He likes CBC and Canadian Tire."

"Canadian Tire always reminds me of my father, even though I hated when he'd take us there as kids. I'd get so bored, though when I was older, he'd leave me in front of the paint chips and I'd look at the colors. That Canadian Tire smell—you know what I mean?"

"Yeah."

"It just takes me back." She smiled faintly, recalling those shopping trips she'd dreaded, when her father would get all manner of things for his home improvement projects. The stash of Canadian Tire money in a jar on his desk. "But back to your father."

Ryan's hand was on hers now. A brief squeeze, not lingering, but any contact from him felt like a big deal.

She swallowed and continued to look through the replies to his father's tweet.

"Do you think your father expected this response?" she asked.

"I'm certain he didn't. My father isn't well versed in the ways of social media. I don't know what he'll think of this. He's uncomfortable that any part of my success is because I'm, well, attractive. He wanted me to be an engineer or similar. God, I can't believe these comments." Ryan started reading out some of the responses. "'I wish more Asian fathers on TV looked like this' . . . Oh no, someone is calling my dad a 'sexy beast.' I can't take it anymore." He shoved the phone in his pocket.

Lindsay laughed again.

Ryan gave her an are-you-kidding-me? look as she sipped her bubble tea. One of the bubbles went down the wrong way, and she started coughing.

"You okay?" he asked.

She held up a finger. She would be . . . soon.

He shifted his chair around the table and put his hand on her upper back. She kind of wanted to keep coughing so he'd leave his hand there, but that would be ridiculous.

At last, she recovered.

Ryan didn't move his chair.

And then she whispered, "Silver fox alert!" hoping to make him laugh, and it worked. They were both clutching their stomachs and laughing.

When Ryan finally stopped, he said, "What's your opinion?"

"He's your father. You're closer to my age and much more my type, don't worry."

"Is that so?" He gave her a look. "I'm your type?"

She swallowed.

He was still sitting next to her, not on the opposite side of the table. She leaned toward him, just a tiny bit, but he didn't move at all.

He cleared his throat. "Any plans for the rest of the week?"

She tried not to be disappointed. It had been silly to think he might kiss her, both now and earlier, when he'd touched her nose. He was Ryan Kwok, and she was . . . well, she liked herself and thought she looked cute in the outfit she'd put on today—not for his benefit, of course—but she was an ordinary woman. It was enough that they were friendly, that he wanted to spend time with her outside the bakery.

"Oh, you know," she said. "Working. What about you?"

"I'm scanning all of our family photo albums," he said, "and Mel is coming to Toronto."

"Melvin Lee?"

"Yeah, he's doing a couple shows at a comedy club while he's here."

Lindsay fiddled with the straw in her drink. "I'm not sure if I should tell you this."

"Then you should definitely tell me. You can't say that and then *not* tell me."

"True." She paused. "My roommate is a big fan of *Just Another New York Sitcom*, and she likes him better than you."

"He *is* funnier than me . . ."

"Yeah, he's *way* funnier. You have the sense of humor of a rock."

Ryan gave her another look, and she giggled.

She took a moment to reflect on how surreal her life was. She was having bubble tea with a movie star. They knew each other well enough that she could tease him. Sure, he wasn't Tom Hanks—in fact, she hadn't even recognized Ryan the first time she met him—but still.

"I mean," Lindsay said, "she thinks he's hot."

"Without my glasses, nobody takes a second look at me, it's true." Ryan mimed taking out a pair of glasses and putting them on, then graced her with a smile of irresistible charm.

Her brain momentarily forgot how to function.

"Do you want me to get you two tickets to his show?" Ryan asked. "We can all grab a drink afterward, if you'd like."

Maybe that was why she'd spoken. Some part of her had hoped he'd make an offer like that. She couldn't wait to see the look on Vivian's face.

But she felt weird about having led the conversation to this point. She didn't want to take advantage of her friendship with Ryan.

"Are you sure?" she asked. "It's not necessary—"

"I insist."

"Are you really—"

"Lindsay," he said, "it's fine. Mel won't have a problem with it, I promise."

Her cheeks heated. She needed to turn the conversation to something else. "Let's take another look at your phone and see what people are saying about your father."

Ryan's gaze shot daggers at her, and for some reason, that look made her clench her thighs together.

Yes, she did very much like "hanging out" with him.

# CHAPTER 14

Tuesday was gloomy, so Lindsay and Noreen didn't sit on the patio at Fantastical Brewing. Instead, they sat inside at the bar, next to a mural of a dragon.

The bartender handed a pint of Unicorn Tears Sour to Lindsay and a pint of Hoppy Hippogriff IPA to Noreen.

"I've never seen him here before," Noreen whispered to Lindsay. "He's cute, isn't he?"

The bartender in question was a muscular East Asian man, probably in his late twenties. His long hair was tied back, and he had a serious expression.

"Yeah," Lindsay said, with less enthusiasm than he deserved.

Noreen nudged her shoulder. "You're single, aren't you?"

Lindsay shrugged.

"That's okay," Noreen said. "I found the perfect guy for you, and I've already arranged a date for this Saturday."

"Noreen!"

"What? You don't trust my judgment? You said you want to date again, didn't you?"

Lindsay spun the glass between her hands. "I have plans for this Saturday. Ryan—"

"I do love that you're on a first-name basis with him."

"—got tickets for Melvin Lee's comedy show. They're friends."

She'd been a little doubtful it would happen until Ryan had texted her earlier this afternoon with the info.

"So, you want to go on this date another time?" Noreen asked. "Or no, because you're making heart eyes at Ryan? He must like you, too, if he invited you to the show."

"When we were having bubble tea yesterday, I told him my roommate is a big fan of Melvin Lee's. That's why Ryan invited us. You're not mad?"

"Why on earth would I be mad?"

"Because I'm going with Vivian, not you."

Noreen waved this off. "You know I'm not big on stand-up comedy. I'll meet the infamous Ryan Kwok some other time." Her eyes were dancing. "You had bubble tea together?"

"It's not like that."

"I think it is." Noreen leaned in and whispered, "My best friend and a movie star!"

"We're friends. I don't think he thinks of me in that way."

"You sound uncertain."

"He did wipe lemon curd off my nose."

"Always a strong sign of feelings."

"And sometimes he looks at me as if . . ." Lindsay shook her head. "It's just the way he is, maybe? I'm not sure. I keep telling myself it's foolish—"

"Why? He could like you."

"I don't know." How could someone like her really fit in his world? Besides, she couldn't forget what he'd said in that interview. "But I can't think about any other guy right now, so you'll have to put off the blind dates for a while."

"All right, I get the message." Noreen lowered her voice and started singing, "Lindsay and Ryan, sitting in a—"

Lindsay smacked her friend's shoulder. "Stop it! You know, that's one of the advantages of not living with you anymore. I don't have to listen to your terrible voice when you sing in the shower."

"Hey!" Noreen said, pretending to be affronted. "My voice is *not* terrible."

"This time, I admit it was more your song choice."

Lindsay sipped her beer and contemplated Ryan. Yes, they got along and maybe he was attracted to her. It was within the realm of possibility.

And if he propositioned her, she'd sleep with him.

She couldn't imagine him wanting more than that, but maybe he'd want to have some fun, and she trusted him to treat her well.

Yep, she could have a little more fun before she tried to have a real relationship.

She recalled seeing him with wet hair yesterday, and she pictured him wearing just a towel slung low on his hips, like in that one scene in *That Kind of Wedding*. And then he'd go to her. She'd be naked in a four-poster bed—this was her imagination, after all—and he'd slip under the covers and slide his hand between her legs . . .

No, she had to stop fantasizing before she got carried away. She'd leave that for later, for when she was in bed with one of her trusty toys.

For now, she was at the bar with Noreen.

"How's married life?" Lindsay asked. "You've gotten used to living together?"

Noreen sighed dreamily. "It's great. Marc's not as good about taking out the green bin as you are, but otherwise, it's practically perfect."

Lindsay had never doubted her friend was making a good choice by marrying Marc Mathieson. It was nice to hear it was going as well as she'd expected.

She hoped that one day, she'd have something similar.

*You haven't had a real relationship in seven years.*

True, but today, she couldn't help feeling hopeful.

An image popped into her mind of her and Ryan in the kitchen together. Not at Kensington Bake Shop. No, a home kitchen, maybe making some kind of pasta sauce . . . He'd feed her a spoonful, then get some on his shirt and have to take it off . . .

"What are you smiling about?" Noreen asked.

"Oh, just thinking we could have a lemon meringue donut. How do you feel about that?"

"I'm sure that's what was on your mind."

Lindsay shrugged, and Noreen didn't push her anymore.

"Let's try it as a special tomorrow," Noreen said.

Lindsay nodded and sipped her beer, her lips puckering. It was sour but fruity and delicious.

Yes, everything seemed wonderful right now. A long day of work was behind her, she was out at a bar with her best friend, and she had plans for Saturday night. And though she was excited about hanging out with her roommate outside of home for the first time and meeting Melvin Lee, she was most excited about seeing Ryan more than once in a week.

Perhaps she should be worried. Because Ryan's presence in her life would be temporary.

But that was no big deal, right? It was just a little crush. No sense worrying about it.

"YOU'RE GOING TO *love* me," Lindsay said as Vivian stepped out of her bedroom.

Vivian was wearing a navy pantsuit with a pale pink blouse today. Lindsay could absolutely not pull that look off, but Vivian could.

"Yeah?" Vivian said. "What's up?"

"Melvin Lee is going to be in town for a few days, and Ryan got us tickets to see him do stand-up at a comedy club. How great is that? He says we'll get a table right at the front, and then the four of us will hang out after."

Vivian looked slightly alarmed. "You want me to *hang out* with Melvin Lee?"

"Not alone. I'll be there. What's wrong? Are you intimidated?"

"I don't know," Vivian said slowly. "You're not supposed to meet your heroes, right? It'll shatter the illusion. Not that Melvin Lee is my *hero*, but he's my favorite comedian. What if he's actually a jerk? And I saw his show the last time he was in Toronto."

"Come on, it'll be fun! Ryan's really cool, and the two of them are good friends, so I bet Melvin Lee is cool, too. It'll be fine. Ryan says Jory Tyler is a jerk—"

"That was a surprise to you? Jory Tyler has 'douchebag' written all over him."

"—but like I said, he's friends with Melvin Lee. I bet he's not a jerk. Will you be disappointed if he's just an ordinary guy?"

"No, that would be nice."

"When are you going to get this chance again?"

Vivian was silent for several seconds. Lindsay wanted to talk and hurry things along, but she suspected Vivian wanted the silence to think, so she let her have it.

"Okay," Vivian said at last. "You're right."

"You don't need to be nervous."

"But I don't like meeting new people. I find it stressful, even when they aren't somewhat famous. I'll do it, but I *will* be nervous. I'm glad you'll be there."

"Excellent. It'll be good, you'll see. Ryan is very easygoing."

Vivian gestured for Lindsay to come inside her room. "I want to show you something." She went to her computer and pulled up an illustration.

Lindsay stood beside Vivian and quickly figured out what she was looking at. The illustration was of a scene from Episode 3 of *Just Another New York Sitcom*. Melvin Lee was kneeling beside a capybara. Ryan—sans glasses—was leaping backward. Juan Velazquez was looking scholarly, probably reciting capybara facts.

Lindsay had never gotten into fan art and fan fiction and the like, and she didn't know much about art, but she loved this. Somehow, it captured the mood of the scene just right.

"Did you do this?" Lindsay asked.

"Yes."

"It's incredible. You should show it to him."

Vivian blanched. "Um, I'm not sure . . ."

"I was kidding!"

"I posted it on JANYSers United, so it's not like no one's seen it, but . . ."

"Don't worry, I'll say nothing."

"I did one more." Vivian pulled up an illustration of the Rube Goldberg machine episode. Unlike the previous picture, there was only one person in it: Melvin Lee.

Geez, Vivian really did seem to be a superfan. But she wouldn't to do anything stupid on Saturday—she was far too self-conscious for that. She hadn't even wanted to go, for that matter.

"If you change your mind, it's okay," Lindsay said, "but I do think it'll be fun."

"Don't worry, you talked me into it. You want to go out for dinner beforehand?"

"Sure. We can go to Tasty Shrimps R Us."

Vivian glared at her.

"I'm kidding!" Lindsay said. "You can pick the restaurant. I'll eat anything."

She exited Vivian's room a few minutes later. She would have been happy to talk for longer, but she got the sense Vivian wanted more time to decompress after work.

Lindsay made herself an omelet and watched TV while she ate. Saturday night would go well, wouldn't it?

# CHAPTER 15

"Give me your phone," Mel said.

Ryan shoved his phone in his pocket. "No way are you getting those fingers on my phone. I remember what happened last time. I still have nightmares about it."

"What happened the last time I stole your phone?"

"You called my mother."

"Right. I did." For a rare moment, Mel looked solemn.

"The previous time, you tried to set up a Twitter poll from my account."

"Yes! The 'Are my abs sexy?' poll. I think the options were 'yes,' 'no,' 'hell yes,' and 'not as sexy as Ryan Reynolds's.' But I didn't post it."

"Because I grabbed my phone back just in time."

"No, I *could* have posted it, but I didn't want to embarrass you." Mel managed to sneak Ryan's phone out of his pocket.

Ryan tried to grab it back, but it was a little awkward, seeing as they were sitting on the large rock in the park in Yorkville and he was carrying a cup of coffee, which he was trying not to spill.

When the two of them were together, Ryan often felt like the serious one. The Bert to Mel's Ernie. Similar to the roles the two of them had occupied on *Just Another New York Sitcom,* when they'd first met. Which was different from the role Ryan usually had in relationships—of any kind. Friendships, family . . .

Mel held the phone to his ear.

"Who are you calling?" Ryan hissed.

"Oh, hi, Mr. Kwok," Mel said into the phone.

"Did you call my *dad*?"

"My name is Mel, and I'm calling on behalf of the Silver Fox Club. We'd like to invite you to join our organization . . ." He cracked up. "Yes, it's Melvin Lee. How did you know? . . . You're right, we did speak a few times before. How are you enjoying Twitter? I suggest the poll function . . ."

This continued for five minutes, and to Ryan's distress, he was jealous. Based on the pauses in the conversation, Dad was saying more to Mel than he usually said to Ryan.

At last, Ryan pulled the phone away. "Sorry about that, Dad."

His father was chuckling. "It's okay."

"I'll call you later, all right?"

Dad grunted, and Ryan ended the call.

"Your dad's cool," Mel said. "It's hard to understand the problems you have with him."

Ryan gripped his coffee cup. "You're not his son. He has different expectations of me. You know what that's like."

Mel sobered. "That's true. I do. Some things were okay for everyone else, but not for me, according to my dad."

A couple of young women were looking at them. When Ryan shot them a smile, one of them approached, laughing nervously.

"I can't believe it. I'm a big fan of you two. You're friends in real life? Not just on TV?"

In response, Mel put Ryan in a headlock and gave him a noogie. Ryan exaggerated his wince.

"Would you mind if my friend took a picture of us?" she asked.

"Yeah, I'd mind," Mel said.

"Sorry, I—"

"I'm kidding! It's all good. Sit down." Mel slapped the rock next to him.

The woman handed her phone to her friend, who snapped a picture.

"Now you have to take a photo for me," Mel said. "It's only fair." He handed the woman his phone and pulled something out of his bag.

Ryan was a little alarmed. What did Mel have up his sleeve?

But Mel simply handed him a sheet of paper that said "Ryan Kwok." Mel had another one that said "Melvin Lee."

"People get us mixed up sometimes," Mel explained. "So we gotta take a picture to clear that up. Hold the paper over your abs, Ryan. You know where those are, don't you?"

The woman took a couple of pictures before returning Mel's phone.

"Now autograph the paper for the nice lady." Mel handed a marker to Ryan. "Try your best to make your signature more legible than usual."

"At least it's not completely illegible like yours is," Ryan said.

They signed their names and gave the papers to the woman who'd taken their picture.

"Have a nice day!" Mel said before turning to Ryan. "I gotta upload these to Twitter."

"OMG. Ryan Kwok?" A young woman, probably about twenty, approached.

"Your fan club has arrived," Mel whispered.

Ryan spent a few minutes talking to people while Mel did whatever he wanted to do on social media. When the last of Ryan's so-called fan club left, he sipped his lukewarm coffee and looked around. There were half a dozen other people sitting on the rock, and lots of people walking by.

"Oh, look!" Mel said. "Your dad has already replied to my tweets."

**@RyanKwoksFather:** *Thank you for the clarification on who's who. I wasn't sure.*

Ryan felt a stab of pain. Here Dad was, talking to Mel on the phone, replying to his tweet almost right away, yet he always sounded put out when Ryan tried to contact him.

"How's your dad doing?" Mel asked. "And you?"

"I call him, and the rare times he answers, he insists he's fine. Doesn't understand why I'd want to check up on him."

"And you?" Mel repeated.

"I'm . . . not great. It's always *there*, you know? But I'm better than before."

Ryan didn't want to talk about this in depth now, but he was happy his friend was here.

Mel punched him in the shoulder, which was one of the ways he showed affection.

"What about these women coming to my show?" Mel asked. "You trying to have a threesome afterward?"

"Mel . . ."

"I'm kidding! One of them is your baking instructor, right?"

"Yeah. Lindsay."

"You're turning pink just saying her name."

"Am not."

"You're not," Mel conceded, "but I had you worried there for a minute, didn't I?"

"You're a pain in the ass," Ryan muttered. "Please stop being so loud."

"You really are irritable today, but that's okay. You're in looooove," Mel sang. "Is that the problem?"

"It's the last thing I need with everything happening in my family. I can't manage the people who are already in my life."

Things with his father were a mess. He didn't know how to help Jenna.

Adding a relationship on top of that?

"Plus," Ryan continued, "I keep making a fool of myself in front of her. We met when I knocked over a tray of donuts, and I dumped whipped egg whites all over my head at the last lesson."

Mel laughed. "She's really got you all twisted up. Can't wait to meet her."

"Don't be an ass."

"Me?" Mel put a hand to his chest and opened his mouth wide in shock. "I would never. Who's the other woman?"

"I haven't met her. She's Lindsay's roommate, and she's a big fan of yours and *Just Another New York Sitcom*. I don't know if I should say this—"

"I like where this is going."

"—because it might go to your head, and we all know that's the last thing you need—"

"Hey, I'm not the one who has people salivating over my abs."

"—but she thinks you're the more attractive one of the two of us."

Mel's eyebrows shot up. "Is that so?" He stroked his nonexistent beard. "I'm intrigued." He put one hand behind his head, the other on his waist, and struck a pose.

"What are you doing?"

"Practicing my sexy look. I would think you, of all people, would recognize that."

"Someone's taking a picture."

"So? Let them." Mel finally returned his attention to his coffee, which was probably cold. He was quiet for all of about three seconds before saying, "I'm thinking of starting a podcast."

"To be honest," Ryan said, "I'm surprised you don't already have one."

"I know, I know. It's shocking. You want to be my first guest?"

"Sure."

"You think your dad would agree to be on my podcast? Either with you or by himself?"

"You want my *dad* on your podcast?"

"Why not?" Mel said. "He's achieved minor notoriety on Twitter."

"He's only tweeted a handful of times. I don't even know what the two of you would talk about. You want to learn about engineering or home repair or nature documentaries? He told me I should be the next David Attenborough."

"Don't worry, I'll guide the conversation to other topics. 'How does it feel to have a son with famous abs? Did you know what a silver fox was before someone called you that on Twitter?'"

"I can't wait," Ryan deadpanned.

"Anyway, we'll see. Still not sure about the whole podcast thing. It feels like everyone has a podcast these days."

"It's felt like that for years."

"You could start one."

"No, thanks."

"It'd give you something to do right now," Mel said, "other than learn how to bake."

"I'd prefer to be the occasional guest on a podcast rather than having one of my own."

Later that day, they were having takeout in Ryan's condo when Mel discovered pictures of them had surfaced on Instagram, including one of Mel giving Ryan a noogie and one of Mel striking his sexy pose.

Someone speculated that they were in love.

"What should I say in response?" Mel asked. "'As flattered as I would be, Ryan is in love with someone who saw him dump egg whites on his head.'"

"Please give me your phone. Now."

Mel laughed. "Nah, of course I wouldn't do that to you. Did you really think I would?"

"I'm never a hundred percent sure with you."

"You know I'll mention you're in the audience on Saturday."

"I would expect nothing less," Ryan said with a smile. "Thanks for being here."

"Anytime."

Although parts of Ryan's life were still a mess, he was glad he was able to enjoy himself sometimes. Like today.

And on Mondays with Lindsay.

# CHAPTER 16

"D o you have that one friend who's, like, inhumanly good-
looking?" Mel said into the microphone, the spotlight shining
on him.

Ryan sipped his diet cola and watched his friend onstage.

He knew exactly where this was going.

"Like, whenever you two are together, everyone's always staring at them, and not at you? You could be doing some crazy fucking shit, inventing time travel, I don't know, but nobody's paying
attention because they're all looking at the piece of eye candy next
to you?

"Okay, maybe you don't all have that friend. But I do. My man
Ryan Kwok is here!"

Mel gestured to Ryan, and Ryan stood up and waved, then sat
down again.

"I love you, Ryan!" somebody shouted.

"See what I'm dealing with?" Mel said. "Ryan, come onstage
and take off your shirt."

There were a bunch of cheers from the audience.

"See? Everyone wants Ryan to take off his shirt. But I don't get
quite as many requests." Mel raised the hem of his shirt, just an inch.

"Woo-hoo!" shouted someone in the back.

"Should I?" Mel said. "Nah. I'm not drunk." He picked up his water glass and had a sip. "I'm the short, fat, funny sidekick, and that's okay. I'm just glad Ryan gets to be the sexy hero, because when we were growing up—him in Toronto and me in New York—we didn't see leading men like us in Hollywood movies. Asian guys rarely got to be *cool*. Which is bullshit.

"Anyway, when Ryan was little, he told his dad he wanted to play James Bond when he grew up, and his dad was like, 'No, you're going to be an engineer.' You know what Asian parents are like." He paused. "But not all Asian parents are the same."

Ryan tilted his head to look at Lindsay, who was wearing a floral summer dress. It was nice to see her out tonight, in a different part of his life. She sipped her drink and chuckled at Mel, and Ryan's heart warmed. He'd be content to watch her all night, but she might find that a bit weird.

"People often ask if I'm sure my parents are Asian," Mel said, "and I'm like, 'You think I don't fucking know?'" He paused. "But I understand why they ask. If you were expecting stories about me getting ninety-nine percent on a math test and my father asking where the other percent went, I'm sorry to disappoint you. First of all, because I never got above ninety on a math test. Come on, don't stare at me like you've never seen an Asian guy who's bad at math! I'm not the only one. But I'm a good driver, I promise.

"One time, I got a sixty-seven on a difficult math exam, and I was so proud of myself. I passed! Woo-hoo! My parents weren't disappointed, either. They didn't tell me I'd never get into Harvard and become a neurosurgeon with those marks. Instead, they gave me a speech about how we all have different strengths. I can see some of the white people in the audience nodding along, and many of you Asians being like, 'What the fuck is he smoking?'

"In fact, I've smoked a bunch of things over the years. Even

smoked a joint with my mother once. I know, I know, you're skeptical. But my mother really is Asian. She's pretty cool, you know.
When I was three years old, I told her I wanted to be a squirrel when I grew up, and she patted my head and said, 'You can be
anything you want to be.' When I was five, I told her I wanted to
be a wrestler, and she patted my head and said, 'Well, that's a bit
dangerous, but you can be whatever you want.' When I was a little
older, I loved watching *Seinfeld*, this obscure show from the eighties
and nineties . . ." Mel pointed at someone in the audience. "Yeah,
you've heard of it before?"

Ryan enjoyed watching the audience under Mel's spell, but
most of all, he enjoyed being next to Lindsay and listening to her
laugh—she had a lovely laugh.

"So when I was six or seven," Mel continued, "I told my parents I'd like to be a comedian like Jerry Seinfeld, and what do you
know? They told me to follow my dreams and even laughed at the
terrible comedy routines I subjected them to. Maybe they were just
pleased my new career plan didn't involve being beaten up on a
regular basis, or foraging for nuts and living in trees and having a
bushy tail.

"I know some of you are still skeptical. The thing is, my parents were both born in the US, and I expect that's part of the reason, though not all of it. My mom grew up in New York; my dad
grew up in a small town. His family ran the town's Chinese restaurant, and my dad was The Asian Kid at school. That was his iden-
tity. And my mom had really strict Asian parents that fit the
stereotype. They wanted her to be a doctor and marry a nice Chinese boy. My mother rebelled. She became a librarian—which was
a quasi-respectable career, but not what they wanted for her—and
she did marry a Chinese boy, but she swore that when she had kids,
she would be the opposite of her own parents.

"Sure enough, my parents were all rainbows and unicorns and

'You can follow your dreams!' Well, maybe not the rainbows—we'll come back to that later. When I started high school, they put a box of condoms in the washroom and told me to be safe. Which is very different from some of my Asian friends' experiences. Their parents told them they couldn't date in high school because it might distract them from their studies, and they couldn't date in university. Couldn't even date in med school. And then, suddenly, they're thirty and their parents are mad they're not married? Yeah, not my parents."

Lindsay laughed again, and Ryan couldn't help wondering what her parents had been like when she was younger. He wanted to know everything about her. And if he was honest with himself, he wished he could hold her hand under the table.

"Another reason people are surprised to learn my parents are Asian," Mel said, "is because my mom and dad are divorced. Shocking, I know. And I'll tell you another thing. I'm the reason they're divorced. 'Melvin, don't say that!' you cry. 'That's not true. You need therapy.' Well, maybe I do, but instead I'm up here trying to make people laugh. Maybe if you pay me enough tonight, I'll be able to afford that therapy.

"Anyway, what happened is that when I was sixteen, I told my parents I was bisexual. I was pretty sure they'd be okay with it. My mom was, but my dad wasn't. Turns out, my father thinks being queer is okay for other people, but not for his son. He's fine with LGBTQ rights as long as it doesn't affect him.

"My mom was awesome. She was like, 'Melvin, that's cool, honey. I love you no matter what. Do you think Brad Pitt's hot?' And my dad wasn't so awesome. I guess he'd rather I'd have grown up to become a squirrel. So, my parents had this big fight. It was intense. It literally lasted a month. At the end of it, Mom decided she couldn't be with a man who wouldn't accept me as I was. And that was that. I've only spoken to my dad twice in the last fifteen years. Now, don't look at me with pity." He pointed to the back of the room. "One out of two isn't bad. It's more than many kids have. But like I said, I caused my parents' divorce. Mom tells me it's not my fault, and it probably would have happened eventually anyway, but I still feel like it's my fault." He held up a hand. "Okay, okay, stop holding up bills, trying to pay for my therapy. I'm all right. I just told a hundred people—wait, how many people are in the room?—this story. That must mean I'm okay with it, right?"

Ryan knew a lot of things that never made it into Mel's stand-up. Like the fact that he'd had therapy. His father's rejection had hurt him an awful lot, and he'd been profoundly depressed for years.

Mel shared pieces of himself. He stood up there, honest, genuine, loving the attention of the audience.

It was the truth, but not the whole truth.

"All right, all right," Mel said. "Stop shedding tears, everyone. I'll talk about something a little lighter now. You know how all East Asian people look the same? Like how Bruce Lee looks like Yo-Yo Ma, who looks like George Takei? Yeah, you at that table to my left. I see you nodding. You know what I'm talking about. You're Asian, and you think all Asian people look the same, don't you? No? Oh, you're nodding at the fact that white people think we all look the same. Which doesn't make sense to me. Like, have you *seen* white people? For example, there was this show many, many years ago. Called *Game of Thrones*, I think? Another super-obscure show. Anyway, there were so many white dudes with beards in that show and I couldn't tell them apart. I had no idea what was going on. It was so confusing!

"You remember my friend Ryan? I introduced him at the beginning. Some of you are probably still staring at him and drooling, not paying any attention to me. I know you are. We're about the same age, and we look nothing alike. Nothing. Alike. Like I said, he's the hot one, and I'm the short sidekick. Yet not all that long ago, there was an announcement that I was going to voice the character of a killer penguin in an upcoming film. Don't you think I'd make a good penguin?" He struck a pose and said, "Chirp, chirp. Do penguins chirp? I'll have to research that later." He pulled out his phone and pretended to make a note. "A website used a picture of Ryan Kwok when they announced that Melvin Lee had gotten the part, and I was pissed! People were going to see this picture of me, then be disappointed when they met me in real life and realized I wasn't super attractive. Not like I'm down on my looks—my mother always told me true beauty is on the inside and all that kind of bullshit. When I objected, she said something about different kinds of beauty. So, I've always been a bit full of myself and thought I deserved to be in the spotlight. But just objectively, you know? Ryan has a chiseled jaw and chiseled abs that I don't have. It's a fact, and I'm okay with it. Ryan, come on up, take off your shirt, and prove I'm not lying about those abs."

"I'll strip for you later!" Ryan called out, and people laughed.

But the reaction Ryan cared about was Lindsay's. She was laughing as well, and she was also blushing, which pleased him a rather stupid amount.

"Yeah, yeah, man," Mel said. "But in case anyone is wondering, he's straight. Try not to be too disappointed."

Mel went on to talk about some of the roles he'd played over the years, small parts in movies and TV shows. He also told an entertaining story about the first time he tried durian and described some of his experiences with online dating.

"And that's all for tonight. You've been a great audience. Or maybe you want to boo me but you're being polite because you're Canadian, I don't know. Remember to follow your dreams! Whether you want to be a squirrel, a wrestler, or just a comedian with a hotter friend, anything is possible!"

• • •

**"THIS IS LINDSAY** McLeod, my baking instructor," Ryan said. "And Vivian Liao, her roommate. Ladies, the man who talked your ears off for the last hour is Melvin Lee, as I'm sure you know."

Melvin Lee held out his hand, and Lindsay shook it, followed by Vivian.

Lindsay felt a touch shy. When she'd met Ryan, she'd had no idea he was an actor . . . and then she learned who he was . . . and *then* she watched his TV show and movies.

But she'd known who Melvin Lee was before tonight.

She didn't watch much stand-up, but she'd enjoyed his set. She'd particularly enjoyed the parts where he'd made fun of Ryan, enjoyed how Ryan played it cool. *Oh yeah, my friend is talking about my six-pack in front of a crowd, no big deal, it's all good.*

She'd thought about slipping her hands under Ryan's dark gray T-shirt and learning his body by touch. He could wear a potato sack and look mouthwatering. It was unfair.

Lindsay, on the other hand, had spent more than an hour getting ready, which was a long time for her. She'd changed outfits three times and struggled to put on more makeup than she usually wore.

Then she and Vivian had gone out for dinner at a Thai restaurant, which had been mostly good, despite a few awkward moments when neither of them was sure what to say.

In contrast to Lindsay's summer dress, Vivian was wearing gray pants—similar to the type she'd wear to work—killer black heels, a white shirt with a bow, and a vest. She looked fabulous, and when she'd shaken Melvin's hand, she'd been as cool as a cucumber.

No *Oh my God, oh my God, oh my God! You're my favorite comedian ever, I even got a tattoo of your face on my lower back, want to see it?*

Lindsay imagined it would be pretty weird to be on the receiving end of that.

Someone from the venue came over and spoke to Melvin Lee, who stood up. "There's a more private area we can go to on the upper floor. How does that sound?"

Five minutes later, they were seated upstairs. Melvin Lee was across from Lindsay, Ryan was to her left, and Vivian was to her right. The space wasn't huge, but it was separated from everyone else by curtains. Lindsay's knee bumped against Ryan's, and she immediately moved back.

"So, ladies," Melvin said, "how'd you like the show?"

"You can tell him that he sucked," Ryan said. "It's fine. He can take it."

"I don't know about that, man. My ego is like a fragile glass flower."

Ryan snorted.

"I enjoyed it," Lindsay said. "I'm glad I got the chance to come. Thank you."

"Hey, you've had to put up with this guy here." Melvin cuffed Ryan. "You deserve a little high-class comedy in return for your sacrifice, though I'm sure you enjoyed watching him dump those egg whites on his head."

"He told you about that?"

Lindsay wondered if Ryan had told Melvin anything else about the baking classes. Or Lindsay herself. What might he have said to his friend?

Melvin put his hands together as though praying. "Please tell me you have pictures of this. Please."

Lindsay laughed. "Sorry to disappoint you."

"Thank God," Ryan said. "You give anything like that to Mel, and it'll be all over social media in two minutes flat."

"Nah, man, I know you want to keep the whole learning-to-bake thing on the down low for now. I'd just keep them for my own private amusement. Or blackmail purposes. You know, normal shit like that."

"So normal," Ryan murmured, and Melvin cracked up.

Melvin Lee was about five-seven, and his inky hair was longer at the top than on the sides. He was wearing a flowered shirt today and he was all smiles, looking more or less like he did on TV.

Lindsay preferred Ryan, but she could see the appeal, and it was fun to see the two of them interact.

"And what about you?" Melvin turned his smile to Vivian.

"It was good," Vivian said, then had a sip of her drink. She always looked so polished. "I'd seen most of it before, aside from the part where you pointed out Ryan Kwok in the audience."

"But I'm more charming in person, aren't I? Not sure the Netflix special shows the full extent of my animal magnetism."

"What kind of animal?" Ryan asked. "A skunk? Or will you chirp like a penguin again?"

"I'd seen you in person before, actually," Vivian said to Melvin Lee. "When you were in Toronto a year ago."

Melvin crossed his arms over his chest. "So you really are a fan." He put his finger to his lips. "Wait a second. Vivian Liao. Your name sounds familiar."

"Really?"

Lindsay could have sworn she heard a wobble in Vivian's voice.

Melvin snapped his fingers. "I've got it." He pulled his phone out of his pocket. "You did this, didn't you?"

The picture on Melvin's screen was familiar. It was the illustration Vivian had done of Melvin puzzling over his Rube Goldberg machine.

He pointed to the signature in the bottom right. "Vivian Liao."

Vivian looked mortified.

Okay, maybe "mortified" was a bit strong, but Lindsay could understand her discomfort.

"That's pretty cool," Ryan said with an affable smile.

"Where did you get that?" Vivian asked Melvin.

"A friend sent it to me. Don't be embarrassed! The show has lots of fans, and you're hardly the only person who's created fan art. Are you an artist? Is that what you do for a living?"

"No, I work in finance."

Melvin made a face. "You're, like, one of those people who make the stock market run? Working for the man and everything?"

"That's not quite how I would describe my job, but—"

"Why work in finance when you're such a talented artist?" Melvin tapped the picture on his phone. "Unless finance is your true passion." He made a *yikes* expression.

Lindsay felt sweat form on the back of her neck. She'd thought the night had been going well, but she had a bad feeling about this.

"Hey, do you guys want to stay here, or should we head out?" Ryan asked. "Bubble tea? Late-night dumplings?"

But Melvin wasn't paying attention. "So, what is it, Vivian?"

"I prefer art, but—"

"You had strict parents who stuck up their nose at something like that? They would have preferred you be a neurosurgeon, but finance or law would be okay, too?"

"Mel," Ryan hissed.

"Or maybe I'm wrong," Melvin said. "Maybe you're working toward a different career, just keeping your finance job to pay the bills for now."

"I like my life the way it is," Vivian said, lifting her nose slightly, "and I shouldn't have to justify it to you."

"I'm not trying to be an ass—"

"Then you've grossly misjudged your words."

Ryan grabbed Melvin's arm. "Mel, she's right, you *are* being an ass. Let's head to the bar and get you another drink or some water."

"No, let me finish. I'm trying to be encouraging. I made it." Melvin jerked his thumb toward Ryan. "He pissed off his dad and spent a few years working as a barista with only the occasional acting job, but he made it. Why can't you do it, too?"

"Why should art be my dream?" Vivian asked.

"Well, you already said finance isn't your passion . . ."

Ryan hauled Melvin out of his chair. "We'll be back in ten minutes, Lindsay."

Her heart did a little somersault at his low voice, directed right at her, but then she snapped out of it. That wasn't important right now.

As Ryan and Melvin walked away, she turned to Vivian.

"Let's leave," Vivian said.

# CHAPTER 17

It was after midnight. Lindsay was usually in bed at this time, since she had to wake up early for work. But she'd encouraged Vivian to go to Melvin Lee's show tonight, and she felt like she owed her roommate some company.

They were currently at a Japanese cheesecake café, which Lindsay had been surprised to find open at this hour on a Saturday. Vivian was drinking tea and scarfing down the light, airy cheesecake, and Lindsay was eating at a slower pace, trying her best to keep her eyes open. Coffee would be one solution, but then she might not sleep at all tonight.

"I'm so sorry," Lindsay said. "You weren't sure you wanted to meet him—"

"And my worst fears came true." Vivian sighed. "Ryan Kwok was nice, though, and just as good-looking as he is on-screen. I wasn't disappointed in *him*. I'm not sure why all those women in *JANYS* don't respond to his charms when he's not wearing glasses." She chuckled.

Lindsay supposed that was a good sign.

"I'm happy for you," Vivian said.

"Happy for—"

"I saw the way he was looking at you."

Lindsay swallowed her cheesecake, then coughed. "What do you mean?"

"He clearly likes you."

Well. Lindsay couldn't say it was all in her imagination now. Someone else had seen the occasional looks Ryan gave her and interpreted them the same way. But it wasn't like he'd made a move.

"Yeah, Ryan really was a sweetheart. Why are they friends? Ugh." Vivian paused. "Do *you* wonder why I don't pursue art?"

"It's none of my business. Everyone has their reasons."

"I don't love my job, but I'm good at it, and I don't mind putting on nice clothes and going to the office every day. And you know what I do love? A steady paycheck."

"Completely understandable."

"I'm not rolling in cash, but I have a nice lifestyle, and when I draw, I can draw whatever I want. Fan art for *JANYS*... although I don't know if I'll be doing that anymore—"

"I'm *so* sorry." Lindsay couldn't seem to stop saying it.

Vivian waved this off. "The point is, I get to do exactly what I want and spend exactly as much time as I like on it. I don't have to hustle. *He* thinks I'm cowardly, but I'm not. I've thought this all through." She had a bite of cheesecake. "I'm happy with my life now. It's the first time I've really gotten to live how *I* want."

"Yeah?"

"When I was a kid, I missed out on a lot of fun. I'm the oldest of four, and I was always expected to look after my younger siblings. And then with my ex . . ." Vivian was quiet for a moment. "But perhaps we shouldn't have left when Ryan led Melvin away. God, I can't believe I'm calling them by their first names."

"I texted Ryan, remember? He said he understood."

For the next couple of minutes, they focused on their cheese-cake. When Vivian finished her slice, she looked at the remaining half of the cake, shook her head, and set down her fork.

"I know I can be cold and not very friendly at times. I didn't used to be like this. Not to the same extent, anyway." Vivian laughed without humor. "If I'm nice . . . I'm afraid people will take advantage of me, or read too much into it."

"I know what you mean," Lindsay said. "When I was a wait-ress, there was a regular who was convinced I was in love with him, just because I smiled at him the way I smiled at everyone else."

"Yeah, men suck sometimes." Vivian looked at her phone. "They're closing up any minute. We should ask them to box up the rest of the cheesecake."

They headed home. Lindsay had a quick shower and toppled into bed. Though she wasn't in the best state of mind, she was ex-hausted and had to be up in less than five hours . . . and she fell right to sleep.

"LINDSAY!" MOM SAID, her voice booming over the phone.

Or maybe her voice wasn't booming. Maybe she was speaking at her normal volume and Lindsay's head was just in a bad place today.

She felt like she was hungover, but she wasn't. She'd only had two drinks last night. However, she hadn't gotten enough sleep, and then today, she'd spent nine hours on her feet at the bakery.

At least now she was home and lying on the couch, her head on one of Vivian's sensible throw pillows.

"What's new with you?" Mom asked.

"Um . . . We made a fishing cake today," Lindsay said. Better than talking about last night. "It was for a man's sixtieth birthday. Blue frosting, green reeds along the sides, fish on the top."

Her dad had enjoyed fishing. Lindsay felt a slight twinge at the thought that her father hadn't lived to see his sixtieth birthday. Hadn't gotten to see—and taste—all the amazing donuts and cakes she could now make.

But she was used to such twinges. She'd been living with them for years.

"What about you?" Lindsay asked. "What have you been up to? Still seeing Harold?"

"Yes, and it's going *very* well."

Lindsay was a bit frightened to ask what that meant.

Luckily, Mom didn't say anything inappropriate. Instead, she went on about a French bistro that she and Harold had gone to last night and its amazing crème brûlée. Then she said something about an izakaya they were going to try, and she spoke of it as though it was this special new thing that had only just landed on Canadian soil.

"Mom," Lindsay said, exasperated, "izakayas have been here for years. I went to one when I was in university."

"Is something wrong today? You're not usually so huffy."

"I'm just tired. Had a long day yesterday and didn't get much sleep."

And hearing about Harold was still a tiny bit weird, even though she'd told herself multiple times that this was a good thing.

"Okay, sweetie," Mom said. "Good thing tomorrow is your day off. You can relax. Ooh, but you have those baking classes with the movie star, don't you?"

"I do."

"Why don't you sound enthusiastic? I thought they were going well."

"Like I said, I'm tired."

Mom spent the next ten minutes giving Lindsay advice on how to get a good night's sleep, how to conceal dark circles under her eyes, and all sorts of other fun stuff.

Afterward, Lindsay remained lying on the couch and closed her eyes. She still had to figure out what to do for tomorrow's baking lesson. They were halfway through their lessons now and were moving on to cakes, but what sort of cake should they make?

She could give Ryan a few options, and he could pick from those. She'd send him a text. Best to know what they were doing ahead of time so she could have everything prepared.

But this couch of Vivian's sure was comfortable—much more comfortable than the futon at her old apartment. And what was with this pillow? It was so soft and fluffy.

She'd relax here just for a few minutes . . .

Lindsay awoke three hours later when Vivian gently shook her shoulder.

So much for "just a few minutes."

# CHAPTER 18

"Here's the plan for today," Lindsay said.

"I'm listening." Ryan crossed his arms over his chest.

To be honest, this wasn't an unconscious movement. He was doing it because he knew his biceps looked nice like this. And he'd purposely put on a black T-shirt that was a touch tighter than his other clothes. When he'd posted a picture of himself wearing this shirt on Instagram, he'd gotten more than a few likes.

*Why are you doing this? You can't have her.* He wasn't in the right headspace for a relationship right now, and besides, it would be complicated, given what his life was like.

But he couldn't seem to help it.

Her eyes, to his delight, dropped to his arms, and her voice faltered.

A black shirt wasn't the most practical thing to wear when baking. If he got flour on it, it would stand out more than if he were wearing a lighter-colored shirt.

But that was what the pink apron was for.

Though, knowing himself, he'd get flour on his dark shirt anyway.

He looked at Lindsay and wondered absently—okay, not so absently—whether she'd also picked today's outfit with him in mind. It was the hottest day of the year so far, and she was wearing a tank top. It was hardly a skimpy tank top, but it was still lower cut than the shirts she usually wore.

He couldn't help hoping this was for his benefit.

"All right," she said, regaining her composure. "As you requested, we'll make a chocolate fudge cake, with chocolate buttercream between the layers and on the outside. And for extra fun, we'll make it a drip cake, using chocolate ganache."

"What's a drip cake?"

She pulled out her phone and showed him a cake with white frosting and artful, dark brown "drips" down the sides. He had to lean close to get a good look, and he tried very hard not to be distracted by her nearness.

Okay, maybe he didn't try all that hard.

He wouldn't have to move much to nuzzle the spot where her neck met her shoulder . . .

"You get the idea?" she asked.

"I don't know if mine will look that nice, but sure."

He flashed her a smile that could make panties melt, according to the reviewer who hadn't liked his movie but had started #StarringRyanKwoksAbs.

And Lindsay was not immune.

Her mouth opened and she released a shaky breath. He watched her breasts move up and down beneath that rather tight tank top. This was almost as bad as when she'd wrapped her lips around that thick bubble tea straw last week.

An erection would be inconvenient now, but it was happening anyway.

Fortunately, after he changed his smile to something a little less sexy, she moved away from him and started arranging the ingredients.

"The first thing to do," she said, completely professional now, "is preheat the oven. Don't forget to do this, and make sure you set the right temperature. No 'well, three-fifty is basically the same as four-fifty, whatever.' It's easy to set the right temperature, so why not do it?"

From the sounds of it, she'd watched the latest season of *Baking Fail*.

"And remember to grease the pans," she continued. "I don't know why people keep forgetting this on *Baking Fail*. It's very simple and will save you a lot of hassle. You want your cakes to come out cleanly, don't you?"

"Of course," he said, like a good pupil. He loved how she was so confident and competent. She was an expert, and she acted like it.

"You got me?"

He looked her right in the eyes. "Yeah, I got you."

Her breath caught, just a tiny bit. He imagined the camera zooming in on their faces, capturing their responses to each other.

He imagined the audience saying they had "good chemistry."

Lindsay had him grease three pans. They were making a triple-layer cake, which sounded awful fancy to him. Once mixed, the batter was poured into the pans, then put in the oven.

"Thirty minutes," she said, "then you'll test to see if it's done."

"And what do we do while they're baking?" he asked.

In a movie, this was where she'd shoot him a sexy wink and say, *I have a few ideas.*

But she didn't do that, nor did he. She was his teacher, and he was keeping his hands off her. Being a good student.

Though he did feel the need to talk about Saturday night. It had been in the back of his mind, even if she wasn't treating him any differently from usual.

"I need to apologize again for Mel's behavior," Ryan said. "He was totally out of line."

"He was."

"And the next morning, he did feel bad about it."

This was the truth. They'd had a spat on Saturday night, but yesterday morning, before Mel headed to the airport, had been better.

Mel, Ryan suspected, still wasn't a fan of Vivian's life choices and would never be able to wrap his mind around the idea of someone not minding a job in finance. But he'd admitted that he'd been out of line and shouldn't have said what he said.

Lindsay nodded. "Don't worry, I won't hold it against you."

"I'm his friend, though. He's usually not like that—not that it would matter to Vivian."

"I'll tell her." She smiled, and he was relieved she wasn't upset with him. "Okay, while the cakes are in the oven, you can start on the buttercream."

She stood distractingly close as he made the buttercream. Although, he wouldn't lie, if she was anywhere in the kitchen, it was still distracting. She was so pretty, yet no-nonsense . . .

Would he learn better from someone he didn't find so attractive?

He shoved that out of his mind. No point thinking about it. He didn't regret his decision to take baking lessons from her. He'd learned quite a bit, and with her in his life, everything had begun to feel bearable in the past few weeks. He'd started looking forward to things again.

Mainly, he looked forward to spending time with Lindsay, it was true.

Under her watchful eye, he completed the buttercream and took the cakes out of the oven.

"Don't overbake the cake," she said, "or it'll be dry. Now let them cool for a little before we turn them out of the pans."

"And then put the buttercream on?"

Her eyes widened. "No. Do you want runny buttercream? Don't frost the cake when it's warm. I don't know why people keep making that mistake on the show."

He chuckled at the horror in her voice and recalled how he and his mom had made the same error with their cupcakes.

He helped Lindsay clean up the kitchen as the cakes cooled, though she didn't let him help as much as he'd like—she seemed to have a particular way she wanted things done, and he couldn't help finding that rather cute.

God, everything she did, he found it cute or endearing or sexy or *something*.

"All right," she said, "now you can make the chocolate ganache, and we'll let it cool to room temperature while we frost the cakes."

Lindsay only had to correct him twice as he prepared the chocolate ganache . . . which was actually quite a bit for something that only had two ingredients, especially considering he'd made it twice before.

She got out a cake stand that rotated, like a lazy Susan.

"Why does it rotate?" he asked.

"It'll make decorating easier. You'll see."

She showed him how to spread on the buttercream with the icing spatula between the layers. She made it look simple, like it required no concentration, but he'd seen contestants make a mess of this on *Baking Fail*. At one point, she put her hand over his on the spatula handle—apparently, he wasn't doing it properly.

Her hand was warm on his, making it even more difficult to

focus on spreading the buttercream correctly, especially when she was standing so close to him. He didn't think the touching was strictly necessary, but he wasn't complaining . . . and she probably wasn't doing it because it was necessary, but because she wanted to.

The thought caused a rush of pleasure.

And she wasn't *just* his baking instructor now. He liked that he'd seen her outside the bakery, both at the bubble tea shop and at the comedy club, and he wanted to see her in even more places.

The fervency with which he wanted her practically undid him.

He nearly dropped the spatula, nearly sucked the stray bit of buttercream off her thumb. Nearly slid his hands into her deep brown hair and kissed—

"Is something wrong?" Lindsay asked, stepping back.

*Nothing.*

*Everything.*

"I'm fine," he said.

She looked skeptical but continued with their lesson. "Now we need to put buttercream on the sides, since we're not doing a naked cake . . ." She put a hand to her mouth.

Oh, hell.

He'd—barely—managed to keep quiet when she found excuses to touch him, but he wasn't going to let that go.

He put down the spatula. "Did you say something about naked cakes?"


YES, LINDSAY HAD mentioned naked cakes. Clearly, she hadn't been thinking straight. This wasn't the best topic of conversation around Ryan Kwok, but it was difficult to think clearly in his presence—especially when he was wearing that dark T-shirt that clung to his muscles—so she just opened her mouth and words came out.

"Naked cakes are . . . well . . . they've become popular in the past several years. You don't put frosting on the outside, so you can see all the different layers. There are also semi-naked cakes, which are . . ."

To her horror, she'd forgotten. She wasn't even sure she'd be able to make chocolate ganache right now.

Ryan's lips quirked in a way that said, *I know exactly what you're thinking.*

"What are semi-naked cakes, Lindsay? Is that what happens when I take off my shirt before I eat some cake?" He reached around to the knot he'd tied at the back of his apron.

Oh God. Did he intend to get semi-naked in the kitchen?

He laughed softly. A laugh that wouldn't be broadcast to the rest of the world.

A laugh just for her.

"I think you'd like that," he said. "Wouldn't you?"

She swallowed. "Come on. You know a *lot* of women would like that."

He didn't contradict her.

He just laughed again.

She wasn't going to resist; she'd already decided before that she wouldn't.

And though she was happy to take whatever he wanted to give, she was really, really annoyed at herself for forgetting what a semi-naked cake was.

Well, that wasn't true. She could picture it, but her brain refused to construct a sentence.

Maybe if she tried very hard . . .

"It's when there's a bit of buttercream on the outside, but not a ton, so you can still see the cake in some places."

*Ha, take that, sexy movie star!*

Ryan looked perplexed. "What?"

"Semi-naked cakes. That's what they are."

He seemed to have trouble understanding and forming sentences, too.

It made her feel like the most powerful woman in the world.

"I still think you'd prefer my definition." He lifted his eyebrows.

When she nodded, he raised his hand slowly, as if he was moving through molasses, and cupped her cheek, pushing back the strands of hair that had escaped her ponytail. Gently, so gently, his focus all on her. Her skin prickled at the contact.

"Mondays are my favorite day of the week," he told her.

She didn't say anything, just breathed heavily into the small space between them. She could feel the heat rolling off his body, and he was touching her deliberately.

It wasn't a touch that could be passed off as inconsequential, nor was it done with an excuse—like when she'd adjusted the way he was using the spatula, or when he'd wiped lemon curd off her nose during their last lesson.

His other hand joined the first one on her face. He smoothed her hair before cupping her other cheek, and he looked at her with those dark eyes, more intense than usual.

A notch appeared between his eyebrows. "Is this okay? You've gone rigid. I thought . . . but if you don't want . . . that's totally . . ."

"I want," she said.

She wrapped her arms around his waist, and he dropped his head and kissed her.

First, an experimental brush of his lips, but then he opened his mouth against hers. It was somehow tender and deep at the same time. She stood on her toes to meet him, to get a better angle.

She wanted to take all that she could from this moment.

"You taste like chocolate buttercream," he murmured against her lips.

"I had to taste it to make sure you did an adequate job."

"Mmm. I think I did a more than adequate job."

"Cocky."

He smiled against her lips before kissing her again. He swirled his tongue into her mouth and she gasped, pressing herself more firmly against him, wrapping one leg around his.

His hands moved to her hips to keep her steady, and hers moved up to his neck. He pressed her against the edge of the counter, and she almost bit him when she felt his erection at the apex of her legs.

It made her greedier, and it made everything a little sloppy—but in a good way.

Because it was Ryan, and she'd wanted him for a while now.

He pulled back slightly and tipped his forehead against hers.

"Lindsay," he said, stroking his hand through her hair again. "Will you go on a date with me later this week?"

A *date*?

She hadn't expected that.

She'd seen his interviews, and she didn't think he was interested in dating; she'd just thought he'd invite her back to his place. But a single date probably wasn't anything serious to him. He only wanted to have a fun night out.

A small part of her did want the whole fairy-tale romance with a movie star, to be the Hugh Grant to his Julia Roberts, but she hadn't even managed a relationship with a regular guy in years. She couldn't imagine this working out, even if it was what he wanted. Which it wasn't.

She certainly wouldn't say no to one date, though.

"Sure," she said. "Thursday evening? I'm taking this Friday off."

There was a pretty clear implication there.

"Sounds good to me," he said.

He couldn't seem to resist kissing her again, and she wasn't complaining. He kissed her as if it was the easiest thing in the world, like kissing was simply the right thing to do when the two of them were together.

An errant thought popped into her head: it was weird to kiss someone she'd seen kiss other people close up, on-screen no less. Who'd kissed someone as famous as Irene Lai.

Whatever.

For now, he was kissing Lindsay, and she would enjoy it, the pressure of his mouth against hers sinfully perfect. Even better than the cake they were making.

He put his hands on her shoulders and stepped back. She missed the contact, but she did like the way he was looking at her.

"Now, shall we get back to the cake?" he asked. "Isn't that what we were doing before you deliberately used 'naked' in the conversation?"

"I did not *deliberately*—"

He laughed as he started applying buttercream to the sides of the cake. When she got her bearings again, she helped him with the bench scraper, standing behind him and putting her hand over his when he used it for the first time, her body closer to his than it would have been if they'd done this an hour ago. They didn't bother with a crumb coat.

Then it was time to drip the chocolate ganache. She'd originally planned to show him what happened if the ganache was too warm, but it had already cooled to the right temperature.

"I just use a spoon for this." She got some ganache on her spoon and let it drip down the side of the cake. "Now you try."

Except he used a little too much ganache. It wasn't bad, but it wasn't perfect.

Eventually, he got the hang of it, and after they had enough drips down the side of the cake, she had him fill in the top with chocolate ganache and pipe little swirls of the buttercream on top.

"Voilà," she said. "What do you think?"

"It's pretty awesome." He snapped a few photos with his phone.

"I'll box it up for you."

"Uh-uh. We have to taste it first."

"But then it won't look as pretty for whoever you want to give it to."

He shrugged. "I don't care. I want to eat a slice with *you*."

He wasn't touching her, but those words made her skin sizzle.

She put a generous slice of cake on a plate before putting the rest of it in a box. Then she finished cleaning up the kitchen, and when she went downstairs, he was making lattes. She stood by the door for a moment, watching him work.

He caught her looking and gave her a slow, easy smile that nearly made her legs collapse underneath her. Then he carried the lattes over to a table.

"Are we going to share?" he asked, nodding at the cake.

Right. She'd only brought one slice of cake. A big slice, but only one nonetheless. Like they were splitting dessert at the end of a date.

"Uh, yeah," she said.

"Sounds good to me." He grabbed one of the forks, picked up a forkful of cake with lots of buttercream, and held it to her lips.

It was delicious, and it was even better because he was feeding it to her. When she released a quiet moan, his eyes seemed to bore into hers.

One part of her still couldn't believe this was happening. That he'd kissed her. That he looked at her like this.

But she knew it was real.

It might be temporary, but she'd enjoy the hell out of it while she could. And then, once she'd gotten that out of her system, she'd be ready for a real relationship with another guy.

She hoped.

For now, though, Ryan Kwok was the only man she could think about.

# CHAPTER 19

Ryan walked home at a brisk pace, sunglasses covering his eyes, a box of cake in a paper bag in his right hand.

A middle-aged woman looked at him curiously. Because she recognized him? Or because he was whistling?

Yes, he was whistling.

He stopped when he realized what he was doing.

He was in a good mood, though. He had a date with a lovely woman on Thursday. He'd kissed her today, and it made him feel more alive than he had in ages.

Dating was the last thing he needed, which was why he'd been holding himself back from her . . . until today, when she'd started talking about naked and semi-naked cakes, and he couldn't stand it any longer.

He could make this casual, but a part of him did want more than a couple of dates and sex, however difficult it would be.

He wouldn't let himself dwell on that now. First, he needed to plan this date. He'd told Lindsay that he'd think of something and text her in the next couple of days.

When he got home, he removed the cake from the box. It was nearly perfect, aside from the slice she'd removed for them to eat.

Aside from the slightly wonky chocolate drips and the misshapen swirls of buttercream, owing to his lack of skill, not hers.

But it made him smile, because he'd made it with her—and it tasted pretty damn good, too. When he looked at it, he thought of their kisses. Her lips against his.

Not that he needed a cake to remind him of her kiss, but still.

He thought of the way he'd pressed her against the counter when she seemed weak at the knees. That little moan when she'd felt his cock between her legs . . .

Ryan should have asked her to come home with him, rather than waiting until Thursday.

If she were here right now, he'd pull off that tank top. Lay her back on the counter and drip chocolate ganache down her breasts, then lick it off. Unbutton her jeans and slip his hand into her panties, feel how wet he could make her.

After he'd put the cake away and texted Jenna to see if she'd like some chocolate fudge cake and a visit from her brother tomorrow, he jumped in the shower.

He told himself it was because he was sweating after his walk home in the hot weather. Not because he wanted to imagine having a shower with Lindsay.

Even though, once he was in the shower, that was all he could think about.

He'd never had someone else in this shower with him, but it was easy to imagine, the water running through her long hair, soap suds over her body. Kissing her beneath the spray.

He tilted his head back as he grasped his cock. He imagined it was her hand on his erection instead, imagined her guiding him toward her entrance.

He made a strangled sound at the thought of making her come while she was in his arms, of spilling himself inside her . . .

And then drying her off and bringing her to the bedroom and thrusting into her once more, her hair wet and her skin glistening.

What noises did she make when she orgasmed?

He hoped to find out soon. She'd made a point of saying she was free all Friday, as though she planned to stay the night . . .

He came in his hand and the water washed everything away, but he wouldn't be able to stop thinking about it.

THURSDAY AFTERNOON, LINDSAY flipped the sign from "Open" to "Closed," then walked to the table at the back and sat across from Trevor.

The table where she'd eaten cake with Ryan a few days earlier.

Trevor bit into a lemon meringue donut, which also reminded her of Ryan.

Normally, she'd be happy to talk to her brother at the end of her workday, but today was no ordinary day. She had special plans later.

"Mom didn't come home last night," Trevor said.

"Oh?" On another day, Lindsay might have cringed, might have gotten worked up and had to remind herself that it was okay, her mother was allowed this.

But today, it didn't bother her. Her mind was firmly on other things.

"She didn't come home the night before, either," Trevor said. "In fact, she hasn't slept at home for four nights. She's been at Harold's."

Lindsay shrugged. "She can have her own life."

"But . . ." Trevor made the sort of face a baby might make when trying turnip for the first time. "I met him earlier."

"Yeah? What's he like? Is he an Asian doppelgänger of Dad?"

"Not at all."

Lindsay breathed out a sigh of relief. It would be easier to see her mother with someone who wasn't like her dad.

Though she wasn't too bothered by anything right now, except the fact that Trevor was still in her bakery and she had to get ready for her date.

"And he's soft-spoken," Trevor said.

Yeah, quite the opposite of their father, who'd had a booming voice and a hearty laugh. A laugh she hadn't heard in a painfully long time.

"Does Mom seem happy?" Lindsay asked.

Trevor took another bite of his donut. "Yeah, I guess?"

"Well, that's all that matters." She discreetly looked at her watch. "If he's a decent guy and she's happy, what more can we want?"

"But do I have to know about it? Do I have to know she's probably"—he dropped his voice—"having sex?"

"This is what happens when you live with your mother. Not that I think there's a problem with you living there, but it's the price you pay. If you hadn't told me that she hadn't come home in four nights, I wouldn't have known."

Which reminded her. She should tell Vivian that she didn't plan on being home tonight, so her roommate wouldn't worry.

Trevor looked like he wanted to tear out his hair.

"Lindsay!" Noreen called as she pushed open the door from the kitchen. "You're still here? Shouldn't you be getting ready for your date with your movie star . . . Oh, hi, Trevor."

Lindsay put her head in her hands.

"I'm sorry," Noreen said quietly.

"You're dating a movie star?" Trevor asked.

"It's only a first date," Lindsay said.

"Mom said you were teaching a guy how to bake. Is this him?"

"Uh, yeah."

"I don't believe this," Trevor muttered. "First Mom, and now you."

"Just because we're related to you doesn't mean we can't date. Stop being such a prude."

Trevor switched to Big Brother Mode, which was a little jarring as he was two years younger than her. "Make sure you tell Noreen where you're going. Call me if you get into trouble."

"I doubt you'd stand a chance against him," Lindsay said. "He has biceps like pomelos. And he's a good guy, so you have nothing to worry about. I know him."

"Do you really? He probably has tons of women hanging off him, legions of adoring fans . . ."

"Trevor, stop it. I can do whatever I like. You need to get going so I can head out and primp for this date. I hope there's no sock on the doorknob when you get home."

Trevor's brain was probably close to exploding, but he did as requested. Perhaps he was afraid of what else would come out of her mouth if he stayed.

As soon as her brother was gone, Lindsay headed to the back to collect her stuff, then hurried home, excitement thrumming through her veins.

# CHAPTER 20

Lindsay had picked out her outfit two days ago, but now she was second-guessing herself. She was wearing a navy A-line dress with cap sleeves. She liked dresses, but she didn't wear them to work, and she didn't go out a ton, other than having drinks with Noreen. It was good to have a chance to wear this one, which she'd picked up on sale for forty bucks and had only worn twice. There was a thick belt around the middle, which gave her a nice figure, and she'd paired it with peep-toe heels.

She stood in front of her full-length mirror and gave her hips a little shake.

It looked classy but semi-casual at the same time.

Where was he taking her?

He'd said they'd go out for dinner, and he'd assured her there was no need to be formal, but she'd never gone on a date with a movie star before.

She opened her closet again and debated another dress. She had a black off-the-shoulder cocktail dress with a flouncy skirt. To her, that felt quite fancy, but maybe it would be more appropriate . . .

Her phone rang. It was Ryan, asking her to let him in.

Shit! She didn't have time for a new outfit. She put on some drop earrings, ran a brush through her hair, grabbed her purse, and hurried to the front hall. She was slipping on her shoes when there was a knock at the door, and even though she'd anticipated that knock, she jumped.

Lindsay opened the door, and Ryan leaned against the door-frame and gave her a slow smile—as well as a slow perusal of her body. His eyes traveled down from her face to her chest, to her cinched-in waist . . . and back up.

She swallowed. He was looking at her like she was the heroine in a movie.

And he was here, in her apartment, the sleeves of his pink collared shirt rolled up to reveal his forearms. Even though his pose might seem casual, he probably had a very good idea of how people reacted to it. Many men weren't aware of the magic of forearms, but he was.

He touched the collar of his shirt. "You seem to like me in pink."

Why did he think that? He'd look good in any color of the rainbow.

Oh, right. The apron.

Before she could speak, he pulled her close and slid his hands over her shoulders, down her upper arms. Then he cupped her cheeks, like he'd done the first time they'd kissed.

"I didn't wear any lipstick," she said. "Because—"

He cut her off with a kiss, a kiss that seemed to grow and grow with each press of his lips against hers. As soon as she moaned and tried to wrap her body around his, he stepped back.

"We should head out," he said, his voice perfectly normal. "Since I made reservations."

"You have much better self-control than I do."

He must be used to having nearly anyone he wanted. It wasn't a special night for him.

"No," he said, leveling her with a look. "I do not."

His gaze held hers for a moment, until she was practically trembling, and then he took her hand in his and led her out of her apartment.

**HE SHOULDN'T BE** nervous, but he was.

Sure, Ryan knew he looked relaxed, but inside, it was a different matter.

It had been simple hanging out with Lindsay at the bakery and the tea shop. But a date, at a nice restaurant . . .

Yet, he'd really wanted to do this.

He wouldn't let himself think too much about what it meant, or what would happen after tonight—or tomorrow morning—was over.

It was just a little hard with these damn nerves. Though he was in good company, since she was clearly a bit nervous and didn't hide it well.

He would tell her to relax if he didn't know that would make her clam right up.

They'd already split an appetizer, and she'd drunk most of her cocktail. Something with maple and bourbon. He'd stuck with water. As a general rule, he tried not to drink calories, aside from protein shakes, but sometimes he made an exception for bubble tea and lattes. Otherwise, it was water, black coffee, and tea.

With alcohol, there was also the issue of how red in the face he got, so he generally abstained, though he'd tried a sip of Lindsay's drink.

The waiter arrived with their main courses. "Wild boar ragù with pappardelle for the lady." He set Lindsay's plate in front of her. "And the venison for the gentleman. Is there anything else you need?"

Lindsay shook her head, her earrings swaying. "I'm good, thank you."

"Me, too," Ryan said.

It was a cozy restaurant on Portland, and he'd requested a more private table. Indeed, the table they'd been given at the back was nice. It wasn't in a room of its own, but it was set off a bit from most of the restaurant.

*Rather romantic*, he thought, looking at the small vase of wildflowers in the center of the table. Not that he had much personal experience with romance. Most of what he knew was from, well, movies and TV.

"How is it?" he asked after Lindsay had finished her first bite.

"It's really good," she answered with a smile, then dabbed at her mouth with a napkin.

He was glad the food was tasty, and she looked absolutely lovely, but he couldn't take this anymore. The slightly stiff politeness . . . it wasn't what he'd wanted for tonight.

So he did the first thing that came to his mind: he undid a button on his shirt. Then another.

She raised her eyebrows.

"Was I mistaken?" he asked. "You said nice things about my shirtless scenes in *That Kind of Wedding.*"

Her mouth opened and closed a bunch of times. "You don't have anything on under that, do you?"

"No," he said casually, putting his hands on the third button.

"Ryan!"

He winked at her.

"Are you trying to make me choke?" she asked.

"Trying to lighten the mood."

Her face fell. "I'm sorry. I'm not used to all of this." She gestured vaguely around them. "The food really is good, though."

Maybe they should have gone somewhere else. He'd just wanted to take her somewhere nice, that was all, and it was easier to have a little more privacy here.

He leaned forward and placed his hand on her knee, just under the hem of her skirt—one of the advantages of her wearing a dress. He brushed his thumb over her skin.

"Ryan!" she admonished again. "Eat your food before it gets cold."

"Yes, ma'am."

"And before I combust."

He graced her with a crooked smile. He enjoyed when she talked back to him.

Everything felt a little easier after that, though on the other hand, it wasn't easy at all. Anything either of them did to change their relative positions to each other . . . Well, he was aware of her every movement.

After they finished their main courses, she asked if he was interested in dessert, or if he'd eaten too much chocolate fudge cake already this week.

"I thought we could go somewhere else, if that's okay with you," he said. "I rarely have ice cream, and there's a rolled ice cream place near here. You want to try it?"

Her face lit up, and it fucking slayed him.

"Good," he said. "I was afraid you wouldn't be interested in ice cream because you're all about lemon meringue cupcakes and"—he shuddered—"matcha tiramisu donuts."

She laughed. "Come on. Almost everyone loves ice cream."

When they left the restaurant, he slid on his sunglasses. It wasn't fully dark yet—it was just past the longest day of the year—but it was dusk. They soon arrived at the busy rolled ice cream place. There was a line of at least ten people, and he held her hand as they waited.

He'd tried not to think about having more than tonight with her, but now he couldn't seem to help it. Walking around the city together. Taking her out for dumplings and ice cream and coffee. Introducing her to people other than Melvin. Taking her to the Golden Globes . . .

He felt like he had no space in his life for a relationship, yet maybe this was exactly what he needed. Maybe, even though he was kind of flailing right now, it was something he could handle emotionally. Maybe he shouldn't hold himself back.

He'd always tried to be an optimist when it came to his career, even when it seemed like there was so much working against him. He could try to be optimistic here, too.

"I think we should share," she said. "Which one would you like?"

She didn't ask what he'd been thinking about.

He could kiss her.

"Yeah, let's share," he said, his voice a little scratchy. "You pick whatever you want."

"No, you said you hadn't eaten ice cream in ages. You should choose. In fact, I won't allow you *not* to choose."

"Bossy, are we?" he murmured, leaning closer to her. Another inch, and he could nip her earlobe, but he wouldn't do that here. "All right." He read over the options, trying not to be distracted by Lindsay's presence next to him. "How about the taro-coconut?"

"Sounds good to me. That's what I would have picked."

He was entirely too pleased with her words.

They ordered, and she thrust out her credit card before he could stop her. He'd paid for dinner, so he'd let her pay for ice cream if that was what she wanted. They watched one of the workers dump a few things onto a cold metal surface and prepare the ice cream. Once finished, the seven cylindrical rolls of ice cream were placed in a white cup with fresh fruit, a triangular waffle cookie, and two Pocky sticks. It was drizzled with condensed milk and topped with shaved fresh coconut.

There were no empty seats inside and the small patio was full, so Lindsay led them to a bench in the nearby parkette.

The best part about the bench was that he got to sit right next to her, his leg pressed against hers. Her knees were visible from under her dress, and he wasn't usually turned on by knees, but he liked every part of her.

He held the cup between them and dipped his plastic spoon into the ice cream, getting a small piece of kiwi and a raspberry as well.

It was good.

It was really good.

It was just . . .

He put a fist to his forehead.

"Brain freeze?" Lindsay asked.

"Yeah. Been a long time since that's happened to me."

"But so worth it." She wiggled her hips against him.

"Yeah, so worth it."

When he looked her in the eyes, she ran her tongue over her upper lip. He wanted to kiss her so much, but surely he could wait five minutes until they'd finished their ice cream.

"I've never had rolled ice cream before," he confessed.

"No?"

"I wonder how someone came up with the idea." He picked up one of the Pocky sticks and had a bite. "My mom used to put these in my school lunches occasionally."

"My mother didn't. She would have considered them too Asian. She was very concerned about us getting teased for our lunches, like she had when she was a child. We got sandwiches and pudding, or occasionally Oreos."

"Where I grew up, our food was nothing out of the ordinary. At least half the kids were Asian."

"Not where we lived in Newmarket. It wasn't entirely white, but mostly white."

They finished their ice cream in comfortable silence. Ryan was distantly aware of the traffic and other noises of the city, but they didn't matter. He threw out the empty ice cream cup, returned to the bench, and pulled her close to him.

"Thank you for tonight," Lindsay said. "This was fun."

"You make it sound like I did you a favor, but I think it's the other way around."

"Stop being such a charmer."

He put a hand to his chest and pretended to be insulted.

She rolled her eyes.

"I had a good time tonight, too." He didn't give her a chance to respond; he simply kissed her. He wrapped his arms around her and held her against him, so he could feel her beating heart against his, and his lips melded with hers.

And that was enough to make him forget all the doubts he had about the two of them. Because when he was kissing her, it felt right.

He slid his hand up to the outside of her thigh and squeezed.

"Lindsay," he murmured. "Come home with me?"


**LINDSAY WAS IN** Ryan Kwok's condo.

He lived in a two-bedroom unit. More security than her building, and it was in Yorkville, but it wasn't some palatial mansion on the Bridle Path. She supposed he didn't have Julia Roberts's or Jackie Chan's level of fame. Wasn't commanding twenty million a movie or something like that.

But one day . . .

Oh, she *believed* in him.

"Does it meet your approval?" he asked, sounding a little anxious, or possibly that was her brain's erroneous assumption.

"It's nice," she said. "I love your kitchen." She was all about nice kitchens.

Her body was thrumming with awareness. She wanted to undress him, touch things she'd only seen on the big screen—along with thousands of other people.

But although she wasn't usually shy about such activities, it was hard to make the first move. Easier to run her hands along the granite countertops.

He came up behind her and rested his chin on her shoulder. "Tell me if I ever do anything you don't like. Or if there's something you want. Okay?"

How many women had he said such things to?

Probably lots.

She didn't mind. She was under no illusions; she was here with her eyes wide open. Here to have a night of fun with him. Maybe it would turn into a few more nights, but she had no further expectations.

Well, she expected him to treat her respectfully, and he was.

He was a decent, good-looking guy who'd show her a good time. Nothing more.

But . . .

She shoved that down. She just had a little crush on him, because it was hard not to be caught up in it all when you'd gone on a date with an up-and-coming movie star, wasn't it? But she could handle herself.

His lips were warm on her neck, and she arched back.

Oh God. Just feeling the length of his body against hers . . . it was intense. When she rubbed her ass back against his cock, he growled. It was such a heady feeling, knowing she could affect him like this.

With one hand, he undid the belt on her dress and shoved the dress over her head. As soon as it dropped to the floor, he removed her bra and massaged her breast. She tilted her head back and parted her lips. When he circled his thumb around the hardened peak of her nipple, she shuddered—or he shuddered, she couldn't tell.

He spun her around to face him and picked her up easily, his hands under her ass. He walked into the bedroom, flicked on the lights, and deposited her on the bed, falling on top of her and kissing her hungrily. She squirmed underneath him, seeking the pressure she craved. *Touch me. Please.*

His hand climbed up her bare leg and rested on her inner thigh for a moment, as if in question. When she bucked her hips upward, he slipped his hand into her panties, trailed his fingers over her slit.

"Fuck," he said as he slid his hand through her wetness.

She began unbuttoning his shirt, needing to touch him as well, but then he slipped a finger inside her, and that was too much, how could she possibly undo a button when he was touching her like that?

Finally, when she was able to function again—sort of—she finished with the buttons and placed her hands on his chest.

He graced her with a lopsided cocky smile. It might have made her roll her eyes, except he really did look like a freaking god . . . and, oh my, he'd slid a second finger inside her, and the blunt tip of his thumb was circling her clit. She was soaked.

She hurriedly reached for his belt, then unzipped his pants and thrust her hand inside his boxers, needing to undo him the way he undid her.

But the heat, the hardness of him, unraveled her further.

She pumped his cock a few times, and he shut his eyes and swallowed hard—she was watching him carefully, attuned to his every reaction, even as she was overwhelmed by having his hand between her legs.

He pulled off her panties, and she felt a moment of self-consciousness at being fully naked in front of this man, who was supporting himself above her, his shirt unbuttoned and pants open. This man so many people thought was fucking fine, but his reaction to her—and the need in her body—soon pushed that self-consciousness aside.

"Fuck, you're gorgeous," he said. "So gorgeous." He buried his face in her breasts, sucking one peak into his mouth while his hand drifted between her legs again. He pumped his fingers inside her and rubbed her clit, and it was like there were paths of arousal crisscrossing all through her body, down to her toes.

She arched her hips up abruptly and gasped.

"Did you come?" he murmured.

She nodded, incapable of speech.

"I'm good, aren't I?" he said, probably to annoy her.

She rolled him off her—well, he let her do it. If he didn't want to move, she wouldn't be able to move him. Because . . . look at those freaking biceps.

Now it was her turn to finish undressing him, and she made quick work of it, even with the last of that orgasm pulsing through her body. As soon as she wrapped her hand around his dick, he groaned.

"You have to stop," he said. "I'm . . ."

He lifted her up and set her away from him—there was lots of room in his king-size bed. Then he opened the top drawer in his night table and pulled out a condom.

He was going to be inside her soon, and she wanted it, craved it with an intensity that nearly frightened her. She told herself it was because she hadn't had sex in a couple of months, but really, a couple of months wasn't that long.

"You good?" he asked, his hands poised to tear open the packet.

She nodded, and he rolled on the condom. She felt like they were on the precipice of something important. He ran the tip of his cock over her entrance before slowly pushing inside, and she gripped the blankets.

He didn't start thrusting right away. Instead, he gently pushed her slightly sweaty hair back from her face and looked at her in a way that made her chest ache. He bent his head and kissed her slowly on the lips, and as the pace of his kiss increased, he began to move within her. Deep, so deep, rolling his hips against hers. His lips on her neck now, biting lightly, maybe more than lightly, possibly leaving a mark, she didn't care.

He was all around her, everywhere, his mouth and hands making her feel so much.

She wrapped her legs around him tightly, holding on with all she could. The angle gave her clit some friction, but not quite enough . . .

And then his hand was between her legs, the pad of a finger on her clit, and she cried out and jerked to the side.

There was no cocky smile on his face this time.

"Lindsay," he said. "I won't last long. I'm going to . . ."

He buried his face in the pillow and growled as he came inside her.

And afterward, he looked at her as though she was everything.

# CHAPTER 21

When Ryan woke up on Friday morning, it wasn't even seven o'clock, but Lindsay was already awake. She was looking at something on her phone. It seemed to be a video of vegetables. Huh?

But then someone sliced through the cabbage with a big knife, and instead of cabbage inside—as one would sensibly expect—it was chocolate cake.

The sweet potato next to the cabbage also turned out to be a cake.

Ryan rubbed his eyes and looked again. Perhaps he was still half-asleep.

Some fruit appeared on-screen. A mango and a peach. These, too, were cake.

"Good morning," he said to the woman watching this strange video.

"Good morning." Lindsay paused the video and set her phone on the night table. The night table on the other side of the bed, the one that was almost never used. "Did you enjoy the illusion cakes?"

"They were kinda freaking me out, to be honest. I thought I was dreaming for a moment. Do you make cakes like those?"

"Nah, not really my thing. Those were done by one of my class-mates in college. She's talented, isn't she?"

"It's amazing, but does anyone actually commission her to make such cakes?"

Lindsay's cheeks pinkened.

"What is it?" he asked, slipping his arms around her.

"When you came to the bakery . . . for the second time."

"The first time being when I knocked over all those donuts."

"Yes. Though I'm rather glad it happened now." She gestured between them.

He started kissing his way down her neck.

"Stop it!" She slapped him playfully. "I was telling you a story."

"So you were. Please, continue."

"The second time . . ." She giggled as he pressed a kiss to her collarbone. "Before you asked about baking lessons, I was, for some reason, imagining you wanted a butter pecan cake in the shape of your abs."

He burst into laughter. "How on earth—"

"Don't ask why I was thinking about that, but I was." Lindsay glanced at the phone she'd discarded on the night table. She hadn't put on any clothes last night after they'd had sex, and neither had he. The sheets had slipped down to her waist, and he was glad she wasn't self-conscious about that.

Her breasts really were lovely in the morning light. Nice and plump.

"Wouldn't that be something," she said, "if I could make a cake that looked like your abs, six-pack and all?"

"To do them justice, I think you need to do a lot more touch-ing." He brought her hand under the sheets, to the body part in question.

She laughed, and he turned her onto her side. He lay behind her and ran his hands over her skin, loving the simple pleasure of having her in his bed first thing in the morning. Of hearing her laugh first thing in the morning.

He couldn't bear the idea of this not happening again.

"How are you feeling?" he asked.

"I'm doing well."

"Just 'well'?" He slipped his hand between her legs. "I'm going to make you forget all about cakes that look like cabbages."

"If you're sure you're up to the challenge . . ."

"Oh, don't you worry. I am."

He rolled her onto her back, slid down her body, and gave her a long lick between her legs. He kissed her inner lips, her clit, and then he slipped a finger inside her as he continued to focus on her clit.

God, she tasted good.

He'd wanted to do this for a long time.

He kept licking her, acutely aware of every hitch in her breathing, every movement in her hips, the way she was now gripping his hair with one hand. He pumped his fingers inside her, faster and faster, and then she bucked her hips and came.

"Ryan," she cried, her hands scrambling to hold on to him. "Fuck me."

He didn't need to be told twice. He rolled on a condom and turned her on her side again. He entered her from behind, all the way to the hilt in a single stroke. But after that, his thrusts were more leisurely than they'd been last night. He undulated his hips and reached his hand around to play with her breasts, and then between her legs. Kissed her freckled shoulders, her neck, her back, wherever he could reach.

"Yes," he said into her hair, "just like that."

His orgasm overtook him as he held her tightly, and he called out her name.

He went to the washroom once he'd recovered. After cleaning himself up, he headed back to the bedroom, figuring they could spend a couple more hours together in bed. Then he could make her something for breakfast. Did anyone ever prepare food for her? Likely not often.

After breakfast . . . well, returning to bed would be an option, or if she wanted to go out, that was fine, too.

But when he sauntered back into the bedroom, Lindsay wasn't in his bed. No, she'd put on her underwear and was turning her dress right side out. Her gaze drifted over to him, and she seemed momentarily distracted, but then she turned her attention back to her dress and pulled it over her head.

"Do you have something to do today?" He thought it was her day off, though of course she could have better things to do than spend the day with him.

She didn't answer his question. "Last night was lots of fun."

"And what about this morning?"

"That was fun, too. Thank you."

This sounded far too formal.

"You can stay longer," he said.

She shook her head and gave him a weak smile. "I don't think that's a good idea."

"Why not?" There was something he wasn't getting here.

"Are you used to women doing whatever you want them to do?"

He circled his arms around her and pulled her onto the bed with him. "Are you embarrassed you slept with me?"

She sputtered, then composed herself. "You don't know me very well. I'm not embarrassed about that at all."

"I want to know you better."

She wriggled out of his arms and sat cross-legged on the bed with a sigh. "If I stay, I'll get other ideas, and that wouldn't be for the best."

"What kind of ideas?"

"You know, relationship ideas. Like that we could really be together, which I don't think you want."

"But what if I did?"

She stared at him. "I can't take you seriously when you're not wearing clothes."

He smirked and walked over to his dresser, where he put on boxers and a T-shirt before coming back to bed.

"Okay, serious talk," he said. "I want to do this again. I want to keep seeing you."

"Really?"

"You think I would lie to you about that?"

"I don't, but you're a good-looking *movie star* who must have interest from lots of women and probably takes advantage of that. I don't think you're an ass about it. I think you're discreet and respectful, but—"

"There aren't as many women as you're imagining. Some, yes, and I'm always clear about what I can and can't offer. I don't play games. I don't lead people on. So, when I say I want to keep seeing you, I mean it." He suddenly wished he hadn't been as successful in his career, wished he was still a no-name actor—or that he'd met her several years back—so it would be easier for her to believe.

She was quiet, and he gave her time to think. Didn't touch her, even though her leg was begging to be touched, her cheek to be caressed.

"Would you be interested in having . . . a relationship?" she asked.

He nodded.

There were still doubts at the back of his mind, but she made him feel like he might be able to make this work.

"Oh," she whispered. "But I've seen and read your interviews. You've said . . . that's not a priority for you."

"Things change," he said. "I'm not sure how good I'll be at it, since the last relationship I had only lasted two months and that was a while ago. And, more than that, because I'm not in the best place emotionally, with my mom's death and all, but I do want to try." *With you. You've changed me.*

She was silent again. She didn't look at him but toward the window, though the curtains were closed.

"I haven't been able to have a relationship since my dad died," she said. "That was seven years ago, so I'm in no position to judge. Not that I haven't had sex with a bunch of men in that time—I have."

She looked at him, like she was daring him to have a problem with that, but he didn't.

"When I sleep with a guy," she continued, "I don't usually feel like I'm in any danger of falling for him."

"But my good looks and charm and sexy, sexy abs that aren't made of cake are too much for you to handle?" He gave her one of his patented lopsided smiles, unable to stop himself from joking, but then he said, "Why haven't you had a relationship in a while?"

"It's hard for me to get close to people. Hard for me to be vulnerable."

He hadn't gotten that sense from her. Was she different with him than she was with other people? Was he special?

He felt stupidly pleased.

"Okay," he said. "Neither of us knows what we're doing, but we can still try. We can take it slow. If you're willing. But you should know that being with me is more complicated than being with most people, since I'm a little famous."

She enclosed his hand in hers, which he figured was a good sign.

He smiled at her tentatively, uncertainly.

And then she said the very best words.

"Let's try."

Somehow, he felt like it would work out, despite everything.

"Thank you." He tackled her onto the bed. "Shall we fix this disturbing situation now?"

"Disturbing situation?"

"The fact that you put on clothes." He trailed his hand under the hem of her dress, feeling incredibly lucky that he got to do this, and she laughed.

And then he got to the top of her legs, and she made other noises . . .

**"I MIGHT HAVE** been a bit presumptuous," Ryan said as Lindsay took a seat at the breakfast bar in his kitchen.

"What do you mean?" She had no idea where this was going.

"I don't really keep breakfast food at my place. I have a shake each morning. But I was hoping you'd stay overnight and figured I ought to have something for you to eat in the morning . . ."

He started pulling stuff out of the cupboards and fridge. Two types of cold cereal, the boxes unopened. Oatmeal. Milk. Bread and jam. Eggs. Plain yogurt. Strawberries and blueberries.

"I hope you see something you like," he said.

Oh God. He was making her heart melt.

He stood at the counter, behind all the food, but despite his casual stance, he looked a bit uncertain. She couldn't help coming around the counter and wrapping her arms around him.

"Unless you don't eat breakfast," he said. "Then—"

"I definitely eat breakfast. I start work before seven most days. I need some sustenance to keep me going." She reached for the yogurt and berries.

"I'll make it for you," he said. "You sit down and relax."

"It's just yogurt. I can do it myself."

"It's just yogurt. Unlike meringue, it's something I'm fully capable of handling."

He washed the berries and got out a glass cup. He spread a layer of yogurt at the bottom, followed with blueberries and chopped strawberries. Then more yogurt, and another layer of berries. One last layer of yogurt, and three blueberries on top. He handed it to her, along with a spoon.

"Do you want anything else?" he asked.

"Coffee?"

He started the coffeemaker before making his shake. It looked the opposite of appetizing, but she was curious, so she asked to try a sip.

She nearly spit it out.

"You have one every morning?" she asked in horror.

He shrugged. "You get used to it. And they're really not so bad."

"Mm-hmm."

He laughed at her skepticism.

He sat on the stool next to her, and they ate their breakfast— well, he drank his. When the coffee was ready, he poured them each a mug and took out milk and sugar for her.

She loved watching him walk around the kitchen.

Okay, to be fair, much of the time she spent with him was in a kitchen. But at the bakery, she was in charge; here, it was different. It was his place, and he was taking care of her in little ways. Plus, he wasn't fully dressed—he was still just wearing a T-shirt and boxers.

There was something so delightfully ordinary about this.

Lindsay was reminded of her childhood, of coming downstairs to find her mother and father drinking coffee and reading the newspaper together.

She'd thought she'd have to leave as soon as possible this morning if she had any hope of keeping her heart intact, but he'd surprised her.

He wanted this.

She looked at him and smiled, and he smiled back. She felt so giddy that she practically bounced in her seat.

"I should wash up," she said after draining her coffee.

"There are a couple unopened toothbrushes under the sink."

She headed to the washroom, where she washed her face and found a new red toothbrush. She brushed her teeth, then set her toothbrush in the holder next to his. Having a toothbrush at his place . . . was that moving too fast?

But it didn't make her feel uncomfortable.

No, she felt like she could do this. She could get over her issues with dating.

She returned to the kitchen and hopped up on the barstool next to Ryan. He turned his phone toward her and showed her what he was looking at.

It was a shirtless, ridiculously jacked Asian man on Instagram. Lindsay read the caption under the picture.

"Holy shit," she said. "That's Albert Nguyen?" She peered at his face—he did indeed look familiar. He'd been on a sitcom for a few years, but he'd been lean and lanky then, and his character had been a dork.

"Yeah," Ryan said. "He got cast in a superhero movie a while back—do you remember? Apparently, he's been following a careful fitness and diet regimen ever since to get himself to look like this. I know exactly how much work it can be."

"He probably can't eat chocolate fudge cake."

"No. Having zero percent body fat is tough."

Lindsay turned from the photo to Ryan. Ryan was, alas, wearing a shirt, but she remembered how he looked underneath that T-shirt, and besides, she could still see his forearms and biceps, which were plenty nice.

"You're better-looking," she said.

"You don't need to stroke my ego, Lindsay," he drawled.

"But seriously, he's too bulked up and chiseled. He doesn't look real."

"People are giving me shit online."

"What?"

*Looks like there are some new abs in town. You need to get working on your crunches.*

And #StarringAlbertNguyensAbs was trending.

For the last half hour, she'd been able to forget she was dating a movie star. She'd brushed it aside when he'd said that dating him was a little more complicated. Ryan was just the hot guy who wanted to be with her and gave her incredible orgasms.

But now, she couldn't forget.

Tons of people had seen him shirtless. When he posted selfies online, people went crazy over them. And despite the utter perfection of his body, despite the fact that he drank nasty shakes for breakfast to maintain it, people were now telling him it wasn't enough?

This wasn't something she could relate to. At all. She couldn't imagine people on social media discussing her like this. It would give her serious issues.

"Does this . . . bother you?" she asked.

"Nah. There's room for more than one Asian actor with nice abs."

She suddenly wondered if actors like Ryan were in danger of getting eating disorders. Probably. It wasn't something she'd ever thought about before.

She didn't belong in his world.

"Oh, by the way," he said. "I'm not posting publicly about you or Kensington Bake Shop or our dates for now. And it's not like I have paparazzi following me everywhere, but people do sometimes recognize me when I'm out."

"Right. Okay. That would be for the best."

He put aside his phone. She wondered how he dealt with social media when he had hundreds of thousands of followers on both Twitter and Instagram. He wouldn't be able to look at all his notifications. He probably got a lot of hate, too. People could be awful.

She had trouble comprehending what his life was like.

He could date women who were as famous as he was. Women who had the time and money to ensure their bodies were works of art, rather than spending ten hours a day in a kitchen.

She thought of Irene Lai and the bikini scene in *That Kind of Wedding*. That woman was freaking *toned*. And the actress who'd played the bride had been a knockout in her cheongsam at the reception.

Lindsay swallowed and looked down at her forty-dollar dress.

"Hey," Ryan said, placing his hands on her knees. "What's up?"

"I'm slightly intimidated by your life," she admitted.

"I'd tell you not to be, but I'm not sure it'll help. I know some of it can be a bit much. But don't doubt that I really do want to make this work."

He pulled her onto his stool. It felt a bit precarious, but he was leaning back against the counter, and she doubted they would topple over. Plus, he must have some special moves and would be able to catch her.

"Okay," she said quietly. "Okay."

• • •

*I'm not usually attracted to Asian men, but I'd date him.*

Ryan scrubbed a hand over his face and sighed as he read over the tweet, accompanied by a picture of Albert Nguyen. A couple of women had said something similar to Ryan before.

Even though he was famous in part for how he looked, he still had his insecure moments. They didn't last long, but they still happened. He'd grown up not seeing men like him get the girl in Hollywood movies, and many people hadn't considered Asian men attractive at all. He'd occasionally had things said to him that . . . well.

It didn't bother him, of course, that Albert Nguyen had rockhard muscles, but some of the related backhanded compliments and comments did bother him a bit.

Not that Ryan talked about it often, and he didn't use the way Asian men were desexualized to shit on Asian women. Unlike, say, Ricky Shen, who'd said some misogynistic crap over the years.

Yet, as Ryan doom-scrolled, he still felt like today was a very good day.

Because of Lindsay.

He wanted to wake up to her looking at cabbage cakes in his bed again. Preferably naked, but he was flexible. She'd been about to leave after they'd had sex, but then they'd talked it out and decided to . . . try.

No horror show on Twitter could change the fact that today had been a good day. She'd left not long ago, and he was already looking forward to the next time he could wrap his arms around her and kiss her and hope his life didn't intimidate her too much.

She was probably home by now. He wondered what she was up to.

The idea that she might be thinking about him, too, made his heart fucking flutter.

# CHAPTER 22

When Lindsay got back to her apartment that afternoon, she immediately hopped in the shower, and her body felt different than it had before. First of all, because she was a bit sore—she wasn't used to having sex five times in twenty-four hours—but it wasn't only that. Somehow, it just seemed different, now that *he'd* touched her everywhere.

Afterward, she went to the grocery store to get ingredients for a cake.

At six o'clock, Lindsay was in her bedroom, but she came out when she heard her roommate return home.

"I made something for you," Lindsay said. "It's in the fridge."

Vivian padded over to the fridge and opened it up. "A blueberry cheesecake?"

Lindsay was used to Noreen, who was more effusive and excitable, but she thought Vivian seemed happy.

Her suspicions were confirmed when Vivian immediately cut herself a big slice and put it on a plate. No eating out of the pan for Vivian.

Lindsay helped herself to a smaller slice, and they sat down at the table together.

"How does it compare to your ex's?" Lindsay asked. "You can tell me it's not quite as good, I don't mind, but I hope—"

"It tastes exactly the same, but this is better because I didn't have to see his face."

"I take it you're not still friends."

Vivian let out an uncharacteristic snort. "Ha. As if."

The blueberry cheesecake seemed to act like a social lubricant for Vivian, the way alcohol worked for some people.

"We broke up for two reasons," Vivian said. "The first was that he wanted children, and I didn't. I was clear from the very beginning that I didn't want kids, so it's not like I misled him. But then I realized he thought I'd change my mind."

"Ugh. I hate when men think you don't know yourself."

"Occasionally, people do change their minds, but I've known since I was sixteen." Vivian paused. "With all the time I spent looking after my younger brothers and sister, I realized I didn't want to go through that again. And I'm really not a fan of the baby and toddler stages. Toddler logic and tantrums?" She shuddered.

They ate in silence for a little longer, and then Vivian said, "The second reason . . . I started wondering if I was bi, and when I told him, he got pissed. He thought that meant I couldn't be faithful to him."

Lindsay shook her head. "Yeah, he sounds like a real keeper."

"That's part of the reason I liked Melvin Lee's stand-up. Because he's Asian, and he talks about being bi . . . Why did he have to be such an asshole?"

Lindsay didn't bother answering this rhetorical question.

"Oh, your date was last night!" Vivian said. "I totally forgot. When did you get home?"

"A few hours ago." Lindsay's cheeks heated slightly.

"I assume it was good? Are you going to see him again?"

"Yep." Though now that she thought of it, they hadn't made

any plans. That was okay. At the very least, she'd see him on Monday for their sixth baking lesson.

Perhaps she'd have him make a semi-naked cake.

She chuckled, but then she thought of Vivian's story. So many things could go wrong in a normal relationship, let alone one with a guy like Ryan Kwok.

She was being insecure, like Vivian's ex.

But it was only natural to be a bit insecure when you were dating a movie star, right? Besides, everyone had their insecurities, and she wasn't using hers as an excuse to be a jerk.

For now, she'd try not to worry.

She stuffed a bite of cheesecake in her mouth. She didn't have to maintain a body like Albert Nguyen's to get ahead in her career, and she would take full advantage of that.

When Vivian went to her room after finishing her slice of blueberry cheesecake—Vivian appeared to be one of those restrained people who wouldn't eat half a cheesecake in a single sitting—Lindsay pulled out her phone and looked at Ryan's Twitter page. He'd posted a picture of himself with his shirt unbuttoned, a ridiculously charming crooked smile on his face. Not a superhero, but I still think I look all right.

Lindsay rolled her eyes.

His public persona was confident and smooth, but she knew he was more than what most people saw. She also knew he was an attentive lover.

*I slept with him last night.*

*He made me coffee and a yogurt parfait this morning.*

She grinned at the memory.


**LINDSAY DIDN'T FEEL** like staying in that night, so she convinced Noreen to meet her at Fantastical Brewing, after the cake-decorating class Noreen was giving at the bakery. Unfortunately, there was a large group occupying the patio, so they sat inside at the bar.

Halfway through her second glass of Bigfoot Imperial Stout, Noreen said, "You know what you don't see enough of? Donut and beer pairings."

They'd already covered Lindsay's date with Ryan, and Noreen was pretty tipsy since the imperial stout was over ten percent ABV.

"Seriously!" Noreen said. "The chocolate espresso donuts would pair well with this one, *donut* you think? Haha, see what I did there?"

"What would you pair with this?" Lindsay asked, holding up her Real Loch Ness Ale.

"Oh, who knows. But the Unicorn Tears Sour could be good with something fruity. The crème brûlée donut with the milk stout? Here, let me write this down in case I don't remember all my brilliant ideas tomorrow." Noreen pulled a notepad and a pen out of her purse. "Ooh, we should do a joint beer-donut event! Buy a beer and a donut, get more than half your calories for the day."

Lindsay laughed. "Don't mention the calories."

"We have to think of more ideas. What would go with the matcha tiramisu donut?"

Lindsay surveyed the tap list. "Not sure any of those would be appropriate."

A bartender walked over. "You ladies work at Kensington Bake Shop, don't you?"

"Yes, we're the owners," Noreen said. "This is Lindsay, and I'm Noreen."

"I'm Isaac."

"Hi, Isaac!"

Noreen spoke louder than usual, even though that wasn't necessary to be heard over the background noise of the bar.

Yep, Noreen was definitely tipsy.

"I could ask the boss man if he'd be interested in your idea," Isaac said.

"I don't know," Lindsay said. "We were just fooling around—"

"Really, I think it could be fun. Who doesn't love donuts and beer?" He flashed them a smile.

"See? This guy gets it," Noreen said to Lindsay. "It would have to be done here, though, since we don't have a liquor license, or much seating." She pulled her business card out of her purse and handed it to Isaac. "Tell him to email me."

"Sure thing." Isaac turned to the other bartender, who was currently making a cocktail. "What do you think, Adam?"

Adam was the Asian guy with long hair whom they'd seen last time.

He grunted.

"Chocolate espresso donuts and Bigfoot Imperial Stout," Isaac said. "Doesn't that sound good?"

Adam grunted again.

"As you can see," Isaac said, turning back to Noreen, "Adam is thrilled with your idea."

Adam's lips twitched—barely—but he said nothing.

"If you like the Bigfoot," Isaac said, "have you tried our Centaur Baltic Porter?"

"Of course!" Noreen said. "We come here all the time. Me and Lindsay, I mean. I think you're the one who's new."

Noreen was a friendly and slightly oblivious drunk. Normally, she'd be able to tell that Isaac was interested in her, but not today. Lindsay, however, didn't miss Isaac not so discreetly checking if Noreen had a ring, and his smile tightened just a fraction when he saw it.

"What kind of donut should we pair with the Baltic porter?"

Noreen asked Adam. "We can make a donut version of anything. We recently made lemon meringue donuts as a special."

Adam just shrugged.

"You're playing a losing game," Isaac said.

"Game?" Noreen frowned. "What game am I playing?"

"Trying to get Adam to talk."

Adam chuckled, but no words escaped his mouth.

Lindsay suspected that dealing with someone who only communicated in grunts would get frustrating after a while.

Ryan, on the other hand, was nothing like that.

She smiled as she thought of him.

When they finished their beers, it was just after ten. Not super late, but Lindsay and Noreen both had to work in the morning. Lindsay made sure her friend got an Uber, and then she walked east, back to her new apartment, which was finally starting to feel a little like home, even without the mismatched throw pillows.

There were lots of people out and about. Sitting on patios, enjoying the warm night. Standing on the sidewalk and smoking cigarettes. Waiting in line outside a brand-new liquid nitrogen ice cream shop, which reminded Lindsay of having ice cream with Ryan the previous night.

Not long ago, she'd felt like she'd stalled in life, while everyone was moving on without her, but maybe, just maybe, that wasn't true anymore.

# CHAPTER 23

**R**yan whistled as he grabbed a bar of soap from under the bathroom sink.

Wait a second. Something was wrong here.

The box of soap was wet.

He pulled out everything from under the sink. A lot of it was damp. He grabbed a small bucket and put it underneath, then turned the faucet on high.

He soon heard a drip.

Well, that was unfortunate, though the bucket would catch the water for now, and he did have a second washroom.

He returned to the living room and grabbed his phone. Since he was the opposite of handy, he didn't even bother looking up YouTube videos. He was about to search for plumbers in Toronto when he got a better idea.

He grinned and called his father.

Miracle of miracles, his father picked up.

"Hi, Dad."

"Hi," Dad said gruffly.

"What are you doing?" Ryan asked.

"Reading."

"What are you reading?"

"Aiyah, why are you calling me?"

"I have a problem, and I thought you could help me with it."

"A problem?" Dad sounded intrigued.

Yes, Ryan was happy about this situation now. It was a good excuse to call his father, and Dad preferred sorting out problems over small talk and discussing his feelings.

"My bathroom sink is leaking."

Dad proceeded to ask a bunch of questions, only some of which Ryan understood. But he pretended he didn't understand anything.

"Why don't you come over and take a look at it?" Ryan asked. "You can pick up the photo albums while you're here. I finished scanning the photos."

"Wah, do you have nothing better to do?"

"I thought getting the family pictures digitized was important."

"I can get them some other time," Dad said. "I am busy right now."

"What's more important than fixing your only son's sink?"

"Why don't you call someone else to fix it?"

"Who do I call?" Ryan asked. "An electrician?"

On the other end of the phone, his father made a sound of mental anguish. "No wonder you flunked out of engineering. Fine, I will be there in an hour."

Ryan smiled. He'd done it! He'd convinced his father to visit him.

Before setting down his phone, he looked at the photo his father had posted on Twitter a few days ago. It had been one of his mother's favorites. Ryan, age seven, was practicing his kung fu moves—gleaned entirely from watching movies—on his dad, who was making a comical expression, clutching his chest as though he'd been severely injured.

Ryan had put all of the scanned photos on an external hard

drive for his dad, which he'd give to him today, but he'd emailed a few of them last week.

He hadn't expected one to show up on Twitter for Throwback Thursday. Yep, his dad had even tagged it #TBT.

Ryan had no problem with his dad posting this picture, but now that it was on social media, he wondered what other people would see when they looked at it. A cute picture of a boy and his dad, right?

They wouldn't know that it was one of the few pictures of just the two of them. They wouldn't know that when he was a child, Ryan had told his mother he didn't like being Asian. Because his only chance to make it big was to learn martial arts, which Dad had forbidden.

There was so much that a simple photo didn't convey.

What did other people assume about their relationship, based on their tweets? It was probably far from reality.

Dad showed up when he said he would, carrying a big toolbox and complaining about the traffic. It was the first time he'd been to Ryan's place by himself. Ryan felt a stab of pain at the fact that his mother wasn't following his father through the door.

"Show me the problem," Dad said, dispensing with pleasantries.

"Wouldn't you like to sit down and have a cup of tea first?"

Dad looked appalled by this suggestion.

"I'm kidding," Ryan said. "Okay, here's the washroom . . ."

Dad looked under the sink. He silently worked for a grand total of . . . three minutes.

"It's fixed now," Dad said to Ryan, who was leaning on the doorframe.

"We don't need a father-son trip to Canadian Tire to get parts?"

"No, I just needed to tighten a nut. You should be able to fix it yourself. It was very simple."

"But why learn when I have you to call?"

As soon as he spoke, the smile slipped off Ryan's face. Because he *wouldn't* always have his father to call. Like he no longer had his mother.

"So tell me," Ryan said, rocking back on his heels. "What's a nut?"

Dad stood up. "I hope you're just pretending not to know." He didn't look at Ryan; he seemed distracted by something on Ryan's counter.

It didn't take Ryan long to figure out what his father was looking at.

There was a toothbrush holder . . . with two toothbrushes in it.

"I alternate toothbrushes. One for the morning and one for the evening."

Dad looked at him like he'd sprouted a second head, which had been Ryan's intention. Sometimes, he couldn't help it. It was too easy to get on Dad's nerves.

"I'm seeing someone," Ryan said. "It's convenient for her to have a toothbrush here." Lindsay had only stayed one night so far, but he hoped there would be many to come.

"Oh," Dad said. Nothing more.

*You're doing this all wrong*, Ryan wanted say. *You're supposed to ask what her name is, and what she does, and how long we've been seeing each other, and when you get to meet her.*

That was what his mom would have done. Ryan would be inundated with questions right now, and he hated that his mother wasn't here to ask them.

Though if his mother were still alive, he probably wouldn't have called his father down to look at his bathroom sink. He wouldn't be worried about his father, alone in that house with his grief, and it was difficult to get Dad to even talk to him.

Like now. Dad wasn't saying anything.

Ryan hadn't been expressly forbidden from dating in high school, but his mother wouldn't have been thrilled with the idea. Same in university. He was supposed to wait until he had an established career, then immediately find the right woman and get married, even though he had no dating experience. That would have been the ideal situation, according to his mother. Very similar to what Mel had said in his stand-up routine.

Mom had started bugging Ryan about dating two years ago, and he'd never had anything to tell her. She would have been very happy about Lindsay.

He swallowed. Tried to think of something to say.

Dad was still looking at the counter. "I should throw out your mother's toothbrush."

Just that simple line, but it felt like a big deal.

"It's still in the toothbrush holder?" Ryan asked.

"Yes."

Then Dad strode down the hall, and the conversation was over.

Ryan followed him. "Since you came all this way, you should stay for tea."

"I only paid for an hour of parking."

"Sorry, I should have told you how to use my visitor parking and registered your car. But it only took you a few minutes to fix my sink, so you've got time."

"All right," Dad grumbled.

Ryan made a pot of tea, then grabbed the bag of photo albums and pulled out an external hard drive. "All the photos are on here. Will you post one again for Throwback Thursday this week?"

Dad sat down at the kitchen table, a puzzled expression on his face. Then the confusion seemed to clear. "Why are we talking about this?"

"What, you think that what happens online stays online?"

"Hmph."

"You didn't seem to mind when Mel called and invited you to join the Silver Fox Club."

"Melvin Lee is a nutbar," Dad said.

"A nutbar. Fancy vocabulary. And what am I?"

Dad grunted. "You are less of a nutbar than he is."

"Thank you?" Ryan poured them each some tea. "Not gonna lie, I was horrified when I saw all those people calling you a silver fox."

Dad chuckled, apparently enjoying Ryan's discomfort. "I didn't know what a 'silver fox' was. I had to look it up."

"Why did you post those pictures of us? Not the kung fu one, but a couple of weeks ago—"

"Someone asked if you'd inherited good looks from me. It seemed rude not to answer."

"People are rude—very rude, not just ignoring questions—on Twitter all the time."

"Yes, I have seen this behavior."

"And you think civilization as we know it is coming to an end?"

Dad swallowed some tea, then stood up. "I don't know why we are having this conversation. I should be going."

He'd been here less than half an hour, but Ryan didn't stop him. He said goodbye to his father at the door and gave him a hearty slap on the back, thanking him again for fixing his sink.

Dad left, and Ryan felt, for once, like it hadn't gone terribly?

He'd actually gotten his father to visit him.

Then he glanced at the kitchen counter, feeling like there ought to be a box of food he didn't need—that's what his mom would have brought—before heading to the washroom, where his sink was no longer leaking. He looked at the two toothbrushes.

**Hey, you want to come over after dinner?** he texted Lindsay.

• • •

**LINDSAY WAS IN** Ryan's bed. They'd had sex, and now they were just chilling out, naked.

Ryan certainly wasn't complaining. It was nice to lie in bed with her, to trail his hand up and down her body, to hear her talk about her day at work and her plans for donut-beer pairings at the nearby brewery.

"I hope it's not going to bother you," she said. "My job, I mean. I work a lot, including almost every Saturday and Sunday."

"Of course not," he said. "I'm glad you have a career, and I don't think it's less important than mine. But if you want suggestions for donut-beer pairings, I can't provide any, seeing as I know nothing about beer. Are you going to pair the matcha tiramisu donut with anything?"

"There's a new beer called The Floor."

He tickled her, and she laughed. Somehow that led to more kissing. Him on top of her.

God, he hoped he could make this work.

Some people might think it was foolish for him to lack confidence: he was a reasonably successful actor and considered quite attractive. But that didn't build a relationship. After years and years of never being good enough for his father—well, perhaps he wasn't as confident as he'd otherwise be.

"If I suck at this," he told her, "you tell me, and I'll do better, okay?"

She nodded before pressing her lips to his again.

And for the second time, she stayed the night.

# CHAPTER 24

O kay!" Lindsay said as she tied her apron. "Today, since it's strawberry season, we're going to do a three-layer lemon cake filled with strawberries and a Swiss meringue buttercream. So far we've been making American buttercream; this one's a little trickier, as it involves egg whites, which are cooked with sugar. Then I'll teach you how to color the buttercream and create an ombré effect on the outside of the cake. How does that sound?"

It was two twenty on Monday afternoon. They usually started their lessons at two o'clock, but they were a little late today.

She and Ryan had been together since nine o'clock last night. She'd gone over to his condo after dinner, then they'd had sex . . . and talked . . . and had sex again. This morning had been more of the same, and when he'd gone to the gym for a quick workout, she'd stayed at his place and relaxed for a while, before he came back and they had lunch.

And then more sex.

Which was why they'd arrived at the bakery together . . . and a little late.

But now that she was here, she was in teacher mode. She was determined to be professional and not get distracted by the fact that he was wearing a Henley and looked more delectable than their cake would—even though their cake would be pretty freaking awesome, because she was good at what she did.

What was it about Henleys that made them look so good on men?

Especially Ryan.

He made a point of slowly rolling up his sleeves to display his forearms. Like he was trying to make her forget how to speak.

When her mouth opened and no words came out, he smirked.

"You're so full of it." She attempted to shove him, but he was too strong to be swayed.

It was weird to be dating, period. But it was particularly weird to be dating a guy who was so stunning and knew exactly how good-looking he was, though he wasn't unbearably vain.

And she could play this game, too. She reached under her apron and pulled down the hem of her V-neck T-shirt so that it showed a good amount of cleavage.

Predictably, his gaze went to her breasts.

They would never get any work done at this rate.

"What do you think of my plan?" she asked.

"When did you tell me your plan? Before you tried to distract me with your breasts?" He crossed his arms over his chest, which showed off his biceps, as well as his forearms.

"You started it."

"What, by doing this?" He shoved one of his sleeves down, then slowly rolled it up.

"You're having far too much fun."

"Aw, I think you enjoy it."

Then his arms were around her, and she raised herself onto her toes to kiss his lips, thrilled she got to kiss this guy. He was so—

She heard a throat clearing and immediately jumped away from Ryan.

"So this is what you're doing in your baking lessons." Noreen stood at the door to the teaching kitchen.

"No," Lindsay said. "We do actual baking."

Ryan stepped forward, his arm extended. "You must be Noreen. I recognize your picture from the website. Nice to meet you."

Noreen shook his hand, looking a little starstruck. Probably in part because Ryan was still displaying his forearms.

"What are you doing here?" Lindsay demanded. "We're closed on Mondays."

Noreen's lips twitched. "Yes, I'm aware of that."

Ugh, her best friend was enjoying this far too much.

"Why are you here?" Lindsay repeated.

"Oh, I was just out for a walk on my day off and figured I'd pop in to see how your lessons are going. Since I'm the one in charge of the baking lessons here, I wanted to make sure you're doing a good job."

"She's doing an excellent job," Ryan said.

"Has she even told you what you're baking yet?"

He scratched the back of his head and graced Lindsay with a lopsided, slightly sheepish smile, the sort that worked extremely well for his character in *Just Another New York Sitcom*. "Something with cake."

Noreen snorted.

"There's also strawberries and lemons," Ryan said, "and buttercream, but a different type than what I've made before. Plus some kind of decoration I didn't understand. Amber effect? Was that it?"

"Ombré," Lindsay said.

He wrapped an arm around her waist.

"I'll be impressed if you manage to accomplish all that," Noreen said.

"We've finished lots of things over the past few weeks," Ryan said. "Like, a chocolate fudge cake. And lemon meringue cupcakes, which I did all by myself."

"I heard you dumped egg whites on your head."

Ryan shrugged. "Might have happened."

He was acting like a cool, endearingly clueless movie star right now. Playing it up more than usual, in contrast to their date last week.

Except there was also something endearing about how he'd been a little unsure of how to act on that date. The first half of their dinner had been slightly awkward.

She liked *everything* he did. It was superbly unfair.

"Well," Noreen said with a smirk, "the chocolate fudge cake and the lemon meringue cupcakes were before you started sleeping together."

"Noreen!" Lindsay hissed. "Don't you have a husband to bother?"

"He's at work, which is why I'm here. But now that I've met you, Ryan, I'll head out. Don't be a jerk to her, okay? I'm watching you." She pointed two fingers at her eyes, then at him. "I'm sure you know more famous people than I do, but I can still do damage."

"I believe it," he said. "You could throw donuts at me."

Lindsay took her best friend's arm and led her downstairs.

"The camera doesn't lie." Noreen fanned her face. "He looks as good as he does in the movies, and he seems quite taken with you. You're super cute together."

"Uh, thanks."

Noreen touched Lindsay's shoulder. "I'm leaving now. Have fun. Take a picture of the cake and send it to me. I need proof, or I'll assume you spent all afternoon making out."

"Why are you being such a pain?"

"It's not every day I get to tease you about dating a movie star." And with that, she left.

Lindsay headed back upstairs, where Ryan was looking at something on his phone.

"Just learning what an ombré effect is. Seems pretty fancy." He whistled.

"It's not that hard," Lindsay said. "You can do it. You just need to focus."

He pointedly looked at her breasts.

"On something other than those." She tried to sound annoyed, but it was hard to be annoyed when Ryan Kwok was looking at her like that.

"I like when you're bossy."

Okay, so maybe she hadn't completely failed at sounding annoyed.

"Before we get started," she said. "I want you to know . . . I'm not going around telling everyone that we slept together. Noreen and Vivian just know I didn't come home until the afternoon following our date. I live with Vivian, and Noreen is my best friend . . . it's not like I shared intimate details."

"It's okay. I trust you. And Noreen has nothing to worry about. Well, maybe that's not true, but like I said, just tell me if I'm not doing a good job at this, okay? I really want to treat you as you deserve."

Whenever he was a little vulnerable like this . . . that's what slayed her the most. Even more than when he wore a Henley and rolled up his sleeves, which was quite a feat.

"All right," she said. "Let's get started."

She showed him the recipe for the cake, and he read through it carefully and asked a couple of questions, focusing entirely on baking now. She was still slightly disarmed because the way he concentrated was pretty hot, too.

"I'm not helping you make the cakes, but don't worry, I'll correct you if you're doing something wrong. Like, if you forget to preheat the oven or grease the pans. So don't forget."

"Or what?" he asked, eyes dancing. "You'll kiss me to show me the error of my ways?"

She suddenly stiffened, which didn't escape his notice.

He abandoned the recipe and walked over to her. "Did I say something wrong?"

"It's just . . . I've seen you banter with women like this on-screen, then kiss them. And I can't help thinking this is all an act. That you're just good at creating chemistry with someone."

She nearly covered her face. He was going to think she was frightfully insecure and wonder why he was dating a *normal* person.

"Lindsay," he murmured, clasping her hand. "I'm not *acting* with you, I promise. I don't know what I can do to convince you, but I'm not. This is the first time I've ever wished, even for a second, that I hadn't been successful as an actor. Because then you'd believe me."

"Sorry. I'll stop distracting you with my insecurities—and my breasts. Now, get to work."

"Yes, ma'am."

He managed to get three cakes in the oven without any major incidents. There was a minor incident, though—he cut himself while zesting the lemons, and she, of course, had to tend to his very shallow wound.

"Now it's time to make the strawberry filling." She handed him another recipe.

"Only four ingredients. Easy-peasy." He winked at her.

His winks were dangerous. She was sitting on a stool as she watched him work, and she couldn't help squeezing her thighs to-gether. He noticed, and he winked again.

"This is so not fair," she muttered.

"What, that I have to bake and you get to sit there looking pretty?"

"I'm supervising."

He planted a quick peck on her lips, then started slicing the strawberries.

Given the number of times they'd had sex in the past twenty-four hours, she shouldn't *still* be horny, yet here she was. Definitely still aroused. Definitely thinking about when he'd gone down on her first thing this morning . . .

"Shit," he muttered, pulling her out of her pleasant memories. "I cut myself. Again."

She took out the bandages she'd put away not long ago and tended to his—once again, extremely shallow, but bloody—wound.

"If I didn't know better," she said, "I'd think you were doing this as an excuse to get me to touch you."

"I don't need to resort to such extremes."

He waggled his eyebrows, and oh God, why was she so aroused? Why was there so much left to do today?

She half wanted to tell him she'd finish the cake herself, since she could do it faster than he could—that was what her diploma and several years of experience had gotten her. But the whole point was that he was learning how to bake, so she couldn't very well take over.

He finished cutting the strawberries, and Lindsay breathed out a sigh of relief. He shouldn't have to cut—or grate—anything else today. Next, he combined the strawberries and other ingredients in a saucepan.

The oven timer went off, and Ryan sauntered across the kitchen, put on oven mitts, and pulled the cakes out of the oven.

"Let me have a look," she said, "to make sure they're done."

This was not simply an excuse to press up next to him . . . no, certainly not.

Though he did give her another kiss on the lips. And not a quick kiss.

Well, perhaps it would have been quick, but then she circled her arms around his neck and pulled him back down for more. Just another few seconds. Or several seconds.

As the cakes and strawberry filling cooled, they moved on to the buttercream.

Once the egg whites and sugar were whipping in the stand mixer, she said, "This will take about ten minutes, though if you want to dump it over your head and make a mess again, you can stop earlier."

"If we have ten minutes . . ."

And then he was kissing her again. He backed her up against the counter, his arms around her waist as he slipped his tongue into her mouth. She moaned against his lips, and he chuckled, oh so low.

They did, eventually, manage to get the egg whites whipped to stiff peaks. She showed him how to add the butter a tablespoon at a time, after switching to the paddle attachment.

"Wow, this is such a long process," he said.

"Yep, and we still have to color it and frost the cake." She instructed him on how to layer the cakes with the strawberry filling and buttercream. "Now it's time for the fun part."

"Fun? I thought it was all supposed to be fun."

She swallowed. This was when they'd kissed last week for the first time. Right before they did the sides of the cake. So much had happened since then. They'd gone on a date . . . she knew what it was like to have him inside her . . .

But they had a cake to finish.

"First, apply the buttercream to the sides," she said. "A thin layer. This is called the crumb coat. Then while it's in the fridge . . . we'll use gel food coloring to . . ."

She couldn't focus anymore. He was holding a small spoon

with buttercream up to her lips, and his other hand was on the small of her back.

Why were they at the bakery?

Why weren't they in bed?

She parted her lips, and he slid the spoon into her mouth. After she'd swallowed, he licked off an errant bit of buttercream on her top lip, and that lick, unsurprisingly, turned into a kiss. A gentle kiss at first, with him cupping the back of her head, but soon it deepened.

She pulled away. "I'm giving you baking lessons." That was as much to remind herself as to remind him. "We can do that . . . after you're finished."

"Do you find me irresistible when I'm walking around the kitchen?"

"Dammit, Ryan, just start on the crumb coat!"

He laughed, but he did as she said.

She helped him color the Swiss meringue buttercream—four colors, from light to dark pink—then he took the cake out of the fridge and started piping rings of the colored buttercream. She tried not to admire his forearms and biceps as he did so.

Tried, but didn't succeed.

Still, she was an expert. She showed him how to smooth out the icing, fill in holes as needed, reminded him to clean off the tools between swipes.

At last, they had a pretty decent cake.

Was it up to her usual exacting standards? No. But it was much better than most of the stuff she'd seen on *Baking Fail*.

"Now we need to decorate the top," she said. "I was thinking fresh strawberries?"

He quickly washed two strawberries, sliced them—without cutting himself this time—and laid them in a circle in the center of the cake. Then he washed one more strawberry and put it in the middle.

"Do you want to eat a slice now?" she asked.

"No." He held her gaze. "I want to take ten gazillion photos and put them on Instagram, since I'm so proud of myself for baking and decorating this cake when I was horny as fuck."

"Did you just say . . ."

"Did I just say what, Lindsay?"

He wanted her to repeat his words, damn him.

"That you're horny as fuck?" she said.

"Might have done," he said innocently, as he started removing his clothes.

No, his apron. He was only removing his apron. She did the same and hung it on a peg, bumping into him in the process.

An accident. She hadn't done that on purpose.

But then she was in his arms again, and he was kissing her, and God, why was he so good at this? His hands slipped beneath her T-shirt, touching her skin above the waistband of her jeans. It was enough to nearly make her combust, and at the same time, it frustrated her.

She wrapped a leg around him and tried to climb him like a tree.

He laughed softly, in a way that made her insides turn into runny strawberry filling, and then he unbuttoned her jeans.

"No!" she said, suddenly coming to her senses.

He instantly stepped back.

"We can't do it in the kitchen," she explained. "No, no, it's all wrong."

"You don't want to be bad with me, Lindsay? I thought you did."

"Not here. There are health codes, you know."

She grabbed his hand and led him to the office at the back of the second floor. It was very small, but likely still bigger than the supply closet in *That Kind of Wedding*.

He kept kissing her lips as he shoved a hand into her jeans. When the tip of his finger touched her sensitive skin, she gasped. He ran his finger along her entrance before plunging inside, and she released an obscene moan, which made his eyes darken.

"Yeah?" he said, pulling his face a few inches back from hers. "You like that?"

It was a rhetorical question.

With his other hand—gosh, he was so talented with his hands—he pulled her shirt over her head and tossed it on the tiny desk. Her bra followed a moment later. She arched her chest when he took one nipple in his mouth and swirled the tip as he pumped his finger inside her.

"You're remarkably coordinated," she said, to piss him off. "I didn't expect it after your performance earlier."

"You make it hard to concentrate," he murmured. "That's why I now have two bandages on my fingers." He wiggled the hand that had been cupping her breast. "You're dangerous."

She needed to touch him.

She hastily undid his pants and wrapped her hand around his cock, reveling in the nonsense sounds he made. When he removed his hand from her jeans, she made a noise of frustration, but his gaze held hers as he licked the moisture off his index finger, then his middle finger, before licking his thumb and sliding his hand back down, his thumb now on her clit.

"Oh my God, oh my God," she sobbed.

She shook in his arms as her orgasm racked her, and she arched her body as much as she could, her head hitting the wall.

"Oh my God," she said one last time as she slid to the floor.

She looked up at him, and she could swear she saw a smirk touch his lips.

Hell, she wasn't letting him get away with that. She was bringing him down with her.

She shoved down his pants and boxers, revealing his erection. Even though she was still recovering from her orgasm, she managed to suck him into her mouth, almost down to the base, and he stumbled back against the wall in the cramped office. She palmed his ass with one hand—of course, he had a very fine ass—while wrapping her other hand around the base of his cock.

She squirmed as she sucked him, desperate to feel his hands on her again, but she focused just on him. On the little sounds he made, the way he sifted his fingers through her hair, then tightened his grip when she took him particularly deep.

"I'm going to . . ." he said, his words coming out in a strangled rush.

She gripped his ass with both hands and pushed him against her face, and he came inside her mouth with a muttered curse before sliding onto the floor next to her.

He couldn't seem to stop touching her as his breathing slowed, his hands on her naked breasts and in her hair. At last, he tipped his head against the wall and closed his eyes.

She felt far too pleased with herself, but she also didn't feel like she was done, even though they'd fucked this morning and last night. He made her insatiable, and she seemed to do the same to him.

"You want to find somewhere a little more comfortable?" he asked. "A bed, perhaps?"


**NORMALLY, LINDSAY WOULD** have been happy to walk to Yorkville, but it seemed of the utmost importance that they get there as quickly as possible. They climbed into the back seat of a taxi, and then Ryan said, "Oh shit, the cake!" and she ran back into the bakery to get it, kicking herself for delaying her sexual gratification for another minute.

At his place, they went straight to the bedroom. They un-dressed in a hurry before collapsing into bed together and rolling around naked. He slipped a hand between her legs and pushed a finger inside her, and she was still so wet for him. And the length of his godlike body was pressed against hers.

She'd definitely lost all powers of speech now.

"I need to be inside you," he said.

She nodded. She needed that, too, desperately.

He grabbed a condom, rolled it on, and then rolled her onto her stomach. He entered her from behind, both of them groaning as he seated himself deep inside her.

It was just his body and hers, moving together. He pushed into her, over and over, and she gripped the pillow and buried her face in it. When he slid the hair back from her neck and kissed her there, the tenderness of it nearly undid Lindsay, even as his other movements were hardly gentle.

"You're amazing," he murmured, and she felt like she was the most amazing freaking woman on the planet. She was so glad she could make him feel like this.

She turned her head to the side so she could kiss him, and he slipped his hand underneath her hips to touch her clit. She cried out, the noise swallowed up by his kisses, and then he cried out, too.

Afterward, she felt sated. Finally.

She expected it would last maybe half an hour. She'd never felt as ridiculously consumed by lust as she did around Ryan, and spending more time with him didn't lessen it.

In the past seven years, when she wanted sex, she'd find a guy, sleep with him a few times to take the edge off her need, and that was that.

But it was different with Ryan.

An intense craving specific to *him*. Nobody else would do, and it wasn't simply because he was such a fine physical specimen.

Uncertainty and fear curled through her, but it had nothing to do with his fame this time.

She wasn't used to having such a relationship with a guy. She'd kept her distance, ever since her ex had dumped her one month after her father's funeral. She hadn't let people in.

And though she and Ryan had agreed to take it slowly, her heart didn't seem to have gotten the message. This hardly felt slow.

Even though she hadn't shared deep, dark secrets with him today, even though she'd been physically intimate with many guys in the past, this felt different. Because it was him. Because they couldn't seem to stay away from each other.

She wasn't able to hold herself back, not when it came to Ryan.

"Hey," he said, running his hand over her side.

He smiled at her, a little uncertainly. It seemed like he knew how she felt, like maybe he felt a bit of that, too.

He didn't try to talk about it, though. Thankfully. Not now.

And that just made him worm his way into her heart even more.

"We should get something to eat," he said.

"There's a whole cake sitting on your table."

"I was planning to take it to my sister's tomorrow. We could go out for hand-pulled noodles?"

She almost declared her love for him right then and there.

# CHAPTER 25

"N o, not like that," Jenna said.

She took her son from Ryan and showed him what to do again.

"Rocking a baby to sleep is harder than I expected," he said.

"It's not that you're doing it *wrong*. He's just very particular."

Eventually, after ten minutes of rocking, Ezra fell asleep in Ryan's arms. Ezra was definitely bigger than he'd been the first time Ryan had met him, but he still seemed impossibly small.

"Now, go have a shower," Ryan said.

"Are you sure you can manage?" Jenna asked.

"I'll be fine, don't worry about it."

Ryan tried to sound more confident than he felt. He wasn't used to looking after babies, but he was determined to be a good uncle and a good brother.

He didn't think his father had visited Jenna since the hospital. Winston's family was all outside of Toronto. They'd come last week for three days, and Ryan suspected their visit had exhausted Jenna, so he was determined to make sure today wasn't stressful for her.

She shot him an uncertain look before heading upstairs.

After a few minutes of watching his nephew sleep in his monster onesie, Ryan pulled out his phone and scrolled through Instagram. His favorite Instagram account was now Kensington Bake Shop. There were rarely any pictures of Lindsay herself, but he admired the farm animal birthday cake that had been posted a few hours ago. It had a procession of farm animals and a fence around the sides.

He wondered if Lindsay had worked on this cake, or whether it had been done by someone else. He pictured her deep in concentration as she shaped the animals out of fondant.

Once he finished with Instagram, Ezra was still sleeping soundly, so Ryan went to Twitter, and the first thing he saw was a tweet from Mel, who'd Photoshopped his head onto Albert Nguyen's body with the words, Hope no one expects me to undergo this transformation, because it's not happening.

Ryan barked out a laugh, and Ezra made a sound of disapproval and opened his eyes. His face scrunched up, like he was thinking of letting out a giant wail.

*Oh no. No, no, no.*

Ezra needed to stay quiet, or Jenna would come down, and Ryan wanted her to have time to herself.

"Shh," Ryan said. "It's okay. I'm here."

Ezra did not seem impressed and looked suspiciously at Ryan's face.

Well, perhaps Ryan was imagining the "suspicious" part.

At last, Ezra went back to sleep, and Ryan breathed out a sigh of relief.

Okay, no more laughing. Whether it was the movement of his body or the sound that had woken Ezra up, he wasn't sure, but he'd be very careful not to do it again.

He went to his dad's Twitter account and braced himself for what he might find.

Apparently, Dad had discovered GIFs. There was a GIF of Ryan holding a wrench in *Just Another New York Sitcom*. He was cocking his head with a smile, and the text underneath read: You called for a handyman?

Dad's tweet: Please don't hire my son as a handyman. He can't repair even the most basic things. He called me to help him fix a leak, and it took me all of three minutes.

Ryan chuckled but was careful to be very restrained, so as not to wake the baby. He was tempted to reply with: It was just an excuse to see my father. It's the only way I can get him to visit me.

But he didn't type that.

Instead, he read through the replies, including one that said, How do I hire you as a handyman, Mr. Kwok?

Ryan started having flashbacks to all the comments people had made about Dad being a silver fox. He tossed his phone onto the couch and concentrated on Ezra.

When Jenna emerged an hour later, she looked a little better. As if knowing his mother was there, Ezra immediately woke up, and she fed him.

"Now I have to try this cake," Jenna said. "You want to cut me a slice?"

Ryan cut a generous slice for his sister and a less generous slice for himself. He was pleased at how neat the layers inside looked.

Jenna had a bite and started crying.

He was so ill-equipped to deal with this. "What's wrong?"

"I don't know." She shook her head. "I've been crying so much in the past few days. I don't understand it."

Ezra, who was on the floor in the bouncer, started crying, too, as if in sympathy.

"What do you want?" Jenna asked, exasperated, then turned to Ryan. "I feel like I should be able to tell what he needs from his cry, like it's some magical power moms are supposed to have, but I can't. Am I a terrible mother?"

"No, no, I'm sure you're not. Don't say that." But Ryan doubted such words, coming from him, would reassure his sister.

She changed Ezra, which apparently he did not like at all, then returned to the kitchen, the baby in her arms. He was still crying. She bounced him up and down, and Ryan felt helpless. So he did the only thing he knew how to do, which was to try to make his sister laugh, or at least smile.

Normally, he wouldn't share this bit of information yet. It would lead to far too many questions. But he felt like his sister needed such news, needed an excuse to tease him, so he said, "I'm seeing someone. Lindsay, the woman who's teaching me how to bake."

He didn't hide the smile that came to his face when he said her name, which clearly amused Jenna.

"How long has this been going on?" she asked.

"About a week?"

"You're such a dog! Dating your teacher?"

There was more pep in her voice now, so he considered it worth it.

"Do you have a picture of her?" Jenna asked.

He shook his head, then remembered he could pull up her picture on the bakery's website, so that was what he did. "She's the one on the left."

"Aw, she's pretty." Jenna shoved his arm.

Ezra farted in response.

"See?" Ryan said. "He doesn't like when you push me around."

Jenna rolled her eyes.

"And, Jesus, how does something so small make such a stink?"

"Ezra, want to show Uncle Ryan your poop-explosion-while-changing trick?"

Ryan looked at her in horror.

Jenna smiled at him sweetly.

He was glad she seemed like her normal self. Her tears and helplessness—they had worried him.

"Maybe Ezra and I will take a little trip to the bakery on a Monday afternoon. We'll barge into the kitchen and see what you're up to." She ate more of her cake. "Not that I actually want to catch you making out with a girl. Remember when you were in grade ten—"

"You were supposed to be at university!"

Jenna had been in her first year of engineering at U of T, and she'd been living downtown in residence. But that Thursday, she'd decided to come back to Markham because she wasn't feeling well and preferred to be home when she was sick. So her mom could look after her, and so there was no noise from students partying.

It was after school had finished, but too early for his parents to get home from work, and Ryan had had a girl in his room . . .

Jenna had freaked out, and then, being an evil sister, had threatened to tell their parents, since having a girl in his room had been strictly against household rules. In the end, she hadn't told, but that summer she'd made him cover for her when she went out to meet her secret boyfriend.

"Should we go look at your favorite lamp?" she said to the baby.

"He has a favorite lamp?" Ryan asked.

"Yeah, he likes the one by the couch in the living room. I don't know why, but it seems to fascinate him. Want to take him?"

Ryan carried Ezra to the couch, holding him so he could look at the lamp. Ryan wasn't convinced his nephew had any particular interest in the lamp, but whatever. He wasn't crying—or farting—and Jenna seemed like herself.

He smiled at her over Ezra's head. He hoped they were all going to be okay.

· · ·

**THAT NIGHT, RYAN** called his father.

"I think you should visit Jenna," he said. "We're all the family they have in Toronto, you know. Just for an hour or two on the weekend, or you could take a day off work."

Dad grunted. He wasn't the kind of person who took days off work unless he had a fever. He rarely even used all his vacation—he probably had lots of vacation days saved up.

"I don't want to get in the way," Dad said.

Ryan felt a strange wave of emotion overtake him and sat down heavily on the couch. "If you visit your daughter and grandson for two hours every two weeks, I don't think you'll be a bother."

Dad was acting the exact opposite of what Mom would have been like.

Since this conversation was going nowhere, Ryan changed topics. "I saw you insulted my handyman skills on Twitter today."

"Aiyah!" Dad said. "Why are we talking about Twitter again? You saw my post—"

"Your tweet."

"—so why do we need to talk about it? We both know what it said."

"Fine," Ryan said irritably. Sometimes it was hard to stay upbeat when talking to his dad. "What do you want to talk about?"

"I watched *The Journey of the Baked Alaska* last night," Dad said. "It was on Netflix."

"You hadn't seen it before?"

"I saw part of it when your mother was watching it."

They were both silent for a moment after the mention of her.

"What did you think?" Ryan asked.

Dad merely grunted.

Well, it was about what he'd expected. That, or Dad saying something like, *It was even stupider than I remembered.*

"I like playing unintelligent but pretty characters," Ryan said. "It's the opposite of the usual stereotypes of Asian guys."

"Right," Dad said. Nothing more.

"Okay. I'll talk to you later."

Ryan lay back on the couch, feeling useless.

He was about to text Lindsay but stopped himself. How much were you supposed to text someone when you were in a relationship? He didn't want to seem needy. This was the problem with not having much to do with his time.

Besides, Lindsay was meeting her mom's new boyfriend tonight.

**WHEN LINDSAY STEPPED** into her mom's home, a surprising sight greeted her eyes. Trevor and a man she assumed must be Harold were making wontons in the kitchen?

"Harold, this is my daughter, Lindsay," Mom said.

"Nice to meet you," Harold said.

Harold was thin and had a beard and glasses. She thought Mom had said that he'd come to Canada from China in the eighties.

"Are those wontons?" Lindsay asked. When she was a child, wontons had always come from Po Po. Ever since Po Po's death, Mom had bought them frozen.

Mom grabbed a tattered notebook and led Lindsay into the living room.

Lindsay swallowed. She remembered this notebook.

When Po Po had been sick, she'd written out her family recipes for Mom. Except she'd written them in Chinese, and Mom hadn't had the heart to remind her that she'd never been taught to read or write Chinese. Po Po likely wouldn't have been able to write them in English anyway, as her English had been poor.

It was hard for Lindsay to comprehend not being able to communicate well with your own mother because you barely spoke the same languages, but that was what it had been like for her mother and grandmother.

Mom opened the notebook. A piece of paper, with words written in English, fell out.

"Harold is translating them for me," she said.

Lindsay regarded his neat handwriting. "There are tons of people in Toronto who could translate this. You could have had someone do it years ago if you wanted to make the recipes."

"You think I wanted to show Ma's recipes to some stranger?"

Lindsay hadn't realized these were so personal to her mom, but she could understand.

"I was so embarrassed that I couldn't read it and could barely speak it," Mom said. "That's why I didn't like going to Pacific Mall when you were younger. Everyone would speak to me in a language I didn't understand because the little I could speak wasn't even the right language."

"You were embarrassed?"

"Why are you surprised?"

"I thought you were ashamed of your background."

"When I was younger, yes, but not so much by the time you were a teenager." Mom paused. "Everyone who was my age there . . . they looked like me, but they weren't like me. They didn't grow up here. And when I was a child, it was different. There was no Saturday Chinese school. Maybe if you lived in Chinatown, but not where we lived. Even if there was, I'm not sure my parents would have enrolled me. Your grandfather wanted us to be Canadian, to assimilate, but at school, nobody could see me as being just like the other kids."

Lindsay had thought she'd understood her mother, but she'd been wrong.

"Anyway," Mom said, "I could have found recipes online, but I wanted to make *hers*. If only I'd been interested when she was still alive. We're having wonton soup and doong tonight. Did you know the doong have to cook for hours? I'd forgotten."

"I just remember getting the frozen ones. I guess those had already been cooked."

"I helped her when I was little, but that was so long ago. Ma would often make doong in the spring, and Harold says that was likely for the Dragon Boat Festival. There will be extra for you to take home! I feel like I'm all ready to be a grandmother now."

It was a good thing Lindsay hadn't been eating anything. She might have spit it out.

"You and Trevor don't owe me grandchildren," Mom went on, "but I have two kids, so odds are that at least one of you will have children of your own."

Lindsay made a noncommittal noise. The truth was, she hadn't thought much about whether she'd like to have kids. When she was younger, she'd assumed she would have them one day. Then she'd stopped dating—that was probably why it hadn't been on her mind.

But it was time to think about it. Knowing whether or not you wanted kids—wasn't that supposed to be something you figured out by thirty? She was twenty-nine.

Mom didn't seem bothered by Lindsay's silence. "Harold's daughter is pregnant. It will be his first grandchild. She's due in October." She paused. "It's going really well with him."

"I'm glad, Mom."

"You know he's from the same part of China as my parents? Not the same village, but not that far away. He has an uncle who's been in Canada for a long time and sponsored Harold to come here. I can understand when he speaks because it's Toisanese. Not well, but I understand a little. I haven't forgotten it all."

They returned to the kitchen. Harold and Trevor had finished the wontons, and they all sat down to eat about half an hour later. First the wonton soup, and then the doong, which, yes, were exactly like the ones Lindsay remembered her grandmother making.

The whole meeting-her-mother's-boyfriend experience wasn't as weird as Lindsay had feared, though it was still a little weird. Harold didn't say a lot, and it helped that he wasn't like her father at all, that she didn't feel like he was supposed to be a replacement for her father. Trevor didn't seem as perturbed as Lindsay feared he might, so perhaps he'd had time to get used to the idea of their mother dating again.

After dinner, Mom opened the box of donuts Lindsay had brought.

"Lindsay made these all herself," Mom said. "Isn't she talented?"

"I didn't personally make them," Lindsay said. "I was working on other things today."

"Why are you contradicting me when I'm bragging about you?"

Lindsay was reminded of the day Mom had brought another man into Kensington Bake Shop. It seemed so long ago now.

"She's so good at what she does," Mom said, "that a movie star asked her to teach him how to bake. What's his name again, Lindsay? Ryan Kwok?"

Lindsay nodded and tried not to blush.

"I saw him in *Unraveling*," Harold said. "Didn't he get a Golden Globe nomination?"

"He did."

"Why are you blushing, Linds?" Trevor asked.

"It's only natural!" Mom said. "He's a movie star. He makes women blush."

"How do you cope when you're in the same room? Don't you have to teach him?"

Lindsay shrugged as she sipped her tea.

"What did you make together in your last lesson?" Mom asked.

"We're working on cake right now."

"Isn't he famous for taking off his shirt?" Trevor, unfortunately, was insistent on being an annoying little brother. "Does he do that while you're baking?"

"Of course not. He's completely . . . professional."

Dammit, her voice wobbled on that last word, and now Mom was on her case, too.

"What's happening?" she demanded. "Is he used to getting any woman he wants? Is he taking advantage of you?"

Oh no. Mom was in full Mama Bear mode.

"No," Lindsay said, "but we're seeing each other. He's a good guy, I promise."

*"You're dating him?"*

"Mom! Stop trying to destroy my eardrums!"

Trevor laughed at her discomfort, the bastard.

The next fifteen minutes were a full-scale interrogation. Lindsay tried to answer every question honestly, but some questions were too personal.

Trevor contributed the occasional question, and Harold sat there in silence, sending her a sympathetic look as he ate his carrot pineapple cake donut.

Although Lindsay could do without some of the questions, there was still something nice about it, about certain things not changing even when it felt like everything was different now.

They were a family.

At nine o'clock, Lindsay said she should get going, as she had to work early tomorrow.

"Yeah, I'm sure you're going right home," Trevor said.

She smacked his shoulder. In a loving, sisterly way, of course.

Mom packed up some food for her, and Lindsay headed out. She intended to go home, but for some reason, when she was standing on the sidewalk outside her mother's condo, she wanted to see Ryan.

She sent him a text.

# CHAPTER 26

"People are often surprised that my mom was born in Canada,"
Lindsay said. "Not just white people—Asian people, too. But,
yeah, she was born here in the early sixties, when there were still
fairly racist immigration laws."

They were together in Ryan's bed. There was something luxuri-
ous about simply lying half-dressed in bed with someone and
talking.

She'd never really gotten to do this before Ryan.

Well, she had a little, with her university boyfriend, but they'd
had cramped twin beds. It hadn't been the same.

"She grew up in a mostly white area," Lindsay said. "The other
kids made fun of her, and she rarely saw people like her on TV.
There was no sitcom starring a hot Asian dude who could pick up
any woman he wanted while wearing glasses."

She slipped her hands under the sheet and attempted to tickle
Ryan's abs. He did laugh, but she didn't think it was because he was
ticklish.

"All the Asian guys she knew were related to her. Even when
she went to university in a place with more diversity, she was only
interested in white guys. When she married one, my grandmother

was pissed, though she still came to the wedding. My grandfather wasn't angry. He'd always emphasized they were in Canada now, their children were Canadian." Lindsay paused. "Mom definitely had a bunch of internalized racism, but from what she said today, it sounded like there were other issues, too, especially in the past ten or fifteen years. She's different from a lot of people in the Chinese community here. Different from people like your parents, who came here as adults, right?"

Ryan nodded.

"They probably went back to Hong Kong every now and then, and you've been there, too? My mom's never been to China. My grandparents left in terrible circumstances and never went back." She trailed her fingers absently up and down Ryan's leg. "Harold seems nice, but still, tonight made me miss my dad a little more."

Ryan would understand, but she felt a bit uncomfortable now, because as nice as this pillow-talk business was, she wasn't used to it.

He squeezed her roving hand. "There was a period when I thought being Asian was the worst. Although our neighborhood was very Asian—mostly Chinese—that wasn't what I saw in the English media. I knew how other people regarded us, and it stood in the way of me getting what I wanted, of achieving my dreams. So, yeah, there were times when I wished I was white. Not anymore, though. I won't let myself feel that way just because some people are racist."

"I'm glad," she said. "You're great as you are, even if your buttercream skills leave a little to be desired."

He raised his eyebrows and pretend to look offended, which made her laugh.

"How did your sister like the cake?" she asked.

"Oh, she enjoyed it. And then I told her about us, and she bugged the hell out of me."

"My mom did, too. I started blushing when she asked about the baking lessons and my brother kept pressing the issue."

"I told Jenna because I thought teasing me would cheer her up."

"And did it?"

"Yeah, I think so."

Lindsay opened her mouth to ask about his nephew, but then shut it. She couldn't help remembering her mom's comments on grandchildren, and now, oh God, why was she thinking of Ryan holding a baby, why was her brain running away with itself?

But he would be so cute with a baby . . .

She shouldn't be having these fantasies.

She couldn't help thinking of Vivian, who'd said she never wanted children. Lindsay hadn't known what she wanted, and she still wasn't sure, but the picture of Ryan with a baby—their baby— certainly made a compelling image.

And to think, she'd once thought she could stop herself from falling for this man.

"My dad hasn't visited Jenna since the hospital," Ryan said, "though it's only a half-hour drive. She hasn't said she wants him to visit, but I think she does, and really, doesn't he want to see his grandchild? Even if he's better with older children? I keep trying to get him to visit."

"My mom would be there every week. My dad, too." Her dad had been good with babies, but if she had a baby, he wouldn't meet them.

She hadn't really thought about that before.

Ryan didn't say anything, but he held her a little closer.

She imagined losing a parent halfway through her pregnancy, like Jenna. The excitement of talking about the baby together, and then . . .

Tears came to Lindsay's eyes, but she forced them back.

Ugh, today was too damn emotional. It seemed like her heart

had been on a seesaw ever since she'd started seeing Ryan, and she didn't want to get off, even if it was difficult at times.

He'd be a good dad, though his filming schedule might make things a little difficult. But he wouldn't expect her to do all the work, and he wouldn't consider the time he spent with his kids as babysitting. She could see the work he put in with his family, work that was often done by female family members.

And he'd do emotional labor in their relationship. He wouldn't run from it.

*Why are you so damn sweet?*

They lay in silence for a few minutes, and she absently stroked his hair, overwhelmed that this was her life; she got to touch this man.

And then he said, "I figure I should give you a heads-up. I'm doing an interview for a magazine on Thursday." He named a Canadian magazine she'd never heard of before.

"Does this include a photoshoot where you get to take off your shirt?" She ran her hands over his pecs.

"I'll be fully clothed."

She let out an exaggerated sigh. "Your fans will be so disappointed."

"The reason I want to tell you now—"

"Is that you won't be able to see me on Thursday because you have to work? I understand. We don't have to see each other every day."

"No, because of the kind of interview this is," Ryan said, "I think they'll ask about my love life."

*Oh.*

"I want to tell you what I'll say, so there will be no surprises if you read the piece." He paused. "I plan to laugh it off and say I'm too busy, as I usually do."

Her stomach dropped.

He liked her. He was good to her. Good enough to warn her in advance of this.

But he didn't see her being around long-term, even if he'd emphasized that this was his first relationship in a while, like she was someone special. He was going to say exactly what he had in the interview she'd watched many weeks ago.

"Okay," she said, not wanting to let on that this tore her up inside.

She wished it didn't, but it did.

He drew his eyebrows together until a notch appeared between them.

"Lindsay," he said, "you know why I don't want to mention you, right? It's not because I don't care about you. It's not because I don't want this to go somewhere."

"You don't need—"

"But if I mention you, people might track you down. Hound you on social media. This isn't something I have much experience with, so I'm not really sure. My only other relationship in the past five years—however brief—was with Helen Alvarez . . ."

He trailed off, probably at her expression of shock.

"You dated Helen Alvarez?"

Helen Alvarez was very famous. More so than he was. And ten years older than him.

"Only for two months."

"I never heard about it," she said stupidly.

Stupid, because she hadn't even known who Ryan was until recently.

"It didn't last long," he said, "and her people keep tight control on what gets out about her personal life. I don't want to subject you to any public attention yet, and I don't want it to interfere with what we have, okay? If it gets out, I won't be embarrassed, but I'd rather wait a little longer before too many people know."

It was all very reasonable.

He kissed her and she walked home alone. It was dark, but she felt safe on the major streets downtown, and she didn't see the need for Ryan to drive her.

He said all the right things.

He was very good in bed and went down on her, like, all the time.

But he'd dated Helen Alvarez. She couldn't get that out of her head.

As good as he was to Lindsay, she couldn't help thinking that one day, it would be over, and he'd easily walk away. A few months later, she'd look him up on Twitter and see a picture of him with a glamorous, well-known woman. Even though he'd tried to reassure Lindsay, he couldn't fully convince her.

She should have done a better job of protecting her heart, but she couldn't seem to help it when he was involved.


**THE INTERVIEW HAD** gone well.

Better than the promo tour Ryan had done for *That Kind of Wedding*, not long after his mother had died. He was starting to feel more like himself again. Yet . . . a different version of himself? Because he couldn't be the same after his mom's death.

And after Lindsay.

*You'll probably never be the same again, but that's okay*, she'd told him.

He'd hated lying and saying there was no one special in his life, but it was for the best. For now. That had been the most awkward part of the interview, as well as the follow-up questions, in which the interviewer had asked him about his ideal woman, and he'd struggled not to describe Lindsay to a tee. He'd kept that answer brief.

Now it was Monday again. The day of the week when he always saw Lindsay, which made it the best. She'd had errands to run earlier, so he was meeting her at the bakery at two.

Before heading out the door, he checked his social media accounts. Someone had asked Dad what his favorite movie of Ryan's was, and Dad had yet to reply.

Ryan was sure Dad would reply eventually. He knew what the answer would be.

There was lots of other activity on social media, too. In fact, it looked like someone had taken photos of Ryan wearing sunglasses and walking around Toronto. Lindsay wasn't in the pictures, and he breathed out a sigh of relief.

But then he started reading the tweets. People were speculating on why he was spending so much time in Kensington Market. Apparently, the owner of a nearby café had seen him there more than once, but thankfully, no one mentioned Lindsay.

He should probably talk about this with her.

When he reached the bakery, he was smiling. It was their seventh lesson, and they'd be making a maple walnut cake with cream cheese buttercream and doing some fondant work. But as much as he enjoyed being in the kitchen with Lindsay, he was looking forward to the end of their lesson.

Because then he'd get to take her home.

# CHAPTER 27

Tuesday after work, Lindsay bought sushi and tempura—veggie tempura, not shrimp—and arrived at the apartment just after Vivian.

"Sushi?" Lindsay asked, her heart beating a little fast. Maybe she should have texted Vivian beforehand. "I got enough for you."

"Sounds good," Vivian said.

A few minutes later, they sat down to an early dinner. Lindsay began by helping herself to a California roll.

"It's going well with Ryan?" Vivian asked.

"Yeah, it's pretty good."

"At some point, I guess he'll have to go away to film something."

"He has a movie lined up to start this fall. I think it's filming in Vancouver?" Lindsay hadn't thought about it much. It was a ways in the future. "I hope I can handle a long-distance relationship for a while."

She wasn't used to being in a relationship, so it would be like going back to her regular life . . . but a little different, of course. There would be phone calls and texts. Attempts to remain close despite all the miles between them.

Would she and Ryan be good at that? She couldn't imagine him cheating on her, but perhaps the shine would go off their relationship once he was out of Toronto.

Vivian reached for the tempura. "Do you think you'll still . . . Never mind. Sorry, I'm being a bad friend. I don't want to overwhelm you with my negativity. It's just hard because I had a bad experience with my ex."

Though it wasn't the right moment for it, Lindsay couldn't help smiling.

Because Vivian had said "friend."

"He doesn't want to tell people that we're together yet," Lindsay said. "Like, he did an interview and pretended he was single because he doesn't want to subject me to awkward attention, or for it to interfere in our relationship. I understand, but it did make me feel a bit weird. And someone noticed him spending time in the area, so we had to discuss what he should say on social media about it."

"It's so strange to have to think about such things, isn't it?"

"Yeah, it sure is." Lindsay chuckled. "I assume you're still not making *Just Another New York Sitcom* fan art?"

"I've moved on to Dean Kobayashi fan art."

"Ooh. Good choice."

"Don't let your boyfriend hear you talk about another actor that way!"

Lindsay froze, a tuna roll halfway to her mouth.

*Boyfriend.* She and Ryan hadn't used that term . . . did he think of her as his girlfriend?

The words were a little scary, but she quickly recovered. "Ryan's ego is a healthy size. I'm sure he'd be fine with it."

When Vivian laughed, Lindsay smiled again.

She had a new friend, and she hadn't had one of those in a long time. Plus, a new boyfriend—maybe? This was uncharted territory for her. She was used to everyone in her life having known her *before*. Before her father's death—and also before the bakery.

But Vivian and Ryan hadn't known her back then.

She was glad she was making new connections, something that had eluded her for so long. It was just rather uncomfortable at the same time. To let people in, to let them know the Lindsay McLeod who'd been forged in the wake of grief.

With Ryan, she felt particularly vulnerable. Like she'd given him quite a bit of herself, which meant she'd given him the power to hurt her.

What would happen when he went to Vancouver to film a movie?

And when their relationship became public knowledge?

**WHEN RYAN GOT** home, he took off his shoes and settled heavily on the couch in his living room. Today's visit with Jenna and Ezra hadn't been great. Ezra had cried for most of it, and when Ryan had tried to cheer Jenna up by encouraging her to give him a hard time, she didn't take the bait, which was most unlike her.

He'd suggested she see friends who were also on maternity leave. Friends who'd know what she was going through, unlike Ryan—but she'd said she didn't have anyone and started crying.

And at one point her face had crumpled and she'd whispered, "I'm so bad at this."

The way she'd said it, like she really, truly believed she was a bad mother . . . God, he hated it.

Ryan lay back on the couch and put his hand over his eyes, thinking of how different things would be if his mom were still here. If she'd gotten to hold her grandchild in her arms.

For one, Jenna would probably be doing better, not grieving and trying to take care of a newborn with little help at the same time.

Ryan would see his parents together, rather than calling his dad with the futile hope that they could have a half-decent conversation.

Dad probably wouldn't have a Twitter account, either.

And Ryan might not have decided to spend so much time in Toronto, near his family. There was a good chance he never would have met Lindsay.

It was all tangled up together.

He didn't like the fact that the best thing in his life had only happened because his mother had died. He'd only entered Kensington Bake Shop because he'd seen those women eating cupcakes in front of the bakery. And he hadn't been paying attention because he'd been lost in his memories, and he'd knocked over the donuts.

He pulled up Twitter on his phone. He'd tweeted earlier about his baking lessons at Kensington Bake Shop, without mentioning why he was learning to bake or saying anything about Lindsay. Then he'd shared a picture of the cake he'd made.

Before he'd started decorating the cake yesterday, he'd asked for a theme—it would be more like the competition this way, he'd reasoned. She'd told him to make a penguin cake, but when it was finished, she'd thought his birds looked more like puffins.

On Twitter, he'd included a poll so people could vote on whether it looked like a penguin cake or a puffin cake. He checked the results of the poll now.

"Puffin cake" was currently winning with sixty-four percent of the vote, dammit.

Lindsay would be amused.

The top reply was from his dad: Where is the option for "neither"?

Ryan immediately responded. Failing to impress my father #StoryOfMyLife

A minute later, he regretted it, but his tweet already had dozens of likes. More than one person had replied, including someone who'd tweeted a GIF of him removing his shirt in *That Kind of Wedding* with the text, Don't worry, we love you, Ryan!

Yes, this was his life now. The life of the little boy who'd grown up in Markham, practicing his kung fu moves in the hopes that—

His phone rang. It was Mel, which was surprising, given Mel would usually text first.

Ryan answered. "Hey, what's up?"

"Just wanted to let you know before you saw it online." Mel paused. "Herbie Chin passed away."

# CHAPTER 28

R yan wasn't used to lying in bed with a woman when they hadn't had sex first, but Lindsay was here, trailing her hand up and down his side, and this was all he wanted right now.

"I'm sorry," he said again.

"Ryan, you don't need to be sorry."

He'd been out of sorts since Herbie's death yesterday.

Herbie Chin had been ninety-two. While he hadn't been given all the opportunities he'd deserved, his career had spanned more than six decades. Though he'd worked little in recent years, he'd still had the occasional role. Most people wouldn't know his name, though they'd likely seen him in something. He'd had a wife who'd died a few years ago, three children, ten grandchildren, and a couple of great-grandchildren.

That, Ryan figured, was how he wanted to go. When he was old, after a short illness.

Not due to a heart attack while his daughter was pregnant with her first child.

"We'd been emailing lately," Ryan said. "I'm glad I did that before it was too late. He never told me he was sick."

Ryan was okay with feeling sadness and other emotions. He

didn't try to shove them aside. But he felt like he was burdening Lindsay. How much should he lean on her for support? He liked being able to slide his arms around her and say what was on his mind, but he didn't want to be a bother.

And some of the things he had to deal with were just plain strange.

Once the news had become public, Ryan had tweeted about Herbie, including a picture of them on the set of *Just Another New York Sitcom*. He'd written about how Herbie had paved the way for actors like Ryan, and he was honored they'd gotten to film something together.

This had gotten a lot of likes and retweets, and inevitably, some people had said stupid shit. And also . . .

"I was asked to write a piece about him," Ryan said.

"Are you going to?" Lindsay asked. "You should. If you want to."

"I don't know. Writing things like that—it's not my strength."

"But you have people who can help you, right? I can read it for you, too."

He laced his fingers with hers. "That would be great. Thank you." He paused. "I'm going to the funeral on Sunday."

"Where is it?"

"New York."

"I could go with you, if you like. I know it might be difficult for you, especially since your mom's funeral wasn't all that long ago."

A tear slid down his cheek, and he couldn't help but think that his father would berate him for crying. He thought back to the fact that he'd called Herbie Chin a father figure of sorts in a tweet, and he wondered how his dad felt about it.

His father, whom he'd never, ever seen cry. Was Dad even capable of crying?

But right now, Ryan was here in bed with Lindsay, and she was offering to go to a funeral in another country with him, and somehow, that broke him. He wasn't used to having someone like this in his life.

"No, that's okay," he said. "I'll be staying with Mel, and I know you saw him act like a jerk, but he really is a good friend. Plus, this is your special donut-and-beer-pairing weekend, isn't it? I'm sure you'll be busier than usual."

"Yes, but I could figure something out—"

"No, no. You stay in Toronto. I'll be fine."

"You sure?"

"Yeah."

Just knowing he had her, knowing she'd text him a couple of times to make sure everything was okay . . . that did melt his heart, and he shed a few more tears.

But she didn't mind. Though she wiped his tears away, it didn't feel like she was telling him not to cry. And it all felt manageable.

Not like after his mother's death, when he'd had to numb himself to survive.

Obviously, this wasn't the same as losing his mother, but it was still loss, and it also made him think of her, as Lindsay had intuited.

He threaded his fingers through her hair.

Over the years, he'd acted in many, many scenes that were unlike anything he'd experienced in real life. For example, Ryan had never been in a fight in real life—well, not since grade two—but he'd been in several fights on-screen. He'd also never had a roommate who owned a capybara. Or encountered a zombie.

And this, right now, reminded him vaguely of a scene in *That Kind of Wedding*, but at the time that had been filmed, he'd never been in bed with a woman like *this*.

Which reminded him . . .

Before he spoke, he just enjoyed being with Lindsay in silence for a little longer. Normally, he didn't particularly like silence, but it was different with her.

And then he said, "There were talks of Irene Lai starring in another rom-com, but the project fell through, and I feel guilty about it. Like if I'd done a better job somehow, our movie would have been more successful, and this project would have been given the green light. What I feared would happen—it seems to be happening. I feel like I'm not allowed to star in things that flop, even though it wasn't *that* big of a flop—"

"And every big actor has done some truly horrendous movies."

"Exactly. But you know what I mean."

"Yeah, but it's not all on you, Ryan."

"I know, but still."

"I don't know exactly what that's like, though I can understand."

He could imagine someone else saying those words and it feeling like a brush-off, yet with Lindsay, she sounded like she really did get it.

And he couldn't complain too much. He'd been given chances that, back in the day, would have been unimaginable. Herbie could only have dreamed of starring in a rom-com like *That Kind of Wedding* when he was Ryan's age.

He *was* grateful, but he wanted more. Part of what drove him was wanting to give kids examples of people like themselves in media.

At the same time, it was good for Ryan to have a break. He had the occasional interview and such, but it was nice to be able to hang out with Lindsay like this. To know he could be there at a moment's notice if his father or his sister needed him. Not that Dad would ever make such a phone call, but it was nice to be able to keep an eye on his family.

"Lindsay," he said suddenly, "in case it wasn't clear—because I'm terrible with this stuff—I'm not seeing anyone else. It's just you." He kissed the back of her hand.

"Same here, *boyfriend*."

He liked that label, as long as he was *her* boyfriend.

He rolled on top of her, and he kissed her gently and thoroughly.

NEW YORK CITY wasn't an unfamiliar place to Ryan. He'd spent a fair bit of time here, much of it with Mel, though Mel had never taken him to this bar before. But clearly, Melvin Lee was a regular customer.

It was a good thing he'd arrived with Mel; otherwise, Ryan wasn't sure he'd have been able to find this bar in Chinatown. It didn't have a proper sign, and there weren't even any numbers to indicate the address. This didn't seem like the smartest business decision, but what did Ryan know about such things?

The older bartender—a Chinese man in his late sixties, if Ryan had to guess—asked Mel if he'd like his usual drink, and Mel nodded.

Ryan considered ordering an alcoholic drink, then dismissed the idea. He hadn't had more than a few sips of alcohol in six years. Best to keep it that way. His tolerance was probably even shittier than it used to be. He read over the juices, soft drinks, and other nonalcoholic beverages on the menu and was pleased to see sour plum drink listed.

It was a sign of the solemnity of the day that Mel didn't make fun of Ryan for ordering sour plum drink. It wasn't that Mel ever teased Ryan for not drinking alcohol, but rather that he thought this particular beverage was disgusting. Ryan enjoyed the smoked plums, though.

Instead, they nodded and clinked their glasses together. They didn't say his name, but they both knew whom they were drinking to.

They were still wearing suits, having come here straight from the service. Ryan usually felt comfortable in a suit, but today he kept pulling at his tie. Mel, who was never comfortable in a suit, had already pocketed his tie and had folded his jacket on top of the bar.

"We should get some food," Mel said, then asked the bartender for five-spice beef jerky and marinated tofu.

The bartender didn't try to make conversation with them, didn't inquire about the improbable situation of Mel wearing a suit and not running his mouth.

"I can't believe there were baby pictures of Herbie," Mel said. "There certainly aren't any baby pictures of my grandparents. His daughter gave a good eulogy. I think she takes after him the most."

Ryan nodded as he remembered the eulogy he'd given at his mother's funeral. They'd all gone to a restaurant in Scarborough afterward and even managed to act half-normal, because that was what they had to do.

His phone vibrated. He didn't look at it, instead reaching for a piece of the beef jerky that had been placed in front of them, but when it vibrated again, he picked it up.

Hey, Lindsay said. How did it go? How are you?

A question she meant sincerely, not as a simple greeting. Like the way he asked his dad, though his dad just grunted in response.

It was a nice service, Ryan texted. I'm okay now, just a bit out of sorts.

She sent him two heart emojis, and he smiled.

Of course, his smile didn't escape Mel's notice, and his friend grabbed the phone out of Ryan's hands before he could protest.

There was something reassuringly normal about that.

"Ooh, she sent you hearts!" Mel said. "I knew you liked her. That's what I said last time, and you told me it was the last thing you needed in your life right now."

"I changed my mind."

"More like you couldn't keep your hands off her?"

"She makes me feel like I have more to give," Ryan said, then realized that was the corniest line ever. This was why he had no interest in screenwriting.

The words were true, though.

"Aw." Mel fluttered his eyelashes. "You looove her."

"Stop it," Ryan said, but there was no heat behind it.

Maybe he did love her, but he'd just gone to a funeral. He gave himself permission to wait a little longer before thinking about his feelings.

"I'm also worried," he said, "about the attention she'll get and how she'll deal with my life. People have noticed me spending more time in the area, but they don't know about her . . . for now."

He took his phone back from Mel and sent Lindsay another text. **How was the beer/donut event?**

She replied with a picture of a beer and a matcha tiramisu donut. **Look, it's your favorite! The beer is a Hoppy Hippogriff IPA. We're out of the matcha tiramisu donuts now, and not because someone knocked them all on the floor** ☺

He snort-laughed.

Which, of course, caused Mel to grab the phone out of his hand.

"You have no respect for my privacy," Ryan muttered, taking back his phone yet again.

"What? This looks like an innocent conversation. It's not like you're sexting each other."

Ryan choked on his beef jerky.

"Oh good," Mel said. "My ploy to cheer you up worked."

"I was choking. You think that means you cheered me up? Besides, it's only natural to not be all sunshine and roses after a funeral. Even you were reasonably somber until a few minutes ago."

Mel shrugged and downed half his drink. "Remember his first scene on the show? When he caught you in bed with . . . who was that? The girl from the copy place?"

"You've got the wrong sitcom," Ryan said, but he knew Mel had done it on purpose.

Mel knocked back the rest of his drink, and the bartender had another one ready for him within a minute. "My favorite scene was when he hit you when his cane, and you fell over and broke your glasses. No woman would look at you for a week."

"Not on the show, but in real life, I did okay."

"By the way, the women at the table by the window are checking you out."

Ryan reached for some marinated tofu with his chopsticks. "Of course they're checking me out," he said, adopting the voice of a cocky asshole, the sort he'd played on-screen multiple times. "I mean, look at me."

His phone vibrated again, and he immediately reached for it.

Melvin chuckled. "I'm happy for you about Lindsay, even if you're ignoring me now. What's she saying? Sending you smooches or eggplants?"

Ryan held up his phone, displaying the text and accompanying photo.

The guys at the bar got this beer from the cellar. It has actual matcha in it. Look at the scary green color! It's like the shakes you drink for breakfast.

"Disappointingly PG," Mel said. "I think it's cool she runs a bakery. Was that always her dream?"

"I don't think she seriously thought of it until after her dad died."

"Not seriously, maybe, but it was still her dream, no? Then after his death, she wanted to seize the day and make it a reality. See,

I admire that. Like Herbie—he had to deal with a lot of shit, but he was always chasing his dreams. Unlike that roommate of Lindsay's . . ."

"For fuck's sake," Ryan said. "That again? I thought you admitted you were rude."

"I shouldn't have said what I did, but I don't think I was wrong. It's easy to imagine her getting to sixty and having regrets about working in finance all her life."

"You don't know her. People want different things."

Mel just grunted in response.

Ryan reflected on what he wanted out of life, other than his career. Other than still having his mom.

He downed the rest of his sour plum drink as though it were alcohol that would make him forget. The bartender served him a second glass before he could ask for one, as well as a third drink for Melvin.

Once again, they clinked their glasses together solemnly, as unnaturally bright sunlight filtered through the dingy windows of the bar.

For Herbie.

For not ending life with a sea of regrets.

**"PUT YOUR PHONE** away and drink your green beer," Noreen said.

Lindsay complied. Ryan hadn't texted in a few minutes, but he was at a bar with a friend in New York. And here she was, also at a bar with her best friend.

The donut-beer pairing event had gone well, though Lindsay had needed to put in longer days than usual at the bakery this weekend. But they'd had just enough donuts to make it to six o'clock, and now that the event was over, she and Noreen were relaxing at Fantastical Brewing. The bartenders supplied them with free drinks, which was dangerous.

"The key lime pie donut was my favorite," Isaac said as he pulled a pint. "The chocolate espresso one was good, too."

That donut made Lindsay think of Ryan, but he was constantly on her mind, so that wasn't a surprise.

"What do you think, Adam?" Isaac asked.

Adam, who was wiping down the bar, merely grunted.

"He talks sometimes, I promise. Even if you've yet to see proof of it. Can I get you anything else, Noreen? Or . . . Marc? Was that your name?" Isaac nodded at Noreen's husband, who'd joined them half an hour ago.

Isaac wasn't flirting with Noreen today.

"A Bigfoot Imperial Stout," Marc said gruffly, keeping his arm around Noreen.

Lindsay smiled as she looked at the two of them. They really were good together. She took a sip of her frightfully colored beer and wondered what people would think about her and Ryan. Would they say that she and Ryan were good together? Or that he was way out of her league?

Noreen would never think such a thing, but what about everyone else?

# CHAPTER 29

When Ryan presented his two-tiered summer-themed cake on Monday afternoon, it was a bittersweet moment. He'd looked forward to these lessons for the last eight weeks, and this was the final one.

But a lot had changed in that time. He walked over to Lindsay and kissed her on the lips. She'd still be part of his life, even after *Baking Fail* filmed next week.

In fact, he had special plans for her tomorrow.

Lindsay worked long days, and she was always on her feet. Ryan hadn't heard her complain, but these plans were specifically made with this in mind. He hoped she liked them.

Tuesday afternoon, he put his hands on his hips and looked around his washroom. There was a tray of bath supplies on the counter. He didn't know what she liked, so he'd gotten a few different things.

Okay, more than a few. He might have gone a bit overboard.

He had this image in his mind of a woman having a soothing bath while drinking a glass of wine. But as far as he could tell, Lindsay preferred beer. Unfortunately, Ryan didn't know shit about beer, but he'd gone to the liquor store earlier in the day and picked up half a dozen bottles of craft beer.

Next task: write out a menu.

He figured handwriting would make it more personal, but after three tries, he threw the papers in the recycling bin and opted to type it out and print it on his rarely used printer.

At three o'clock, he was done, and he still had more than two hours before he had to pick up Lindsay. He could think of other things to do for her, but he didn't want to look like he was trying too hard—or that he had no idea what he was doing.

To stop himself from obsessing over it, he called his father. The answering machine came on, and he listened to his mother's message, swallowing hard.

Then he remembered that of course his father wouldn't be home right now. It was the middle of the afternoon on a Tuesday—he'd be at work. But maybe if Ryan phoned his office, Dad would actually talk to him.

So Ryan did exactly that and asked to speak to Stanley Kwok.

It wasn't long before Dad was on the phone.

"Hi," Dad said. "Is something wrong?"

"Why would something be wrong?" Ryan said. "I want to talk to my father. Aren't I allowed to do that?"

"You've never called me at work before."

*Oh.* Yes, that was true, and Ryan could see how that might have made his dad worry there was bad news.

"I won't keep you long. Just wanted to suggest you visit Jenna this weekend. I'm worried about her, and I know you still haven't been to see her."

This morning, Jenna hadn't even laughed when she'd seen Ryan's slightly lopsided cake. He'd covered the cake with blue fondant to represent water; cookie crumbs at the base of the cake were supposed to be sand. Fondant watermelon slices, sunglasses, flip-flops, and an umbrella also adorned the cake, though all the decorations were of dubious quality.

She'd also seemed disengaged in her interactions with Ezra. Yes, having a new baby was tough, but Ryan couldn't shake the feeling that something was wrong.

"I'm sure she's fine," Dad said. "She's a smart woman. She can handle a baby."

"Don't you want to see him? When was the last time you talked to her?"

"Three weeks ago."

Ryan sputtered. His mother would never have gone more than a week without talking to one of her children.

Of course, Dad didn't need to be exactly the same, but . . .

"We can go together on Saturday," Ryan said.

"No. I'm busy."

*Yeah, sure you are.*

Goddammit. Ryan felt like he couldn't do anything right. His dad was bothered when Ryan called him and suggested meeting up. He felt more connection to his dad when he read his tweets.

And Dad and Jenna never saw each other. The last time they'd all been together had been at the hospital.

Why was his family such a mess? Why couldn't he fix it?

*Mom, why aren't you here?*

"Is there some reason you don't want to see Jenna and Ezra?" Ryan asked. "Did you and Jenna have a fight that she didn't tell me about?"

"No," Dad said shortly.

Ryan suspected this was true. Dad and Jenna had never fought. Jenna had been the smart, well-behaved child; Ryan, on the other hand, had been the one who'd wanted to be an actor rather than an engineer.

"Is it because you feel bad that Mom never got to meet her grandson?"

"I have work to do," Dad said. "Please stop worrying about my feelings. I'm fine. Shouldn't you be at the gym, building ab muscles?" And with that, he hung up.

Ryan set his phone down on the kitchen table, massaged his temples, and stared at the menu he'd made for Lindsay.

How could he be someone's boyfriend? How could he possibly make this work when he had no experience? When the non-romantic relationships in his life were a disaster?

What made him think he could figure out how to fit Lindsay into his life?

He returned to his washroom and looked at the bath supplies. They seemed a little sad now, and he was overcome with the urge to shove them off the counter.

He didn't usually have violent urges.

Ryan went back to the kitchen, sat down on a chair, and attempted some breathing exercises. When he was finished, he felt a little better.

The rest of the day was about making Lindsay feel appreciated. He'd focus on that.

**WHEN RYAN PICKED** Lindsay up at the end of the day, he was looking cool in shades, jeans, and a plain T-shirt. Her stomach did a somersault when she saw him. How did that man look so good in everyday clothes?

He took her hand and led her to his parked car, which she could only describe as "black sedan." She didn't know anything about cars, but this was the opposite of a super-cool-movie-star car, and that made her giggle. It also caused a rush of affection in her heart.

God. The simplest things turned her into mush.

When they got to his condo, he handed her a sheet of paper.

"These are your options for dinner," he said. "Pick whatever you like."

Lindsay quickly scanned the four options. "Are you making these for me?"

He chuckled. "No, you know my skills in the kitchen are nothing to brag about. I'll run out to pick it up while you're having a bath."

"Bath?"

"Yeah. You relax in the bath with a beer"—he threw open the fridge with a flourish and gestured to several bottles of beer—"then I'll bring you dinner in bed and you can have a foot massage."

"Do you give great foot massages?"

"I don't mean to brag, but . . ." He scratched the back of his neck. "Well, I've never done one before, but Google has been informative."

He seemed slightly nervous, as he had on their first date. It melted her heart even more, that this man, who seemed confident as he moved through the world, could be this way with her.

Even though his presence was distracting, she managed to read over the menu again. "I'll have the salmon poke bowl."

"Excellent. Now you can pick your beer."

"Ooh, I like this one." She pulled out a bottle of blackberry sour from a local brewery.

"Do you want a glass? Or would you rather drink it out of the bottle?"

"Out of the bottle is good." She figured that would be easier if she was in the bathtub.

He gestured her toward the washroom. There were two toothbrushes in the toothbrush holder, as there had been since the very first morning she'd been here—she now spent about three nights a week at his place.

But unlike last night, there were bath products by the sink. Lots of them. Things he'd clearly bought just for her. She picked up a bottle that had a pink label with a seashell. There were words on the label, but she couldn't read them because her eyes were swimming with tears.

"Is something wrong?" In one step, he was next to her, his arms around her.

"No." She turned into his embrace. "It's just . . . no one's ever done anything like this for me before."

Not that her family and friends didn't do nice things for her. Noreen had taken good care of her when she'd gotten the flu last winter, making her soup and running to the pharmacy as needed.

But Lindsay had never dated anyone who'd done things like this. Maybe it would have happened if she hadn't avoided romance for so long, but she had, and now here she was, with *him*.

He didn't say anything for a long time, just held her, and then he started reading the labels to her, so she didn't even need to do that. She picked the one with the seashell—some kind of milky foaming bath product—and he ran the bath for her. Then he undressed her carefully.

"Are you sure you don't want to come in with me?" she asked.

"Some other time, but today, this is just for you. I'll get your salmon poke bowl. You'll be ready for dinner in forty-five minutes to an hour?"

"Sure."

He helped her into the bathtub before twisting the lid off her beer and handing it to her.

Then he did the most unexpected thing of all: he placed a small bell on the edge of the bathtub.

"So you can ring if you need anything," he said.

"Are you sure you want to give me that? I might take advantage of it."

"Well, you have to give me time to get your dinner, but I don't mind. I'm at your service." He bowed deeply.

When he left the bathroom, she was tempted to ring the bell to bring him right back, but she didn't. She sank under the bubbles, her chin just above the surface of the water so she could drink her beer. It was nice to drink something cold while she was in a hot bath. The last time she'd had a bath had been at her old apartment, and beer had not been involved.

Now she was dating a rather famous actor, who was determined to pamper her after a long day of work and told her she was beautiful.

She cringed, remembering how she'd cried when she'd looked at the bath products.

*Way to act cool, Lindsay.*

But although women's tears terrified some men, Ryan hadn't freaked out. He'd held her. He'd seemed to understand.

She rang the bell, and he came into the washroom.

"What's up?" he asked.

"I just wanted to see you," she said, being cheesy in a way she never had before.

He smiled at her and kissed her forehead.

When he left again, she took a long pull on her beer.

She spent almost half her nights with him. He'd gone out of town for only two nights, and she'd missed him. She was becoming accustomed to having him around.

And she couldn't help feeling like this was a dangerous thing.

But for tonight, she'd enjoy herself.

# CHAPTER 30

If Ryan had known the effect that foot massages had on a person, perhaps he would have done this years ago.

However, a foot massage wasn't something he could imagine doing for someone he didn't know well. It was easier to imagine having sex with a woman whom he'd met earlier that day than giving her a foot massage. There was something particularly intimate about this . . . and it also caused Lindsay to make similar noises to the ones she made when he was inside her.

It probably didn't help that she'd spent the past hour dressed in only a towel.

They'd eaten dinner in bed, and Lindsay had accidentally dropped an edamame bean down her towel dress, which he'd needed to fish out.

With his mouth, naturally.

"Ohhh," she moaned again.

Was she trying to kill him?

"My dick is hard enough to hammer nails," he said, gritting his teeth. "I could be a proper handyman now."

She didn't seem to hear him. She was too busy moaning as he rubbed her foot, using one of the techniques he'd discovered using Google.

This would be the end of him.

When she shimmied a little to adjust her position, her towel dress split apart, and *fuck*, it was a beautiful view. Her skin was so dewy, but her nipples were tight buds . . .

He could be a fairly patient man at times, but this was testing his limits.

"That's it," he growled. "I'll do the other foot afterward."

"After . . . ?"

A moment later, he was on top of her. He slipped his hand down her body, cupping her mound as his middle finger slid inside her. She made some noises that were even better than the ones she'd made earlier, and she certainly squirmed more than she had during the foot massage.

He grinned down at her. "How does that feel? Am I hitting the right spot?"

"Yeah, that's a good . . . spot," she said in a strangled voice.

He thrust his finger inside her before bending down and bringing the peak of her nipple into his mouth. She jerked beneath him.

"What about that spot?" he asked, raising his head.

In response, she cupped the back of his head and brought it down to her other breast. He tugged the brownish pink tip into his mouth as he continued to pleasure her between her legs.

"Ryan," she moaned, raking her nails over his back.

He didn't care about anything but making her feel good right now.

He slid down her body and circled his tongue over her clit before feasting on her. "Is that the right spot?"

Her inarticulate response was certainly gratifying, and when he looked up, she shoved his head back down. He chuckled.

It didn't take long before she was coming apart, bucking against his face, twisting the sheets in her hands.

He moved up her body and kissed her slowly, reverently on the lips as he fumbled for a condom. When he finally managed to roll it on, his hands shaking, he positioned his erection at her entrance and pushed inside.

Sex was different with her than with other women. Not that sex had been bad for him before, and not that his partners hadn't enjoyed themselves—he always made sure of it.

But. This.

This was something else entirely.

She ran her foot over the back of his leg, and he groaned as he pumped inside her.

Her lips were parted, and he needed to kiss them. So, he did. She met him greedily, and that spurred him on. He didn't move faster; rather, he moved deeper. Filling her up, pulling back . . . again and again . . . When he stopped kissing her, he watched every little change in her expression, and then her face contorted in the loveliest way, and she cried out. Her cry reverberated all through him. He slowed down for a moment because this was what she preferred after she came—he knew that now. He knew more and more about her with every day, and he felt so goddamn lucky.

When he started rocking his hips against hers again, it didn't take long before his orgasm overtook him, too.

Later, she curled up against him, and he said, "How about I massage your other foot?"

"Oh right. That's what we were doing when you jumped me."

"The sounds you made were driving me wild."

"That was intentional."

He pulled back so he could look at her. "The foot massage wasn't actually that good?"

"It was very good, don't you worry. I may have been a tiny bit louder than I needed to be, so you'd jump me."

"You could have just told me to skip the foot massage and go straight to sex."

"What would be the fun in that?" She fluttered her eyelashes.

He tickled her until she rolled beneath him again and they were both breathing hard.

"Come over tomorrow after work," he said. "You can have another bath if you like."

She stiffened slightly, and he immediately rolled off her.

"What's wrong?" he asked. "What did I say?"

"It's just." She swallowed. "We agreed to take this slow, didn't we? It doesn't feel very slow right now, that's all. Staying with you three nights in a row . . ."

He didn't want to take it slow anymore.

He'd changed his mind, but she hadn't.

That didn't mean he'd done something wrong. She hadn't dated in a long time, and more experience with his fabulous abs wouldn't get rid of her hesitation.

But he felt perilously close to screwing up, like how he seemed to be constantly screwing up with his father.

Of course he'd give her what she wanted. Give her some time.

"That's no problem," he said, hiding his worry. "I understand. Sometime later in the week, then. But tonight was fun."

"Tonight was all for me."

"Yeah, and that was fun for me, too." To look after someone. To give her something she wasn't used to having. He wanted to do it again and again for her, but he wouldn't push it.

"Thanks," she said, curling up beside him again.

It was only eight thirty, but she was asleep almost instantly.

He set his alarm to the time she needed to wake up for work. Then he ran his hand through her hair, something he knew wouldn't wake her, if he was careful.

He really hoped he could figure this out. Make it work for her. Get her used to being spoiled in little ways so that she wouldn't cry because it was so unexpected.

But then he thought of his father and his sister, and how everything seemed to be out of his control. His mom would have known exactly what to do, but they were like this because she was gone. Because she was no longer here to bring him food he didn't need and knit clothes for Ezra, whom she'd never gotten to meet.

She'd never gotten to meet Lindsay, either.

Never gotten to bug the shit out of him when she saw two toothbrushes in his washroom.

He stayed in bed, even though he wasn't tired, and looked at Lindsay in the fading light, hoping that someday soon, someone would ask about his love life during an interview, and he would tell the truth. He didn't want to keep her a secret, but at the same time, he didn't want her to be so exposed.

After *Baking Fail*. He'd figure it out then.


**LINDSAY WAS WALKING** to work the next morning when she saw the movie poster. She stopped and stared at it.

Her boyfriend with another woman.

She'd seen the poster for *That Kind of Wedding* many times before. Not in this particular location, however—this was a different route from the one she usually took. It was unsettling to come across a photo of her boyfriend in Chinatown, early in the morning as the city came to life.

In the poster, Ryan wore a tux, but his shirt was undone, as was his tie. He was looking back at Irene Lai in a bridesmaid's dress.

*I'm dating that guy.*

And he looked at her like that—well, not exactly. But she thought the way he looked at her was even better.

To most people, he was painfully handsome, slightly cocky, but easygoing. That was his public persona. Not exactly the character he'd played in *That Kind of Wedding*, but close. The hero in the movie was a notorious womanizer, but Ryan didn't have a reputation for that, though some people might assume it. He could be breaking hearts all over the continent if he wanted to.

*How well do you really know him?*

No, she couldn't think that. She trusted him. She knew a side of him that most people didn't—they had no idea how unbelievably sweet he could be. Or that he was slightly awkward and clumsy at times. Knowing the real Ryan Kwok . . . it was like knowing a marvelous secret.

But she kept staring at that poster, and she couldn't help wondering.

The poster would disappear soon. In fact, she was surprised it was still up, since it had been many weeks since the movie's release, and it hadn't been a giant success.

He would move on to his next role, and his star would keep rising.

He was a good guy, but she wasn't part of his world. One day, he'd say something clichéd like, *It's not you, it's me.* He'd tell her that she was a lovely woman and he wished the very best for her.

She couldn't seem to stay away from this man, but when this inevitably ended, she had to make sure it didn't crush her. She needed to put a little more space between them.

She started walking again, past the grocers laying out produce in Chinatown.

*Baking Fail* would be filmed next week, and for some reason, it felt like that could be the end, even though their relationship was so much more than baking now.

But she wouldn't hope for a lot.

That was too risky.

# CHAPTER 31

This was it.

This was the reason Ryan had been taking baking lessons for the last two months, and he was determined to do Lindsay proud. In the grand scheme of things, this competition wasn't important, but he imagined how pleased his mom would have been, and he wanted to be able to donate the prize money in her memory. And show Lindsay that her lessons had been worth it.

He was competing against three other Canadian celebrities. First, there was Logan Burris, bad-boy defenseman for the Toronto Maple Leafs. Next, Leanna Cox, a pop musician. Lastly, Peter Irwin, an elderly actor known for his long-running sitcom *Chinook Diner*, which took place in a small town on the prairie.

Ryan recalled that it was the one sitcom his father had been able to tolerate. Dad would watch three minutes of it before changing the channel in disgust, which was a long time for him.

*Focus, dammit. Don't think about your father.*

It was good to be in front of the camera again. They'd done some brief pre-competition interviews earlier, and now Ryan was standing in front of his workstation. It threw him off that it wasn't exactly like the teaching kitchen in Kensington Bake Shop. And

Lindsay wasn't there beside him, and he hadn't had the option of wearing a pink ruffled apron.

Today, they'd film the donut and cupcake rounds, and then tomorrow, the cake round.

After introducing the judges, Joey Fielder, the host, said, "Are you ready to see the donut you'll be making today?"

"I'm always ready!" Logan Burris raised his fists, though those wouldn't help him in this competition.

They all stood around the presentation table in front of the judging panel, and Joey lifted a large dome to reveal . . .

Something that was supposedly a donut.

"This donut," Joey said, "is called Your Morning Brownie. A yeast donut with a chocolatey filling, dipped in a coffee glaze, topped with a mocha brownie and chocolate cookie crumbs, and drizzled with chocolate ganache. You need to make six of them in seventy-five minutes."

Peter Irwin burst into laughter.

"Too easy for you?" Joey asked.

"In my day, we used to bake fresh donuts and brownies each morning for our parents, before walking to school six miles in a blizzard. Even in the summer. Uphill both ways, of course."

As it turned out, Peter had no idea what he was doing in the kitchen. Contestants on *Baking Fail* usually had a little baking knowledge—which was why Ryan had needed to take lessons— just not enough to do complex tasks in the allotted time.

Ryan was about to put his brownies in the oven, and yes, he'd remembered to grease the pan, when a commotion at the next workstation distracted him.

He'd been doing a pretty good job of focusing on the task at hand, while answering questions and describing what he was doing when the camera was pointed at him. Perhaps it helped that he was used to being in the kitchen with Lindsay, who was quite distracting.

But it was hard not to notice when there was a literal *fire*.

"What were you trying to do, Peter?" Joey asked.

"I didn't know melting chocolate was so difficult!"

"Okay, everyone, take five!" someone shouted.

Ryan tried not to let this ruin his concentration as he sipped some water in the next room, and it wasn't too long before they were filming again.

Luckily, it had been a pretty small fire.

He put the brownies in the oven—hopefully it wouldn't matter that the batter had been sitting on the counter for a few minutes—before cutting the donut dough into circles. He left those to proof, and then it was time for the cookies.

He should have asked Lindsay to show him how to make cookies. This wasn't the first time he'd seen a *Baking Fail* challenge that involved cookies, even though there wasn't a cookie round. Though these were just crumbs, so they didn't need to look at all neat.

"Any advice for our contestants?" Joey asked the judges at the halfway point.

"Make sure everything is cooked properly," said the first judge, an esteemed cookbook writer. Ryan didn't know anything about cookbooks, though; he only knew the judge from *Baking Fail*. "I don't want to be eating raw dough."

Joey turned to the other judge.

"Don't start a fire," she said.

"Why couldn't you have told me that half an hour ago?" Peter asked.

At five minutes left, Ryan was banging on his cookies with a rolling pin to make cookie crumbs. He still had to fill his donuts and glaze them and put everything on top, but all the ingredients were done, more or less.

"Ahhh!" shouted Logan as two of his donuts toppled to the floor.

Ryan banged harder on the cookies, then started assembling everything.

"One minute left!" Joey called out.

Ryan hurriedly cut the brownies into triangles, which was how they were shaped on the example donuts, and put them on top of his half-dozen donuts.

Now it was time for the judging.

Logan Burris's donuts were first. He only had four donuts, rather than six. He also didn't have the cookie crumbs, and his brownie had clearly not been baked for long enough. The first judge, who'd emphasized he didn't want to eat anything raw, told Logan that he hadn't listened to the instructions.

"You know me," Logan said. "I don't play by the rules."

Leanna Cox's donuts were next. They weren't quite golden brown, and there was very little filling, but they apparently weren't completely unappetizing.

And now it was Ryan's turn, and dammit, his heart shouldn't be beating this fast.

"These don't look the most professional," the first judge said.

"No?" The second judge cocked her head. "I think they have a rustic appeal."

"But they do taste excellent, though the coffee glaze is a touch strong."

Lastly, it was Peter's turn. His so-called donuts looked more like softballs covered in brown sludge, and they weren't properly cooked inside.

Based on the judges' comments, Ryan expected to win the donut round, yet a part of him was still surprised when Joey announced it.

The cupcake round, however, did not go so well.

Ryan laughed when Joey revealed the lemon cream cupcakes. Lindsay would enjoy this. They even had lemon curd filling. But after pouring half of the cupcake batter into the tins, he realized the consistency wasn't right. It was too thick.

He started spooning his batter back into the mixing bowl.

"Whatcha doing there, Ryan?" Joey asked.

"I forgot the buttermilk, so I have to add that now." Hopefully this would still work and he wouldn't be too far behind.

When there were five minutes left, he was just finishing the fondant frogs that were supposed to decorate the cupcakes, and he still had to do the buttercream. Crap.

He grabbed all the ingredients and quickly started mixing them, then glanced over at Peter, who couldn't figure out how to use his stand mixer.

"One minute!"

The buttercream was runny, but it was too late to do anything about that now. Ryan slopped some on top of each cupcake, followed by the little fondant frogs.

The judges proclaimed his cupcakes a little dry and weren't impressed with his buttercream. Or his fondant work.

It was no surprise that Leanna Cox won the cupcake round. Hers were clearly the best. Logan's cupcakes had been declared "too sweet" and his curd "very lumpy." Peter's had been described as "not cupcakes, but a mess of sugar, flour, eggs, and butter in a muffin tin."

Ryan would have to do better tomorrow. Whoever won two rounds won the competition, and in the event that nobody won more than one round, it was at the judges' discretion—usually, whoever won the final round.

It would all come down to cake.

**"THE THEME," JOEY** Fielder announced in his booming voice, "is Canada!" He stuck a red-and-white top hat with maple leaves on his head. "What will our contestants make? A giant beaver cake? A hockey cake with the Toronto Maple Leafs logo?"

The guest judge, who was from Vancouver, booed loudly.

"Hey!" Logan Burris said.

"Okay, everyone." Joey held up a hand. "You might not get a fair grade if you make a Leafs cake, so keep that in mind. You have two hours. Ready, set . . . go!"

Ryan picked up his pencil and start sketching in his *Baking Fail* notepad. Should he do a two-tiered cake with lots of red and white? Fondant maple leaves? A polar bear? A lumberjack drinking beer and eating poutine?

No, he definitely didn't have the fondant skills for that last one, and if he did a polar bear, it would probably end up looking like a seal.

Okay. Something with red and white fondant, including maple leaves. He'd make a maple walnut cake. It wasn't one of the basic recipes provided, but he remembered—vaguely—Lindsay's recipe. Maple walnut cake plus cream cheese buttercream—yes, that would be good. Perhaps he could make Nanaimo bars for some added decoration.

He ran off to the pantry to get ingredients. The pantry was filled with all manner of things he'd never heard of before, as well as the basics. Peter Irwin was distracted by the candy, but Ryan wouldn't let himself be like a kid in a candy store.

No, today he was in the zone.

Joey came around to ask everyone what they were baking.

"I'm making a chocolate hockey cake," Logan said, because of course he was making a hockey cake.

Leanna had opted for a Black Forest cake, which she planned to sculpt into a moose.

Joey walked over to Ryan. "What about you? I see you've got some maple syrup out."

"It's a maple walnut cake."

"Canadian flavors, too. I'm impressed."

"What about me?" Peter asked. "I'm making a poutine cake!"

"I can't wait," Joey deadpanned. "How are you going to decorate your cake, Ryan?"

"An extremely detailed buttercream version of Lake Louise. No biggie. Something I can easily whip up in half an hour."

"And what are you really making, Peter?"

"A vanilla sheet cake with a map of Canada on the top."

Ryan was careful not to forget any ingredients today, nor did he forget to grease the pans. Once the cakes were in the oven and he'd set the timer, he started on the bottom layer of the Nanaimo bars, then the cream cheese buttercream for the cake, which, unlike last time, was definitely not runny. Next was the custard-flavored buttercream for the Nanaimo bars.

He might not look as good as Lindsay did in the kitchen, but he sort of knew what he was doing.

"Shit!" someone shouted from the far end of the room.

"What happened, Logan?" Joey asked.

"I had my oven on broil."

Ryan rolled out some white fondant and started cutting out maple leaves. He was removing his cakes from the pans—for some reason, they'd stuck a little, but not too badly—when he looked over at Peter, who was doing the same thing. Except Peter's cake came out much less cleanly.

"Oh no," Peter said, after tasting some of the cake that had stuck to the pan. "I think I forgot the sugar. Crap, I don't have time to make another cake." He ran into the pantry.

Ryan wondered what Peter was getting in there, but he tried to focus on his own bake. He wouldn't let himself feel cocky because it seemed like his was going better than the others'.

"Ryan, are you melting chocolate in the microwave?" Joey asked. "Any tips, judges, so he doesn't start a fire?"

Before anyone could answer, Logan exclaimed, "Oh no, my head fell off!"

"Sorry to say, but you're mistaken," Joey said. "Your head is still firmly attached to your body. No decapitation in sight."

Logan held up a small, headless figurine, made out of modeling chocolate or fondant.

Ryan was applying buttercream to the outside of his cake when the guest judge shouted, "Ten minutes!"

Oh shit.

Ryan pulled his Nanaimo bars out of the blast chiller. The top chocolate layer had solidified . . . mostly. Maybe a couple more minutes. Then he rolled out the red fondant and draped it over the cake, followed by applying his white maple leaves.

Next, it was back to the Nanaimo bars, which he still had to cut up.

"Five, four, three, two, one . . . step away from your cakes!" Joey said.

And now for the moment of truth.

Once again, Logan Burris was first. His hockey cake included a large Zamboni, as well as a model of himself—no longer headless—and a model of a nameless Montreal Canadiens player in a fight. (Well, the Canadiens player was lying, bloodied, on the ice.) When he spun it around to give the judges a better view of the hockey players, the Zamboni tumbled onto the floor.

"At least you're not beating up a Vancouver player," the guest judge said.

Logan's cake was very dry and his buttercream grainy, though it earned the high praise of being "barely edible."

The judges moved on to Leanna.

"It was supposed to be a moose, wasn't it?" the first judge said.

"Looks more like a dog to me," Joey said. "A very sick dog."

Leanna cut into her sculpted cake and served the judges a slice.

The guest judge tried a bite. "You went a bit heavy on the fondant, and it could use more buttercream, but not bad at all."

Ryan's cake was next.

"Where's the picture of Lake Louise that you promised us?" Joey asked.

"Oh, that ended up being just a little too complicated." Ryan flashed a smile. "But if I'd had an extra five minutes, I'm sure I could have pulled it off."

"It actually looks like a cake," the first judge said. "Which should go without saying, but in this competition, that's still an accomplishment."

Ryan executed a bow.

"And you made Nanaimo bars to decorate the top," the second judge said.

They each tried a few bites, and Ryan held his breath, anxious for their verdict.

"Wow." The first judge smiled. "That's nearly good enough to serve my wife. You left the cake in maybe a minute or two too long, but it's pretty tasty."

The guest judge looked delighted to eat something that wasn't completely terrible.

Was it good enough to beat Leanna? Ryan hoped so.

"Thanks, Ryan," Joey said. "Now, Peter, show us your Canada-themed cake."

Peter gestured to the . . . *thing* on his display table.

"Peter," Joey said, "what *is* that?"

"It's a vanilla sheet cake with a map of Canada on top, as promised."

"It looks like Rice Krispies Treats covered in candy."

"There may have been a couple catastrophes in the baking process."

"Only a couple?"

"That's really stretching the definition of a cake," the first judge said.

"It doesn't look like any kind of map I've ever seen," the guest judge added.

Peter crossed his arms. "That's due to the lack of duct tape."

Everyone laughed. Duct tape was how his character had solved all his problems on *Chinook Diner*.

The brave judges tried Peter's concoction.

"How does it taste?" Peter asked.

"No comment," the first judge said.

Ryan was feeling reasonably good about his chances as the judges conferred, and now that he was here, he wanted to win even more than before. His creations might not have been professional quality, but he thought he'd proved he was the best baker here.

Hadn't he?

He restrained from fidgeting as he waited.

"The winner of the cake round," Joey said at last, "is Ryan Kwok, which means Ryan is the winner of our first celebrity episode of *Baking Fail*. Congratulations!" He handed Ryan a lopsided cupcake trophy.

"Thank you," Ryan said.

He really was pleased, especially when he saw the giant check made out to an immigrant and refugee health organization—the one his mother had donated to every year. He couldn't wait to tell Lindsay he'd won, though she'd have to promise not to tell anyone else until the episode aired.

There were still interviews to film, but they took a break and the cakes were offered to the crew. A couple of people helped themselves to Leanna's and Ryan's cakes. Nobody touched Peter's so-called cake. A brave cameraman spent a long time staring at Logan's cake, then helped himself to Logan's modeling chocolate head.

Ryan wished he could go to Lindsay right now, but it would be a few hours before they wrapped up here. He wondered how her day was going.

He quickly looked at his phone. He had a bunch of texts, but nothing made sense until he checked social media.

Oh God. If only he'd been more careful.

What was he getting her into? Why would she want to be with him when she was subjected to *this*?

# CHAPTER 32

U h, Lindsay." Noreen walked into the kitchen and held up her phone. "I think you should see this."

Lindsay turned her attention back to the red velvet cupcakes. "I'm busy."

"It's one o'clock. Take your lunch break. I'll frost the cupcakes."

Usually, Lindsay would have had lunch by now, but Beth was out sick today, and so she was busier than usual. No big deal.

But Noreen sounded really insistent.

"What is it?" Lindsay asked.

"People have figured out that you and Ryan Kwok are dating."

*Oh.* Lindsay's stomach dropped.

She headed to the small office where she and Ryan had fooled around—she couldn't help thinking of that whenever she was here now—and started eating her sandwich as she pulled out her phone.

She didn't have Twitter and Instagram accounts under her name; she just had the bakery accounts. Someone had tagged Kensington Bake Shop. That must be how Noreen had noticed.

Things moved fast on Twitter, and it took Lindsay a while to sort out what had happened.

It had started when someone tweeted, I think I saw Ryan Kwok on a date! accompanied by a photo of Ryan and Lindsay eating ice cream last night. They'd returned to the rolled ice cream shop from their first date, because even though she was trying to keep a little distance from him, she'd thought he deserved a treat after his first day of *Baking Fail*.

A bunch of people had tagged him, but it was possible Ryan hadn't noticed since he was filming today. Plus, he had a much bigger following than Kensington Bake Shop, and she was pretty sure he only got notifications from people he followed. Although she thought he'd mentioned having an assistant to keep an eye on things for him?

Anyway, since he'd posted about taking baking classes here not long ago, someone had likely looked at their website and noticed the photo of Lindsay, the same woman who'd been on the date. That was how they'd figured it out.

Raquel entered the room as Lindsay was scrolling through Twitter.

"Is this true?" Raquel squeaked. "That you and Ryan Kwok are dating?"

Lindsay nodded.

"That explains several of the odd phone calls and inquiries we've had today. I thought they were about him doing *Baking Fail*, which was supposed to be a secret, so I brushed them off, but . . ."

Business had increased slightly in the past couple of weeks. Lindsay hadn't been sure whether to attribute it to the donut-beer event or to Ryan tweeting about his lessons. There had been a couple of related phone calls, but not many . . . until now.

When Raquel left, Lindsay returned her attention to her phone, to all the things people were saying about her.

*Aww, they're cute together!*

*Lucky woman.*

*Is she Asian? I can't tell.*

*The way he's looking at her!!*

*Why is he wearing a shirt?*

*Is she wearing RUNNING SHOES on their date?*

*How did she get a guy like him? What's her secret?* ☺

*Maybe if we cut into his abs, we'll discover they're made of cake.*

*I don't think that's Ryan Kwok. It's Melvin Lee.*

> *It's definitely Ryan Kwok, you dumbass.*

> *I was making a joke about how people always mix them up.*

*I NEED another season of JANYS. Why did that show get canceled??*

*Dean Kobayashi or Ryan Kwok? Who do you think is hotter?*

*Hey, @RyanKwoksFather, did you know about your son's girlfriend?*

> *Maybe she's not his girlfriend. He hasn't said anything about having a girlfriend.*

*Ryan, will you take me on a date? Please?*

There were so. Many. Tweets. Many of them were fine, but some were disturbing. People were commenting on her body. Her clothes.

She hadn't wanted to get in too deep with Ryan, but now the world knew about them.

Okay, they weren't being followed around by the paparazzi like the royals in England, and Ryan wasn't a megastar. But would people be waiting for her outside the bakery today?

Did someone know where he lived? Would they wait to see if she entered his building?

Some of the comments were confirmation of what she knew. In comparison to Ryan—who had his name and face on posters— she was spectacularly ordinary.

Not that she was down on herself. She liked her life. She was proud of her accomplishments. But she wasn't in his echelon, and some people were pointing that out. It was different hearing it come from others rather than herself.

She went back to work as soon as she finished her sandwich, needing to take her mind off this until she could talk to Ryan.

Lindsay didn't let herself check her phone for the rest of the afternoon. She stayed busy in the kitchen. When she left for home, she headed out the back door, just in case.

She didn't look at her phone again until after she'd showered, until she was wearing pajamas and eating instant noodles from the Korean grocery store. Vivian was still at work.

Then, finally, Lindsay looked at Twitter once more.

*Is Ryan Kwok getting a dad bod?* asked a so-called entertainment journalist. The tweet included a picture of Ryan from *That Kind of Wedding*, compared with a more recent shirtless picture from Instagram.

His abs were a little less defined.

They were also still pretty damn spectacular.

*Is Ryan Kwok's new girlfriend to blame for his changing physique?*

There was speculation that he was sitting around eating cake and donuts all day.

Of course, many people were tearing these tweets apart.

*I'd be VERY happy to date a man with this so-called dad bod. He looks amazing either way. I mean, check out his incredible bone structure.*

*The guy on the right looks more fun. Like he's eaten carbs sometime in the past year.*

*Does having a dad bod simply mean you don't have a six-pack that could cut diamonds?*

    *This is an absurd statement. Diamonds are a ten on the Mohs scale of hardness.*

    *Don't you know what hyperbole is?*

*It's ridiculous to expect every man to look like a chiseled superhero. Do you know how much work it takes to maintain a body like that? Is it even healthy?*

*I think his body is exactly the same in both pictures, but there are tricks that can make abs look more defined. Maybe it's just good lighting. Or dehydration . . .*

*I don't understand the love for this guy. He doesn't do anything for me, and no, it's not because I'm racist.*

*Can we please cancel the term "dad bod"?*

*It's time for a new hashtag #RyanKwokNoAbs*

Dear God.

She kept scrolling, her horror growing with every moment.

How on earth did Ryan manage to stay sane when he got shit like this?

She also felt a strange sense of guilt. The reason he wasn't carefully following his diet was because he was going on dates with her. Because they were baking cakes and going out for ice cream together, and those things weren't compatible with having a body like a superhero.

It was his choice to indulge in the occasional donut, though. She wasn't forcing him. And maintaining a body like Albert Nguyen's wouldn't allow donuts and such.

Most people were on Ryan's side. They spoke of unrealistic expectations of male stars and how having no body fat probably wasn't healthy. They said he looked great.

Still, Lindsay couldn't help feeling like she was holding him back. Without her, it would be easier for him to keep up a ridiculous fitness regimen.

Or maybe he wouldn't.

But she wondered if she was holding him back in other ways, too. She was pretty, but she wouldn't be a knockout on the red carpet, and even if Ryan didn't have abs that could cut diamonds, with his looks, he could get a knockout to accompany him to awards shows.

Plus, he was a genuinely good guy.

He was on his way up in the entertainment world, but she didn't have any connections that could help him.

And she didn't like this kind of attention. Perhaps it would help with business, but she didn't need it to succeed. The bakery had been doing fine before this.

She massaged her temples and lay back on the couch, waiting for Vivian to come home or Ryan to call.

**ALTHOUGH IT WAS** dark, Lindsay wore sunglasses and approached Ryan's building stealthily. Not that she really had any idea how to avoid paparazzi, or if there would be any.

She made it inside without incident, but then again, she hadn't noticed anyone taking a picture of her at the ice cream place last night.

Ryan was a sweetheart about the whole thing. He'd already had a long talk with his publicist, or whomever he talked to about such issues. He told Lindsay, over and over, not to listen to idiots on Twitter and that she was beautiful and perfect for him. He assured her that it was good he'd had more cheat meals than usual in the past month, and that he'd been taking the time to enjoy himself.

"I feel like I'm holding you back," she whispered.

"What are you talking about? Of course not. Quite the opposite. In fact . . ." He shot her a lopsided smile. "You helped me win *Baking Fail*."

"You won?" she squeaked, then threw her arms around him. "That's awesome!"

"My cake wasn't too bad, if I do say so myself." Then he sobered. "Are you sure you want to do this with me?"

"Well, if you—"

"I'm asking what *you* want."

The internet, in all its glory, had discovered their relationship—and that was hardly taking it slow. But it had already happened, and he'd done his best to assuage her fears.

When she looked at him now, she didn't see a man whose face and body graced the big screen. She just saw Ryan, and something built up in her chest, and she couldn't say no.

"I want to keep doing this."

His smile fucking lit her up. It was nearly enough to blast away the doubts at the back of her head, though they still lingered.

"If you're willing," he said, "we can take a proper picture together—one in which we're both looking at the camera—and I'll post it. Some people will say terrible shit, but you can ignore the trolls."

He made it sound easy, but she supposed he was used to it. You had to learn to let stuff like this roll off you.

"We don't have to," he said. "If you'd prefer not."

"No, I want to do it." Everyone was speculating. It would be better if they *knew*. Right?

"I'm very good at selfies." He winked at her. "Just saying."

They took a few pictures on his couch, and he put the best one on Twitter and Instagram, and she tried not to obsess over the responses.

*Tried* being the key word.

# CHAPTER 33

The following Thursday, Dad posted another old picture on Twitter, tagged again with #TBT. This was a shot of Ryan running through the sprinkler at the age of seven.

Dad was posting old pictures every Thursday now.

Was he bored?

Was he sentimental?

Ryan scrubbed a hand over his face and had another sip of his protein shake.

His phone rang. It was his brother-in-law, and a thread of fear immediately curled through him.

"What's up, Winston?" Ryan asked.

They got along fine, but in the five years that Jenna and Winston had been together . . . well, Ryan hadn't been around a lot, not until recently. Winston never called him.

"Jenna wants to see you today," Winston said. "She . . . I think she really needs the company. She has an appointment with her doctor this afternoon because we think she has postpartum depression, so if you could make sure she gets to that, it would be great. I . . ." He trailed off, and a minute later, Jenna was on the phone.

"I can't take Ezra to the appointment," she whispered. "The thought of getting him into the car—he hates the car and he always cries—and being in the waiting room with him . . . it's overwhelming." She sighed. "What kind of mother can't even take a short car ride with their baby? I didn't sleep at all last night, though Ezra had a good night. I—"

"Can't Winston take the day off?" Ryan asked.

Not that Ryan wasn't willing to go, but how the hell was Winston leaving for work when she was like this?

"He's already an hour late," Jenna said. "He has an important meeting this afternoon, and he's taking next week off. Please, Ryan. I really need someone else to be here today."

"Of course." This was why he was in Toronto. "I'll look after Ezra during your appointment. If you want to go to the bookstore afterward or meet a friend at a coffee shop, I'll take care of everything."

"You will?" She sounded skeptical, but he detected a tiny bit of hope. He'd mentioned the bookstore and coffee shop because those were happy places to Jenna.

"Yeah, of course," he said, as if he'd looked after a baby a hundred times before.

*Ryan, you don't know anything about babies. You've rocked him to sleep. Once.*

"Um, I'll find someone to bring with me, if that's okay." He wasn't sure she'd be okay with it. She might be self-conscious about anyone seeing her like this.

But she didn't seem to care.

"Yes, that's fine. I just . . . I can't do this for another full day by myself. It's not that I don't love him, but . . ."

"No, no, I totally understand."

He didn't know what it was like to be pregnant, give birth, and devote two months to looking after a baby. But he was good at putting himself in someone else's shoes, and it wasn't hard to believe that would be tough. On top of the grief, which he knew all about.

"I'll—we'll—be there in an hour or two," he promised.

Shit. Now he had to find someone who was free on a Thursday morning to look after a baby.

He immediately called Lindsay. Not because he thought she should come with him—he'd feel guilty asking her to leave work.

When she didn't answer her phone, he called the bakery. They weren't open yet, but fortunately someone picked up, and he asked to speak to Lindsay.

"What's up?" she asked.

It was reassuring, just hearing the sound of her voice.

"My sister is . . . not doing well, and she needs help looking after the baby today. I was wondering if you knew someone who could help me. I can pay them, that's not a problem."

"I have to be at the bakery, and so does Noreen, but what about my mom? My mom's great with babies. And she's retired."

Ryan hesitated. He'd never met a girlfriend's parent before. This wasn't how he'd imagined it happening. "Are you sure you're okay with me meeting your mother?"

"Yep. But I'd prefer to introduce you. She lives nearby, so maybe she can meet you at the bakery, and then you can drive from here? I'm pretty sure she'll say yes."

This *was* a little alarming.

Ryan was usually happy to meet new people. Wasn't the sort of thing that bothered him. But this was Lindsay's mom.

Still, if she could help him look after Ezra, he'd deal. For Jenna.

Lindsay ended the call, and a few minutes later, she texted, telling him to be there in half an hour. He sent a text to his personal trainer to cancel their afternoon session.

Exactly half an hour later, he walked through the bakery door. Lindsay smiled when she saw him, which made his smile broaden.

"This is Ryan," Lindsay said to the middle-aged woman standing beside her. "Ryan, this is my mother, Alice."

Alice shook his hand and looked at him with an assessing gaze. They exchanged a few pleasantries before Lindsay insisted on giving them some donuts, and he led Alice to his car.

Once they were on the road, she said, "I know you're some hotshot movie star, but I only care that you treat my daughter well. Okay?"

He shot her a quick smile before turning back to the road. "I'm doing my best."

"It's not enough for you to *try* to treat her well. You *will* do it."

"The last thing I want is to hurt Lindsay."

Although he'd never met a girlfriend's mom or dad in real life, he had some experience with this on-screen. *That Kind of Wedding*, for example, had included a memorable meet-the-parents scene near the end of the movie.

Unfortunately, he'd had a glass of wine thrown in his face during it, and his character in *Just Another New York Sitcom* had also fared poorly when meeting the parents of a girlfriend.

But surely these things went all right in real life sometimes.

"Well," Alice said, "you better not hurt her. I spent a lot of time googling to see if you had a reputation for being a womanizer."

A choked sound escaped his lips. "What did you find?"

"Very little, but maybe I don't know where to look. But just know, I'm paying attention."

Conversation petered out after that.

He spent most of the car ride making a mental list of horrible things she could do to him if she didn't approve of how he treated Lindsay.

He really hoped Alice was good with babies.

They arrived at the town house in good time, and when Ryan

knocked on the door, they heard various noises coming from inside, but it took a while for Jenna to come to the door. Ezra was in her arms, wailing at the top of his lungs.

"He won't stop," Jenna whispered. "No matter what I do . . ."

"Let me take him," Alice said firmly.

Jenna turned to Ryan. "Who did you bring?"

"This is Lindsay's mother, Alice."

"Lindsay's mom," Jenna repeated. Normally there might be some inflection in her voice, but today, it was flat. Her hair was a mess and it looked like Ezra had spit up on her more than once, but that was to be expected for parents of small babies, right?

It was her tone of voice, the helpless look in her eyes, that frightened him.

*Nothing* could happen to anyone else in his family.

Jenna handed Alice the baby.

"You're so cute!" Alice said to the pinched-up face trying to destroy everyone's hearing. "Look at all this hair." She walked up and down the hall, bouncing the baby in her arms, and he quieted within a few minutes.

"How come he wouldn't calm down for me?" Jenna said. "I walked with him just like that, and he kept wailing. I'm his *mother*." She looked like she was past the point of being able to cry, which was terrifying.

"He's very smart," Alice said. "He knew you needed a break, and that's why he was making a fuss. What's his name?"

"Ezra," Ryan said.

"Ezra! You'll have lots of fun with me and your uncle Ryan today, okay? We'll give your mommy a break." Alice turned to Jenna. "What about your mother? She's in the area, isn't she? Has she been helping you?"

Jenna's mouth opened, but no words came out.

"Our mother died six months ago," Ryan said, wishing he'd mentioned this in the car.

"While you were pregnant? You poor girl. What about your father?"

"I haven't talked to him in weeks," Jenna said. "He never visits."

"I think he's going through some things," Ryan said. "Since Mom died, you know. I call him regularly, but he doesn't usually pick up the phone."

"He's one of these men who cannot talk about feelings?"

"Among other things."

"What about your in-laws?" Alice asked Jenna. "Do they help you? Or do they cause too much stress?"

"They aren't in Toronto." Jenna looked overwhelmed by all the questions.

"Go have a shower and get ready for your appointment," Ryan said. "We'll be fine."

Jenna headed upstairs while he and Alice sat down on the couch. She handed him the baby. He worried he'd do something she disapproved of, but she didn't critique the way he held Ezra.

"Thank you very much," he said. "For coming with me today, even though you don't know me or my family."

Alice waved this off. "It's fine. I like babies, and I haven't gotten to play with one in so long. No grandchildren yet, you understand." She gave him a meaningful look.

He stilled, feeling slightly alarmed. He hadn't known Lindsay for all that long . . .

"I'm teasing!" Alice said. "Don't worry."

He kept comparing Alice to his mom, which he probably wouldn't be doing if Alice were white. Not that she looked much like his mom, and having grown up in Canada, Alice spoke English without an accent.

But she still made him think of his mother. Miss his mother.

Well, he was always missing her, but sometimes he missed her in different ways.

"What do you think of the lamp today, Ezra?" Ryan shifted the baby in his arms so he could see the lamp.

Ezra responded by giving Ryan a slightly curious stare and opening his mouth, and at that moment, Ryan was a goner.

He couldn't help grinning at his nephew.

"Do you remember me, buddy?" He had no idea if babies could remember people they saw once a week.

He decided to try a little game.

He held a baby blanket in front of his face, then pulled it down, widened his eyes, and said, "Peekaboo!"

Ryan wasn't sure whether Ezra understood the game, but he still managed a tiny smile. Ryan didn't think he'd ever seen his nephew smile before, and it was delightful.

He did it again, and Alice took a picture.

"Don't worry," she said. "I'm not putting it on social media. Just sending it to Lindsay."

Ezra soon tired of the game, but he was content to grab the blanket, decorated in turtles.

Jenna came back downstairs and gave them instructions, not all of which Ryan understood. After she left, Ezra, perhaps sensing her absence, became fussy, but Alice said he was probably just tired. She showed Ryan how to change a diaper, and then he put on the carrier, where Ezra would snooze. At first, there was a bit of wailing, but the baby soon quieted.

"All right," Alice said approvingly. "Can I borrow your car?"

Ryan raised his eyebrows.

"There's not much food in the house," she said.

When had she looked in the fridge? He hadn't noticed.

"I thought I'd go grocery shopping, then make some meals for them, okay? I will explain how to feed him if he wakes up while I'm gone."

Ten minutes later, Ryan was alone with Ezra, who was still peacefully napping, his fist under his chin. Ryan thought his nephew looked cuter as time passed. Newborn babies were tiny and slightly odd-looking, but Ezra was getting quite handsome now.

Ryan pulled out his phone and texted Lindsay, thanking her again and letting her know everything was okay. As soon as he sent the text, however, Ezra woke up and started fussing, so Ryan sang "Twinkle, Twinkle, Little Star." He breathed out a sigh of relief when Ezra fell asleep once more.

When Alice returned an hour later, Ryan was attempting to feed Ezra, with little success.

"I'll take over while you put the food away," she said. "He's probably not used to taking a bottle."

She managed to coax Ezra to feed, then handed him back to Ryan and started trying to find things in the kitchen.

"You really don't need to . . ." Ryan began.

"It's no problem. It's nice to have something to do for once."

She bustled about the kitchen, making both pasta salad and chickpea salad in half an hour, occasionally taking breaks to play with Ezra.

"Thank you so much," Ryan said again. "I really appreciate it." He took out his wallet and handed her some cash. "For the groceries."

She waved this away.

"I'm a rich movie star. I can afford it." He shook the cash in his hand.

"Ah, fine," Alice said, "since you're a *rich* movie star, I'll take it."

Ryan refrained from saying he wasn't really *that* rich because he didn't want her to give the money back.

When Jenna got home, she didn't say much about what had transpired at the doctor's appointment, and he felt like it wasn't his business to ask. But she mumbled something about therapy, and she was holding an Indigo bag with books in it.

She reached for Ezra as soon as she washed her hands, and this time, he didn't wail. He happily slapped her cheeks instead. She didn't say anything to him, but she looked slightly better than she had earlier. Of course, one appointment and trip to the bookstore couldn't fix everything, but it was a good start.

"Would you like us to stay longer?" Ryan asked.

"No, Winston will be home in a couple hours. I'll be fine until then."

"Are you sure?"

"Yes, *Ryan*."

He was pleased she sounded so annoyed with him.

"I can help you tomorrow," Alice said.

"Oh, you really don't—"

"But I didn't get enough time to play with you today, did I, Ezra?" She booped the baby's nose. "I'll come after lunch."

"I can drive you," Ryan said.

"No, you visit on Monday or Tuesday, now that you're an expert on babies. Tomorrow is Lindsay's day off, right? You can spend it with her."

He stifled a laugh at her bossing them around and trying to arrange their lives, when they'd only met a few hours before. But in truth, he rather liked it.

Because, yeah, it did remind him of his own mother.

"Give me your phone," Alice said. "I'll get your dad's number and tell him to visit."

Ryan and Jenna looked at each other.

"What? My late husband was great with babies." She paused. "You knew about Lindsay's father, didn't you?"

"I knew he had passed," Ryan said. "I didn't know he was good with babies."

"Make your dad do something for you," she said to Jenna. "It will be good for him, too. Get him out of the house. He had two children, so surely he knows something about babies."

"I'll call him." Ryan didn't want to unleash Alice on his father.

"Why won't you give me your phone? Does it have nude photos of my daughter?"

This conversation had taken a horrifying turn.

The only positive thing was that Jenna chuckled at his pain, damn her.

**RYAN CALLED HIS** father when he got home. Disappointingly—but unsurprisingly—there was no answer.

He heated up his dinner and checked social media, and it wasn't long before he stumbled upon a Buzzfeed article titled "12 Reasons Why Ryan Kwok's Father Is the Best Dad on Twitter." The article included twelve of his father's tweets and discussed how #relatable Ryan and his father's relationship was.

Ryan couldn't help laughing.

Obviously, the media getting a skewed perspective on something was nothing new, and what you showed to the world was often different from the full truth.

> *@RyanKwoksFather, why are you better at replying to tweets than answering my calls?*

Ryan deleted the words rather than tweeting.

He wouldn't let family drama play out on social media. Social media was for posting thirst trap pictures of himself and the occasional funny observation. Tweeting about his movies and interview appearances, and supporting other Asian people in the entertainment industry. He didn't post his whole life on there.

He looked down at his phone and realized his father had retweeted the article.

*You're definitely home, Dad. Why don't you answer when I call?*

Then his phone buzzed. A text from Lindsay: Would you like me to come over tonight?

# CHAPTER 34

Lindsay suspected Ryan could use a treat after spending half the day with her mother, so on the walk to Ryan's condo, she picked up bubble tea. They'd only had bubble tea together once, many weeks ago now, but she still remembered what he'd ordered. She got a small one of those, as well as honeydew milk tea with pearls for herself.

When she arrived at the door of his suite—without any paparazzi sightings, thank God—he opened it up and smiled at her. He looked a little tired, and her heart squeezed.

"I brought you bubble tea!" She held up the peach green tea with jellies, half-sweet.

"You're the best." He leaned in to kiss her, making sparks shoot all the way up her body.

They sat down on his couch with their tea.

"How's your sister?" she asked.

"I think the break was good for her, and hopefully the doctor will help. Her husband is taking next week off, so that's good, and your mom insisted on going back tomorrow."

"I hope my mom wasn't too, uh, domineering."

"She wanted to call my dad, but I wouldn't let her."

"She texted me and said she liked you. Said you weren't as pretentious and full of yourself as she feared."

"I'm glad she liked me. That's important to me." He held up his beverage. "Thank you for bringing this. Did you do it because of the thread on Twitter?"

"What thread?"

A smile tugged at the corner of his lips, and he picked up his phone and showed her.

Someone had made a thread of "Ryan Kwok as Bubble Tea." There were ten tweets, each showing a picture of bubble tea on the left and a picture of Ryan on the right. The color of the tea had been matched to his outfits. The first tweet had been retweeted a couple of thousand times. He scrolled down to something that looked like it could be honeydew milk tea, and next to it was a smiling Ryan, wearing a pale green dress shirt with the top two buttons undone. The color wouldn't look good on most people, but he pulled it off. The next tea was a light orange and it was paired with a shirtless picture. Of course there was a shirtless picture.

People made posts like this about her boyfriend. It was still dizzying to think about.

Yet despite it all, Ryan was a well-adjusted guy. He was wonderful in so many ways.

She thought of how he looked after his family. When he'd called her this morning, there had been barely a moment's hesitation when she'd suggested her mom. She'd thought she'd gone too far with that suggestion, but she couldn't think of anyone else—and he'd agreed. He'd just wanted to help his sister.

In contrast, the boyfriend who'd dumped her a month after her father's funeral had the emotional intelligence of a rock. Well, no. That was probably unkind to rocks. Though to be fair, they'd been in their early twenties. She was older now, and Ryan was a couple of years older than she was.

He was in tune with how people felt, and he always listened, always tried to be supportive and kind. Okay, they'd had a bit of a tiff when they first met and he knocked over her donuts, but he was honest and tried to do the right thing. She was sure that had contributed to his success, in addition to his looks. He had good people skills, but he wasn't completely smooth and charming all the time. And the way he'd bought her all those beers and bath products because he didn't know what she'd like . . .

"I love you."

She hadn't meant to say that. Hadn't even consciously thought it before the words escaped her lips.

She didn't take it back, though. Because it was true.

Lindsay did love him, and it wouldn't have happened with just anyone. It had been seven long years since she'd had a relationship, but somehow, she'd been able to get close to him. She'd tried to pull back, because it had been hard to believe they could last, but now she believed. If people occasionally posted pictures of them together on Twitter, she could deal with it. She'd ignore the ugly comments. It was a small price to pay.

She threw her arms around Ryan, and he gently hugged her back.

But he didn't say the words, and his smile had disappeared.

*Oh.* It was as if the bottom had fallen out of her stomach.

She'd thought he'd easily return her words; she'd *felt* like he loved her. But now her doubts came roaring back. Sure, he was good to her, and he'd never intentionally hurt her, but maybe he couldn't love her. Maybe he wouldn't want to be with her longterm. He needed someone, well, more like him—as she'd thought before.

She had a fortifying sip of tea. "I should go."

"Don't," he said, wrapping his hand around her wrist.

That word was enough for now. She didn't go.

He pulled her into his lap and embraced her. Though she felt a little better, her mind was spinning.

They hadn't been together all that long. Perhaps it took him a while to fall in love, and he'd return her words in time.

But she wasn't comforted by that thought.

She should have known better than to get involved with someone like him, but at the same time, she couldn't bring herself to leave.

HE DID LOVE her. That was the worst part.

But Ryan hadn't been able to say the words. They'd stuck in his throat—and that wasn't like him, not being able to get the words out. This woman really had him twisted inside out.

She had him wanting to say something he'd never said to anyone before.

Not even his family. They didn't exchange "I love yous." His father was allergic to hugs and any expression of feelings. His mom had showed her affection by calling him every other day and, when he was in Toronto, by bringing him food he didn't need.

Then there were romantic relationships. Or his lack thereof.

*I love you.*

Those words were terrifying, in part because he knew how it felt to lose someone he loved, but also because he kept fucking up with people he loved. How could he possibly have a good relationship with Lindsay when he couldn't fix his family? When his best hope of hearing from his father was to tweet at him? When he'd never had a relationship like this before?

He turned toward her in bed, watching her chest rise and fall as she slept. She'd brought him bubble tea a few hours ago, and the small gesture had made him glow.

They'd had lazy sex, but he wouldn't be surprised if he woke up in the middle of the night and she was gone. He could feel her slipping away.

Fuck, why hadn't he been able to say the words? Or talk to her about it?

He looked at the clock. He'd been lying in bed for two hours, wide awake. Maybe it was partly because he hadn't done his workout today, but he knew that wasn't most of it.

It was because of the woman beside him, who deserved better than what he'd given her.

She deserved to know how he felt, but it was easier to take off his shirt and post pictures for the world to see than it was to say three short words.

# CHAPTER 35

I'll be in Toronto next week. Want to have lunch on
Thursday?

Sure, sounds good, Ryan replied. It would be nice to catch up
with Irene. He hadn't seen her since the promo tour for *That Kind
of Wedding.*

He finished his shake and sat down on the couch. It was six in
the evening on a Friday—Dad should be home now.

He called, and his father answered on the second ring.

Well, this was a nice surprise.

"What do you want now?" Dad demanded.

"Can't I just call my dad?"

"Why do you have to call all the time?"

"I'm only trying to talk to you twice a week," Ryan said. "How
are you doing?"

"Aiyah, why do you always ask that?"

"Because your wife died six months ago and you never talk
about it. Because I care and I genuinely want an answer. Because
I'm your son."

"We never used to talk twice a week."

"Mom and I talked more than that. Often not for long, but we did talk regularly."

"You and I never did."

"Maybe we should have. Now she's gone, and we have no idea how to communicate with each other. You never tried to understand me, even a little. You'd just huff and say I should go back to engineering."

Dad grunted.

"You don't call Jenna, either. She's not doing well. She needs support. But did you know that? Probably not, even though she's exactly the daughter you wanted. Studied what you approved of, got a job in that field. I visited her to help with Ezra yesterday, and I brought Lindsay's mom with me."

"Who's Lindsay?"

"The woman whose toothbrush you saw in my washroom."

"Ah. The one who appeared in those pictures with you, eating ice cream."

Did Dad sound bitter that he hadn't heard more about her before seeing the picture on Twitter? But why should he know more, when he never tried to talk to Ryan?

"You shouldn't have involved someone else in family matters," Dad said.

Ryan rarely got angry, but dammit. "Who was supposed to help? You? No, you were at work—which is fine, I don't blame you for that. But Jenna needs you and you're never there. You're her *father*, and yes, I know you've been struggling—"

"I'm not struggling," Dad snapped.

"Right, because you can never admit to having feelings."

Dad grunted again.

It was like speaking to a bad-tempered brick wall.

"So, that's how it is?" Ryan said. "You're not going to talk at all. No, you just post pictures of me as a child online."

"Leave the internet out of this."

In a different situation, that might have made Ryan laugh, but he wasn't in the mood.

Why couldn't they even have a conversation?

Why did she have to die?

"I miss her," Ryan said. "A lot. I wish I could tell her about the baking lessons and being on the show. I wish she could see it. I'm sure she would have gotten a kick out of it."

Dad still said nothing.

"Fine. You can have what you want. I won't bother trying to talk to you anymore. But you should call Jenna."

And Ryan hung up.

He kept his phone in his hand for five minutes afterward, even though he didn't look at the screen. Some optimistic part of him hoped his father would call him back and apologize for being a cantankerous old bastard.

He wasn't surprised when that call didn't come, but he couldn't help being disappointed.

Of course he'd talk to his father again, but he'd wait a month or so. Clearly his dad wasn't interested in being a big part of his life, unlike his mom. And that was okay. It would have to be okay, because that was what he had.

He slumped on the sofa and considered asking Lindsay to come over. He could make her something for dinner, take his mind off things. Maybe have a bath with her, using one of the many products on his bathroom counter. Or all of them, like some kind of Franken-bath. It might leave them smelling strange, but they'd smell strange together.

Then he could wrap her in his arms, press his nose to the crook of her neck—which might smell like some combination of coconut, rose, grapefruit, and lavender—and tell her about . . .

But he felt like he wasn't worthy of that.

He couldn't tell her that he loved her. He still couldn't get those words out or explain to her why he struggled with them. Yet, he wanted her comfort.

No, he wouldn't do that to Lindsay.


**"I'M SORRY ABOUT . . ."** Ryan trailed off, forgetting his words, not for the first time in the past few days. His brain had been mush lately. Good thing he wasn't filming *For the Blood* yet. He'd probably forget all his lines.

He was sorry about the rom-com that had been in development, the one Irene was supposed to star in, the one that was no longer getting made. But he'd forgotten the name of the project—he only remembered it was based on a bestselling novel.

Irene knew exactly what he was talking about, though.

"It's all right," she said. "You know this happens regularly. And it's not your fault."

They were at a restaurant patio near his condo for lunch, sandwiched in between important appearances Irene had to make while in Toronto. The patio was full of well-dressed people and expensive food. Irene was always well-dressed when she was in public, and today was no exception. He didn't know the designer, but her black dress looked quite chic.

*That Kind of Wedding* hadn't been Irene's first lead role in a film, and she'd become famous for playing Dr. Eve Xiao on a long-running TV show a decade earlier.

Whereas Ryan's show had been canceled after one season.

So when people glanced in their direction and whispered, he suspected most of them were recognizing her, not him, which was totally cool by Ryan.

He lifted a forkful of salad to his mouth. It was a "warm salad" but he always thought of salad as being served cold—what exactly made something a salad?

"Ryan?" Irene said.

"Sorry." He'd drifted off again.

"How are you doing? With your mom, I mean."

"Not great," he admitted, "but it's become more manageable over time, and I'm glad I've taken these months off."

"And you have a girlfriend now."

"I do." He smiled, but it felt forced.

If Irene noticed, she didn't say anything. She had a bite of her own salad—which wasn't the warm variety.

Feeling uncomfortable talking about himself, Ryan asked, "How's Bennett?"

"He's fine. On tour right now. But I've been getting harassed more online since our relationship became public. You know, as an Asian woman dating a white man, I'm a traitor, apparently. I knew this might happen, which is why I told Bennett I wanted to wait a little longer to announce it . . . but I understand. It's hard to keep under wraps."

"Jesus," Ryan muttered. "I'm sorry." The ways in which people could be terrible still surprised him at times, even though they shouldn't. It wasn't like he hadn't seen this happen before.

He squeezed Irene's hand, then withdrew.

And out of the corner of his eye, he saw someone taking a picture.

# CHAPTER 36

*Did romance blossom on the set of* That Kind of Wedding? *Irene Lai and Ryan Kwok spotted canoodling on Toronto patio.*

Against her better judgment, Lindsay read the article on the gossip site.

She knew it was nonsense.

She trusted Ryan. Some people might say she shouldn't—how could a guy be that inhumanly good-looking and also trustworthy?

But she did. And he'd told her about this lunch beforehand. He'd even invited her to come and meet Irene, saying they could eat somewhere near Kensington Bake Shop, but she'd felt a bit weird about the whole thing and declined. Though she'd like to meet Irene Lai, it would feel like she was using him for access to his famous friends.

There were two photos on the website. One was merely a picture of Irene eating a salad. No "canoodling" going on there.

In the other photo, Ryan had his hand over Irene's, but Lindsay assumed this was a brief, friendly pat. She'd touched Ryan that way, too, before anything had happened between them. Irene and Ryan had spent many weeks on set together; they were allowed to be friends.

Irene also had a boyfriend. Bennett Reed was the front man of a band that Lindsay had never particularly liked.

Yep, both Irene and Ryan had publicly acknowledged they were dating other people, but after a single photo of them on a patio, there was talk of them fooling around together?

If they were cheating, they were idiots to do it in such a public venue. Yorkville was likely a good place to get noticed in Toronto, and wasn't this particular restaurant known for being popular with celebrities?

Of course, some people thought straight men and women couldn't be friends, so . . .

Lindsay couldn't help searching "Ryan Kwok" on Twitter and reading what people had said about him today.

*I can't believe Ryan Kwok would do this to his girlfriend.*
*I refuse to believe it.*

*Ryan Kwok can get it, even with his dad bod.*

*Irene Lai is hotter than that baker he was supposedly dating.*

*They were definitely dating. He posted a picture of them together, and they looked cozier than he does with Irene Lai.*
*I don't think he's cheating.*

*Way to go, Ryan! Dr. Eve Xiao, eh?*

*Who is Ryan Kwok? Never heard of him before.*

*I didn't know Ryan Kwok was Canadian!*

*Irene Lai is a slut.*

*Irene Lai has no class.*

> *WTF is wrong with you? Irene Lai is the epitome of class.*
>
> *Stop using words you don't understand.*
>
> *#DoubleStandards*

*I think Ryan Kwok has a thing for exotic women.*

> *Are you serious?? He's an Asian man who's dated Asian women! Don't fucking call them exotic. What is wrong with you.*
>
> *Why don't Millennials know how to use punctuation?*

*I have no idea what's going on with Ryan Kwok's dating life, and I don't trust tabloids. But at least he's always been supportive of Asian women and hasn't thrown them under the bus. Unlike another Asian actor, who shall remain nameless . . . \*cough\* Ricky Shen \*cough\**

*Asians are taking over Hollywood.*

> *Two Asian actors have lunch together in Toronto and you think Asians are taking over Hollywood?? You're racist.*
>
> *I can't be racist. I'm married to a Korean.*

The comments were nauseating.

Multiple people had called the bakery this afternoon, asking for a comment from Lindsay, and that was when she'd learned about these photographs. But she hadn't allowed herself to look online until after work.

Ryan had also texted her, saying they should talk. He'd assured her there was nothing happening between him and Irene.

Suddenly, Lindsay couldn't help wondering how many times he and Irene had kissed.

Because they *had* kissed. For work.

There had been three kisses in the movie, if she remembered correctly. How many takes were needed to get each one right? How many people had been present when they were filmed? If she watched the movie now, would she flinch when she saw him make out with another woman?

Perhaps she would.

But she could deal with this, though it might take a little time to get used to it. *She* was the one he kissed in private. *She* was the one who ate dinner in bed with him.

And she was positive there was nothing between him and Irene, even if they'd had excellent chemistry on-screen.

And yet.

Even if he was hers for now, Lindsay imagined him ending up with someone more glamorous. He would never *say* she wasn't enough for him, but other people would.

*Who cares what those people online say? So many idiots feel free to say any stupid thing that pops into their head.*

The problem was that he might come to that conclusion, too, even if he'd be nice about it.

After all, he didn't love her.

She'd simply been convenient. In the right place at the right time. He'd needed someone in his life who'd listen—but at other times, help him forget—and she'd filled that role.

But that role wouldn't last forever.

She loved him, and he hadn't been able to say it back, and that was okay, it really was, not everyone fell in love at the same rate, that shouldn't mean anything . . .

Still, she couldn't help thinking of the interview she'd watched way back when, and she couldn't shake the feeling that he was just having a little fun with her, nothing more. There wasn't anything wrong with it, but the longer it lasted, the more she'd hurt.

She might have to end things now.

Instead of texting him back, she went on Twitter and read more stupid stuff that people had said. Yep, this was some quality adulting.

Ryan had tweeted twice.

*Would it distract everyone if I took off my shirt?*

*But seriously, Irene and I are not together. We're good friends, but we're both seeing other people.*

There was a noise in the quiet apartment, and Lindsay jumped. Right. It was just Vivian's key in the lock.

Vivian entered and slipped off her shoes. She was carrying a couple of plastic bags, which she placed on the kitchen table. "I brought sushi."

Why did Lindsay need a boyfriend when she had friends to bring her food?

From the odd look on Vivian's face, she must be doing this because she'd seen the pictures. Lindsay got them both plates and started digging into the sushi.

"So?" Vivian said, after watching Lindsay eat a quarter of the sushi. "You can't tell me you believe those gossip columnists."

"Of course not."

"Then why do you look like shit?"

"You brought me sushi just to tell me that I look like crap?"

Vivian sighed. "This is a lot for you to deal with, but I assume you'll get used to it, and once you and Ryan have been together for a while, people will lose interest."

Lindsay stuffed another piece of sushi in her mouth. "You think we'll stay together? You don't think he'll cheat on me with a supermodel or something like that?"

"Do *you* think that will happen?"

"No."

"Well, then. Ryan's been good to you, hasn't he?"

Lindsay's cheeks heated as she remembered the last night they'd spent together.

But that wasn't enough for a successful relationship.

# CHAPTER 37

As soon as Lindsay stepped into Ryan's place, he wrapped his arms around her.

She loved being in his arms. It felt so safe, in a way that nothing else did.

*But that's an illusion.*

"Hey," he said. "I'm so sorry about today. Everyone's reaction to me and Irene eating lunch together, in a very public location—that was completely out of hand."

"I trust you. That's not a problem. And I love you."

She paused, still hoping he'd return her words, but he didn't.

"But I'm not sure how this can work in the long-term," she said, forcing back her tears. "Because you're . . . not like me. There's a hashtag about your abs. You're in movies. And soon you'll be an even bigger star than you are now."

"You think that?"

"Yeah. Because you have an easy, honest charisma, and you're obviously very talented. You were nominated for a Golden Globe."

He chuckled. "Dad asked why it couldn't be an Oscar instead."

She managed a smile.

Yes, they were smiling with each other, as they often did. They did genuinely like being around each other and they had fun together. In some ways, it felt simple with him, but it really wasn't simple.

She swallowed. "I can't handle your lifestyle. The gossip . . ."

"I know what you mean." He looked down. "I read what people said online."

*But if I knew you really loved me, I could deal with it.*

She couldn't manage to say that, though. She stepped back from him.

"And I know one day"—her voice wavered—"you'll go for someone more like Irene Lai."

"There's never been anything between us—"

"I know. But someone like her, or Helen Alvarez. It's not that I have poor self-esteem, but I'm not like them, and I don't think you feel the same way about me that I feel about you. I'm an enjoyable distraction for you—"

"Lindsay, you're not just a distraction."

"—but nothing more," she finished. "And I don't blame you for that. I don't blame you for asking for a relationship rather than letting me leave that first morning, but now, it's not working for me."

"I . . ." He scrubbed a hand over his face. "I don't . . . Okay."

It was very, very quiet.

A foolish part of her had thought he'd immediately fight for her. He'd kiss her and tell her that no, she was wrong. She was all he needed; he didn't need anyone famous. They would figure this out together.

But that didn't happen, and her chest felt like it was caving in on itself.

"I've had a good time with you," he said, "but I agree. My life is a lot to handle and we should both take some time to think about this. We can talk about it in a month?"

He spoke calmly. She reminded herself that he was a good actor . . . but she didn't think he was acting here. He simply wasn't all that affected by this.

*Disagree with me, dammit.*

He didn't say anything more. Instead, he pulled her close and kissed her forehead, and she couldn't help fearing she'd never feel for someone else the way she felt for him. A peck on the forehead would never ignite her like this again.

But those were just the silly thoughts of a woman who hadn't dated for seven years.

She took the elevator in a bit of a daze, but once she hit the street, she started running, needing to get to the safety of her apartment as fast as possible. She cursed all the red lights that slowed her down.

But at last she was home—her new home, which really did feel like home now—and she finally cried.

They were taking some time apart. It wasn't officially over, but it seemed like it was. Even if he'd said they should both do some thinking, she felt like it was all on her to figure out if she wanted to deal with his fame. And if his feelings were what they seemed to be, she couldn't imagine changing her mind. Sure, he'd said she wasn't just a distraction, but he hadn't said anything more than that.

Yes, it felt like the end.

**THAT NIGHT, WHEN** it was time to get ready for bed, Ryan noticed the second toothbrush in his washroom. The bath products he'd bought for Lindsay, most of them unopened.

He went to throw them in the garbage, but then he stopped himself.

He hadn't been raised to throw out unused, perfectly good

items like this, even if they made his heart ache. His mom would tell him it was a waste of money.

His dad would tell him scented bath products were stupid.

Or, more likely, he'd say nothing at all.

The next day, Ryan opened the fridge to get his lunch and noticed the beer bottles he'd bought for Lindsay. Although he could get rid of the beer, he couldn't get rid of the breakfast bar where they'd eaten together. Couldn't get rid of the bed where they'd spent so much time.

Well, technically, he could. But that would really be a waste, and he wouldn't let himself do it. He wouldn't throw out the beer, either. One day, Mel or someone else would visit and he'd serve it to them. For now, he'd push the bottles to the back of the fridge and ignore them.

But every time he opened the fridge, his gaze went right to the beer.

*I'm an enjoyable distraction for you . . . It's not working for me.*

Those words had pierced his heart, but he'd stopped arguing with her. Kept himself from saying all the things she'd wanted to hear. "I love you" would have been beyond him, but he could have assured her that he really cared about her, he hadn't felt this way before. He'd played characters who loved like this, but he hadn't known how it truly felt.

Until now.

There were so many things he could have said, but he didn't want to see her name get dragged through the mud online. Lindsay admitted it bothered her. So, rather than asking how he could fix it, he'd let her believe what she wanted and pretended this wasn't tearing him apart.

Still, he'd said they should take a break rather than end it because it was too painful for him to say those words. They would've been as hard as "I love you."

But it was probably over.

It would suck for a little while, but if he could survive the death of his mother, he could survive this. He had eight weeks until he went to Vancouver to film *For the Blood*, and he had preparation to do. Good. That would help take his mind off Lindsay.

As for his family . . . well, he was now seeing Jenna twice a week, and he was getting better at looking after Ezra. Alice came regularly, too. She and Jenna got along well.

Lindsay's mom. Right. He might see her again at Jenna's, although they generally visited on different days to spread out the help that Jenna got. Seeing Alice could be awkward, but she was good for his sister, and that was the most important thing.

That afternoon, after a brutal workout, he still felt like moving, so he walked in the general direction of Kensington Market and told himself that was *not* where he was going. Friday was Lindsay's day off, anyway, and normally they'd be seeing each other now . . .

Instead, he went to Rise and Shine, the coffee shop where he'd worked all those years ago. He talked to the owner—his old boss—and her wife for ten minutes and took a picture with someone who recognized him. Then he had a coffee, and he remembered Lindsay telling him that she used to study here in university.

Every little thing reminded him of her. The memories exhausted him emotionally, even as his body wanted to keep going.

And *this* reminded him of filming *Unraveling*. That role had been really hard on him.

He went home and stopped himself from posting stupid shit on Twitter, but he couldn't stop the annoying ache in his chest.

He was about to go to bed early when his dad tweeted.

Saw my son at the bus stop today! The tweet included a picture of a *That Kind of Wedding* poster at a bus shelter.

Ryan stared at the tweet in confusion. His father never took the bus. Or used exclamation marks. And he was acting like he was proud of Ryan for making this rom-com that had gotten less-than-stellar reviews.

People could act so differently in public—including on Twitter—than they did otherwise.

Ryan didn't reply to the tweet.

Instead, he lay in bed, staring at the ceiling and wishing Lindsay were next to him.

She wasn't the sort of person who'd ever craved being in the spotlight, and he didn't see how being with him would ever make up for the stupid things others might say. Like, sure, he was nice to look at, but he didn't know much about being a good partner, and he couldn't even manage to be a decent son.

Yes, this was for the best.

# CHAPTER 38

S hit!" Lindsay exclaimed.

"What happened?" Noreen asked.

"I dropped a donut on the floor."

Luckily, it was only a single donut.

Unluckily, it was a matcha tiramisu donut, so it gave her major flashbacks to the day she'd met Ryan.

And now she was harboring fantasies of him running into the kitchen in a pink ruffled apron, knocking over all the donuts, and kissing her.

It was a really bad sign that she was fantasizing about donut destruction. Usually, she was in her element in the kitchen, but not today.

Noreen gave her a look.

"What?" Lindsay said.

"How about we go out after work? Some beer to ease your heartache?"

"I'm not heartbroken."

Noreen narrowed her eyes. "You're such a bad actor."

*Actor.*

Everything made her feel like crying, but Lindsay wouldn't let herself cry.

"I can't go out after work," she said. "I'm supposed to do something with Vivian."

"You could ask her to come to the bar with us."

"All right. I'll do that."

Lindsay texted Vivian during her lunch, then pulled up Instagram.

Oh God. Pictures of her ex-boyfriend's abs wouldn't help her get over him.

Looking at his Twitter account wasn't the best idea, either, but she wanted to be sure he hadn't said anything about their relationship.

As expected, he hadn't.

She had to stop thinking about him all the time, but how did you stop thinking about someone when you loved them? How did you get over them?

Time. That was probably the answer, wasn't it?

She'd just have to wait this out.

After work, she and Noreen headed to Fantastical Brewing. They'd been at the bar for ten minutes when Vivian showed up.

Lindsay took a break from pouring alcohol down her throat to introduce her friends, who'd never met before.

"Noreen, this is Vivian, my roommate. Vivian, this is Noreen, who runs the bakery with me."

Noreen and Lindsay were sitting at the bar; Vivian took the seat on Lindsay's other side.

"What's good here?" Vivian asked.

"The Centaur Baltic Porter and the Bigfoot Imperial Stout are my favorite," Noreen said. "If you like strong, dark beers, I recommend those. Lindsay is drinking a Unicorn Tears Sour."

JACKIE LAU

Vivian eyed Lindsay's red drink. "I think I'll have that one."

When Isaac came around, she ordered her beer. He set the pint in front of her a few minutes later, and Vivian took a dainty sip. She was wearing jeans today—Lindsay didn't think she'd ever seen her roommate in jeans before—but paired with a blouse that made it look like a sophisticated casual outfit.

However, the face Vivian made when she tasted the beer was anything but sophisticated.

"You don't like it?" Noreen asked.

"I've never had a sour beer before, and it's too sour for me."

Lindsay promptly burst into tears.

Vivian wouldn't have tried that beer if it hadn't been for her, and oh God, she missed Ryan so much.

Vivian placed a stack of napkins in front of her, and Noreen laid a hand on Lindsay's back.

"I'm so sorry," Lindsay said. "I should have warned you about that."

"You're crying because I don't like the beer?" Vivian asked. "It's no big deal. I can still drink it, then I'll try something else."

"I have to go to Eunice's wedding next Saturday."

"The idea of going to a wedding makes you upset," Noreen said, "because you'll be thinking about Ryan?"

Lindsay sniffed.

"You never told me why you two broke up."

"Technically, we're just on a break," Lindsay said. "But he doesn't care about me the way I care for him."

"How do you know?" Noreen asked.

"When I said I loved him, he didn't say it back. I know it hadn't been long, but still . . ." Lindsay put her head in her hands. "I don't know. I'm just so bad at this. I have no experience with relationships."

"But you have experience with other types of—"

"You mean friendships? I hadn't made new friends in years. Until Vivian."

Lindsay smiled weakly at Vivian, then caught the attention of the bartender. Isaac walked over, and she ordered a Hoppy Hippogriff IPA. Maybe if she drank something that didn't literally have "tears" in its name, she wouldn't cry.

"I was questioning our relationship," she told her friends, "but in the end, it was Ryan who suggested we take a break. That was *his* idea."

"It's just hard to believe," Noreen said, "after the way you two were together when I barged into your baking lesson."

"And the way he looked at you in the comedy club," Vivian said.

"We weren't even dating then," Lindsay said.

"I know."

"But these things happen sometimes." Noreen touched Lindsay's shoulder. "No matter the outcome, I'm glad you did this—I know it was hard for you. Feel good about the fact that you tried."

Lindsay supposed that was true. A few months ago, she'd been getting wedding invitations in the mail, meeting her mother's date at the bakery, and feeling like the world was moving on and she was stuck.

She didn't feel that way anymore.

Now she just felt . . . sad.

She couldn't imagine dating again in the near future. For a while, she would be his, even if they weren't together.

"Next time," Noreen said to Lindsay, "if you doubt someone's feelings, try having more of a conversation. At least you'll have more answers than you do now. Communication is important."

Lindsay hadn't had any serious intention of ending their "break," but she wondered if she should try to talk to Ryan again. Ask him exactly how he felt.

For a minute, she allowed herself the fantasy that he'd sweep her off her feet—in a private location with nobody taking pictures—and tell her that he was just scared because he'd never had a relationship like this before . . .

Wait. That didn't seem so far-fetched.

Maybe he *was* scared, and that was why he couldn't say the words.

Because she knew Ryan. Not just his persona; she *knew* him. He'd lost his mother earlier this year and struggled to have a relationship with his father without his mom, and he didn't usually do romantic relationships . . . Yeah, it would make sense for him to be scared. Afraid of fucking up, especially since his life was more public than most people's.

Except Ryan was usually good at talking about things, and he was fairly self-aware.

Hope sprouted in her chest, and she didn't squash it. She wouldn't obsess about it, wouldn't let herself dream about the sorts of scenes that only happened in movies.

But she could allow herself a little hope.

Once she felt stronger, she'd visit again, and they'd have a proper talk. She needed to be clear about her feelings, too. Perhaps he'd also believed he was doing the right thing, not wanting to pressure Lindsay after she'd said the public attention bothered her.

They hadn't put all their cards on the table, and they needed to do that.

She had a sip of her IPA. She was slightly buzzed, and it was a warm night, and she was out with her friends at her favorite bar. Life wasn't too bad. Even if her heart felt like it had a hole in it.

Like a donut.

She chuckled, and her friends seemed cheered by her laughter.

She was moving forward, and somehow, she'd find a way to continue.

Hopefully with Ryan, but if not . . . she'd still survive.

• • •

**"HOW CAN YOU** eat that when it's so hot and humid?" Trevor pointed to Lindsay's bowl of Taiwanese beef noodle soup.

It was a Monday, and they were having lunch at a restaurant near her apartment.

Monday used to be the day she saw Ryan, but now . . . well.

It was still nice to see her brother.

"What's wrong with my choice of meal?" Lindsay slurped her noodles. "Besides, it's heavily air-conditioned in here. I might need to put on my sweater."

"You carry a sweater with you in August?"

"Yeah. Because some places are cold inside."

Trevor looked at her like she was nuts. "Soup in the heat of summer is just wrong."

Lindsay shrugged and went right on enjoying her soup.

"How's Mom?" she asked a few minutes later.

"I don't see her much."

"But you live together."

"She's at Harold's most of the time," Trevor said. "When she's not, she's helping your boyfriend's sister, and she's got various other social engagements, too. Honestly, I can't keep track."

"You've gotten used to Mom dating?"

"Yeah, and I guess Harold's okay."

"That was super enthusiastic."

Trevor lifted a shoulder. "Being glad she found Harold . . . it was like being glad Dad was dead. I know it doesn't really make sense, but that's how it felt. Like we were erasing him."

"It doesn't have to be logical for you to feel that way."

"Yeah. Exactly." His lips quirked, but his eyes looked sad.

And oh, she knew how he felt.

"She's less of a busybody now, which is nice," he said. "She's not constantly asking what I'm doing with my life or if I've met any nice girls in the two hours since I last saw her. She seems to enjoy helping with the baby, too."

"Yeah, I think that was good for everyone involved."

"She has more people to fuss over. Spread it around." He laughed a little. "She's got Harold's kids, too. And all those recipes of Po Po's to try."

"So, you don't see Mom enough for her to drive you mad, but you still enjoy some good cooking. How lucky for you."

He held up a chopstick as if he was going to toss it at her, but he didn't.

"How do you do it?" he asked. "How do you keep going?"

She was somewhat alarmed by this. "What's with all the serious talk today?"

"I guess it's because I have too much time on my hands. Nothing to do but think."

"What happened to video games? Last I checked, they were still a thing."

"Oh, I play video games, don't worry. But only, like, six hours a day."

"Slacker," she muttered.

He leaned forward. "Dad died, and you immediately started working toward your dream of having your own bakery. You got your diploma, worked hard . . . you made it happen. I goofed off, and it took me six years to finish my degree."

"I did what I needed to do."

She didn't know how else to explain it. After losing her father, she'd needed something big to work toward. Then in the evening, after another day of school . . . or another long day of work . . . or another disappointing look at a rental unit . . . she would imagine telling her father about it. How she'd made some minuscule step forward.

Then she'd imagine what he might say in response.

*You know how I feel about pies, Lindsay. They're nowhere near as delicious as cakes. Except for lemon meringue.*

Sometimes, she'd play memories in her head. All those teddy bear tea parties she'd made him attend when she was four or five, which she'd taken for granted at the time—she'd only been a small child, and she'd assumed her father would always be there.

She couldn't recall when she'd stopped talking to her dad at the end of her day. Sometime after Kensington Bake Shop had opened. Once she'd "made it."

Of course, it wasn't like everything had been rosy as soon as the bakery opened. There had been long, long days of work. But they'd built up their business and gotten a little attention.

She hadn't made new friends or dated during that time, but she had her family, her friends from before, and she'd maintained those relationships.

She still missed her dad, and sometimes it was pretty bad, but she wasn't alone.

Her brother had coped differently, and there was nothing wrong with that. Unlike her, he'd been better at meeting people and having fun.

"What would Dad think of you dating a movie star?" Trevor asked.

She considered the question. "He would pretend to be super unimpressed, even though he would definitely be a little impressed. And then, after he'd eaten too much lemon meringue at Thanksgiving, he'd ask if Ryan had ever met Harrison Ford and if he could introduce them."

Trevor laughed, and Lindsay laughed, too, her heart feeling a little lighter.

Yes, she'd give Ryan a bit more space, and then she'd try talking to him one more time. At the very least, she'd be able to tell her father that she'd gone after what she wanted.

She regarded Trevor. "Why did you ask how I did it? Do you have plans for your life that I haven't heard about yet?"

"You'll have to wait and see."

As a sign of sisterly affection, she put more food on his plate. "I guess I will."

She'd have to wait and see about a few things.

And tonight, she'd curl up with some popcorn and *Indiana Jones and the Last Crusade*, one of her father's favorite movies.

# CHAPTER 39

R yan was in New York again.

After too many depressing days in Toronto, he'd wanted to get out of the city. And so he'd come to visit Mel, hoping it would take his mind off Lindsay. He wouldn't see the beer in his fridge, nor would he roll over in the morning and expect her to be next to him.

Yet he was still thinking about her all the time, even in New York.

It sucked.

He was just here for three nights. He didn't want to be gone too long, in case Jenna needed him.

He looked down at the shitty latte that Mel had made with his new espresso machine and thought of Rise and Shine—and the lattes he'd made for Lindsay.

Yesterday, on their way out for dinner, they'd passed a twenty-four-hour donut shop—you could find anything in New York—and he'd thought of Lindsay then, too.

"All right," Mel said as they sat at his kitchen table, "we're going to talk about what it's like to be an Asian actor in North America and how people are always asking for your views on diversity. Then a bit on male bodies and the pressures stars face and why you don't want to bulk up much more than you already have."

"I'd be miserable," Ryan muttered.

"You already *are* miserable, which is why we're not recording the podcast yet. Because even though it's partly about those things, it's mostly you and me goofing off, and right now, I think you'll bring everyone down, even with me being my usual entertaining self. You're too mopey."

"I'm not mopey," Ryan said, though he knew it sounded unconvincing.

"Right."

"And you know I can do a decent job, no matter what mood I'm in."

"I know, but I'd prefer if you were in a better mood first."

Ryan sipped his subpar latte. "You should have let me make the lattes."

"Quit changing the subject. We were talking about your mood."

"Yeah. And what a joy that was."

"Are you finally going to tell me what happened with Lindsay? Actually, you know what? I'll make you tell me. We're not recording the podcast until you do."

Ryan rolled his eyes. "Fine. She was upset about what happened with Irene. Not because she didn't trust me, but, you know, all the comments online. And she thinks she's just an enjoyable distraction for me."

Mel's expression was comically surprised. "Which is obviously not true. Wait, are you saying you didn't tell her she was wrong?"

"I protested a little, but I suggested we take a break."

"So, it's your own damn fault you're moping around New York? I've been so nice to you—"

"Uh, yeah, when you shook me awake at seven this morning, that sure was nice."

"—because I thought she'd broken your heart, but you're the reason—"

"She wanted this!" Ryan said. "She agreed."

"And if you'd told Lindsay how much you care for her, she probably would have kissed you and let you take her to bed."

Yes, that had been tempting, but . . .

"You like to think of yourself as a good-looking but average guy," Mel said. "But even though you're no Ryan Reynolds, you're not just any ordinary guy you meet at a bar. Not surprising she'd find that intimidating."

"She told me she loved me, and I didn't say it back."

"But you do love her, don't you?"

Ryan didn't say the words. He simply nodded.

"Then why the fuck—"

"I'm not good at saying those things."

"Even if you couldn't say the words, you could have told her—"

"No. I'm not good at that stuff. I'm not good with people."

Mel smacked his hand against his forehead before standing up and sauntering around the room. "Look at me! I'm Ryan Kwok!" He made his voice super low; it didn't sound anything like Ryan's voice. "I love taking off my shirt and everyone loves me! Women say I'm charming! But I think I'm bad with people."

"Can you cut it out?"

Mel sat back down. "This is so far from the truth I don't even know what to say. What's wrong with that brain of yours? Have all your brain cells been absorbed by your abs?"

"You know what I mean."

"No, I don't."

"I'm bad at relationships of all kinds," Ryan said. "I can't seem to do anything right with people I'm close to. My dad—"

"If we're talking about dads, mine's barely talked to me in fifteen years. I have you beat."

"But your father is a homophobic asshole."

"Lots of people have complicated relationships with their parents. You're not special. And it's not because *you* haven't tried to have a relationship with him." Mel paused. "Look, I get that losing your mom was rough on you. She was pretty cool. Even if she had her reservations about you pursuing this career, she was supportive, and everyone thought it was beyond adorable when you took her to the Golden Globes. And you know what she'd do right now?"

"You only met my mother two or three times. I don't think—"

"She'd smack you. Not hard, of course. Maybe just with her words. She'd say you were being an idiot, and she'd also say your dad was an idiot."

Ryan smiled weakly. He could imagine her doing exactly that.

"I suspect you were an excellent boyfriend," Mel said, "even if you clammed up when it came to telling Lindsay you love her. It's like you want to be a noble hero, sacrificing yourself for her, but why?"

"She doesn't deserve to be dragged online. I don't want her to deal with that if she doesn't want to."

"I know you well, and I bet she'd be better off with you in her life. Yes, there are disadvantages, but there are lots of great things about being with you. Although you'll have to help her deal with some of the attention, I think the worst of it will die down soon. I feel like you're throwing this away because your dad is a stubborn old bastard, and also because you're struggling with loss."

"She helped me with that," Ryan said quietly. "Her dad died when she was twenty-two, and she understood."

"Your mom's not here to talk some sense into you, so I gotta do it instead."

"It's weird to hear you being serious for so long."

"I do my best."

"So, you think I should try to get her back?"

Mel slapped him on the shoulder. "Yeah, man. That's what I'm saying. Let her know how you feel, and she can decide, but I think if she really knew you loved her, she'd change her mind. And next time I come to Toronto to see you and Lindsay and her friends, I'll keep my rude thoughts to myself."

Ryan drained his latte and considered it.

The last couple of weeks had shown him that his feelings for Lindsay weren't going anywhere. He hadn't expected it to be so intense, but it was.

And just like he'd always felt he had to be perfect in his career, couldn't star in a movie that got middling reviews, he'd felt like he had to be perfect with Lindsay. But she didn't expect that. He'd been a good boyfriend for the most part, right? He thought he'd treated her well, and she made him want to do everything he could for her . . . but that didn't mean he had to be perfect.

He could have talked to her about everything. Promised he did care for her, very much. She would have understood, wouldn't she have? He could have told her that yes, the gossip was difficult, but he wanted to figure it out with her.

There was a strange feeling in his stomach. It was either hope . . . or that terrible latte making its way down.

"You could declare your love on the podcast," Mel said. "Let the whole world know."

"God no," Ryan said. "Lindsay wouldn't like that."

"I know, man. I was kidding."

"All right, let's record the podcast so I can get back to Toronto and see her."

But what should he do to win her back?


**RYAN WAS STILL** mulling over that question as he walked up to his building on Sunday evening, having switched his flight so he could return to Toronto a day early. Tomorrow was Monday, so that would be the perfect time to see Lindsay.

He was trying to find inspiration from movies, but the problem was that, first of all, many such scenes in movies involved airports—and Lindsay, to his knowledge, wasn't going on a trip anytime soon. Second of all, a lot of them were very public.

No, he needed another idea.

As he stepped into the lobby of his building, he was surprised to hear yelling. His building was usually quiet.

"Nobody buzzed you in. You snuck in behind someone else."

"Aiyah! Are you accusing me of trespassing? I'm here to see my son. I tried calling him, but no answer."

"Okay, we'll try again, but if I can't get in touch with him, I'll have to ask you to leave."

"I'm worried something is wrong. I haven't heard from him in a long time."

What on earth . . . ?

Ryan hurried to the front desk and put a hand on his dad's arm.

Dad was so surprised that he spun around, about to clock whoever had touched him, but realized it was Ryan before it was too late.

"Ah, here he is," Dad said. "I guess he was traveling." He nodded at Ryan's suitcase.

"Yes, this really is my father," Ryan said to the concierge. "I'll take him upstairs. Sorry for the trouble."

They didn't speak in the elevator, though Ryan could practically hear the thumping of his heart over the *ding* of the elevator when they got to his floor.

Once home, Ryan offered his dad a beer, since he actually had some in the fridge.

Dad drank his beer in silence at the kitchen table while Ryan got himself a glass of water, thirsty after traveling.

"So," Ryan said, sitting down across from his father. "You were worried about me?"

Dad grunted.

For fuck's sake. Ryan had been touched that his father had worried, but now they were back to the same old thing.

"I said I was going to stop calling you, Dad. You rarely picked up, and when you did, you were never happy to hear from me. So I decided I didn't need to talk to you twice a week, as I'd been trying to do. You know, after Mom died. Because *I* was worried about *you*, even though you acted like that was ridiculous."

Dad hesitated. "That's not true."

"What's not true?"

"That I wasn't happy to hear from you."

"Well, you sure did a good job of hiding it." Ryan was frustrated, yet his father's words still warmed him. Little scraps were all he'd ever had from his father.

Dad sighed. "You were always more like her, but after she died, you took over her role."

"What do you mean?"

"She was always the one reaching out to people. Keeping the family together. Asking how people were feeling. Arranging dinners. It was all her. The more you pushed, the more you reminded me of her, and it hurt."

"Oh," Ryan said faintly. "Your heart isn't made of stone. How nice to know." He hadn't meant to be so sarcastic, but he couldn't seem to help it.

Dad looked like he was about to . . . cry? There were no tears falling, but his eyes glistened.

No, that couldn't be right. Ryan must be seeing things. But just in case, he grabbed a tissue box and set it on the table.

Dad glared at it.

Ryan was sure of it now—his father's eyes were definitely wet.

"I realized," Dad said, "that I barely had a relationship with my kids, separate from her—you were right about that—and I felt guilty." He looked away. "She was two years younger than me. She was always in better health. Why did she have a heart attack and not me? It doesn't make sense. I haven't even been to a doctor in ten years . . ."

"Um, aren't there various tests you should have at your age? Prostate or colorectal cancer screening?"

"Maybe. I don't know these things."

Ryan put a hand to his head. "*Dad.*"

"Okay, okay. I will go." Dad paused. "I feel so guilty that I'm here and she isn't. It doesn't seem right. She was the better person, always. Not some bad-tempered man who always complained about how his son was disappointing him."

"What about Jenna? You don't even visit her and Ezra. She could use a little help."

"Ah, but I don't know how to look after babies. I told you. I am better with older kids."

"Surely you have some experience."

"That was so long ago," Dad said. "Plus, I didn't do much when you were very little. I feel bad about it now. Your mom did everything. Like I said, she was a much better person than me. When I think of going to see Ezra without her, I . . ."

At that point, his stoic father started crying, which was the first time Ryan had ever seen such a thing. He suspected Dad had decided at the age of three that crying was childish and hadn't done it since.

Ryan wanted to put a hand on his dad's shoulder, but he thought such an acknowledgment of his father's tears would freak the man out and turn him back to his usual ornery self.

At last, Dad said, "I shouldn't cry."

"Why not? Men can cry. Have you ever watched K-dramas?"

"No. They are playing with your emotions. I won't be manipulated."

"When I visited to get the photo albums," Ryan said, "what were you watching? You seemed embarrassed about it."

"Ah, whatever, I have no dignity anymore. I was watching your show."

"*Just Another New York Sitcom?*"

Dad nodded sheepishly. "I still think it's kind of terrible and stupid."

"Gee, thanks."

"But it's entertaining, when you turn your brain off. And sometimes, I don't want to use my brain these days. I tried to watch your movie in the theater, too, but I had to leave."

"You thought it was too stupid?"

"No, I was crying too much. Making a fool of myself. I didn't last half an hour." Dad had a gulp of his beer. "I met your mother at a wedding. We had mutual friends who were getting married. She was the emcee—she was very good. See, you're definitely more like her. But there were no penguins at that wedding."

Ryan stared at his father.

His parents met at a wedding? His dad cried actual tears in a movie theater?

He suddenly felt like he didn't know anything about the world.

"So instead," Dad said, "I left the theater, went home, and watched six episodes of *Chinook Diner.* I've seen all twelve seasons in the past few months."

"You're binge-watching sitcoms?"

"I know, it's shocking, but now I get why you want to make shows and movies like that. To make people laugh, even when their world is falling apart. I know it takes skill, and you are . . . good at it."

"Thank you."

"But part of the reason I don't watch much TV is that I'm very bad with faces. Some shows have too many characters, and it takes a long time before I can tell them apart. But I can tell you apart from other people, so it's easier to watch things you are in."

"Oh. So that's partly why you prefer books and documentaries." Ryan paused. "I think you should consider therapy."

"Because I'm bad with faces? I don't think—"

"No, for everything else."

Dad looked alarmed by the suggestion. "I don't see how it would help."

"Well, you can try. It doesn't mean you're weak. And you're the only parent we have now, so make sure you take care of yourself and that includes mental health. Don't just talk to me on Twitter. By the way, why are you on Twitter? You hate social media."

"It's easier than talking on the phone. It doesn't remind me of how you are like your mother. And because I'm your dad, people are paying attention to me. I'm all alone in the evenings, so sometimes it's nice to get attention, even from strangers on the internet. Does it bother you?"

"No. It was just . . . unexpected. You can post whatever you like."

"There was even a Buzzfeed article. Did you see it?"

Talking about Buzzfeed articles with his father . . . yeah, this felt like an alternate reality.

"I did," Ryan said.

"They said I was funny. The best dad on Twitter. I'm not the best dad in real life, so that was nice. But when you didn't tweet for a week or call me, I was worried. If your mom said she would stop calling, she wouldn't have meant it, but you did."

"Do you understand how difficult it is to have conversations with you?"

Dad just sipped his beer in response.

"I was going to call you eventually," Ryan said, "but not for a few weeks. I was in New York this weekend, and I didn't take my phone off flight mode when I landed. That's why I didn't answer. I'm sorry I made you worry."

"I cannot lose you, too." Dad looked right at Ryan as he spoke, but then he turned away, as if this expression of emotion was too much for him. "I brought you some food."

For the first time, Ryan noticed the plastic bags from the Chinese grocery store near his dad's house. It was a mishmash of stuff.

"Let's talk about something happier," Dad said. "You're still seeing Lindsay?"

"You don't believe I'm cheating on her with Irene Lai?"

Dad scoffed. "You wouldn't do that." He had a bunch of expletives for gossip columnists, which made Ryan chuckle.

His father was obviously anti-gossip-columnist.

"Lindsay and I are on a break," Ryan said.

Dad looked nearly as alarmed as he had at the suggestion of therapy. "I've been watching sitcoms. I know bad things happen when people are on a break."

"Don't worry, I'll sort it out." Ryan said that as much to convince himself as to convince his father. "You know I don't have much experience with romance—or maybe you didn't know that. Plus, I felt like every other relationship in my life was a bit of a mess—"

"Aiyah, is this because of me?" Dad put a hand to his forehead. "If I can be married for more than thirty years, then I'm sure you can have a relationship. You are better at this stuff."

"You can meet her, if you like."

"I will think about it."

"You don't want to?"

"I might scare her off. She already has to deal with gossip columnists."

"I think it'll be okay." Ryan paused. "Would you like to take a picture together so you can have new content for your Twitter account?"

"Ah . . . I guess."

Ryan pulled out his selfie stick, which probably horrified his father, but Dad didn't say anything. They had to take several pictures because Dad had a tendency to look constipated in photos.

"You know what we should do?" Ryan said. "Re-create that kung fu picture. Sometimes people do that—re-create childhood photos. It can be pretty funny."

"I guess it would be entertaining for my followers. I have eight thousand now."

It took a while to get the angles right, but the final result was hilarious, and Ryan chuckled at the idea of Dad thinking about his followers.

"I've never used the camera on my phone," Dad said. "Where are the photos stored?"

So Ryan had to show him that. And how to post a photo from his phone to Twitter. He also suggested Dad try texting, if he didn't always feel like talking on the phone.

"I should go," Dad said. "Now that I've seen proof you weren't eaten by a giraffe in Alaska. Maybe we could . . . go to Jenna's together sometime this week? I will take a day off. I have so many days saved up. Your mother was always bugging me to take more time off—and actually retire—but I never did."

Ryan swallowed. "Okay, I'll talk to Jenna, and you can see if you're up to it."

"I will think about therapy, but I make no promises."

Dad gave Ryan a strange look and stepped closer to him.

Was Dad going to give him a *hug*?

That seemed impossible, but after everything his father had said today . . .

Apparently, a hug was too much. Instead, Dad gave him a pat on the back, which was more than Ryan had gotten since he was, like, six. He'd take it.

After his father had left and Ryan had put away the food that he didn't need and didn't fit his diet, he sat down on his couch and had a good cry. The sort of cry his character had near the end of *Unraveling*, but no one was recording this time.

He cried for his mother and everything in his life that was tangled up.

He wished he could wrap his arms around Lindsay. Wished they could support each other. She was the one he wanted to talk to about everything—both the good and not so good.

But first, he had to win her back.

He'd better start on that.

# CHAPTER 40

At noon on Monday, Lindsay was about to start making a blue-berry cheesecake for Vivian. A surprise for her roommate on their planned movie night.

Lindsay wasn't sure which movie they'd watch. Something without Ryan Kwok.

It hurt whenever she saw pictures of him and heard his voice, yet she kept looking at his social media and googling his name. This morning, she'd even listened to a podcast he'd recorded with Melvin Lee. He'd been as relaxed and charming as usual, and he had lots of intelligent things to say between all the easy banter with Melvin.

And Ryan had, briefly, been hers.

Maybe he would be again.

She planned to have another talk with him, but she kept put-ting it off. Because it was possible she'd be rejected, and hope was better than rejection. Plus, he'd said they'd re-evaluate in a month and it had only been a couple of weeks, so maybe she should give him more time.

She was getting out the ingredients for the cheesecake when her mother called.

"Lindsay!" Mom said. "I'm taking you out for bubble tea now."

"Do I have a choice in the matter? I was going to do some baking—"

"On your day off? We're going out, and that's an order. I'm in front of your building."

"You're so demanding," Lindsay muttered. "Okay, I'll be down in five minutes."

She might have protested further, but it was rare for her mom to stop by unexpectedly. She put on some proper clothes—jeans and a tank top, rather than pajamas—and headed downstairs.

Mom was waiting for her on the sidewalk. She smiled as she took Lindsay's elbow and guided her to the right. It seemed like she had a particular tea shop in mind to try. There were so many within walking distance of Lindsay's apartment; that was the great thing about living in downtown Toronto.

As she followed her mother, who was walking briskly today, Lindsay thought back to seven years ago. Her mom had kept on with her life, but she'd seemed perilously close to breaking. They all had. Lindsay had thrown herself into her dream of owning a bakery because she'd needed that to keep her going.

Things were better now.

Mom stopped at a little tea shop that Lindsay had never been to. There were only three tables, and they managed to snag one. While they were waiting for their orders, Mom went to the washroom, and Lindsay looked at Twitter again. Ryan had retweeted two photos of him lifting his leg to kick his father, who was leaning backward. One from his childhood, and one that was clearly much more recent. Lindsay hoped that meant things were better between them.

"Here you go!" Mom plonked their bubble tea on the table.

Lindsay quickly put away her phone.

"What were you looking at?" Mom asked.

"Nothing."

Mom didn't call her out on her obvious lie.

Today was a weird day.

Lindsay sipped her taro milk tea. It was tasty, but everything was a bit flat right now; she couldn't fully enjoy it. Not when she kept missing Ryan.

"How are things?" she asked her mother.

"Pretty good. Harold finished translating all the recipes. I'll email them to you."

"It's still going well with him?"

"Mm-hmm."

"I'm glad." Lindsay really meant that; she didn't just think she ought to be glad. Her feelings about it were simpler than they'd been before.

After they finished their bubble tea, Mom insisted they go shopping, which was surprising as Mom didn't particularly like shopping.

This was truly bizarre.

At last, Mom declared it was time for her to meet up with Harold, and Lindsay headed home with the smiling bubble tea plushie that Mom had bought for her in Chinatown. She'd make a Havarti grilled cheese for lunch, then get started on the cheesecake.

When she stepped off the elevator and onto her floor, it smelled like a bakery. What—

"Hey, Lindsay."

Lindsay shrieked, then realized who it was.

Ryan.

Ryan Kwok was standing outside her door.

And, like the first time they'd met, he'd startled her.

"I'm sorry. I should have thought this over a little better. I, uh . . ." He scratched the back of his neck, giving her a nice view of his arm muscles. He was wearing a short-sleeved Henley—she definitely approved.

And she grinned when she saw what was on the tray in his other hand.

"Did you make these?" She pointed at the dozen chocolate espresso donuts.

"I did. I had to buy a deep fryer. They turned out reasonably well, even if they're not as pretty as yours."

"Fortunate I didn't run into you and knock them over." She let him into the apartment, and they took off their shoes before heading to the kitchen.

"What are you holding?" he asked.

"It's a bubble tea plushie." She put it on a chair. "My mom insisted on getting it. I don't know why. Wait—that's the reason my mom was acting weird today, wasn't it? You asked her to take me out so you could surprise me."

He nodded as he set the donuts on the table. "Lindsay, I . . ."

He seemed nervous. She'd seen him interviewed by big names—yeah, she'd watched far too many videos of him—and he'd never been like this. Her heart squeezed.

The both sat down, and she took his hands in hers.

"Go ahead," she said.

"You're so much more than a fun distraction. You're the one . . . here." He pulled their joined hands to his chest, over his heart. "But I've never done this before, and I was convinced I'd make a mess of it, especially since my fame made you exposed. So, I let you think I didn't care."

Where they were joined, she could feel him shudder.

"This year has been tough," he said. "I lost the one person who'd always supported me. It's no excuse, but I want to tell you what happened. I might come across as confident, even if I'm not all that confident when it comes to certain things and believed you were better off without me. I believed I couldn't do it, but I was wrong. I can do this, and I promise to give it my everything, if you'll take me back. I'll do all that I can to make this work for you." He raised their hands to his mouth and kissed her fingers. "I love you, Lindsay. I loved you when you said those words to me, though I couldn't say them myself. But I can now. I love you. And I don't want one of the co-stars from my movies—I just want you. That isn't going to change."

"I . . ." It was hard to speak. She was overcome by the conviction in his voice. "I love you, too. I still do. You're very lovable, you know. I freaked out when you couldn't return my words, but I thought about it later . . . and I understood. I should have tried to talk about it more with you."

"I'm not sure I would have done the greatest job of talking it out then, but I'll do better from now on. Unfortunately, you *will* get some attention, and people will say nasty things online, because they always do. I hope you're okay with learning how to deal with that, and you might want to spend less time on social media. That's one of the downsides of being with me. I won't pretend otherwise. But I can get you someone to talk to about it, and I'll make sure you always know how much I care for you, no matter what people say. If you don't think it's worth it, I understand, but I need you to know exactly how I feel."

She nodded. "Thank you. It's totally worth it, if I can be with you."

His face split into a grin, which lit her up even more than his smiles usually did. It was a smile just for her, and not for any adoring fans. She got to see him in ways nobody else did, and for that, she felt like the luckiest person in the world.

"I'm afraid of screwing up," he admitted, "but I have to be

okay with screwing up in small ways here and there, rather than running from it. Nobody can be perfect. I can just promise to love you and always try to do right by you."

He pulled her onto his lap and kissed her. She hadn't kissed him in so long, and oh, she'd missed this so much. Being in his arms . . . it felt right.

This wasn't what she'd expected when a good-looking stranger had knocked over her matcha tiramisu donuts.

And certainly, in her wildest dreams, she'd never imagined dating a movie star.

She'd just wanted to be able to have a relationship again; she hadn't thought it would be with someone like him. Going forward, she wouldn't let her insecurities get the best of her.

Lindsay believed in his love, and she tried to show that in her kiss.

When she slid her hands under his shirt, he pulled away. "Let's eat our donuts, and then we'll go to my place before Vivian gets home."

"Does Vivian know about this?"

"How do you think I got inside the building? She came over during her lunch break."

Lindsay picked up a donut and bit into it. A big bite so that she got some of the filling. "This is delicious."

"It's your recipe, and you were a good teacher. I only got one small burn while deep-frying them." He showed her a tiny mark on his wrist, and she kissed it to make it better.

When he shifted beneath her, she moaned. She couldn't wait to be in bed with him again.

"Fuck," he muttered under his breath.

It still amazed her that she could do this to him, but she didn't doubt he found her sexy.

She tore off a small piece of her donut—a piece coated in a generous amount of ganache—and fed it to him, moaning again when he licked her fingers.

"I think we can manage a quickie here," she said.

"I like the sound of that."

Usually, she savored her donuts, but not today. She finished it quickly so she could return to kissing him. He devoured her like she was even more delicious than the world's best donut, and when he swept his tongue into her mouth, she squirmed in his lap.

He leaned back, just enough so she could see his cocky smile.

"Why aren't you kissing me?" She knew from experience that he could do many great things with that wicked mouth of his, and she didn't want to wait any longer.

He laughed softly. "I wanted to look at you for a moment. You're beautiful."

He pressed an open-mouth kiss to her neck, then one to her temple.

"Don't worry, Lindsay," he murmured. "I'm just getting started."

# EPILOGUE

### A few months later . . .

"Y ou didn't tell me that Peter Irwin was on the show with you," Dad said.

"I didn't tell you anything about this episode," Ryan said, "except that I was in it."

"And Logan Burris!" Jenna exclaimed. "I hope he beats you."

Ryan gave her a look, and she laughed.

They were at Jenna and Winston's house to watch Ryan's *Baking Fail* episode on TV. Jenna, Winston, and Ezra were here, of course. As were Dad and Lindsay, as well as Alice, Trevor, Harold, Vivian, and Noreen and her husband. Even Mel, since he was in town—he was guest starring on a TV show. He and Vivian were cordial to each other, but the fact that they were sitting at opposite ends of the room was likely not an accident.

Ryan had offered to have the viewing party at his place, but Jenna said it would be easier to put Ezra to bed if they had it here. They'd ordered pizza for dinner, and Lindsay and Noreen had brought donuts and cupcakes.

Ryan still baked on occasion, though it had been a while. He'd been busy lately. He was in talks to star in a rom-com for a streaming service—he was super excited about the script, and hopefully it would happen soon—and in the middle of filming *For the Blood*. But he had a few days off, which allowed him to come back to Toronto to spend time with Lindsay and his family . . . and see their reactions to the show.

He was currently seated at one end of the sofa, Lindsay curled up beside him. Ezra was in his arms. The little guy looked tired, but when Ryan said, "You're cheering for Uncle Ryan, not Logan Burris, aren't you?" Ezra opened his toothless mouth and smiled.

Ryan had asked Lindsay earlier if she wanted to have a baby one day, and she'd said yes, but not for a few years—and that sounded good to him.

"You want a matcha tiramisu donut?" Alice asked Ryan as she helped herself to one from the dining room table. "I understand they're your favorite."

Lindsay snorted.

Ryan shook his head. "I'm good, thanks."

"Wah," Dad said. "Peter Irwin is very stupid."

"Yeah, like you'd do a great job making donuts."

"I know better than to start a fire in the microwave!"

His relationship with his father had improved in the past few months. They spoke once or twice a week, and their conversations were better than Ryan asking, *How are you?* and Dad grunting or getting angry in response.

It wasn't perfect, but it was certainly better.

Dad had finally found a therapist whom he liked. He visited Jenna, Winston, and Ezra every weekend, and he was particularly good at putting Ezra to sleep by reading aloud to him. Apparently, the literary novels he preferred were quite soporific.

"Ah look, you won the donut round," Dad said.

"Even though your donuts were slightly misshapen," Jenna teased.

Ezra went to sleep before the cupcake round, and Ryan pulled

Lindsay into his lap. He didn't mind if she was a little distracting—after all, he already knew what happened.

"Oh my God!" she said. "Those are almost like the lemon meringue cupcakes I had you make. There's even a lemon curd filling. You better have won this round."

"You'll just have to wait and see," he whispered, pressing a kiss to her cheek.

He'd arrived back in Toronto last night. She'd come over straightaway and they'd spent the evening in bed. He hadn't seen her in two weeks, and God, it had been good to hold her again. He'd missed her a lot, but they'd spoken every day. And every day, he'd told her just how much he missed her and loved her.

She was getting used to dealing with his lifestyle, and they hadn't received any major attention online lately—much to his relief. However, Irene hadn't fared quite as well. He made a mental note to talk to her soon.

"Oh no," Lindsay said. "What did you do to your buttercream?"

"I didn't have enough time to figure out what went wrong. Those frogs took a while. And forgetting an ingredient in the cupcakes cost me precious minutes."

Ryan wished he could whisk her away to somewhere private right now, although he did enjoy watching this with his family.

"You clearly have no idea what a frog looks like," Mel said. "Your frogs appear to have abs. Seriously, that's wrong, man."

Dad grunted. "They look like aliens."

"I think they look like tortoises," Lindsay said.

"Ah, you are right. They are tortoises."

"Do you know how hard it is to make frogs out of fondant?" Ryan asked.

"Yes," Lindsay said sweetly. "We did a frog and lily pad birthday cake once, and I think it turned out well. What do you think, Noreen?"

"Yeah, I was pretty pleased with it."

Ryan fake glowered at his girlfriend.

But although the mood here was light, he couldn't help thinking of his mom. How much she would have loved watching the show with them. He wished she could have met Lindsay.

Who seemed to know exactly what he was thinking about and squeezed his shoulder before turning back to the screen, just in time to see Leanna Cox win the cupcake round.

Fortunately, Ryan did redeem himself, though everyone would have to wait another twenty minutes to see it.

Out of the corner of his eye, he noticed his father was on his phone. "Are you live-tweeting this?"

"No," Dad said, "just a single tweet expressing my disappointment. You know nothing about biology. Didn't you have to dissect a frog in biology class?"

"I didn't take biology in high school, but that wouldn't have helped me make a fondant frog anyway. Completely unrelated skills."

The cake round began, and Dad was so distracted by Peter Irwin's extreme incompetence that he barely commented on Ryan's.

"Your cake's not too bad, Ryan," Vivian said. "Your maple leaves are a little wonky, but they're clearly maple leaves, which is more than can be said of other things happening in that kitchen."

At last, it was time for the contestants to present their cakes to the judges, and Ryan felt slightly nervous, despite knowing the outcome.

"Leanna Cox's moose is even worse than your fondant frogs," Jenna said.

Ryan tilted his head. "Thank you?"

"Yeah, it's pretty terrible," Mel agreed. "Looks like a dog that got high before being run over by a truck."

"I'm sure that's what she was aiming for."

"You're definitely going to win," Dad said to Ryan. "She was your only competition, but you won the donut round, and your cake is clearly the best."

"I agree," Alice said.

Still, everyone was silent as they waited for the host to announce the winner.

And then Ryan's family and friends cheered as Ryan-from-four-months-ago accepted the trophy on-screen.

Yes, that lopsided cupcake trophy meant something, even if it was for a baking show featuring people who barely knew how to bake. It represented something he'd been able to do in his mom's memory.

And now he was here with Lindsay and the people who were important in their lives. She'd be next to him for the parts of his life that the world saw . . . and also the other parts. He'd be with her for the good times, the bad times, and the messy times—he wanted to face them all together.

"Congrats." She kissed him on the lips.

"I couldn't have done it without you," he said.

He was one lucky guy, no matter what happened in his career. Getting the girl in real life was better than getting the girl on-screen. Who could have predicted that knocking over a tray of matcha tiramisu donuts would lead to love?

Perhaps someone should put that in a movie . . .

## ACKNOWLEDGMENTS

I started writing in 2010—though I decided I wanted to be a writer long before then!—so it has been a long journey to get here.

Thank you to my agent, Courtney Miller-Callihan, for believing in this story.

Thank you to the whole team at Berkley, including my editor, Kristine Swartz—it was a joy to work with you, and you pushed me to make *Donut Fall in Love* the best that I could.

Thank you to the romance writing community. I've met some people at conferences; others I know online. I've been a member of Toronto Romance Writers for several years, and that has been invaluable to my development as a writer and led to many friendships. Thank you to Farah Heron and Jenny Holiday, who run the awesome Facebook group "Northern Heat" with me.

To my husband, who has been with me for over a decade, since before I started writing and before I discovered romance novels. I'm sure you're a large part of the reason I enjoy writing stories about love, and you've been endlessly supportive of my writing journey in so many different ways. When I first met you at university as my new housemate and we proceeded to barely talk to each other for four months, I never expected it to work out this way, but I'm glad it has.

I'm also thankful for the support of the rest of my family, including my parents. My father, who is always reading a book, often a very long one, and who has heard a lot about the publishing world from me over the years. My mother is no longer with us, but one of the last things I told her was that I'd started writing a novel—one that will never see the light of day—and I wish she were here today.

Thank you to all my readers, who have made my writing career possible. I'm so lucky to be able to share my stories with you.

Photo by J. Mitchell

**JACKIE LAU** decided she wanted to be a writer when she was in grade two, sometime between penning "The Heart That Got Lost" and "The Land of Shapes." She later studied engineering and worked as a geophysicist before turning to writing romance novels. She is now the author of over a dozen romantic comedies.

Jackie lives in Toronto with her husband, and despite living in Canada her whole life, she hates winter. When she's not writing, she enjoys gelato, gourmet donuts, cooking, hiking, and reading on the balcony when it's raining.

Ready to find
your next great read?

Let us help.

**Visit prh.com/nextread**